To Pete.

Thank you for believing in me.

STORMS OF TOMORROW

Ulana Dabbs

Twitter: @UlanaDabbs

PART I

GREY LANDS

Sorrow is a trial that awakens the heart.

—the Priestess of Da'ariys

I

An absence of deeper emotions didn't hinder Estel's skills as a hunter in Grey Lands. In her twenty years she had no need for sentiment, but even so she had to listen to another of Lea's lectures—a well-rehearsed routine that would drag on and on until her adoptive mother spied a flicker of understanding in her face. Sometimes, to get away, she'd act out the feeling that would please Lea, while her own mind wandered the wilderness.

'How could you say that to her?' Lea's voice went up a notch. 'I thought you were friends with Mara.'

Friends… Could listening to Mara's endless chatter about men and love be called friendship? Estel didn't know. 'It was the truth,' she said. 'Every Greylander knows it, including you.'

'Knowing and telling are two different things.'

'Are they?' The fire in the hearth cracked with sparks, as if affronted by the callousness of her reply.

Lea threw her earth-soiled hands up in the air. 'The girl is dead. Does it mean anything to you?'

Estel considered the question. Why would anyone take their own life and that of their unborn child because of a man? She struggled to understand it and refused to lie just to please Lea, but the longer she stayed in the hut, the less time she'd have to hunt. The skies, visible through the round window, turned the colour of thick smoke and if she delayed much longer, the ashfall would make it impossible to track down the grey sika. 'I need to go,' she said.

Lea slumped onto the bench, sweeping the floor with the hem of her green robe. She lowered her face into her grey palms. 'What did I do wrong? I tried to be a good mother and teach you the ways of Chour. I'm certain that deep inside you are whole. If you'd only look within yourself, try harder—'

'I'm not a Greylander,' Estel said, knowing this exchange would resolve nothing, but pressing on regardless. 'You should accept that and let me be.'

Lea was up on her feet again and the wooden floor rasped beneath her weight. In her wide eyes and trembling chin, Estel recognised the old hurts and disappointments. 'But how can I? How could I ever accept that my daughter's heart is empty?'

'I'm not your daughter.' Lea's emotions were like dense fog, saturating the hut and scrambling Estel's thoughts, turning the small space into a suffocating grave. She never felt like this in the wilds. There lay freedom, without the need for feelings and justifications of who she was.

Lea grabbed Estel's arm with surprising force. 'You're no better than the mrakes roaming these lands. They feel nothing except hunger for flesh. Is that who you are? A soulless night hag?'Lea's grey fingers dug into Estel's flesh, leaving imprints in her ivory skin.

In the silence that followed, Lea's question hung in the air like a net, ready to catch Estel's answer and hold her to it. She reached for the knife at her belt. The curved edge, sharpened only days ago, reflected the light from the burning hearth, and for a moment it looked like the blade itself was aflame. Ignoring the questioning look in Lea's eyes, she set the knife to the inside of her arm. Her muscles tensed in response and light veins stirred beneath the surface of her skin, as if challenging the threat. With clenched teeth, she applied pressure. The blade slit into her, parting the skin in its wake, and when it met the throbbing vein, silver liquid spilled from the wound, slithering between Lea's fingers, shimmering like a multitude of tiny jewels.

Lea let go of her arm with a cry.

‘I can’t feel what you feel because I don’t belong here,’ Estel said in a calm voice. ‘You want me to be something I’m not.’ She wiped the knife on her leggings, tainting the leather with streaks of silver. Without so much as a glance at Lea, she sheathed the blade, crossed the hut, and pushed the door open. The acrid air stirred her lungs and she welcomed it.

***

Estel knew every inch of the forest—a map of the curving paths and snaking rivers etched in her memory from seasons of exploration. She navigated her way through the foliage with ease, scaling over the gnarled tree roots and avoiding the treacherous mires. Sheltered by the grey leaves of the dab and olsha trees, she felt more at home here than she ever did in Lea’s hut. As a little girl she’d run to the forest seeking refuge from the children in the village, who teased her about her looks and were vexed when she ignored their provocations. They wanted her to react, to cry or lash out, but all she did was stare at them, unable to grasp why taunting her gave them so much pleasure. On the day they circled her and smeared her face and arms with soot, laughing and shouting that she was now grey like the rest of them, she fled to the wilds for the first time to be away from the mockery she didn't understand.

Was that what Lea wanted her to become? Would Lea have been pleased if she defended herself and screamed abuse? If that was the way of Greylanders, she much preferred to spend her time in the forest, hunting and honing her bow skills. The forest didn't care about the colour of her skin, welcoming her into its greyness.

Out of the corner of her eye she spied the fox again. It trotted at a safe distance, stalking her like a shadow, its fur as silver as her own hair and eyes. It was a wonder such a creature could survive in the harsh landscape of Grey Lands. More than once she tried to capture it, but the fox evaded her attempts, as if it knew where she planned to set her traps. For a while they played this hunting game and she even resorted to her bow. But the fox was always one step ahead, eluding every arrow she sent its way, until she was forced to admit defeat.

Even though she was curious why the fox chose to follow her all these years, with no way to communicate, she had no choice but to accept its companionship, and in time got used to having the silver shape trot the wilds beside her. The fox never crossed the village boundary and stayed well away from other Greylanders, including Lea, which suited Estel fine. She didn't feel like explaining its existence to her adoptive mother, suspecting that the mystery of the wild animal would further deepen the rift between them.

When the forest path divided, Estel crouched to examine the soft earth with her fingertips. Among the wide and rounded hooves of the wild jik, she spied the heart-shaped tracks of the grey sika. A smile stretched her lips as she traced the curved impressions. Her prey had a tendency to startle even before the arrow was loosened, but today, with fog as an ally, luck was on Estel's side. Her skin tingled when she pressed her palm to the imprint of the sika's hoof, awakening her senses to the sounds and smells around her. The air carried the faint scent of a dead campfire—a sure sign that ash would fall soon and cover the ground in a layer of flakes, concealing all tracks. A bird drummed on a tree bark, filling the forest with rhythmical thuds, and far to the east, a lizard slithered between the leaves. The images came to her in slow motion, as if time itself eased off, gifting her an opening to study the surroundings.

Estel closed her eyes and sharpened her ears. She recognised the light footwork of the grey sika in a snapping noise in the distance. It was close, so close she could almost feel the bristly coat under her fingers and hear the grunting. Keeping low to the ground, she shook the bow off her shoulder and followed the tracks, weaving through the woods and around the grey bushes. More out of habit than need, she sent a quick prayer to Chour, asking the bog to conceal the scent of the fox lurking nearby.

The grey sika was visible through the gaps in the trees and Estel marvelled at its antlers, branching out like spikes on a magnificent crown. As if sensing the huntress's presence, the animal raised its head and its black eyes scanned the environment. Estel nocked an arrow on the bowstring and slowed her breathing. With one shot available to her, she wasn't about to waste it. Inching the bow forward, she pulled back on the string. Her muscles tightened and her blood hummed in her ears like a rushing river. When she stopped her breath and aimed, her senses merged with the sika's and her own heart quickened in time with that of her prey. The world slowed and Estel's arrow found the lethal spot on the sika's body. When released, it would bite into the lung and liver—a deadly combination.

When she was about to let the arrow free, a stab of pain to her right arm made her jolt. The movement warned the grey sika of her presence. In a rush of panic, the animal darted across the open ground and into the woods.

'No, not now…'Estel whispered, but the pain cut through her like a knife through a bowstring. She stumbled as the agony scorched her upper arm and chopped the supply of air to her lungs. The bow clattered to the ground and she clutched her arm with a cry.

Hands trembling, Estel ripped her bracer off and tore the linen sleeve, exposing symbols that pulsed with life just beneath her skin. There were five of them, shaped like letters from some ancient language she could never hope to decipher. She wrapped her hand over them but even through the thick leather gloves, the heat was unbearable, like touching live iron. Crimson spiked her vision and when her legs gave way, she crashed to the ground. She clawed forward, digging at the leaves with her fingers, fighting the pain to remain conscious until it was too much to bear and blackness finally swallowed her.

***

Cupping her eyes against the blinding light, her mind grasped at the weak thread connecting her consciousness and unconsciousness. The pain dulled her senses, diminishing her control over them. Her right arm continued to burn, but the worst of the ache had subsided, leaving a throbbing sensation in its wake. She tried to move, opening her eyes and blinking hard as her focus returned and brought with it a realisation: she was in a familiar chamber that woke memories of the visions that plagued her for the past ten years.

The floor beneath her was cool, made of smooth, sand-coloured stone. Carved faces of strangers dressed in warrior garb, clutching all manner of weaponry from swords and spears to bows and mallets, stared down at her from the ceiling. Across from her, a large tapestry hung off the wall. Woven on it was a green field with people in white robes clustered around a long, narrow object. One end of it resembled an arrowhead and the other the tail of a fish. Shards protruded from its sides and top, reaching into the sky like sails on a ship. A red square marked the side of the contraption and gracing the sky above it were three silver moons.

A voice sliced through the air like a sabre, and she turned to face the man who owned it as he entered the chamber. Like the people on the tapestry, he was dressed in white, and his shoulder-length hair shone silver. Este felt a jolt of recognition, but it was faint and it faded too quickly, leaving wisps of confusion.

‘Where am I?’ she asked, struggling to her feet. Dizziness stirred her insides and she feared she would pass out again, but the man steadied her with his hand. Like hers, his skin was ivory and at his touch, the pain fled her body, replaced by feelings of strength and courage. ‘Are you…?’

‘You’re too weak to sustain the connection.’ The stranger spoke in an unfamiliar language and yet she understood every word. It was the first time he’d said anything to her. In all her previous visions, she felt his presence and glimpsed his shadow as it clung to the walls, but never was his image so clear.

‘I know you,’ she said. ‘I’ve seen you before. Always hiding, always out of reach… What is it that you want with me?’

‘It’s important that…you must go to him…tomorrow is…’ His words were breaking and the brightness that spilled across the room consumed his image.

She groped after him and managed to catch his shoulder. ‘Not again,’ she pleaded. ‘I feel your presence in a way I’ve never felt anyone before. Why are you summoning me? What’s the meaning of these visions?’ She was full of questions without a way to force the answers.

The man flinched back with a grimace of uncertainty. 'You've waited far too long… who you are… Remember.'

He faded fast and she could do nothing to stop him. Her consciousness seized her, pulling her back, forcing her to reconnect with the body that lay abandoned on the forest floor. She tried to resist, but the man was right—whatever power was at work here, she wasn't strong enough to wield it. Like a suffocating curtain, the blackness that hurled her into this vision wrapped her again and she was gone.

II

The acrid smell of ash brought Estel back to consciousness. She laid where she fell, sprawled in a pool of grey leaves, with nostrils full of hoary residue. Her head turned into a tipplers' party, full of clattering mugs and booming voices that grew louder when she attempted to move. Groaning, she felt her way to the closest tree and rested her back against it. There was no telling how long she'd been out, but the ashfall came and went, covering the ground with a grey quilt. Nightfall crept into the forest.

Estel coughed and wiped the sweat off her forehead. One look at her arm confirmed that the symbols were gone as if they were nothing but a desert mirage. When her vision adjusted to the gloom, she met the silver eyes of the fox. It sat on its haunches, spine straight, ears erect, looking back at her.

'What do you want?' she asked. Her throat was raw and dry. 'Were you watching me all this time?' The animal continued to stare and Estel waved her hand. 'Go away to wherever you belong. I've nothing to offer you.'

She leaned her head back against the trunk and for the first time became aware of the colour of the air—instead of the usual greyish sheen it was imbued with violet. She knew it wasn't twilight, and her senses swelled with suspicion. She got to her feet and scanned the forest. It was quiet, too quiet, for even her sharp awareness failed to detect any sign of life. Estel looked around for her bow and found it among the leaves, covered in ash but otherwise undamaged. She swung it onto her shoulder and made her way back to the village.

The air on her cheeks seemed alive and despite the lack of wind, it brushed against her face with the touch of a light breeze weaving in and out of her hair like a purple ribbon. The closer to the village she got, the thicker the mist about her grew, and the violet trapped in it became more vivid. It resembled a solid strip of fabric, but when she tried to grab it, it twined with her gloved fingers. At the sight of a blue glare flickering through the trees, Estel picked up speed.

The village was aflame. A strange blue fire spread far and wide, engulfing every house in a blazing inferno. The heat washed over her as she closed the distance, bringing the screams of the dying Greylanders with it. Estel dropped to her knees and scrambled to the hill overlooking the village. From there, she peered over the edge at the destruction unfolding in front of her. The villagers fled their houses with hands clasped over their heads, and their cries reminded Estel of the slaughter barns where the young goats were butchered in honour of Chour during the Festival of Boarders. She often wondered how Greylanders, seemingly filled with compassion and quick to criticise her lack of emotional attachments, could commit such acts in the name of their bog. She dared to question Lea about it in the past, only to be silenced by the woman's unrelenting scorn.

In the commotion, Estel recognised Armon, the trapper who taught her how to handle a bow and schooled her during their first hunt together. He was a man of few words and cared little about people's opinions. To witness him on his knees, pleading and wailing amidst the smoke and trampling of boots…

Whoever ambushed the village possessed powers even the best hunters couldn't match.

Estel searched the flames, skimming over the familiar faces until she found them. Cloaked in the violet haze that twitched and shimmered with their every move, the riders and their horses swept through the settlement like a purple storm, cutting down men, women, and children. From her vantage point, she counted six of them. Their skin seemed transparent, exposing the blackness of their veins and organs, as if there were no barrier between their insides and the outside world. The riders wielded swords, but not just any swords. Theirs were forged from the mist itself and wherever they struck, the violet ribbons followed them like smoke from incense burning at Chour's altar.

Estel took a deep breath, letting go of tension from her muscles, and focused on enhancing her vision, for only a clear mind would allow her to get a better view of the mysterious riders. One by one, she cut off the screams of people, the roaring of fires, and the acrid smells of burning and blood. They faded like the man in her visions. Like in the forest, the world around her slowed and everything came into sharp focus. Her earlier experiences taught her that she could only sustain this state for a limited period of time, so her eyes rushed past the suffering villagers and stopped at the sight of the first rider.

His muscles sprained and twitched beneath his flesh, and the violet sheen of his skin glittered like silver dust. Despite the slaughter he brought with him, Estel couldn't help but admire the rider's otherworldly appearance. His horse, as striking as the rider, crushed its front hooves into a fleeing villager, smashing the man's skull and splattering red onto its master. The purple skin absorbed the blood, separating it into droplets that merged with the black liquid in the rider's veins. Set against the black sockets, the creature's pupils glinted like violet jewels, reminding Estel of deep and treacherous caverns from which there would be no escape if one happened to be trapped in their depths.

Just as her vision began to blur, the riders parted, making way for a woman astride a black horse. Estel fought dizziness—a warning that her concentration was waning. She focused her remaining energy on the new rider, taking in the black cloak and boots, which looked unremarkable next to the transparent flesh of her companions. But when the woman let her hood slide down her back, Estel gasped.

Her power was spent, and the link was broken.

When her senses rushed back, she found herself with her shoulders pressed against the rock, surrounded by the din of slaughter as the riders rode forth, serving the hand of death to everyone who dared to live. Mixed with the burning timber, the stench of sweat, urine, and faeces swamped the valley and assaulted her nostrils.

Estel gagged. She knew she should be afraid, that any human in her place would be, considering what she witnessed moments ago, but aside from the trembling caused by the misuse of her abilities and a faint pinch deep inside her ribcage, she felt little else. The fox sat at a safe distance, shrouded in the violet fog, its silver eyes fixed on hers.

Apart from the shade of her hair and eyes, the woman among the riders was an exact image of her. If she didn't know any better, she could've been fooled into believing they were born of the same labour. Against the ivory skin of the woman's face, her hair flowed down her shoulders, black like a moonless night, with the same blackness mirrored in her eyes. Her lips were thin and grey like the ash covering Grey Lands, cheeks sharp and set high, divided by narrow nostrils that ended in a pointed tip.

Estel touched her own face as if seeking confirmation or disproval. She didn't know which. How could there be another one of her? The woman looked so similar and yet so different, and the sight of her stirred Estel's memory about how Lea had found her as an infant, wrapped in a dirty blanket, and abandoned at the edge of the forest. She was lucky that Lea chanced upon her before her hungry cries drew mrakes. With her features so different to those of other Greylanders in the village, it wasn't difficult to guess that Estel didn't belong in Grey Lands, but the mystery of her origins was never solved. Every time she tried to breach the issue with Lea, her adoptive mother would dismiss her with half-answers and shrugs. Seeing this stranger brought back the questions and doubts that had haunted her for twenty years. If there was a connection between them, Estel was sure the woman would have the answers.

Estel got to her feet. Lea….was she even alive? Could anyone withstand the destruction brought on by those creatures? The village was still ablaze, but by now the blue fires had devoured most of the huts, and with nothing else to burn, lessened in intensity. The riders disappeared toward the eastern horizon, and the violet mist followed them, making room for the night. Apart from the creaking and snapping of burning timber, silence wrapped the valley in a cloak of stillness.

With the fox at her heels, Estel made her way down the slope until she reached the ruins of the first house. The animal came to a halt at a pile of sapphire embers where the front door once stood.

'I guess I'm on my own,' Estel said into the shadows of the dying village, coughing from the smoke that scratched at her throat.

The deeper she ventured, the more disturbing the signs of assault. The riders had set fire to everything that could catch, turning the village into a wasteland that held no memory of the squabbling she had shared with Lea only hours ago. On the ground, she found scattered items used by Greylanders in their feeble attempts at defence: field rakes, iron axes, buckets…as if any of these tools were a match for the power that had descended upon them. But the most disturbing sign was the lack of bodies. From atop the hill she witnessed a slaughter and yet there were no bodies in sight, as if the mrakes had swept through the settlement and devoured them. Estel refused to trust this eerie silence, treading carefully, ears set on catching any suspicious sounds.

When she neared Lea's hut, faint moans drifted her way from beyond a collapsed wall. In the light of the dying fire, she glimpsed a piece of a green robe and was soon dragging the scorched timber off her mother's body. One of Lea's legs was twisted outwards and half of her face covered in soot, mixed with blood that seeped from the gash on her head.

'Lay still,' Estel said, kneeling down next to her. 'I'll get you out.' She looked around for something suitable to build a stretcher, but Lea grabbed her hand.

'I failed…' Lea sucked the air in through her bruised lips.

'Keep your strength. Whatever it is can wait till later. We must get you out of here before—'

‘No.’ The strength in Lea’s voice ceased Estel’s efforts, and for the first time she really looked at her adoptive mother.

Pain warped Lea’s face and Estel’s heightened senses revealed a deep suffering behind the woman’s marred face. Every inch of her body was an open wound, prodded without mercy by the slightest exertion, and she saw how much it cost her to form words. Perhaps the stretcher was no longer needed.

‘When I found you in the forest…I made a promise.’ Lea’s body went into a spasm. Her consciousness was slipping away.

‘What can I do?’ Estel flinched at the sound of calm in her voice. Even if there was nothing she could do, after twenty years of care and devotion, Lea deserved better than a half-hearted question. But she had little else to offer, and her mother knew that.

The thought took her back to the day when she accompanied Lea to a funeral. The house and people were dressed in black and every stone in the fence surrounding the hut was painted black in the name of Chour—protector of borders and human possessions. Holding Lea’s hand, she walked to the coffin where a woman lay, her hands across her chest, wearing a white headscarf. Estel remembered the wrinkles on the woman's greyed skin, her sallow cheeks, and thin lips that resembled scorched parchment. Lea paid her respects and nudged Estel to follow her example. She did, but watching the family and friends who gathered to mourn the woman, she felt like an outsider who stumbled into the wrong village. She didn't comprehend the sorrow that saturated the air, nor the tears that flew freely from every eye in the room. She remembered squeezing her own to evoke the same sensation, but like now, they stayed dry as earth during drought. Later that night, Lea shamed her for being callous and selfish. Listening to her mother's ragged breath and witnessing her passing into the afterlife, she knew she should feel something more than just apathy. Lea was about to cross the threshold to the world of Light Nav, to join the bogs and boginyas of her fate, but Estel didn't care. Her chest felt as cool as stone.

'Twilight Hunters…' Lea whispered. 'They came for you.'

'For me? What would they want with me?'

'There's no time…You must go to Suha… seek out the seer—' The coughing fit cut her off and the blood from her mouth splattered down her chin. Her eyes stilled, and she looked past Estel, into the forest. The rapid rise and fall of her chest ceased and a whisper escaped her lips, 'Chour me…' For the last time, she asked her bog for protection from the darkness and daemons that lurked beyond, and for his guidance on her upcoming journey through the Light Nav.

A part deep inside Estel tried to recreate the reactions she witnessed in others when something bad happened. She owed Lea that much. She tried to recall a time when she felt sad, but nothing came to mind, for the feeling was unknown to her. In an effort to force tears, she focused on her breathing and rubbed her eyes at the same time, and when that didn't work, she scrunched her eyebrows and made her lips tremble. These were all the signs she spied on the faces of Greylanders when they were upset about something or other. As a last resort, she attempted to cry by wailing and whimpering, but neither her eyes nor her heart listened. She surveyed the remnants of the village and hung her head, defeated.

After a few moments of silence, she squared her shoulders and faced the wreckage with a look of defiance. 'If I was like you, this would break me, so I'm glad I can't feel things the way you do. This is no time for weakness. Strength is what I need if I'm to find my way in this world.'

A rustling nearby made her aware of the silver fox. It never crossed the village border before, but tonight it followed her, as if to witness her inner battle.

'The time has come for me to move on in search of my own kind,' Estel said. She looked at Lea. 'The person who held me back is on the way to face her own trials.' It felt strange talking to an animal, but even stranger to know that she was alone and free to go where she pleased. She savoured the thought for a moment.

Lea spoke of a seer in Suha, but Estel knew nothing of the province that lay far to the west, and even less about the people who lived there. Greylanders rarely travelled outside the boundaries of their land, and the visitors were few and far between. Grey Lands, with their ashfalls, clammy rain, and the monotone landscape didn't attract outsiders, and even when the occasional pedlars wandered here, the villagers' reserved way of treating strangers hastened them on their way.

The fox didn't move, but sat, staring at her in its usual intense way, as if trying to tell her something.

It made her weary. 'You've been following me since I can remember,' Estel said. 'Like a permanent shadow of my life. Did Lea know of your existence? And if so, who gave her the right to hold things back from me, secrets that weren't hers to keep?' The questions floated across the empty village and Estel knew she wouldn't find the answers here. Crouching in the dark, with Lea's dead body at her feet, wouldn't solve anything. It was time to cast aside the life of a Greylander and follow her own path wherever it might lead.

She felt at her best alone, not having to worry about people and their burdens. 'I'll have to cross the sea, which means you can't follow. This is where we part.'

The fox cocked its head and a little whine escaped it. Estel felt a stab in her lower abdomen, as if someone nicked her with the tip of an arrow. The sensation was similar to what she experienced when Lea let out her final breath, but it was so faint that she refused to give it a thought. Instead, she got to her feet.

'Such a persistent vixen like you deserves a name, so for what it's worth, here's my parting gift. From this day, you'll be known as Srebro. A name befitting your striking colours.'

The fox blinked at her, eyes glowing in the darkness like silver beads.

Lea's body was no more than a silhouette against the blackness of the night and dying flames. Estel considered her options. They had a small amount of coin buried under one corner of the hut—courtesy of rare trading opportunities provided by pedlars from the province of Kvet to the north. She didn't know how much they'd be worth outside Grey Lands, but judging by the careful way with which Lea stored them, it may be enough to buy a passage to cross the sea on one of the vessels docked in the harbour town. Her adoptive mother was saving the coin to pay for a patch of land so Estel had a place to settle when she found a suitable companion. Lea wouldn't need the money anymore. With one final glance, Estel turned her back on Lea and felt her way through the charred beams to where the coins were buried.

'Are you going to just leave her there? For the mrakes to feast upon her flesh?' The whisper stopped her in her tracks.

Estel spun around and snatched the knife at her belt. Her senses groped at the blackness around her, searching for the person who uttered the words, but the village appeared as still as before. Daemons roamed these lands by night and she was aware of the dangers one faced if caught outside with no shelter for safety. But why would any daemon be interested in Lea's fate?

She scanned the surroundings, but only the skeletons of scorched huts stared back. Srebro was gone, too. Easing the knife back into the sheath, Estel resumed her walk. If something was after her, she stood little chance of defeating it with only a knife in the dark, so instead she turned her attention back to the task at hand. She found a shovel and began turning over the soil.

The digging seemed twice as loud and every few shovelfuls she stopped to scan the night. Her thoughts turned back to Lea and the voice. The body would attract scavengers and mrakes, but she had no time to work a grave and perform the parting ritual. In any case, Lea was on her way to the other side, to stand the trials that would grant or deny her a place in the Light Nav. Grave or no grave, her adoptive mother was on her own, having to answer for her deeds on Daaria. Estel hoped that her devotion to Chour would be enough to carry her through.

The tip of the shovel hit something solid. She cast the tool aside and parted the soil with her hands to reveal a small iron chest. When she shook it, the rattling under the lid assured her the coins were still inside. Luck was on her side. But could she call what happened to the Greylanders lucky? She shrugged the thought aside. It was no use to think about it. Even if she had been here when the Twilight Hunters ambushed the village, she wouldn't have been able to do anything, so why would she trouble herself with things she had no control over?

And perhaps it was for the best. She had her freedom now, and if she had stayed much longer, there was a danger that Lea's emotional handicaps would sap her strength and turn her into a weakling. Estel lifted her chin and tucked the iron chest under her armpit. Tonight, the chains confining her to Grey Lands were severed at last, giving her a chance to discover where she came from and why her parents had abandoned her. With her heart empty of ties and unburdened by grief, she was ready to seek answers.

III

Dawn was breaking, and the mist lifted, bringing the greys of the land into focus. Estel took a lungful of air and the particles in it stirred her airways and brought upon a cough. The ash was ever-present in Grey Lands, permeating the air, settling on the leaves and trees, and turning the landscape into a place that resembled the gateway to Dark Nav. She often wondered what deeds would cast one into its blackness, where the eternal fires consumed the souls of those who failed to live out their purpose on Daaria? She shuddered, not from fear, but wonder at the bogs and boginyas who decided one's fate. How would she perform during her own trials? Was she worthy to claim a place in the Light Nav, or would she be cast down into the depths of Dark Nav? It was impossible to know while her soul was still trapped in her body.

With the chest tucked under her arm, Estel left the village in haste. She didn't want to stay longer than necessary and turned only once to appraise the scorched shadows of her former home. In the light of dawn, the scattered beams resembled charred bones, and bleak memories gaped back at her through the shattered doors and windows. In her peripheral stood the stone boundary, erected to protect the settlement from those who meant harm, its proud stance had become incongruous, ironic as it enveloped the wreckage before her eyes. Estel thought of it as constraining, a border confining the villagers to the ash and gloom of their land, but few shared her sentiment. Lea's body was there too, resting amidst the wreckage of her home, exposed to the elements and predators, and for a brief moment she considered going back. If it was the other way around, her adoptive mother wouldn't hesitate, but Estel refused to engage in a losing battle of thoughts and focused on the road. She didn't know how far the sea harbour was, but from what little Lea told her, it'd take days to get there. In Grey Lands, villages were few and far between, so it was unlikely she'd come across other Greylanders. Until she reached the safety of the harbour, she'd have to rely on her sharp senses and her ability to wield the bow to stay fed and alive. This was a true test of her skills and she was eager to find out if Armon's teachings were as useful as the trapper himself.

Her mind returned to the mysterious woman who rode among the Twilight Hunters, and their striking resemblance to one another. Were they connected somehow? Did Lea know about her? Estel had so many questions and no one to answer them. No one, that is, apart from the seer, who she knew nothing about. Even his name was a blank.

A worm of frustration squirmed in the pit of her stomach, but she squashed it before it had a chance to grow. At times, Estel wished she could feel nothing at all. She couldn't be brought to sinister bouts of shame, or find herself lost in love, sorrow, or fear, and that would serve her well on this trip into the unknown. But as hard as it was to admit, she felt less and less in control of the pangs that manifested when she most needed a clear head, disorienting her with some lesser semblance of emotions.

The sun edged higher, forever shrouded in the orange haze, and the road ahead was straight and narrow, with occasional boundaries elevated on either side. Grass poked through the stones with grey fingers and the hills to the west rose and fell, overlaid with rocks shaped like stone giants suspended in their slumber. The elders in the village told tales about the creatures of great physical strength that laid claim to Grey Lands before the bog, Chour, conquered them by waking the guardians that dwelled inside the great volcanoes to the north. With their aid, he reclaimed the land and offered it to the Greylanders. To the east lay the forest, with trees like warriors in silver armour, marching alongside Estel in a straight line. Mist snaked between their trunks and whenever she looked past them, she had a strange sensation that something stared back. Hours had passed since she left the village. Hunger awoke in her belly and refused to be ignored. She had an ample number of arrows in her quiver and her bow was still in one piece, so with a resigned sigh, she left the road and headed into the forest.

Closer up, the trees, with some of their bark stripped and branches free of leaves, looked lifeless. The deeper she went, the heavier the mist, and soon, her hair was plastered to her forehead and clothing soaked. It took most part of the morning to chase and shoot down a hare and a quail. She found the tracks of volks, which explained the lack of smaller game. Greylanders despised these predators. They hunted in packs and had the ability to clear out the area of all life in a matter of months. Estel didn't want to be delayed by them.

She shaved down a stick from a branch of the olsha tree, loaded the hare and quail onto it, and made her way back to the road. The wind stirred the treetops and the surface of the sun turned grey—a sign of a storm brewing to the west. It'd bring the ashfall her way, so she needed to find shelter before nightfall.

She halted at the sound of rustling behind her.

Her first thought was of volks, but when she turned around and sharpened her hearing, only wind sighed back. She resumed her trek, but at the crackling of dry leaves somewhere to her right, she lowered the stick to the ground and reached for her bow. With eyes trained on the shadows between the trees, she drew an arrow and set it to the bowstring. She delayed the draw and sought a clear aim, knowing too well that a shaking arm wasn't going to help her to execute a perfect shot when the intruder decided to strike. She had to learn this lesson the hard way when Armon took her into the woods to test her skills for the first time. They hunted a volk who bothered the goats grazing around the settlement. She never knew her heart could be so loud as it drummed against her ribcage while her sweaty palms slipped up and down the bow. Before they tracked down the volk, Armon instructed her when to draw and release, but her trembling hands betrayed her. When she loosened the arrow, it annoyed the volk rather than injuring it, and if not for Armon's skills and quick thinking, she wouldn't be aiming at anything today.

A shape moved between the trees and she let go of her memories. With one assured motion, she pulled back the string and aimed. As the storm drew near, visibility was getting worse and she was glad for her abilities. Her arms tensed and she held her breath. She was about to loosen the arrow when the threat came clear of the shadows.

Estel breathed a sigh of relief. It was Srebro.

'What are you doing here?' she asked, lowering her bow. 'Silly animal. I almost killed you.'

Srebro didn't move. Her fur was damp from the mist and her muzzle was tinted with blood.

'I see you've managed to satisfy your hunger.' Estel appraised her hare and quail. 'Good. I won't have to share.' The appearance of the fox was a welcome relief from the events of the previous night. She knew they'd have to part ways when she reached the sea harbour—no one would admit her aboard a ship with a wild vixen at her side—but even so, it was good to see the fox unharmed. Srebro followed her around since her first venture to the woods and abandoning her was harder than leaving Lea's body. 'We need shelter,' Estel said.

As if on cue, Srebro turned around and trotted back into the woods, the white tip on her silver tail flashing like a flagpole.

'Wait,' Estel called after her, but the fox didn't stop. She considered her options. Lighting fires on the open land was risky and could end up attracting daemons, but following the fox through the unknown wood trail didn't appeal to her either. Before she got a chance to make her choice, Srebro poked her head back through the trees. Her eyes trained on Estel as if she were trying to tell her something

'All right then,' she submitted, following Srebro into the woods.

The fox led the way, but when her silver fur blended with the mist, Estel was left to rely on her senses to navigate the forest. As well as the need to find shelter, a great dose of curiosity spurred her. She spent enough time in the wilderness to know that animals preferred to steer clear of humans, so Srebro's odd behaviour made her revaluate the way she perceived the fox—as nothing more than a scavenger, feasting on the entrails of the animals Estel hunted down. At first, she reasoned that Srebro's need for survival drove her behaviour. Estel's bow was a reliable source of food after all, but trekking through the dense forest, it was clear there was another side to the fox.

The grey light of the afternoon faded as the forest clasped Estel in a dark embrace and there was nothing for her mind to hang on to—no familiar landmarks, or sounds other than the calling of the wind. With the gusts growing more forceful, she had to stop and secure her hair into a tail to prevent it from catching on branches and shrubbery.

The storm was closing in and Estel tasted ash on her lips. Just as she thought that Srebro tricked her and she lost her for good, the fox emerged from the shadows.

'Where are you leading me?' Estel asked. Her voice sounded empty and she felt like a trespasser.

Srebro yawned, sniffed the ground, and trotted deeper into the forest.

Waiting for an explanation was useless, so Estel followed. With the main path far behind them, it was too late to turn back.

A shack came into view as a rectangular shadow in the bleakness of the clearing and Estel approached it with caution. It seemed abandoned, but with the Twilight Hunters searching for her, she didn't want to take chances. She drew her knife and with her back pressed to the wall, inched to the door. The planks felt wet against her palm and the rotten splinters jabbed her skin. Her sharpened senses confirmed that dampness and decay were the only occupants of the shack. She eased the grip on the knife and elbowed the door open. In the dimness, she spied an overturned stool and the edge of a table. The windows were barred with flat boards, but the time had eaten the wood away, letting the ash through the gaps. Acrid smell lingered inside, and she didn't need light to see that whomever lived here was long gone. Estel backed out of the shack.

Srebro sat nearby, licking her front paw, but from time to time, she'd lift her head as if to confirm that Estel was still present. Estel ignored the animal and went in search of wood to light the fire. Her fingers touched the familiar shape of the tinderbox in the pocket of her jerkin. It was a custom in Grey Lands to offer a newborn a box containing tinder, flint, and steel for kindling fires. The elders insisted that light was the only thing capable of chasing away darkness and the daemons it spawned, and despite the fact that Estel wasn't a Greylander, Lea demanded this custom be extended to her. She succeeded. The rite was performed, and the elders presented Estel with her own box.

She returned to the clearing with a handful of logs and twigs and set about lighting a fire. Her movements were well rehearsed, for birthing of flames was considered a rite in itself, requiring great precision. Estel arranged the charcloth in the bottom of the tinderbox and struck the flint against the steel time and time again until a shower of sparks stirred up tiny embers. She encouraged them, blowing gently as they fell onto the charcloth and caught the edges of the splint. When she was satisfied with the strength of the newborn flame, she set the splint to the twigs.

Lazy at first, the blue flames licked the wood, but every time they attempted to give up and die, Estel brought them back to life, blowing air until they sprang to a full-blown flame and began dancing erratically. She fed the flame's hunger with more branches until it was sated and began devouring the life-giving wood.

Satisfied, Estel spent another hour gathering more fuel before she sat down to tend to the hare and quail. Her hunger, pushed aside by the chores, returned in force, noisier than before. Srebro watched her intently as she worked the hare's hide, pulling out the hind legs and removing the tailbone. When she opened the cavity and pulled down the organs, the fox sprang to her feet and edged closer to the flames, licking her muzzle.

'It seems I must share after all,' Estel said, beckoning Srebro closer with her bloodied knife. The fox went down on her belly, crawled up to the entrails, and snatched a piece of intestine then dragged it away into the safety of the darkness. Estel pursed her lips. Perhaps with time the vixen would become more trusting of her. But the thought was immediately followed by another: In a matter of days, she'd be looking for a ship to cross the seas, and Srebro's trust would mean nothing to her.

When the hare was roasting over the fire, Estel turned her attention to plucking the quail. As the silver feathers fell at her feet, her thoughts turned to the journey ahead. In the chaos of the previous night, she had little time to consider how other humans would react to her appearance. Up until now, she was surrounded by people who had accepted her presence among them, but she had little knowledge about life outside of Grey Lands. What would strangers think of her? Would they mock her, or attempt to do her harm? Due to the enclosed way of life favoured by Greylanders, she had no opportunities to travel, and the rare peddlers who passed her village were more interested in coins than in people who traded them. She didn't fear death, but she wasn't about to make it easy for strangers to kill her. Just because she lacked knowledge about the world didn't mean she'd face it unprepared.

Estel appraised her work. The touch of the quail's goosy flesh on her skin was a stark contrast to the softness of its feathers, but the bird was ready. She impaled it onto a long branch and placed it over the fire. The aroma of charred meat blended with that of the ash and she was glad she didn't have to sleep outside, exposed to the forces of the upcoming storm.

Srebro finished with the last of the entrails and scuttered back into the woods, leaving her to eat alone. There was a comfort in knowing that the fox was somewhere out there. It made the forest look less ominous. Estel much preferred Srebro's company to that of humans, or spirits.

When the meat was ready, she cut a palm-sized piece and savoured the smoky taste. It warmed her stomach and appeased its hungry rumblings. Each bite eased the tension in her body. When the food turned into a pile of bones at her feet, she licked the last traces of fat off her fingers and stretched. Tomorrow she'd have to spend some time crafting arrows to fill her quiver, but for now, she needed rest. Estel walked to the hut and opened the door.

In the faint light from the campfire, the single room looked even more ruined. The blankets bunched in the corner formed a makeshift berth, with branches and twigs tied beneath to keep it away from direct contact with the floor. The gap in the wall was stuffed with a piece of animal skin, shaped into a tight ball to keep the draft at bay. Mingled with the odours of rot and ash was another scent, similar to that of the incense Lea used to burn to chase the dampness away. It made the presence of the previous occupant linger between the walls like the memory of a fading spirit.

Estel secured the door and with her knife close at hand, settled onto the berth. She laid for a while, eyes wide open, and listened to the sounds of the forest. The wind rattled the loose planks on the roof and the sky growled with the gathering storm. To come awake wrapped in an ash blanket wasn't something she looked forward to, but it was far better than faring the storm up in a tree branch. She cleared her thoughts and focused her mind on the breath flowing through her nostrils. When it balanced and deepened, she sensed the sleep stretching its fingers for her and she was ready to surrender herself to it.

Then, like a volk's jaw locking around the throat of its prey, that painfully familiar pain tore through her upper arm once again.

Her eyes flew open. 'No!' she screamed into the night, but her skin burned stronger than the fire that consumed her village. The symbols shone silver through the linen of her sleeve and she rubbed them in a mad attempt to find relief. It was futile. Her movements grew weak, and the shack became distorted by clouds of red and black.

Helpless, she sank into it and the pain repelled her consciousness.

***

Estel opened her eyes to the familiar room and the tapestry that still hung from the wall in front of her. But something was different—the silver-haired man in white robes was already here. His back was turned, hands clasped behind him as he stared at the mysterious ship woven into the tapestry.

'What do you want?' she asked him. Her voice was a croak and when she touched her nose, her fingers came away silver. She was bleeding.

'You are weakening,' the man said, and his tone sent a surge of energy through her. He turned to face her. His silver hair flew past his shoulders, glinting like the symbols on her arm. 'You must learn how to control it, or you will die.'

'Control what?' She tried to stand up but the room swayed, and her knees betrayed her.

'Conserve your energy. You will need every drop of it before it's over. I can do little for you here, but heed Lea's advice and seek out Ashk. He who knows our kind will unveil what lies ahead.'

‘Why don’t you tell me who you are? You summon me here, speak in riddles just so you can send me away. Why?’ She rolled up her sleeve. ‘What are these marks?’

His eyes widened. ‘It is not I who summon you…’ His silhouette and voice began to fade. ‘Think hard. Remember who you are…’

‘You said it before, but I don’t remember anything. I’m an orphan, an outcast who doesn’t belong anywhere.’ Even as she said the words, she despised them. They made her sound weak. If she could just gather enough energy to focus, she’d recall who the man was, but her arm throbbed again, and the blackness advanced in a suffocating wave, preparing to snatch her away.

‘You are more than that. Your potential is unrivalled, and it is time… your present is our future.’

As the vision faded, the room turned white and the stranger’s face became translucent, but before it faded completely, she glimpsed something in his silver pupils that reminded her of the expression in Lea’s face moments before she drew her final breath.

***

A sound tugged at the edges of her consciousness like a farmer tugging at the reins on his stubborn mule, and no matter how hard she tried to ignore it, it wouldn’t go away.

At first, she thought of Srebro. Perhaps the fox had returned and rummaged through the leftover bones, but when her hearing became more focused, she recognised the repeated sequence to be part of a song. Someone sang outside the shack in a low voice. Estel unwrapped her mind from the tangles of sleep and opened her eyes. As soon as she did, a wave of nausea washed over her. The throbbing inside her skull surpassed that in her arm, and her ribs felt as if a giant pressed his foot upon them. Her body shook with fever that coated her forehead in sweat. This was the worst she had ever felt after a vision. The man said something about her dying… Maybe this was it? Every aching part of her found the thought appealing. To plunge into nothingness, free from pain—that was a notion she could get behind, and if it weren't for the song beyond the shack's window, she'd welcome it.

The night was fading and the grey of dawn streamed through the hole in the roof. Estel found her bow and sat up. She took a lungful of air, but when her boots touched the ground, the shack spun around in a dizzying twirl. Only the sheer strength of her will prevented her from crashing to the ground and alerting the singer. Ignoring the trembling in her fingers, she set an arrow to her bow and inched to the door. It was still barred. Outside, the female voice rose and fell with a rhythm of the song, but it wasn't a tune she recognised. It reminded her of the mourners in the village when they prayed to Chour to grant a safe passage for the deceased. Maybe the owner of the shack returned to reclaim her shelter? With a sharp intake of breath, she drew the bow and kicked the door open.

The song died. Estel trained an arrow that looked all but ready to imbed itself in a girl who sat cross-legged at the edge of a dying fire. Srebro, curled up in the space between them, slept peacefully.

'Who are you?' Estel asked, fighting to keep her arms steady. Daemons were known to take human form to deceive those they preyed upon. There'd be no room for error and she'd have to be quick.

The girl looked up from the fire and Estel judged her to be no older than eight years. She wore a white dress, stained with ash and grime, and sewn into it were insects with wings in colours Estel never knew existed. Some resembled the shades of water in the purest river, others held the glowing flame of a scalding poker, while those closest to the hem reminded her of green herbs sold by pedlars passing through her village. Hugging the girl's waist was a pink belt. Below her knees, the dress met a pair of socks that disappeared into brown sandals, with tiny flowers stitched to the corner of each strap. Her light hair was tied in a tail, but loose strands escaped down her shoulders in waves. Her left cheek was smeared with dirt and her blue eyes met Estel's in a curious, but tired expression.

'What are you doing here? 'Estel asked again, forcing her voice to remain steady. There was something familiar about the girl, but Estel struggled to identify what it was.

The girl got to her feet, seemingly unfazed by the arrow pointed at her heart. She cocked her head as if trying to judge her chances.

Srebro stirred in her sleep but didn't show any signs of waking.

'What is it that you're after? Food?'

The girl shook her head and took a step forward. Clutched in her hand was a soft brown toy, but it looked nothing like those made by the women in Estel's village. This one had a round face and ears, tiny paw prints on the bottom of each foot, and two buttons for eyes. Another one was sewn into its extended belly. The toy looked worn, with some of the seams torn in places, exposing bits of what looked like dried grass.

'Stay where you are,' Estel warned.

The girl's appearance and calm demeanour was out of place in the gloom of the forest. The closest village was Estel's own and she didn't recall a child resembling the girl in front of her. To be sure, Estel asked, 'What village are you from?'

The girl shook her head again, as if struggling to understand the question. The toy dangled from her hand, watching Estel through its button eyes.

'I don't want to shoot you,' Estel said, 'but if you don't tell me who you are, I'll have no choice. For all I know you're a mrake, trying to deceive me.'

The girl flinched and hugged the toy to her chest. Her mouth turned down and her chin trembled. Estel knew the look from her many disputes with Lea. Wherever the girl came from, she was no daemon, for those creatures were incapable of tears. A bit like herself.

That thought tasted sour.

She lowered her bow. 'No need to cry.' Her words sounded awkward. She didn't care much for children and her own experiences with those in the village taught her little about how to behave around them. Her fingers flexed around the bow. Estel wanted to be somewhere else, where she didn't have to deal with this child. If she left her behind, the volks, or other predators, would have their way with her and the girl would stand no chance against their powerful jaws. But she couldn't take her with her. Estel struggled to provide for herself, let alone worry about a little girl.

'What's your name?' she asked.

No response.

'Start talking, or I'll nock that arrow back.' Estel's patience was wearing thin. She was still weak and hurting from the vision. A long road separated her form the harbour, and here she was, wasting the precious hours of daylight talking to a child she cared nothing about.

'Arleta,' the girl whispered at last. Her eyes were round, staring at Estel in a way that made her uncomfortable. *'Jestesmy zwiazani. Moje zycie jest w twoich rekach.'*

Estel frowned. 'I don't understand.' The girl's words filled her with strange longing. It felt as if a part, deep inside her, deciphered them, but her brain failed to catch the meaning. 'Do I know you?'

The girl nodded.

Estel pursed her lips. 'I don't recall seeing you before.' An ache pressed down on her forehead and she couldn't afford another loss of consciousness. If she fainted here, she'd be left at the mercy of this strange girl and it was a risk she was unwilling to take. With Arleta's eyes following her every move, she secured her bow on her shoulder and retrieved the chest from the hut. Srebro stirred, lifting her head to sniff the air, but paying no attention to Arleta. When Estel walked past the girl, the fox sprang to her feet and disappeared into the forest.

'Odchodzisz?' Arleta's voice was no more than a whisper, but Estel heard the words as if the girl spoke them into her ear.

When she turned, the girl stood where she left her. The question hung in the air and even though she couldn't understand its meaning, it made her hesitate. The strap of Arleta's left sandal was undone and Estel felt a sudden urge to go back and fix it for her. Berating herself for such simple thoughts, she called out, 'I can't take you with me. It's too dangerous. Go back to your family.'

She didn't have to justify her actions to this strange child who invaded her campsite and disturbed her sleep. She didn't like the way the girl made her feel—alert, on edge. Even if she let Arleta come along, how would they communicate with each other? With a final shrug, Estel turned away and headed back to the road.

Fighting her way through grey shrubbery, she listened for the sound of footsteps. If Arleta was anything like the children in the village, she'd follow Estel and make a nuisance of herself. Why couldn't people just leave her alone? The image of the brown toy with its button eyes stuck in her mind—and the way Arleta held its paw, as if the dead thing could shield her from dangers lurking in the wilds. Children were silly beings, wasting their time playing foolish games instead of learning survival skills. When she was eight, she found her first knife and slept with it tucked under her pillow. She told Lea that having it close helped her chase away bad dreams. Estel snorted. She couldn't dream. Her strange visions were the closest things to a dream and even they came only in fragments, too vague to make much sense.

The road came into view. The sun watched the forest through a grey haze above her and the trees swayed around her, their rustling an answer to the whistling of the wind. The air smelled of moist earth.

No sound of footfalls.

It was for the best that Arleta didn't follow her. Estel had nothing to offer her and the girl would slow her down. Besides, there was the language barrier. Estel shook her head as if to affirm that her reasoning was just, but the tingling in the pit of her stomach persisted.

IV

Days came and went. Another ashfall covered the land in grey flakes and tainted the air with the smell of charcoal. Estel wrinkled her nose—the particles irritated her airways, making her sneeze more often. The ash was the one thing she wouldn't miss. Lea once told her that only Grey Lands suffered from such freakish weather and it was the reason why all who settled here developed grey skin. 'Beyond the sea, the climate is more forgiving,' she'd say. But she never travelled farther than the village boundary and everything she had learned about life outside it was from the passing pedlars.

Estel knew of some Greylanders who forsook their traditions by disobeying Chour's commandments and leaving the village to find a better life in Kvet. When no one heard back from them, their families agreed that their impiety must've angered Chour and so he sank the boats who allowed the cursed men aboard. Considering the circumstances that forced Estel to follow a similar path, she hoped that Chour would be more forgiving in her case.

Five days had passed since she saw the mysterious girl. The land to each side of her was barren, with no signs of human activity: no smoke ribbons, no farm fields, and no animals other than the predators roaming the wilds. A pack of volks followed her trail for a while, but she managed to scare them away by climbing a tree and shooting burning arrows at their raised hackles. Even though the fire chased them away, Estel stayed where she was, keeping vigil until the early hours of dawn. She spent the following nights in a similar fashion, hidden in the grey safety of leaves and branches.

Srebro followed but kept her distance. From time to time, Estel glimpsed flashes of silver through the gaps between the rocks, or weaving in and out of bushes. She couldn't help but wonder at the fox's insistence on trekking after her, for when they reached the harbour, they'd have to part ways forever. She wished her abilities allowed her to communicate with animals, so she could explain their predicament and urge the fox to turn back. It was too dangerous for Srebro to wander into the harbour. The bond they forged was unsafe. Not because she needed the fox, Estel told herself, but because if the animal grew too accustomed to easy pickings she wouldn't survive on her own. Srebro's growing attachment would make her less vigilant and more trusting of humans.

Some nights, perched high upon a tree, Estel spoke aloud into the darkness, trying to explain why the fox should stop following her. ‘For all the years I spent hunting in the wilds, I’ve never seen another silver fox. If anyone spotted you, they’d hunt you down, capture you, and tear away your fur from your skin.’

Estel looked down, hoping for some kind of reaction, but Srebro didn’t even stir in her sleep.

With a sigh, Estel trained her eyes on the darkening skies, and with nothing to occupy her mind, her thoughts turned to the black-eyed woman and the creatures she commanded. Twilight Hunters, Lea called them, with organs exposed by their translucent skin and eyes like violet gems. The nightfall they brought with them was a living, breathing thing that latched on to her hair and turned the air into a thick mist.

If it was true that the woman came looking for her, why not ask the villagers peacefully? Why the slaughter? Estel hoped that the seer, Ashk, would have the answers for her, but the only hint of his whereabouts was the province of Suha.

‘How am I going to find one man in a foreign land?’ she asked the sleeping fox. ‘Not to mention that I don’t even know how to get there. How many Ashks live in Suha? And even if I find him, how will I know he’s the right one?’

The sound of her voice disturbed a bird on a nearby tree and Srebro lifted her head. She sniffed the air and without a glance in Estel's direction, went back to sleep.

What was she doing talking to a wild fox in the middle of the night, anyway?

Her neck and back felt stiff from balancing on a tree branch, but the effects of her latest vision subsided, and her strength was back. After each trip to the other side, the recovery took a little longer. She never forgot her first vision. It took her unawares, when Lea was out working the fields, leaving Estel to tend the hearth. She was no older than the girl in the colourful dress, but her adoptive mother entrusted her with small chores from time to time. She remembered feeding the fire with branches she gathered earlier that day and watched the flames as they devoured the wood. When they grew in heat and size, the vision came. It was as fleeting as the grey sika in full flight and filled with blurry images of the tapestry. When Lea returned home, she found her daughter with half of her hair smouldered by the fire. The hair grew back, but Lea never stopped worrying, and for that reason, Estel kept any future visions to herself. But did her adoptive mother know more than she let on? Did she know about the strange silver marks on her arm? And what about the man from her visions?

'He looked and felt so familiar,' Estel confided to Srebro. 'If only I could take charge of the vision and question him instead of quivering like a leaf in the wind.' But the interaction sapped her energy every time, and without it, she couldn't even control her senses. Finding Ashk—the only person who would know what to do—became more urgent.

***

The taste of wind, infused with salt and wet grass, was a sign that she neared the sea. Estel couldn't stop licking the briny residue off her lips until the skin cracked and filled her mouth with a tang of silver. Stone borders erected around the harbour reminded her of those safeguarding her burned village. Beyond them, covered with rough shingles, the M-shaped roofs resembled miniature valleys and hilltops that rose and fell, as if trying to outdo each other in height. Smoke escaped in clouds from their chimneys, merging with the grey haze. Lanterns secured to the walls and doorways illuminated the cobbled paths. Every house was a mixture of grey and brown stone with planks in black stripes that formed crisscross patterns on the walls.

Estel had never seen so many buildings clustered in one place.

She stopped at the corner of a house where shadows had grown thicker, and leaned on a cold stone. She considered her options. To expose her true appearance to strangers seemed risky. How would Greylanders who lived here react when they saw her? People in her village grew accustomed to her ivory skin, but it took time. She remembered too well the questioning looks her silver hair and eyes caused when she was growing up. After the lengthy journey to the harbour, her clothes were worn, and the ash trapped in her hair disguised its silver tone. Dried mud caked the sleeves of her shirt and the exposed parts of her skin turned pallid. One sniff of her armpit made her flinch.

An idea forged in her mind.

Her filthy appearance could serve her well in her quest to obtain passage on a ship, and with a bit of work she'd look like a Greylander who'd fallen on hard times.

Concealed by the shadows of the wall, Estel blended the ash and earth and smeared her neck, face, and arms with grime, taking care to treat every inch of her skin. When she was satisfied with the results, she stepped onto the main path. What little camouflage she could gather would shield her from the curious eyes of the harbour-dwellers. It was time to look for a ship to take her beyond the sea to Kvet.

Before setting forth, she looked around for Srebro and spotted her hidden in a cluster of tall grass. Estel crouched close enough for the fox to hear her. 'I know I've said it before, but this is where we must part. This time for good. I'm bound for Kvet and you can't follow me there.'

Srebro regarded her with her silver eyes. She looked like a statue, and yet again, Estel was struck by her unusual appearance. She regretted leaving the fox behind but had no choice.

'Stay away from humans,' she warned. 'Like me, they're hunters, and believe me when I say that a fox like you is a hunter's dream.' She gave Srebro a little nod and turned to the town. When the muscles in her chest tightened and breathing became difficult Estel blamed it on the traces of ash in the air. She adjusted her bow and started down the street, but a few strides later she turned around to find the tips of silver ears poking through the grass.

'Farewell, Srebro, and stay alive,' she whispered.

Upon closer inspection, the houses weren't as sturdy as they looked from afar and many roof shingles showed signs of disrepair. Long cracks ran down the doorways and paint flaked away from the window frames. The cobbled street was a curiosity and felt strange beneath the soles of her boots—like walking down miniature earth mounds. In her village, the stones were considered sacred and only used to erect borders, which left the roads at the mercy of ash, rain, and wind. Hastening down the mud-free streets, she wondered how long they took to build and how many Greylanders opposed the idea.

At the side of each house, wooden barrels were buried halfway into the ground, and judging by the smell, they were filled with refuse. Why one would choose to keep such a stinking waste so close to one's quarters was beyond her.

Estel walked deeper into town and the traffic of people and animals increased, but to her relief, most didn't pay attention to her. Perhaps they thought her one of the beggars who roamed the streets. She passed two such men on her way and when one of them approached her, the stench of sweat and grime was more overpowering than the waste from the barrels. She cast her head down and heeded no attention to his pleas for coin. Her indifference earned her a curse and a shaking of his fist.

Used to the calm of her village and the freedom of the wilds, she found the narrow alleyways disorienting. The sheer number of winding corners and choices she had to make at each of them sliced her brain into small pieces she struggled to fit together. The people going about their chores were like a swarm of insects buzzing inside her brain, and she could do nothing to chase them away. In the wilderness she relied on her senses, but here the sounds and smells repressed them, leaving her exposed to the environment, unable to think. She caught her foot in a piece of tangled wire and lost her balance. A stack of crates saved her from crashing down onto the cobbles. In desperation, Estel closed her eyes and counted her breaths to still her mind and quiet the ringing in her ears. Her village life failed to prepare her for so much activity. How was she to face the world if her knees quivered under her before she even left Grey Lands? She had to regain control. And fast. It was only the first bend in her journey and she couldn't afford to fall apart. She was stronger than this. Besides, she had little else to go back to.

With a final intake of breath, she opened her eyes and one by one, took in the details around her. A stray dog ripped at a bloody bag, but as the seams were about to give, a man wearing an apron burst from the house, yelling curses, and chased the dog away with a cleaver. Farther up, a woman swept her porch, singing to the wide strokes of her broom. The squeaking of wheels echoed through the street as another man pulled his cart, its contents secured with a grey cloth. The longer she focused on the details, the steadier her breathing grew, and dizziness began fading away. As long as she continued to bracket the events unfolding before her, she'd remain in control.

Estel shook away the tension and resumed her walk down the street.

The night descended upon the harbour, weaving shadows through the alleyways and urging people to seek shelter indoors. The waterfront stank of wet sea grass and fish. Estel fought for balance as she navigated her way down the wet cobbles to a small outbuilding, where a torch cast an orange light on a cluster of people. From their striped shirts, she determined they were sailors, or captains of the vessels anchored at the docks. In the darkness, the ships with their folded sails and bared hull masts, resembled a web made of ropes that tried to catch the moon between the yards.

'I'm looking for a passage across the sea,' Estel said.

The men ignored her and carried on talking among themselves.

‘I’ve coin,’ she said, raising her voice. The mention of coin seemed to pique their interest.

A man with a black beard sneered. ‘You look like a beggar to me, woman. Go away before I call my sobakas to bark you away.’

His companions laughed and one of them spat at her boot.

Estel ignored him and addressed the bearded man, ‘I’ve coin, and I can work the decks if you promise me safe passage to Kvet.’ To prove the truth of it, she shook the contents of Lea’s box, hoping it held enough silver to sway him.

The bearded man scratched his cheek. It was hard to tell in the fading torchlight, but his clothes looked more valuable than those of his companions. His leather boots gleamed as if freshly polished and his shirt was white under the brown of his coat. The belt secured at his waist had silver holes punched through the leather. She had a feeling that if anyone had the power to admit her on-board, it was him.

‘Coin, you say,’ he said, and winked at the men. ‘How could a beggar like you afford passage on one of my vessels?’ He leaned close and Estel braced herself for the foulness of his breath but was surprised when a scent of pivo washed over her. The man indulged in expensive spirits. 'Have you been stealing?' he boomed at her.

Despite her lack of fear, she had to play her part and recoiled from him, as if terrified.

Her reaction twisted his lips into an ugly smile. 'Well?' he pressed her for an answer.

'My father left home bound for Kvet and we haven't seen him since,' she said. If she was to persuade this man, a lie might be her best option. 'I fear that if he doesn't come home, my mother will die from grief.'

'And you want to go looking for him. In Kvet.' He stared her up and down and something in his dark eyes warned her that he didn't take well to being crossed. Even though she didn't fear this man, she had no wish to fight him either. Part of her wanted to give up and find another way, but she stood her ground.

'Have you ever travelled outside Grey Lands?' he asked.

She shook her head.

'Open the box,' he ordered, and when she did, he snatched it from her hands and peered inside. 'Do you know how many nights it takes to cross the sea?' When she said nothing, he snapped the lid shut. 'As many as the number of your fingers and toes put together. There's hardly enough here for one night's voyage.' He handed the chest back to her. 'Hurry along before I lose my patience.'

He exchanged glances with his men and Estel realised they thought her a simple village girl, with no understanding of the world. Perhaps they were right, but even so, she could use their view of her to her advantage.

She grabbed the man's hand. 'I'm begging you. That's all I have left. My father needs help and if I don't cross the sea, I'll lose my mother as well.' She hoped that her voice sounded desperate enough to made him rethink his decision.

He pulled back his huge arm and struck her chest with a force so hard, it took the wind out of her lungs. She staggered back and almost fell into a tangle of nets.

'First lesson. Never lay your filthy hands on me,' he said, advancing on her. 'Do you think I give a rotten arse about your father?' He snatched the box and thrust it back at her. The coins spilled across the path and the sound of silver clattering off the cobbles turned heads. Suddenly, everyone was interested in the squabble between the captain and the beggar girl. 'If I see you again, I won't be so generous.' He turned to his men. 'We sail at first light.'

Estel had never killed a man before, but his arrogance made her want to reach for the knife at her belt and sink it into his heart.

She gathered the coins back into the box and got up. Relieving the ache in her chest and the burn in her throat with shallow breaths, she considered her options. Whatever she came up with to get on this thug's ship would require more than an innocent lie. She had until dawn to think of a way, but exhaustion had set in alongside the pain. She retired back into town with the box pressed against the throbbing skin of her torso, and, unwilling to part with its contents, she scouted a dark corner between two houses to sleep. Affording her a clear view of the street, she drew her knife and sank down onto the cobbles. If anyone tried to ambush her, her blade would be the first to greet them. The thought was comforting, and she closed her eyes. With no dreams to distract her, her mind worked on the ploy to get aboard the ship.

V

The sound of a bell jolted Estel from her sleep. Its peal echoed through the alleyways like the roar of a daemon. The fog was thick, and the harbour looked as if the clouds fell from the sky during the night and nestled on the streets. She sprang to her feet. Sleep tricked her, and she had lost precious hours—the ship would be leaving soon, and she must be on-board when it did. She grabbed her bow and coins and rushed back to the waterfront.

The streets were coming alive. Greylanders, spurred by the ringing bell, emerged from their homes to seek Chour's blessing at the temple before the day's labour. Shrouded in a cloud of mist, the home of worship towered over the neighbouring houses with the bog's face carved into the entrance made of old stone. The bell swayed back and forth in the opening above. As commanding as the temple looked, Estel had no time for formal prayers. But a little plea wouldn't hurt, she reasoned. 'Grant me the passage on that ship,' was all she managed, doubting that almighty Chour paid any attention to her present troubles.

When she reached the waterfront and the outbuilding, she searched for the bearded man. The docks hummed with life. The men who manned the ships called out to one another as they loaded barrels onto the decks. In the daylight, the vessel from last night seemed greater in size, swaying with the flow of water beneath it. A golden bird with outstretched wings decorated the bow and its beak alone was as long as Estel's arm. It gave an impression that if freed from the wood that trapped it, it would plunge into the sky and claim the vast expanse as its hunting kingdom. Estel marvelled at the work of a skilled hand that chiselled the bird's feathers and shaped its talons.

'You again.' A voice at her ear. She recognised one of the men who accompanied the bearded captain yesterday. His forehead was bathed in sweat, and black grease covered the stubble on his chin. He must've seen her from the deck while loading cargo.

'I'm taking this ship,' she said, trying to sound bold.

The man sniggered and made a tooting sound. 'Krag doesn't tolerate insolence. I wouldn't tempt my fate if I were you.' His face came close to her neck. 'By Chour, you stink. I doubt any ship in this dock would be willing to take you.'

'You heard the captain last night. I can barely afford to pay for my passage, not to mention such luxuries as a bath and a clean bed.'

A cunning smile twisted his lips. 'If you're willing to part with the coins, I can have a word with Krag to see if we could make an exception this once.' He wrapped a strand of her hair around his finger. 'But the work on deck is hard…'

Despite a little voice whispering in her ear that she shouldn't trust this man, Estel said nothing.

'Come with me,' he said at last, and she followed him down the cobbled path to the ship.

Walking up the gangway, the figurehead looked even bigger and the vessel itself wider. It was like boarding a floating city made of flat planks of timber with grey sails instead of banners. Estel had never seen so many ropes tangled and wound in ways that defied comprehension. When her feet touched the deck, the ship rocked beneath them as if testing her balance.

'Wait here,' the man ordered.

The sailors on-board stopped what they were doing and gaped at her as if she were some kind of exotic animal. They winked and exchanged jokes, tugging at their mates' sleeves, until Krag appeared accompanied by the man who led her here.

'To work,' Krag yelled. When the men dispersed to resume their duties, he narrowed his dark eyes at her. 'I thought I made myself clear last night, but Flip tells me that you keep on insisting to sail aboard my ship.'

She met his stare. 'You did, but I must get to Kvet.'

Flip whispered something in Krag's ear and even though she couldn't make out the words, from the way he licked his lips, she guessed it wasn't anything good. Bracing herself for another shove, Estel planted her feet on the ground.

Krag laughed and patted Flip on the shoulder. 'Go and tell the boys they'll have a new mate on-board.' When the sailor scuttled away, he said, 'You'll work and do what Flip tells you. He's in charge of my men and I don't want any squabbles. Do as you're told and if your luck is as strong as your stubbornness, you might see Kvet's docks. If you get yourself into trouble, don't bother running to me. Oh, and one more thing,' he snatched the bow off her shoulder, 'no weapons aboard my ship.'

Estel waited for him to ask her for the dagger concealed inside her boot, but Krag turned away and walked off. She breathed a sigh of relief. Parting with her bow was harder than she expected—without its weight on her shoulder she felt naked, as if part of her was stripped away. She had to find a way to recover it during the voyage, but for now, it was time to face the ship full of men. Lea warned her about the dangers of such encounters, a place without women was not a place one should ever feel at ease. Estel resolved to keep her reactions in check and stay away from the sailors as much as possible.

Flip beckoned her to follow him and when she crossed the deck, the men whistled and laughed at her back. She ignored them. He led her down the stairs and into the darkness below decks, where the lanterns hanging at regular intervals threw light on a long corridor. Upon entering a large room brimming with benches and swaying with the billowy fabric of numerous hammocks, Estel was assaulted by a dank combination of mildew, sweat, and stale pivo. Her breath caught. She had become accustomed to unchallenged freedom in Grey Lands, and this place made her feel like a hunted animal, trapped in a cage with all ways to escape cut off. It took all her resolve to shut the sensation down. She reminded herself over and over that the voyage was a temporary inconvenience and she'd regain her freedom once the ship docked in Kvet.

Flip patted one of the hammocks in the far corner of the room. 'This is your nest, so keep it clean,' he said, then he waited.

When she placed her chest into the hammock, Flip snatched it and peered inside. Licking his lips, he began stuffing the coins in his pockets. Once emptied, he cast it aside. 'Now, woman, you're under my orders.' He nodded to himself as if pleased with the way he handled the situation. 'Your first task is to scrub this place clean. I want every corner polished and swept. Get to it.'

And so she found herself on-board the ship, and against all odds, heading in the right direction.

***

The open sea was just that—open. Wherever she looked, the wide expanse of water stared back. The waves rocked the ship back and forth and her insides rocked with it. Her sickness came not long after they set sail, and when she threw up on the deck, her first beating followed. Estel hauled water to scrub the area below decks when her stomach heaved and nausea overpowered her. She dropped the bucket and went down on all fours, retching. The moment the yellow spit from her mouth and nose hit the deck, a boot to her backside pushed her face first into the vomit.

'You filthy animal,' Flip yelled. 'I told you to clean the deck, not to puke all over it. And I told you to wash the grime off your skin.' He spat. 'Look at me when I'm talking to you. I gave Krag my word there'll be no trouble and I intend to keep it. Get a hold of yourself, or I'll feed you to the waves. Now, clean it up.'

The only thing that shielded Estel from the man's foulness was her detachment. Flip revelled in asserting his dominance over her, and he reminded her of the kids in the village who took equal pleasure in mocking her. It seemed that Greylanders had more in common than she thought. Watching Flip's sneer and the compulsion with which he licked his lips made her want to grab the dagger concealed in her boot and slit his throat. It was the second time she wanted to kill a human. He was a lesser creature than the animals she hunted. To her surprise, other sailors joined in his jokes and took pride in the assumption that they were her betters.

What was she? A woman. A creature that couldn't even defend herself if they had a mind to assault her. She longed to prove them wrong, but trapped on the open sea and the rocking ship, she stood little chance against the group of them.

She hardly saw Krag. From time to time, he emerged from his cabin, looking as pristine as during their first encounter, to dish out orders and voice his displeasure if tasks weren't completed to his standards. He paid no attention to her and left Flip in charge of her well-being.

Flip followed her around, scouting for opportunities to bring Estel to heel. She caught him leering at her more than once and if not for the dirt concealing her true visage, Estel suspected he'd do more than just stare. Her supply of ash was running low and the man's nagging about her cleanliness became more frequent. He stank himself, but this didn't seem to trouble him. Estel slept little. Any sound caused her eyes to snap open, her heart to pound. In her hammock, with no walls to either side, she felt exposed. At night, listening to the creaking of the ship's timber, she braced herself for an assault. Krag said the journey would take the measure of her fingers and toes, so she marked each passing day by cutting a piece from each of her nails.

Estel soon learned that rank aboard the ship was as important as their unquestioning obedience to the captain. The higher-ranking sailors had access to better quarters and food, but she was at the very bottom of that chain. Her daily rations consisted of a piece of stale bread and a bowl of oats with bits of meat floating among the lumps… if she was lucky. On some days, if Flip was in a particularly good mood, there'd be a chunk of cheese dropped on her plate and a mug of clear water.

When Krag warned her that she'd be put to work, he meant it. All tasks the men frowned upon were given to her—from waste disposal to scrubbing decks and running errands for Flip and other crewmembers. When she asked to try her hand at ropes, she was laughed at and ridiculed. By the end of the day, her body ached in places she never knew existed and climbing into her hammock each night, she prayed to Chour that her own kind was nothing like her present companions.

At first, she used her abilities to her advantage by focusing her senses on the conversations among the sailors and trying to accomplish tasks before they even asked her. But soon, her powers ran dry and she lost her focus. Despite that, she ground her teeth and pushed through the days, doing her chores without a word of complaint. With no fear to hinder her, she could stand her ground and take her punishment, and without shame, she was able to endure a daily portion of humiliation.

On one occasion, when she carried buckets of waste to tip them overboard, one of the sailors crossed her path complaining that she never cleaned up his quarters with such diligence. Estel knew it was a mere excuse for mockery on his part so she chose to ignore him. When she attempted to pass him by, he stopped her with his arm.

‘I was told to seek you out if I’m not satisfied with your services,’ he said, sneering.

Estel fixed her eyes on the deck. She learned that lack of reaction was the quickest way to get rid of unwanted attention. But the man refused to be so easily swayed. He placed his hands on his hips and kicked one of the buckets. The waste sloshed over the rim, splattering both of them.

‘Now, this isn’t the way to behave on a ship,’ he said. ‘Hey, Flip!’ He waved his hand. ‘We’re having some trouble here.’

Estel cursed under her breath. Whenever Flip got involved an otherwise unremarkable event would turn into a spectacle. The man liked to abuse his position to remind her and the crew of his importance.

‘What is it now?’ Flip asked, crossing the deck. He looked at the bucket and spilled waste. ‘You did this?’

The question was aimed at her, but she didn’t look up. To try and prove her innocence was a waste of time. Flip always sided with his men. At the sight of the commotion other sailors joined them and with each new onlooker, Flip’s voice grew bolder.

‘I warned you many times before to pay attention to your tasks.’ He appraised his men. ‘And what do we do when we have an insubordinate member in our ranks? We teach him a lesson, so here's yours.' He kicked at the second bucket and the contents splashed across the deck. The men sniggered.

'Clean him up,' Flip hissed, gesturing at the sailor who started this ruckus, 'then polish the deck.'

Uncontrollable anger flared up in her, locking her hands into fists, but when she wanted to act upon it, the sensation vanished as quickly as it came. She tried to hold on to it, turn it into hate, but it was too fleeting—like trying to catch a strand from a spider's web. With her skin smudged in grey, she blended with the men who regarded her as Flip's dirt slave and if she wanted to see the docks of Kvet, it had to stay that way.

But then came the storm.

***

The wind arose and tossed bruised clouds across the sky, threatening the crew with a change of weather. Angry waves swelled and tripled in size, and a low growl of thunder summoned lightning forks as wide and reaching as the branches of a klon tree, while their skeletal limbs stabbed at the horizon with an electrifying ferocity. Cursing and yelling, the men rushed about the deck, struggling to tie down the sails. Rain slammed their faces with force while the ship panicked beneath their feet, shoved about by the power of the elements.

Estel grabbed the nearest pole, fighting against the storm that stirred her stomach as if it were a pot of soup. The racket from each lightning strike split her skull in half and left her ears ringing. She moaned and retched while the world spun about in a frenzy. The curtain of rain soaked her clothes to the last thread, so thick she could hardly see beyond the length of her arm.

When a hand pulled her to her feet, she didn't resist—her strength abandoned her and just staying on her feet sapped all her energy. Flip shouted at her to get under the deck, but she only looked around in confusion at the chaos. She caught a glimpse of her hair ribbon going overboard, leaving her loose hair at the mercy of the gale. The soaked tips slapped her face like a whip. Flip dragged her to the hatch, but when he opened it, the wind ripped it from his hand. Without warning, he shoved her inside and she tumbled down the staircase, rolling away at the last moment to avoid his feet when he jumped after her. He grabbed her arm and pushed her ahead of him to the sleeping quarters.

When they entered the room, six men regarded her with wide eyes and gaping mouths. Krag was among them, and the look on his face sobered her up. One glance at her bare arm was enough to see that the rain had betrayed her, washing away all traces of her ashy disguise.

Flip wiped the water of his face and shoved her to the floor. 'Here she is, Captain.' His tongue darted over his lips like a fretful worm hooked on a sinker, and then, he noticed her changed appearance for the first time. 'What in Chour's name...'

A few men grunted, but the shock of seeing her true image still lingered on their faces. They looked from Krag to Estel and back, waiting for the captain to speak. It was clear they had never met one of her kind before, but she had no time to ruminate on the significance of this observation.

Krag closed the space between them in two powerful strides, lifted her chin, and turned her face from side to side. Unlike the sailors who didn't seem able to shake the initial shock of her deceit, the captain appeared strong and assured. His eyes had the same look that the men in her village had on the day the elders acknowledged her as a woman.

Estel would've been unaware of the Greylanders who took interest in her, but Lea's constant warnings about the danger of such infatuations made it impossible to ignore them. She remembered a young man, Shym, who started visiting her and bringing gifts and offerings for Lea. When she asked about it, Lea explained that such was the custom if one wanted to court another's daughter, and that the young man was in love with her. By village standards, he was a good match: a devout worshiper of Chour and the owner of a farm. She was seventeen years old, an age when most women in the village expected to find a mate, but the concept of love was foreign to her. Lea tried to explain how one feels when in love and urged her to pay close attention to the sensations in her body when in Shym's presence, encouraging her to act upon them. Estel remembered well the day he put his hand on her thigh. She heeded Lea's advice and stabbed Shym's grey fingers with her knife. Later that night, she had learned that this wasn't the reaction Lea hoped for. Following the incident with Shym, there were no further suitors and Estel was left alone, regarded by the Greylanders as an odd creature, an outsider who refused to integrate with them.

But Krag wasn't Shym and his eyes betrayed more than the look of a whelp in love. His dark pupils glistened in the light of the lantern suspended above her head, and the corners of his lips curled in a mocking smirk. He picked up a handful of her silver hair. 'You said your father crossed the sea in search of a better life in Kvet?'

She managed a nod but kept her eyes on Krag's while her mind assessed the surroundings, weighing her chances of staying alive. Storm sickness still raged in her gut, but she fought the bile back. The sailors formed a semicircle and even though she had the assurance of her knife pressing against her calf, she knew better than to draw it. In the confined quarters, she stood little chance of defeating a crew of this size. She needed to get outside and find her bow. Perhaps if she climbed the mast, she'd keep the men at bay, but as skilled as she was, aiming an arrow in this wind would be close to impossible.

'You see, I know all the ships in the harbour and none of them reported boarding a man who'd match your looks. If indeed such a man came through, the whole town would know about it. After all, we don't see many fair visitors.' He chuckled, and his voice turned dour. 'Do you take me for a fool?'

She did. They were fools, governed by their human weaknesses. Lust and greed drove them, and not for the first time, Estel was proud to belong to a different race. She had no need for the emotions that controlled these men and was done pretending to be a helpless girl.

'I'll get to Kvet with or without your aid,' she said, snatching the knife from her boot. With one quick move, she slashed at his fingers and the shock of it made him let go of her hair. The men gasped as Krag groped his bleeding hand. Estel seized the moment to jump to her feet and up on one of the long tables.

'What are you gaping at?' Krag screamed. 'Get her!'

Spurred by the rage behind the order, the crewmen grabbed their weapons. Estel crouched, her knife moving in fluid motion in front of her. She knew her chances of victory were close to none, but a rush of adrenaline unleashed a wild animal in her. Her heart drummed in her chest and the roaring of blood in her ears drowned the shouting of men as they advanced on her. Three of them held short swords and the other three seized objects at hand—a plank of wood, a bucket, and a piece of rope—to bring her down.

This was her first fight where her adversary wasn't forest prey but human. In her years of tracking and taking down animals in the wilds, the notion of killing a man had always lingered at the back of her mind—something she never admitted to Lea. Chour forbade slaughter of your own kind, but as she got more familiar with human desires, she trained for a day when people forgot the teachings of their faith and instead answered to the primitive parts of their soul. Now she was glad she did. Free from the emotional connection to humankind and their beliefs, her mind was clear and able to focus on defence when it mattered the most.

She aimed her knife at the first man who charged at her with a sword. Estel deflected his attempt at slashing her calf and delivered a stab to the side of his neck. He caught the gushing wound with his palm, staggered, and fell backwards with a look of disbelief on his face.

Estel watched him fall but felt nothing. It seemed that killing a man was easier than taking down a beast in the forest. Without as much as a shift in focus, she turned her attention to the second man. He attempted to knock her down with a piece of flat wood, so she jumped and seized the other end of it. The man lost his grip and the edge of the wood wedged in his chin. The four remaining men cursed and leapt at her in unison. Estel sprang to a nearby bench, narrowly avoiding a bucket that one of them flung after her. Leaping from bench to bench, she reached the far corner of the room, but there was nowhere else to go. The men surrounded her. Estel had no options left to her, but despite that, she refused to surrender or plead for mercy. If she was to die aboard this ship, she'd do so taking as many sailors with her as she could. The thought brought her a strange comfort.

She stabbed at the closest man, but he evaded her knife. 'What are you waiting for, feeble redbloods?' she asked through gritted teeth. 'I can smell your cowardice from here.'

'Stab her!' Flip screamed in rage. He kept close to Krag, following his men's efforts from a safe distance.

One of the sailors threw a length of rope over her head and pulled. Estel lost her balance and crashed onto the table while someone snatched her knife. The first blow caught her in the ribs, taking the wind out of her.

'I want her alive,' Krag's voice boomed in the close quarters.

Swords clattered to the floor, but the four men raged on with frenzied fists and boots that drew back to give each kick a crushing momentum. Instinctively, Estel curled into a foetal position, hands moving up to protect her head and neck. A sharp strike to her stomach caused something inside to shift, and she spewed silver. An endless stream gushed out of her nose, but the men continued to revel in their triumph. Black spots danced frantically beneath her eyelids and agony consumed every inch of her. The nausea she fought so hard to keep at bay burst out through her mouth and down her chin. The cabin turned blurry and her consciousness began slipping away.

'Enough,' Krag ordered. His voice sounded as though he were deep underwater. Squeaking of his boots filled the air as he crossed the cabin. When he leaned over, Estel managed to part one of her eyelids, the other was too swollen and refused to budge. Krag dipped his fingers into her blood, rubbed them together, and smelled the silver. He grabbed her by the hair. 'What are you?'

A cough was her answer. The cabin was spinning, and she no longer knew if it was the storm or her injuries that made it rock with such violence. She closed her eye.

'Get her back on the deck and chain her to the mast,' Krag said. 'Let the rain wash away her stink before you have your way with her. Whatever she is, let's make her first voyage unforgettable.' His words were met with laughter. 'You,' Krag beckoned one of the sailors, 'clean up here and throw the bodies overboard.'

Estel felt herself being dragged down the corridor and back out into the storm that didn't show any signs of abating. The rain mixed with salt water hit her like a multitude of insects with stings, biting deep into her open wounds. The wind carried her moans with it. Her uneventful life in Grey Lands didn't prepare her for such an assault. The men tied her with ropes to the mast and left her at the mercy of the raging gale.

She expected death to come swiftly, but her stubborn body clung to life like fire to dry wood. Her blood ran in silver rivulets down the deck and she struggled to breathe—when the men kicked her, they cracked some of her ribs. Her hands were fastened behind her so tightly that her fingers and arms went numb after mere seconds. She thought of Lea. Was her passing as agonising? Did she feel like her body was drenched in boiling water, scalding her from the inside out? She'd never know for sure. Deep inside, Estel sensed that she should hate the men who beat her so and seek revenge even as she drew her final breaths, but she felt nothing. When she tried to focus and wake the fury inside her, her heart showed a complete lack of interest. Was this what Lea meant when she called her broken and compared her to a soulless mrake?

A low growl stirred the storm and despite the pain, Estel's hearing sharpened. It took a lot of energy to use her abilities in such a state and the bleeding from her nose intensified. She was about to give up the effort when another growl rumbled through the air. The men who manned the rigging didn't look alarmed, so after a few moments, she put the sound down to the humming of blood inside her brain. Or maybe it was another bout of thunder.

The ship rocked violently from side to side. She got used to the motion of the waves, but this was different—it felt like someone or something deliberately shoved the boat. Another snarl followed and this time the men abandoned their tasks and ran to the railing to lean over the edge. One of them screamed and waved his arms at something down below. Estel strained to see through the rain as more crewmen emerged from their cabins to join their comrades at the railing, shouting to one another in panicked voices.

And then she saw it.

A massive tail emerged from the water, as tall as the tallest mast on their ship, and slapped back onto the surface of the sea, causing a rift between the waves. The force of the impact sent the vessel into a rocking hysteria and the men were thrown about the deck like rag dolls. Thanks to her bonds, Estel was spared. Flip and Krag darted across with their weapons drawn, screaming orders at the floundering men.

'It's a zmei!' somebody shouted to her left. 'Here to feast on us.'

Another splash severed the sea, and the zmei's tail rose and coiled around itself, droplets of water clinging to it like swellings on a skin. Its scales were bluish-green and looked like sharp arrow tips that overlapped, creating a body that could cut anything that touched it. Then came the head and Estel forgot all about her pain as she stared into six green eyes—three on either side.

If she only had her bow to hand, she could test her mettle against this magnificent creature. She fought her bonds, but no matter how hard she strained, she couldn't loosen them.

The zmei's jaws gaped open to display a mouthful of twisted fangs that snapped together in a quick succession. One of the crewmembers aimed and threw his spear at the creature, but it bounced off its scales like a splinter. The zmei turned on its attacker. Its giant maw grabbed the sailor and devoured him whole.

Tied to a mast, Estel was an easy target. 'Release me!' she screamed at Flip, who stood with his blade drawn and knees trembling.

The zmei rose higher and it shook itself free of water. When the droplets hit the deck, they bubbled and swirled, growing larger and larger until each took the shape of a man with a zmei's jaw. One of the water ghosts rushed to where Krag stood swinging his blade from side to side in readiness. When he slashed at the creature, the steel went right through and wedged itself into the deck. While he struggled to wrench it free, the ghost grabbed and sucked him inside its watery form until they merged completely. The image of a man trapped in a body shaped from pure sea water, yet solid, was something that even Estel found hideous. Krag struggled inside it like a man drowning, thrashing against the liquid walls, mouth opening and closing, hands clawing down the water. When his jerking stilled, the frame of the ghost splashed onto the deck in a puddle, freeing Krag's dead body before reshaping itself moments later.

Everywhere she looked, the crewmembers were dying in a similar way—devoured and suffocating inside the bodies of water, while the zmei snapped its jaws at those who tried to flee below decks. One of the ghosts advanced her way, and unable to fight for her life, Estel clenched her teeth and waited for the water to suck her in.

Everything froze.

The translucent arms that reached out to seize her became motionless, and the water dripping from them suspended in mid-air. The gaping maw of the zmei stopped inches from a cowering crewmember who had his arms wrapped around his face in a feeble defence. Even the storm came to a standstill. The rain halted in a wall of droplets and the wind, tearing at the sails moments before, ceased.

Estel stared in alarm at a sailor trapped inside one of the water ghosts. His lips were parted in a silent scream and small bubbles escaped them. The bonds holding her a prisoner to the mast fell off her wrists, and she rubbed at the angry flesh where the rope ate into her skin. Hesitantly, she reached with her fingertips and touched the falling rain. The droplets were cold and wet but held their shape.

'What's happening…?' The whisper died in her throat.

Whatever forces were at work were powerful enough to command the world to a halt. In all her years, Estel had never experienced magic such as this. Being trapped in it challenged the truths she lived by and made her question the clarity of her mind. In Grey Lands, she was the only one with the ability to control her senses, which helped her in becoming a skilled huntress. But looking at the powerful head of the zmei about to devour a man two strides from the mast she was tied to, was a proof that much greater force resided beyond the boundaries of her land. Here, aboard the ship bound for Kvet, Estel came to see that the world was a vast place, full of mysteries, and the thought shattered any expectations she might've had when stepping into it. The need for survival filled every cell in her body. She wasn't done yet. Her journey had just begun and she had so much to discover.

A sound broke through the silence—the familiar song. Its all-consuming melody filled the air and stirred the remaining raindrops, causing them to splatter on the deck.

'It's you,' Estel said.

The girl who sat by the fire in the forest walked between the water ghosts, the soft, brown toy clutched in her hand, her lips moving with the song.

VI

Arleta walked with her eyes fixed on Estel's. The winged insects on her dress reflected in the water forms as she passed between the ghosts, seemingly unmoved by the dying men trapped inside them. When she stopped in front of her, Estel's body tensed, bracing itself for some kind of unearthly blow that would thrust her into the Light Nav. But instead, Arleta extended her right hand and opened her dirty palm.

The song, the magic, the girl herself resembled something from an ancient scroll, a tale come to life aboard the ship. The sight of Arleta's little palm and fingers, half the size of hers, filled her with odd sensations. Part of her wanted to reach out and accept the girl's hand, wash away the grime from under her nails, and never again let her wander the world alone. But another part, the one that lived inside her brain, warned her that the girl's sudden arrival didn't bode well. Estel had to fight for her place on this vessel, so how had a young girl managed to persuade Krag to admit her on-board? And where was she all this time?

Despite the conflict between her heart and mind, Estel couldn't deny the force that pulled her to Arleta's hand. To fight the impulse seemed like a wasted effort, and even though her instincts screamed at her to stay away, her shaking fingers reached for the girl's.

The touch sucked her into a star-shaped whirlpool. Estel plunged into a vast expanse with stars and moons scattered like gemstones on the black firmament. The experience pulled her deeper and farther, and despite the whispers in her mind telling her there was no way she could know any of the objects, she recognised and could name them all. Here shone stars shaped into constellations of the bogs and animals, the planets in colours weaved from dreams, and mesmerizing silver paths that crested deeper into the ether. Her blood turned into pure energy that spurred her forward, and she wanted nothing more than to dissolve and become one with the stars, with her body and soul enwrapped in this magic for eternity. The second Estel acknowledged this feeling, it was gone. Elation was ripped from her and she plummeted through the sky, pain returning as she crashed onto hard ground.

The impact knocked the air out of her, setting her ribs on fire. Silver gushed out of her nose while the blood in her throat choked her. The smell hit her first. It was as if a volcano erupted in her lungs, reeking of scorched flesh and acrid vapours. With every intake of air she breathed in fine dust. Debris she fell upon dug into her, and her body felt like nothing more than a broken pile of bones and tissue. Her head swam in a sea of disconnected thoughts. Was she dead? Drowned inside the body of a water ghost?

Groaning, she pushed herself off the ground, catching the flat of her palm on a nail. Its rusted tip went right through and she looked at it for a moment, as if unable to comprehend the damage to her own flesh. The air was the colour of copper, saturated with dense smoke and dust, while the clouds towered above like wide-capped mushrooms. The world was a heap of debris with bits of wood, stone, and glass scattered as far as she could see. A few strides ahead, a red gateway supported by two vertical pillars and topped by a wide arch that curved like a bow, stood high amidst the rubble. A second arch rested under the first, connected to it by a rectangular block. In contrast to the bowed one, its shape was straight and simple.

Estel staggered on her feet—the heat of this place was unbearable, and it felt as if she had been cast down into the bowels of a fiery pit. The skin on her arms stung and when she scratched it, a big red blister formed on the spot. But worse than the physical discomfort was the pressure mounting in her brain. Thoughts, images, and sensations boiled inside it like a stew under a tight lid, but she didn't recognise any of them. Wave after wave of unknown emotions slammed her and she could hardly catch her breath between the assaults. When she couldn't take it anymore, she screamed, clutching her temples with both hands and digging her fingernails into them.

Like a whisper of a promise, the song filled the air, and yet again, Arleta walked toward her through the rubble.

Estel recoiled when the girl closed the distance between them. 'Stay away from me,' she told her in a raw voice.

The girl just looked at her, blue pupils calm and clear, but the whites of her eyes bloodshot, as if she hadn't known sleep in her life.

'What do you want with me?'

'The power is yours to claim, and I'm but a girl whose life is in your hands,' Arleta said in her broken language, and to Estel's dismay, this time she was able to understand the words. Her voice was quiet and there was a grave note in it, a kind of sadness that Estel never heard in the voice of any Greylander.

'I don't know you.' Estel cried out as another wave of emotions rushed through her. 'Please… I can't bear it.'

Arleta stepped closer and pressed her palm to the spot where Estel's heart fought against the confines of her chest. The touch was light, but it stilled every cell in her body, taking away the pain and confusion, and replacing them with a cool rush of serenity. Her heart slowed in its rhythm and she could distinguish every beat.

'Now,' Arleta's voice irrupted into Estel's consciousness, 'choose one. The one that stirs your soul.'

'I don't understand…' Estel said.

In the silence that enveloped them, even her chaotic thoughts stilled, and she was able to pick each of them apart. It was like standing inside a bubble while human emotions swirled outside it in a swarm of energy. She couldn't explain how she knew them, except that she did. Each one called out to her, probing different parts of her being, demanding of her to accept them as her own. How could she fight against such a powerful force?

'Pick one.' Arleta's voice jolted her mind back into focus. 'Look within yourself and find the will to resist the rest. They are all here, in this place, but you aren't strong enough to let them in at once. If you do, they'll devour you and you'll cease to exist.'

Estel brushed her fingers against the swirling energy powered by the emotional currents. It zapped her. She clutched her hand to her chest. 'They don't belong in me. I've no need for them.'

'You are the beginning and you are the end. Whichever path you choose, it'll lead you back to yourself. You are the Creator and you are the Destroyer.'

The cryptic words did nothing to ease Estel's uncertainty. She didn't understand them, but her heart did, for before she had a chance to consider Arleta's words, her hand plunged itself into the energy force. It felt like every bone in her body was ground to dust and every inch of her flesh shredded into a million pieces. Pain was no longer an adequate word to describe the way in which her body fell apart just to be put back together. She screamed as the agony grew more intense until every part of her was alight with it. Her right arm burned, and she ripped the sleeve free of it—a single symbol shone in a blinding, silver light.

She struggled to breathe in the heat and the harsh smell wafting from the ruins. The silver in her blood bonded with the emotion, and together they rushed through her veins like a raging river. She was certain that death had cast its shadow over her when the world began to spin like a waterwheel.

'Sorrow,' Arleta whispered. 'You chose sorrow. Now walk with it and see the future.' Then she was gone.

Estel staggered across the rubble, but despite the violent surge inside her, her vision was clearer than ever.

The crumbling stone, the splintered wood, the glass shattered under an immense rush of power and heat—she perceived this broken world through the eyes of those who lived in it. A hand poking through the debris with flesh scorched to the bone, a body burned beyond recognition—death was everywhere she looked, made inescapable by the numerous corpses, twisted inside window frames and trapped beneath the ruins of houses. And with every step she took, sorrow poisoned her heart. She hastened through the red gate and broke into a run, but it didn't matter how fast she raced, she couldn't escape the feeling of despair as it burrowed deep inside of her, forcing her onto an unfamiliar, harrowing path.

Beyond the gate, a cluster of people with hunched shoulders huddled on the ground, but when she neared them, what she saw sent another wave of anguish through her. The faces that looked up were covered in raw blisters, hair either burned or melted into their scalps. Their eyes looked like black stones, drowning in pools of crimson.

'Help us,' they begged with haunted voices in a tongue she never heard before, and yet understood. Her fingers curled around her chest. If not for the flesh and bone shielding it, they'd have clawed inside it and ripped her heart out to ease the sorrow that seized her.

‘I can’t help you…can’t help…I can’t…’She hastened away from them, licking her lips, which were cracked from the heat. The blood on her tongue tasted unfamiliar, as if imbued with steel.

Someone grabbed at her and she screamed.

A woman on her knees wrapped her hand around Estel’s calf, her grip as feeble as that of a newborn. ‘Water,’ she croaked. Her tongue dangled out of the corner of her mouth, so swollen it could no longer be contained inside. Half of her face looked as if had been boiled in water, inflamed flesh oozing clear liquid. The odour of rot hung thick about the woman. The sorrow in her was agony and the agony was sorrow.

Estel ripped her leg free. Whichever way she looked lay destruction, and far on the horizon, fires consumed the land. She began shaking violently, paralysed by the anguish and her inability to understand or control it.

‘Take it!’ she cried and sank to her knees, palm clasped over the symbol that burned the skin on her arm. ‘I don’t want it.’

When no one responded to her plea Estel raised her voice. ‘Free me from this sorrow, or take my life for I can’t bear it any longer!’

The blackness came over her and the inferno feasting on the land swallowed her into the bowels of heat and torment.

***

'Estel…' The voice came from far away and her first impulse was to hide from it, to remain unseen behind the curtain of darkness that had become her world. 'It's time, Estel…'

She recognised it then. It belonged to the man from her visions, the man with silver hair whose identity she struggled to recall. 'Leave me,' she said, her words cracking like dry kindling. 'I'm dead, drowned in the pool of that which you call sorrow.'

'We haven't much time,' the man said. 'Find your strength and return to your world.'

'There's nothing for me there. I'm broken.'

'If only I could teach you, tell you what you must do.'

'Why can't you? Why won't you?'

'It would disrupt the balance. You must walk your own path, chose your own way, for if you don't, that which you saw will be our future.'

Estel closed her eyes and shook her head back and forth, unwilling to hear his words. Everything she endured since she left the village was an excruciating mystery: the visions, the woman who possessed her image but rode with the Twilight Hunters, the girl who pulled her into the world of death and the pain she inflicted upon her there… Before all this, Estel was so sure of herself and her journey, unafraid to set foot on a vessel that would take her outside the safety of her world. But now, with her heart squashed and wrenched by images and feelings that weren't her own, she could no longer tell what her purpose was.

'The province of Suha,' the man's voice rattled through the darkness of her mind. 'You must go to Suha and find Ashk.'

Must she…? The question followed her into the blackness as the vision faded and her consciousness with it.

PART II
KVET

To free your soul from the shackles of fear,

first you must face it, then defeat it.

—The High Priestess of Vesta

VII

It was the smell—sweet, intoxicating fragrance that could only exist in the Light Nav. When the wispy aroma filled Estel's nostrils, it spread through her like a balm, soothing her injuries and relaxing her muscles. She was dead… she had to be. The sensation was too reassuring, too tranquil to be experienced on Daaria.

But reality returned with a sting, sharp enough to jolt her into the present. She slammed her hand against her neck. A winged insect with black and yellow stripes down its lower body, curled dead on the flat of her palm. She let it fall into the grass.

Estel had let sorrow in, and the silver symbol that appeared on her upper arm immediately after had not faded. It coiled down her bicep like a snake, and something resembling a tear was trapped inside the curve of its body. She scratched the edges of the mark, but her fingernails only reddened the flesh around it.

A rush of warm air soothed her skin, calming the swelling from her bruises. In the distance, the blue sea stretched as far as the edges of the world. Estel couldn't remember how she got here, and it didn't help that her body still felt as if it was aboard the ship, being abused by Krag's men. She examined her skin and probed her bones, but apart from lacerations and bruises caused by the fists and boots of the crewmembers, there were no other injuries.

The memory of the burning world, along with Arleta's insistence that Estel had to receive the sorrow of its people, resounded inside her brain. Deep down, Estel knew the experience had changed her forever, altering her perception of humanity. Until now, she viewed them as frail beings, unable to control their urges, but nothing could have prepared her for the sadness they harboured inside of them. Who would want to expose one's heart to such agony and sadness? Her instincts encouraged her to block the memory of the events she had witnessed there.

She listened, and used her energy to sharpen her senses, but her body was too weak and the dizziness overcame her. When she tried to focus on a cluster of trees ahead, her nose started bleeding. Wiping silver off her chin, she resolved to conserve her strength, unwilling to indulge the questions that hummed in her head like a swarm of flies.

She made for a track that ran parallel to the meadow. Grey Lands' sky was shrouded in a thick, monochrome blanket, but here it was pure and clear with clouds as white as fresh cotton. The sun reigned over this blue expanse in its full glory and every time Estel lifted her eyes, a stab of yellow snapped them shut. It was hard to believe that such a world existed. Even the air tasted fresh on her tongue and every intake of breath calmed the aching in her ribs. High above, birds trilled and swooped across the sky in joyful loops.

The track was wide and well-worn, with hoof and boot prints trodden into the soft earth. A rug of grass, spotted with flowers, separated the left side from the right, winding around hills and valleys that were free of settlements. As the sun moved higher, the heat intensified and her thirst with it. After a while, her mouth dried into a husk and no amount of lip licking would ease her craving. Her coins were lost with the ship, alongside her bow and dagger, and she had landed in a strange place without any idea where to go and what to do.

Something brushed past her ear, making her flinch. At first, she thought it was a flower, swept up by the breeze, but when it flew at her again, she realised it was a creature, with wings as colourful as the landscape. She wanted to scoop it up and examine its marvellous shades, but it appeared too fragile as it fluttered past and merged with the flowers. The more she experienced this world, the less she understood how anyone could accept a life in Grey Lands.

The path took her up the hill. When she cleared it, a cluster of trees beyond caught her attention. They looked nothing like the silver dabs, klons, and olshas she grew up with. These were covered in white and pink buds, attracting insects that buzzed about them in frenzy. For the second time the thought that she was dead and treading the Light Nav crossed her mind. Perhaps the zmei devoured her after all, and everything that happened since then was a part of her afterlife trials. She looked behind and around, searching for evidence of human activity, but the winding path and surrounding meadows were vacant.

Hours later, when the sun began its descent, a clattering of hooves broke the silence. A cart pulled by two horses rode down the hill in her direction. Estel felt a sudden pang of unease roll through her. What if it was someone from the ship? Maybe Krag survived his encounter with the water ghost and was searching for her, convinced that the zmei's arrival was her doing. She had no doubt that without weapons she'd be captured and tortured, but the open countryside offered little in terms of hiding. By running away, she'd draw attention to herself, so with her fists clenched and head down, Estel stepped aside to let the horses pass. But when the cart came within a close distance, the rider pulled on the rains and ushered the horses to a halt.

'You look lost,' the man's voice said.

She lifted her head to assess the threat and her chances, but instead found herself staring into crimson pupils, set against a golden background. She took a step back. The feeling must've been mutual, for his face twisted into a frown.

The stranger recovered faster than she. 'Where are you heading?'

Careful not to invite questions, she shrugged and said nothing. The colour of the stranger's eyes caused her skin to prickle as it reminded her how little she knew about this place and the people who lived here. Silence allowed her freedom to observe and judge.

The man looked her up and down. 'It looks like you had a hard journey.' He shifted on his bench and gestured for her to climb on. 'I'm heading for the city and wouldn't mind some company. My horses are great listeners, but not big on conversation.'

She pursed her lips and the man laughed. 'Perhaps you're no better than them in that respect. Either way, you look in need of assistance and I offer you my cart.'

Estel hesitated and weighed her options. Despite her weakened senses, she didn't detect any threat in the man's demeanour, and her time on the road urged her to accept the relief the ride would bring to her aching feet. She inclined her head in thanks and climbed the steps.

With a click of his tongue, the man spurred the horses forward and they were soon trotting along the track in a steady rhythm. As the cart swayed from side to side, Estel studied the stranger out of the corner of her eye. He appeared older than her, but not by much, and his hair, secured in a tail at the back of his head, was the colour of copper. When he caught her watching, she averted her eyes in haste.

A low chuckle escaped him. 'My name's Zeal.' When she didn't offer hers, he carried on, 'I'm on my way to the city to take part in the archery contest.' He motioned his head at the back of the cart. 'My bow can hardly wait.'

She kept her eyes on the horizon and acted disinterested.

'The city of Kvet is a half day's ride away.' He squinted at the sky. 'Judging by the sun's position, we should reach the gates with the first light of the moon.'

Estel stared at her palms. So, she had reached Kvet. Her ivory skin was disguised under a thick layer of dirt and hardship from her time at sea. To Zeal she must've look like a beggar. Even though he appeared unthreatening and his offer of a ride seemed genuine, she sensed something else. Perhaps it was the way his brows creased whenever he looked at her, or maybe it was a slight narrowing of his eyes, but regardless of the reason, she knew not to let her guard down.

'As you wish then,' Zeal said.

Was it irritation that ran off his words? She couldn't say for sure and resolved to watch him, while keeping herself to herself.

***

They spent most of the ride in silence, broken from time to time by Zeal's whistling. Estel didn't recognise the tune, and its jaunty notes did nothing to ease her suspicions. Since the encounter with Arleta, music of any kind woke weariness in her, as if the girl could be summoned by songs alone. Despite the feeling, she refrained from asking

Zeal to stop, wanting to avoid unnecessary questions on his part.

The sun edged nearer and nearer to where the sky met the earth, while the shadows of the trees shifted across the road like living creatures. The horses snorted to one another, shaking their heads when the reins tightened too much, but Estel found the thudding of their hooves oddly soothing. Despite her promise to stay alert, her exhausted body failed her, her eyelids grew heavy, and she began nodding away. With each bump in the road, she shook to wakefulness to find Zeal unperturbed, his eyes focused on the hills ahead. She was glad that her right arm was out of his line of vision. Even to her, the symbol looked unnatural—too shiny, too perfect—and judging by the curious glances Zeal sent her way from time to time, she didn't doubt he'd ask her about it. Estel wished for a shirt with long sleeves to conceal the mark, but there was little chance of finding one in the wilds. She tried not to think about what would happen when they reached the city. Without money, she'd have to resort to other means to get supplies.

She missed her bow. Ever since Zeal mentioned his own, she yearned to hold the curved wood against her palms and feel the safety granted by owning such a weapon.

A sharp jolt followed by a snapping sound shattered her musings. The horses reared up and Zeal jumped to his feet, trying to calm them, while the wagon tilted and came to a sudden stop. He hopped off and spoke to the horses in a soothing tone, petting one then the other on their sides. Once the beasts settled he turned his attention to the cart.

'For the curse of Agni! It's the last thing we need.' He leaned over and inspected the wheel. 'The bearing snapped,' he announced a moment later. 'We won't be going anywhere.' He ran his grubby fingers through his hair. 'The night is upon us, so I suggest we find a place to set up a camp.'

Without a word, Estel leapt off the cart. Considering Zeal's earlier words, if she walked long enough, she should reach the city before sunrise. Despite her weariness, she let out a long breath and started down the road.

'Where are you going?' he called, hastening after her. He caught her arm. 'You're in no shape to walk that distance on your own. Despite the warm days, the nights in Kvet are surprisingly cold and your clothes are in tatters.'

She jerked her arm free. 'Your earlier hospitality was a welcomed relief, but I won't linger in the dark with a stranger.'

'Oh, I see. You accepted my help, but now that I need help, you're quick to be on your way.'

'I can't help you,' she said in a firm voice.

'Can't or won't?'

'Both.'

Too many things had happened to her in a short space of time. From discovering the woman and her Twilight Hunters who burned her village to the ground, to her erratic visions and encounters with Arleta. Not to mention her narrow escape from death at the hands of the water ghosts. Zeal's troubles were no concern of hers. She needed to be alone, to consider her situation and what she should do next. But here she was, trapped in the middle of nowhere with a broken wagon and a man she didn't trust.

Zeal's jaw hardened, and she could almost hear the grinding of his teeth. 'In that case, go,' he said, and despite the tension in his body, his voice remained steady. 'I can't stop you, but be warned, the roads at night aren't safe for a woman with injuries such as yours. It's not my place to say, but if you don't do something about these cuts, they'll get infected.'

Estel brushed her hand against her face on reflex. The injuries answered with a sting and she winced.

Zeal must've sensed her hesitation. 'Why don't you stay and watch the horses while I go hunting for some meat?' His lips stretched into a hard smile, but she couldn't shake off the feeling it was forced to put her at ease.

Before she could respond, he walked back to the cart and pulled out his bow. At the sight of it, she sucked the air in. It was crafted of supple and graceful wood, not the sandy-coloured barks from which she'd made her own. This wood was unlike any other, in a shade of the deepest wine and seemingly capable of absorbing all light so that it could radiate against the shadows. A black vine wound around the curved limbs and its spikes reminded Estel of fangs from a poisonous snake. The grip was secured with rawhide.

'It's never let me down,' Zeal said, turning the bow in his hand. 'I intend to win the archery contest this year. If I ever get there on time, that is,' he added with a sigh.

Estel stood where she was, unable to take her eyes off the bow. She wanted to hold it, to feel the sleek wood with her fingers. But to show interest would betray her skills, so she forced herself to look away.

'I've got kindling in the back of the cart,' Zeal carried on as if he was confident she wasn't going to leave, 'but you'll have to gather branches.' He pulled out a quiver full of arrows. They too were made of the same wood. He set about stringing the bow.

Estel was tempted to ignore him and be on her way, but something about this stranger and his wondrous bow drew her in. Besides, she might need his help when they reached the city. Without another glance in his direction, she walked to the nearby thicket, picking loose branches on the way. The air smelt sweet and the night invited the half-moon and stars to rule the sky. Curious, she reached out and touched the pink buds on the trees. They felt soft and silky against her skin. What kind of place was Kvet? If she had ever stopped to imagine the afterlife and the world of Light Nav, it'd look like this, with trees dressed in bloom and the air so pure she wanted to get drunk on it. Even grass whispered softly beneath her boots, silken stalks springing back to life after she crushed them with her weight. A bird hooted in the trees. Startled by her approach, small critters fled the foliage.

Estel went back to the cart with an armful of branches. Zeal was gone, leaving the horses to graze free. She considered stealing one and riding to the city. How long would it take for Zeal to catch her? She entertained the idea for a brief moment but decided against it. If he did pursue her, he'd alert the guards and search the city. In her present state, she had no desire to deal with such distractions. The province of Suha lay to the west of Kvet, that much she knew, but how to get there was another matter. Would she need to cross the sea? After her experience on the ship, she preferred not to board one again.

To set the fire boundary, she found some loose stones at the side of the road and arranged them in a circle. With seasons of practice lighting Lea's hearth, she stacked the kindling and the thinnest twigs first, then set about igniting them by striking flint against steel. When the sparks caught, and the fire licked the wood, she nodded to herself—unlike other things in the world, knowledge was forever.

Zeal wasn't wrong when he warned her about the cold. As the night took hold, it brought a chill that found its way into her bones, making them shiver. She enticed the flames, feeding them with the thicker branches.

'So, I wasn't wrong about you. You can light fires.' Zeal came out of the shadows and dropped two hares at her feet. 'The moon is young and the light in the forest scarce. It'll have to do. Besides, I didn't want to leave you alone for too long.'

She stiffened. 'You needn't worry about me.'

'You're right, I don't, but what kind of a man would I be if I let you enjoy the fire all by yourself?' He chuckled, and she sensed his words were meant as a jest, but there was nothing humorous in their circumstances.

Her lack of engagement didn't seem to dampen his spirits as he set about skinning the hares with a joyful whistle on his lips. After a time, she joined him, and soon the two animals were propped over the flames, filling the air with the smell of charred flesh. Estel couldn't wait to sink her teeth into them. The taste of roasted meat and the warmth from the fire wrapped her, and for a short while it was enough—no thinking about the past and no worrying about the future.

When the meat was gone, Zeal fetched a cask of water from the cart and filled a bowl with it. Estel watched as he unwrapped a small bundle and selected a few dried herbs from it. He crushed them into the water and placed the bowl near the fire. When it began to steam, he dipped a piece of cotton in it and approached her. She recoiled.

‘Let me see to your wounds,’ he said. ‘It’s not much. Just some healing herbs from my homeland. They should ease the pain and stop the infection.’

Estel wasn’t happy about letting a stranger near her face, but the meal and warmth took the last of her energy. Red in Zeal’s pupils merged with orange from the fire and the effect was mesmerising. She didn’t protest when he began wiping her forehead. The smell of herbs hit her nostrils and she thought she recognised the bitter scent of salfa. His moves were gentle as he cleaned her face and examined the cuts by pressing around them. The skin of his fingertips felt rough against her cheek.

‘You may need stitches,’ he said, hesitating. His eyes searched hers as if they could give him the answers to some unspoken question. When his fingers brushed against her lower lip, she pulled back.

‘Here, you can do the rest.’ He handed her the cloth and she noticed a little trembling in his fingers.

Estel wiped her neck and arms, doing her best to ignore Zeal’s frequent glances. She wanted to ask him if he met anyone like her in his travels, but her ingrained caution stopped her from doing so.

‘Now that we shared a meal and you allowed me to play healer, can you at least tell me your name?’ Zeal said.

Disclosing her name to a stranger was risky, but he had helped her. What harm could it do? Soon they'd reach the city and go their separate ways. 'Estel,' she said, keeping her eyes on the flames.

'So, Estel, what brings you to Kvet?'

'Is my name not enough?'

'I can see you're in trouble. You don't look like a worshiper of Vesta. In fact, I haven't met anyone who looks like you and I wager that you haven't been to Kvet before.'

His words set her mind on edge. She looked for something to busy herself with and her eyes found his bow. It was a mistake.

'Flamewood,' Zeal said. 'It's made of flamewood.'

The fire reflected in the wood and made it look alive. 'I've never heard of it.'

'That's because it's rare and can only be found in the province of Vatra. If one knows where to look.' He picked up the bow and passed it to her. 'Try it.'

'What makes you think I want to?'

'I saw you looking at it earlier and if I know anything about bows and those who wield them, I'd say you know your way around a bow and arrow.'

'Can you see a bow on me?'

'I don't have to, but here's an idea. I challenge you to a match of skill. Bow against bow.' He tilted his head as if daring her to turn him down. 'What do you say?'

Estel clasped her hands and studied Zeal's face. 'What would you know about my skills, stranger?'

'Do you always answer a question with a question? My offer stands. Come with me to the city and take part in the archery contest. There's money in it for the winner and something tells me you could do with some.'

'I haven't got a bow and no means to make one.'

'Let me worry about the bow. Do you accept my challenge?'

'I don't see how it would profit you. Why insist on competing against me?'

'Not everything is about profit. I should know.' He walked to the cart and found a blanket. 'It's been a long time since I met a worthy opponent.' He offered it to her.

'You don't know me,' she said, taking it from him.

'Agni crossed our paths for a reason, so let us see where this chance meeting will lead us.'

Zeal added more wood to the fire and curled up on his hide. Estel listened to his breathing as it went from quick to slow, until it settled into a steady rhythm of a man asleep. Why anyone would want to let their walls down next to a stranger was beyond her. For all he knew, she was a killer like Krag, intent on stealing his horses and his life. Zeal's insistence on her taking part in the contest heightened her mistrust for him. He seemed so positive she was an archer. The sooner they parted ways the better.

For a time, she watched the flames as they moved to the whims of night's breeze, but soon even she gave in to tiredness.

VIII

The banging woke her with a start and instinctively she reached for her bow. Her palm found nothing but soft grass. It took her a moment to recall the events of the past night. She looked around the makeshift camp and saw Zeal fumbling with the cart's wheel. Estel got to her feet and stretched. She felt rested, and following the herb treatment, her wounds didn't hurt as much.

At her approach, Zeal wiped sweat off his brow and cursed under his breath. 'Damned wheel. I haven't got the right tools. It looks like we'll have to ride the horses after all.'

'If you listened to me last night, we would've been in the city by now,' she said.

'Let me remind you whose cart this is,' he snapped and kicked the wheel. 'We best make haste if we don't want to spend another night under the stars.' He reached into his inside pocket and offered her a bunch of leaves. 'I found these while you slept. Applying them to your wounds should help.'

'Why would you care about my pain?'

He grinned. 'If I'm to win the contest, I'd like to know it was my skill and not your injuries that made it happen.'

She said nothing but worked the leaves into the wounds that hurt the most. It was hard to tell how severe her injuries were, but the skin under her left eye felt puffy and her lower lip was split. There was an oozing cut to one of her cheeks and the numerous bruises on her arms and legs took on the shade of a spoiled fruit. But the worst was on the inside, where the sailor's boots kicked her ribs and stomach.

'It'll sting to begin with,' Zeal said when she discarded the leaves.

He was right. It stung like salt on an open cut, but the sensation soon faded and was replaced by a tingling numbness.

He offered her the reins of the brown mare with white markings on the lower half of its legs. 'I've never been on a horse,' she said. When she took them, the animal shifted uneasily. The feeling of apprehension was mutual.

'There's a first time for everything.' Zeal spoke to the horse in a calm voice while he helped her up into the saddle.

Estel settled, but her calves tightened with every step the horse took— she much preferred her feet to take her where she wanted to go.

‘Her name’s Lulu,’ Zeal said, patting the mare’s neck. ‘You’ll get on well together. She too is prickly around strangers.’

He went on to explain how to handle the reins and take control of the horse. She nodded at his words, pretending to understand what he meant by ‘gait’ and ‘canter’. When he was done, he left them alone to mount his own horse. Estel urged Lulu back to the road. At first the horse was reluctant to follow her lead, and she struggled to convey her intentions through the reins. The animal reminded her of herself when she sparred with Lea over her inability to empathise with others. She steadied Lulu over rough terrain and after a few failed attempts at control, the horse settled into a trot.

The morning sun woke from its slumber to begin its daily climb, and enticed by the warming rays, birds sang their cheery songs. The world around them was so colourful it was hard to believe that Kvet was a real place. Zeal rode his black horse next to hers with confidence she lacked. With his back straight and eyes focused on the horizon, he whistled a happy tune and she wondered how it must feel to have so much joy inside you—or any joy, for that matter. Her strongest emotion manifested when Arleta forced her to walk among the dying in a world made of fire and pain. The memory of that sorrow rattled her more than she cared to admit. She never wanted to experience such feelings again, so she refused to indulge in it. Her hand travelled to the winding mark on her arm—she had to find a way to erase it, for if she didn't, it would taunt her for the rest of her life.

'What's that on your arm?' Zeal asked.

Estel jolted in the saddle. Lulu pulled on the reins and trotted sideways.

'Whoa, be careful with her,' he called. 'Horses are quick to sense their riders' unease. Stay calm.'

'Maybe if you'd stop your incessant questioning, I could focus on riding.'

Zeal snorted but didn't bother with a riposte. 'When we get to the city, stay close and keep Lulu calm.'

'I can look after myself.'

'No doubt, but I'd rather not waste my time looking for my horse in a sea of people.'

She frowned. 'How bad could it be?'

A laugh was his only reply.

Encouraged by the gentle breeze, the flowers on the ground opened up their petals to welcome insects that whirred in circles above them. The sweet bloom teased her taste buds, each inhale leaving a taste of syrup on her tongue. On one side of the road, the forest thickened, and deep green leaves replaced the pink buds. Her eyes followed the sun rays as they forced their way through the crowns to reach the forest floor. A movement caught her eye—an animal of some kind crept at the wood's edge, weaving between the tree trunks. She harnessed her energy in an attempt to focus on it, but her strength was lacking, and it was difficult to control the horse and her abilities at the same time. The tall grass came into sharp focus and she could see a narrow trail between the blades. She followed it with her eyes, blind to all but the scene before her. Just as her vision blurred and the pressure began building in her nose, she spied a paw print and glimpsed a patch of silver fur. Her concentration broke and spots of silver patted the reins.

Estel slid off the saddle, and ignoring Zeal's shouting, ran into the forest, heart racing in her ribcage like a wild horse. Beyond the line of trees, she stopped and scanned the area. Under the abundant crowns, shadows found their solace from the blaring sun, and her vision took a moment to adjust before she navigated her way deeper through the rich foliage. She found the trail in the grass and followed it to a glade.

The silver fox, its head cocked to one side and ears erect, sat in the middle of the clearing.

'Srebro,' she whispered. 'But… I crossed the sea.' She swallowed against the rising lump in her throat, fighting the first swell of sorrow until it broke free and crossed her heart.

The sound of boots tearing through the undergrowth interrupted the moment. Zeal's voice calling her name rang through the forest and Srebro's ears flattened against her skull.

Estel glanced over her shoulder then back. 'We're strangers in this land. It's not safe here.'

There was no way for her to take care of the animal, and all she could do was watch Srebro jump to her feet and flee. But the sadness didn't flee with the fox. It gnawed at the edges of Estel's heart and she was helpless to silence it. Lea spent years trying to wake emotions in her and failed, so how could it be that one glimpse into another's sorrow would alter her so?

The slight creaking of a bow being drawn brushed her ear and when she turned around, an arrow stared back at her.

‘What is it?’ Zeal asked, but he didn’t ease the string. His eyes were focused, lips pressed flat as he waited for an answer.

Estel sensed her choice of response would direct the arrow, so she kept her eyes on his and said, ‘I thought I saw something.’ Her voice was calm and assured. Zeal was a hunter. To ensure Srebro’s safety, it was best to keep her existence a secret. ‘But I was mistaken.’

Part of her wanted to chase after the fox, but another part demanded a confrontation with Zeal. He intruded on her life and stood in the way of what she wanted to pursue. And now, his arrow was trained on her heart—another reason to keep her distance.

Zeal looked around the glade. His chest rose and fell from his run and his clenched teeth made his jaw look more prominent. The stubble that covered his chin was the colour of rust. Estel had never seen a man with such freckled skin, but with his copper hair and strange eyes, she couldn’t imagine him any other way.

She raised her eyebrow at the arrow. ‘Well?’

‘I don’t see anything.’ He lowered the bow, but the scorn on his face spoke of doubt. ‘Next time you decide to run off into the forest by yourself, I’d appreciate a word of warning.’

She said nothing and started for the road.

He grabbed her arm. 'Are you running from someone?'

She narrowed her eyes. 'Should I be?'

'You're on edge. From the moment we've met, you've followed my every move as if I am about to pull a knife and slash your throat. You act like nothing can get to you, but your injuries tell another story.'

He loosened his hold on her arm and she pulled it free.

Zeal lifted his hand as if to touch her hair, but she took a step back. She wasn't about to fall into the same trap that Mara did back in the village. She was the only friend Estel had and even that was too big a word. Mara, who took her own life because of a man, once described the feelings she had for her lover. How his touch set her skin alight, how his promises tasted sweeter than honey, how one look from him would send her heart into a mad quiver. When Estel showed no reaction, Mara began questioning her about love, but Estel had nothing to say. For what was love to someone who couldn't feel it? Following Mara's demise and the circumstances surrounding it, she came to the conclusion that love was the weakest of emotions and she was better off without it. To be spared the constant wrenching of the heart as she understood it was a blessing, not a curse.

Zeal scanned the clearing one last time and motioned Estel to follow him.

They went back to the horses and she climbed the saddle. Riding was a difficult skill that required practice and balance, but she managed to keep straight and after a time the mare accepted her clumsy attempts at control.

No words passed between her and Zeal and she didn't notice any sign of Srebro. The wild country made way to smallholdings, and rich pastures grazed by white, woolly-coated animals. People moved about with tools in hand, tending their blooming orchards and vegetable fields. At last, in the deepening shadows of the afternoon, palisades appeared on the horizon. When Estel first entered Grey Lands' harbour, its size surprised her, but the city of Kvet made a jest of that surprise. It expanded as they closed the distance, claiming the fields and smaller farmsteads. The road narrowed, as if put to shame by the wide bridge separating it from the main gates. It was made of stone and curved over the fast-flowing river like a crescent moon. Two statues graced each corner of the bridge, both resembling a woman holding a bouquet of flowers.

'It's boginya Vesta,' Zeal said. 'They worship her in the biggest temple in Kvet, and in return she blesses them with this weather. If you ask me, it's a great reward.'

Estel noticed the absence of stone boundaries. 'What about Chour?'

He gave her a questioning glance. 'Is he a bog you worship?'

'Don't we all?' She heard him mention Agni before, but surely, all people bowed to Chour above other deities. This is what Lea led her to believe.

'I've never heard of Chour, but then again, I don't worship Vesta either. In my homeland, we honour the bog of fire.' He emphasized the word fire as if it harboured a special meaning.

'Where's home?' she asked.

He laughed. 'Oh, so it's fine for you to ask questions, but if I do the same, all I get is a stony silence.'

She had nothing to say to that. Instead, she turned her attention to the statues. Boginya Vesta had a kind face and a small smile curved her full lips. Unlike Chour's tightly drawn brows, hers were lifted in a questioning kind of way, as if she wanted you to come up and betray all your secrets. Vesta's hair was chiselled from stone with such precision that every curl wound as tight as locks of real hair. It wouldn't surprise Estel if the boginya came alive and spoke to them as they made their way across the bridge.

The clatter of Lulu's hooves rang through the air and below them, the water murmured over stones and moss, rushing down a well-worn bed. The sun shimmered on the surface that was so clear Estel could see every rock and strand of river grass. Fishes swam with the current, their scales as colourful as the flowers of a nearby meadow.

Zeal dismounted, and she followed suit. At the gate, two guards blocked their passage. Estel stayed silent and let Zeal explain the reasons for their visit to Kvet. He told the men they hoped to partake in the upcoming archery contest and to prove he was telling the truth, he patted his bow and quiver.

One of the guards motioned her way. 'Where's her bow?'

It seemed that at every turn someone attempted to delay her, and she had to curb the urge to tell the guards the way of it. But she knew better than to force her passage. It was her experience that humans tended to favour lies over the smallest of truths, so she listened to Zeal's tale about troubles with their cart and the difficult journey through the wilderness. Judging by their rigid faces, the guards were doubtful, but Zeal didn't show any signs of slowing down. His tale grew to include encounters with wild animals and the supplies those beasts snatched from them.

One of the guards raised his palm to stop him. 'You may pass, but if you and your… companion—' he wrinkled his nose '—cause any trouble, we'll find and punish you in accordance with Vesta's laws.'

'No trouble from us, right, sister?' Zeal asked her.

'No trouble,' she agreed, and promised herself that as soon as an opportunity presented itself, she'd abandon Zeal and continue her journey west.

With a grimace, the guards motioned them through the gate. As soon as they led the horses under the archway and into the city's street, Estel halted.

'What's the matter?' Zeal asked.

The sudden noise and surge of activity hit her like a wave, and if not for the solid ground beneath her she would've thought that she was back at sea.

'I… so many people in one place,' she said as her mind threatened to fracture like it did in Grey Lands' harbour.

Zeal adjusted the bow on his shoulder and offered his hand. 'This way we won't get separated.'

She looked at him, then at his open palm. Some of his fingers had strips of cotton wrapped around them to aid bow handling, others were callused. Why would he think that holding his hand would make her feel better? She was about to refuse him when he took her hand in his. It was strong and warm at the same time. He pulled her into the crowd.

The city of Kvet was a vast maze of red buildings with dome-shaped roofs, clustered together like a bunch of friends around a campfire. Visible through the open windows, curtains of white silk swayed on the breeze, and from within, the voices of residents echoed back into the street, mixed with the smell of freshly-baked bread. At the front of each house, in a fenced garden, a tree dotted with red buds grew in a sea of neatly-trimmed grass. The flowers bloomed all around: on the windowsills, by the doorways, at the corner of each house. They lined the pavements and wound around fences, attracting insects and flies with their intoxicating aromas.

Zeal led them through the alleyways and down the market street, where merchants bartered from behind counters heavy with cloth, spices, and trinkets. A woman in a colourful dress sat on a barrel, playing a long instrument with holes down the middle, and the crowd that gathered around encouraged her with clapping. Further down, a group of boys tossed seeds from their pockets to a bunch of white and yellow birds. But the most surprising of all was the variety of humans populating the city. Gone were the ashen skins of Greylanders, replaced by various shades of white, brown, and black, each with a different outfit to match. Kvet seemed to have welcomed every race into its flowery embrace. Zeal's red and golden eyes reflected in many faces that made the man himself look less dubious. Encouraged by such diversity, Estel studied each person, looking for the familiar shades of ivory and silver, but despite the motley that was Kvet's population, it lacked the colours of her own kind.

'The temple of boginya Vesta,' Zeal said when they emerged into a giant square, 'the bearer of spring and goodwill.'

Atop a steep hill and soaring above the city's square, a tower of stained glass rose in the shape of a shard, gleaming like the most precious flower. Above its entrance, moulded from the same glass, was an image of Vesta, watching over those who chose to seek solace between her walls. Women dressed in white robes welcomed worshippers at the gates by placing green and blue wreaths upon their heads.

'We'll stay at a tavern owned by a friend of mine,' Zeal said, leading her and the horses into a narrow street and away from the crowds. 'Warm tub of water is what I need.'

Estel couldn't remember the last time she had felt clean. Perhaps the distaste on the gate guard's face was warranted after all.

'I have no coins,' she said.

'Don't worry about coins, the keeper owes me a favour.'

She didn't know why Zeal insisted on helping her—there were many things she didn't understand about him—but her options were limited. Growing up in the village, she soon learned that humans were creatures of secrets, wanting you to believe one thing whilst their actions often proved that the opposite was true. If she was strong enough to utilise her abilities in full, she'd discover the reasons behind his intentions, but for now, all she could rely upon were her skills of observation.

The tavern was a wide and low structure with a rounded roof and timber walls. From the outside, it was the least colourful building in the city, but it looked orderly and clean. Red candles replaced the flowers in the windows and the main room smelled of roasted meat and sap.

A muscular man came up from behind the counter. Judging by his freckles and eye colour, he too was a native of Zeal's homeland. 'My friend, it's good to see you again.' They clasped hands and he pulled Zeal into a tight embrace. 'How long has it been?'

'Long enough for you to turn this place into a home,' Zeal said. 'We've left the horses outside.'

'Tori,' the innkeeper called, 'stable the horses and feed them.'

Tori, who was busy cleaning tables, wiped his hands on his grey tunic and headed outside without a word. His hair looked dishevelled and his eyes had red circles under them.

'The lad is nothing but trouble since I agreed to apprentice him,' the innkeeper said when the door closed behind Tori. 'All he wants is to sneak out in the middle of the night and frolic with girls. A little bit like yourself before your—'

'Meet Estel,' Zeal cut him off, 'she's here to challenge my bow skills.'

At the mention of her name, the innkeeper's eyebrows shot up, but he soon composed himself. 'I'm Yari.'

He offered his hand in greeting. Estel looked at it but didn't extend her own. Touching hands with strangers wasn't the way of Greylanders, so instead she inclined her head in acknowledgement.

Zeal broke the awkward silence. 'I feel like eating everything in your pantry. Some hot water for a bath wouldn't go amiss either. Agni didn't bless our journey here, I can tell you that.'

'Bogs never do, especially if your faith is lacking.' Yari nudged Zeal in the ribs with his elbow. 'It seems this journey of yours was a rough one. For some more than others.'

Estel sensed that his last words were meant for her, but she chose to ignore them. If Yari wanted to know something, he should ask her instead of hinting. It would change little in terms of her answer, but at least he'd know that she heard him.

Yari led them to a table in the corner of the room.

'Your tavern looks nothing like the other buildings,' she said, looking around the cave-like interior. While she was trapped in this city, she might as well learn more about it. At some point she'd have to look for supplies and information. Starting here was as good a place as any.

'I prefer simplicity to the flowery splendour of Kvet.'

'If that's so then why live here?'

'My homeland is a very special place, but not all can abide by the rules of our bog,' Zeal said. 'For some of us, leaving Vatra is the only way.'

She didn't press him for more—she was bound for Suha and Vatra was of no interest.

Tori came back and Yari gestured him over. 'Get us some medr, a loaf of bread, and pickles to go with it.'

The request earned Yari a scowl, but the boy did as he was bid. The tavern was mostly empty aside from a cluster of men discussing matters in hushed voices, and two black-skinned women who leaned over what looked like a map.

'How did you and Zeal meet?' Yari asked when the food arrived.

'It's a long story and not to be told on an empty stomach,' Zeal answered, and Estel detected a hint of warning in his voice.

Yari cleared his throat but asked no more questions.

When Tori returned with a second platter bearing sliced ham and bowls of fish pieces floating in white sauce, she eyed the food with suspicion. In Grey Lands, most of what she ate came from her hunting and Lea's cooking of the meat. The dishes they shared were simple: stews, oats, and seafood procured mainly from travelling merchants or hauled from the harbour. The fish in her bowl smelled like river grass and the ham was smoked and spotted with fat. If not for the hunger twisting her stomach, she'd have refused the food. Zeal didn't have such qualms and piled his bowl full of pickles and meat.

Tori frowned at that. 'It's best to eat them separately.'

'Medr casks need refilling,' Yari said and ushered him away. 'I'd like nothing more than stay and listen to your tales, but with the contest fast approaching, there's so much to prepare. I'll see to your bath water and we'll talk later.'

Estel bit off a slice of meat—it was salty, but she enjoyed the smoky taste it left on her tongue. Encouraged, she tasted the fish. The white sauce was mild, but not unpleasant.

'Yari's a good friend,' Zeal said, as if she needed convincing. 'He dug me out of a tight spot more than once.'

Tori sent more platters their way with meat encased in peppery jelly and steaming bowls of soup that contained red roots. They ate in silence and washed down the feast with a mug of spicy medr. Estel began to relax and when Yari returned to take her to the bathhouse, she welcomed the thought of washing away the dirt from the road and soaking her worn muscles.

'I found some clothes that should fit you well,' Yari said, leading her to the back of the tavern and down the steps. He ignited a lantern to reveal a square room with a wooden tub in the centre filled with steaming water. There was a gap on the wall the size of two fists put together through which steam escaped in a cloud. 'No one will bother you here, so take your time. I've prepared a room for you. Just take the stairs to the right of the counter. And if you need anything, there's a bell on a bedside table. Ring it and Tori will attend to your needs.'

'I'd rather he didn't.'

'He can be a handful, but he's a good lad. His family fell on hard times.'

'What do you want in return?' Estel asked when he turned to leave. Whenever Lea asked for help, there was always a price attached. Most often she relied on Estel's hunting skills and bartered the meat, but Yari didn't strike her as a man who needed that kind of assistance.

'In return? Zeal is like a brother to me and he brought you here, so you're both welcome to stay for as long as you want.'

'He challenged me to take part in the archery contest.'

Yari smiled, but the smile didn't quite reach his eyes. 'I'm surprised at that for he wasn't planning on entering this season.' He looked at her as if expecting her to challenge him. When she didn't, he carried on, but his voice was less certain. 'But…he must've had his reasons. Be warned, though, he's the best bowman in these parts and no other matches him in skill.'

With that he left the room. Estel removed her tattered clothes and loosened the braids in her hair. When she stepped into the tub, a pleasant shiver ran up her spine. She lowered herself into the water—it was just the right temperature as it wrapped her in a warm embrace. Hanging off the side of the tub was a coarse mitten. A bar of brown soap rested on a stool next to it and its smell reminded her of freshly cut wood. She set about scrubbing the layers of grime that clung to her body since her departure from Grey Lands. Like unsettled mud at the bottom of a lake, the water changed from clear to murky, revealing her ivory skin. In places, her hair had become solid tangles, so she decided to ask Yari for a cutting blade.

She stepped out of the tub and rubbed herself dry with a towel. The clothes left by Yari sat on a stool by the door. The leather on the black leggings looked worn and the cotton shirt had a small hole above the elbow, but both garments were in good enough condition and fitted her well. The black cloth was a stark contrast to her skin tone, but she couldn't do much about it. At least the mark on her arm was covered and the shirt had a light hood to conceal her hair and face if she needed it. She secured her waist with a belt and put her boots back on. Her hair was still damp when she left the bathhouse and found the stairs Yari spoke of. The tavern was busier now. People filed in from the outside to enjoy a drink and talk about the archery contest. As not to draw unwanted attention, Estel put her hood on and made her way up the stairs. Zeal waited at the top.

'Are you who I think you are?' he asked, and she spied a flicker of admiration in his eyes. 'You needed that bath more than me.'

She snorted. 'Is everything a jest to you?'

'It's enough that one of us is grim all the time. I'm here to lend balance.'

She waved her hand at him and carried on to her room, but Zeal blocked her with his body. 'I'm no fool. You don't trust me, and I don't expect you to. Not yet, anyway. But when I challenged you to a match of skill, I meant it. I'd like to take you to a man I know. He's the best bowyer in Kvet.'

She dismissed the first part of his speech. It wasn't a matter of trust. Zeal was a stranger she chanced upon when she needed help and nothing more. ‘I prefer making my own bows.’

‘Just meet the man before judging his work. If you still insist on making one yourself, so be it, but not before you see his wares.’

‘A bow is a costly gift to offer a stranger,’ she said, studying his face.

He returned her stare. ‘Something tells me it’ll be worth it.’

‘You’ll lose.’

‘I can’t wait.’

IX

The crowd suffocated Estel as they made their way into the bowels of the city. The constant shuffling of feet, raised voices, the smell of too many people in one place, it was like being trapped in a room with walls closing in all around. Whilst she wanted to fist her way through the masses as soon as possible, Zeal couldn't curb his excitement, whistling and grinning at the citizens of Kvet as if he knew them intimately. When Estel challenged him about his cheery ways, her rebuke did little to dampen his spirits.

Despite her irritation with the outside world, she felt rested and more alive after last night's sleep. The bed in her room was padded with soft straw and when she sank into it, sleep snatched her at once. When she woke up, the weakness that hindered her senses was gone, and even though her body still ached in places, the worst of it subsided. Her vision was clear and hearing sharp, but at the same time, it was a handicap that heightened her awareness of the city around her. To make matters worse, in this ever-changing landscape of movement and noise, there was nothing to focus her mind on.

The streets were populated with shops selling ground meat stuffed into animal's intestines next to potatoes and beetroots. Some of the bolder traders enticed people to their stalls by promising lower prices for their colourful tubes of silk and cotton. They passed a grey-haired woman offering an assortment of herbs and brews. Her green dress reminded Estel of Lea. Since the day Arleta took her hand and led her into the sorrows of the burning land, she refused to think of her adoptive mother. It wasn't because she feared the memories, but because the little voice that woke inside her that day warned about the consequences of such thoughts. A dark finger of guilt pointed her way every time her mind turned to Lea's final moments. The way she left her body to the mercy of darkness was enough to rattle her heart, and it wasn't a feeling Estel wanted to encourage in herself. It made her feel almost human.

'How far is this bow master of yours?' she asked to keep her mind from further exploring her feelings.

Zeal pointed at the wooden bridge ahead where the river cut the city in two. 'His shop is on the other side.'

A woman wrapped in yellow skirts crossed Estel's path. She held an armful of necklaces and bracelets made from sparkling beads. 'Would you care for one?' she asked in a sweet voice, peering into the folds of Estel's hood.

'The best jewellery for a silver maiden.' She shook her arm, making the beads jingle.

When Estel sidestepped her, the woman rushed to Zeal's side. 'One for your beloved?'

He pushed her out of his way and they picked up pace.

'It's not such a bad idea, you know,' he said, leading them across the bridge.

The planks thudded under their boots and the sun rays transformed the river into gold. 'What idea?'

'To pretend we're together.'

'We *are* together.'

Red touched his cheeks. 'I mean *together*. It'd stop people from staring at you.'

Estel struggled to follow his logic. 'No one is looking at me, and even if they did, how would being "together" stop them?'

'Every man who passed us by was drawn to you. How many people have silver eyes and hair to match? I won't lie, when I saw you by the side of the road, wounded and covered in dirt, I never suspected that underneath all that hid a woman with a complexion unlike any I've ever seen.' He hesitated then added, 'You still haven't told me what brings you to Kvet.'

Estel pulled the hood tighter about her face.

'Why are you so afraid? I can't help you if I don't know what you're looking for.'

She regarded him from the corner of her eye. His face looked sincere enough, but he was still a stranger. 'I can't feel fear,' she said. 'Not the way you do, anyway.' Sometimes telling the truth was the best lie.

Zeal pursed his lips. 'Everyone feels fear. Even the greatest warriors of our time trembled before Agni when he burned Vatra to purge it clean of sinners and soothsayers.'

'Agni is no bog of mine.'

Their exchange was halted by a man in a blue cloak shuffling a stack of rectangular cards. As soon as they walked past the man pulled one from his collection and hastened after them.

Zeal cursed under his breath. 'Damned gazers. Just ignore him.'

'Refuse my words at your peril,' the man said, seemingly unperturbed by Zeal's hostility. 'Fire could never become one with the stars, for its burning hunger destroys all life.' He grabbed Estel's sleeve. 'Death follows those who are bound to the flames.'

Zeal grabbed the man and tossed him to the ground. 'Keep your hands off her, or I'll cut your filthy tongue.'

The gazer held up the card he drew earlier. It depicted a man with half his face hidden behind a white mask. ‘Lies burn stronger than fire and your future is filled with both.’

‘What did he mean by “death follows those who are bound to the flames”?’ Estel asked once they left the bridge and the gazer behind.

‘Who knows?’ Zeal said in a sharp voice. ‘I wouldn’t listen to anything that comes from the mouth of a gazer. They’re known for their lies and deceive anyone who’s foolish enough to believe.’

They stopped in front of a shop with a sign suspended from its roof by a chain. A black bow and arrow painted on a square of polished wood greeted them to Juro’s Archery. When Estel crossed under a low doorway, her nostrils caught a whiff of fresh timber and dye. The light of noon speared through the narrow windows, struggling to pierce the dimness of the workshop. Two lanterns flickered in the corners, elongating the bows and arrows that hung from the walls. A man with a grey beard and a patch over his left eye was hard at work painting patterns on a bow. His hands and face were stained red.

‘Juro,’ Zeal greeted him, ‘still in the business of making trouble.’

'She's a beauty,' Juro said, his voice brimming with pride. In his hand was the most striking bow Estel had ever laid her hands on. 'It's made from a rare material. Some call it glasswood because of the way it traps the light. It only grows in the province of Zyma, to the west. One thing's for sure, you won't find another one like it anywhere in Kvet.'

'I'm not surprised,' Zeal said. 'But the question is how did you manage to get your hands on glasswood from that frozen wasteland?'

'A master bowyer keeps his secrets. They call me the best for a reason.' Juro offered the bow to Estel. 'Here, try her out.'

Estel hesitated while her mind searched for signs of a trap, but her eyes betrayed her, drawn to the gleaming surface. The bow was light blue and shaped like the wings of a bird in full flight. Decorative feathers jutted out from its curved limbs like frozen shards. The arrow rest divided upper and lower parts and wrapped around it was a slice of strong leather to support the archer's grip. Estel turned the bow in her hand, feeling every twist and curve. It was cool to the touch, but light and steady at the same time. Juro strung the bow and she pulled the string, relishing the familiar tensing of her muscles.

Juro smirked at Zeal. 'The girl knows her way with bows. If I were you, I'd start training again.' He gave Estel an arrow with an elongated tip. 'There's the target.'

Without a word, she took the arrow, set it, and aimed at the circle on the wall, painted with five evenly spaced rings. She steadied her breath and focused her eye on the one in the centre. Blood hummed in her ears, drowning all sound. She let her breath out and with it the arrow. It cut through the air and hit the mark.

'Look at that,' Juro said, clapping. 'Where did you learn to shoot so well?'

'How much is the bow?' she asked.

'Down to business then. The bow is not for sale.'

Estel frowned. 'So why show it to me?'

'To see if you're worthy of the gift. The bow holds a special place in my heart and no amount of coin could buy it.'

'Don't play games with me, old man,' Estel said. She had no desire to barter with him, nor to prove herself. She turned to Zeal. 'We wasted time by coming here.'

'If you win the contest, you can have the bow.'

She studied his face, trying to guess what trick was being played here.

'The bow is yours if you prove yourself worthy of it. I can see you have the skill, but so does Zeal. So far, no one has managed to defeat him, so take the bow and try your hand at being the first.'

She hesitated.

'I'm an honest man. You have my word, and Zeal can vouch for me.'

Zeal nodded his agreement.

Estel took the bow and slid it across her shoulder. The weight of it was like a reunion with a long-lost friend.

'You'll need arrows,' Zeal said.

'I only trust the ones I make myself.'

'Good luck,' Juro called to her back as they left. 'You'll need it to best the flame-sworn.'

***

True to her word, Estel spent the next few days scouring Kvet's wilderness in search of the best wood to make her arrows. Having this marvellous bow strapped to her back woke an unusual excitement in her, and for a time she forgot about Ashk and her quest to find him. The contest was fast approaching, and she wanted to be ready. Her muscles were still recovering from her ordeals at sea, and to strengthen them, she hunted for suitable targets and prey to practice. On some nights, she went back to rest at the inn where Yari kept a room for her, but more often, she lit the fire and slept under the watchful eye of the moon. Sometimes, she'd lay on her back watching the glimmering stars that looked like pieces of missing souls, lost in the vastness of the midnight firmament. Wrapped in a blanket and surrounded by the sounds of crackling fire and hooting sovas, she waited for Srebro to make an appearance. It was a mystery how the fox had found her, considering the sea that separated them. The questions nagged at the back of her mind. Did she somehow manage to sneak onto the ship? Even if that had been possible, the vessel was destroyed by the attack of the zmei. How did the fox survive long enough at sea only to then find her here, in a place so far from Grey Lands? Only Srebro knew the answer.

Her thoughts strayed to Zeal. She hardly saw him and assumed that he too honed his skills before the contest. She wanted to ask him about the flame-sworn, and what Juro could have meant by needing luck to face her opponent. Vatrians worshipped Agni, the bog of fire, so it could've been a reference to their fate, but the way the bowyer emphasized the word made her think otherwise. From Yari and Juro's remarks, she figured that Zeal was a worthy archer and his arrows took the victory every year.

Estel ran her hand over the glasswood bow in her possession, wondering how good she really was.

Without the visions to plague her and no sign of Arleta, those few days before the contest were carefree and filled with her favourite activities. Her new bow was light and a joy to wield. She couldn't help but use her magnifying abilities to follow the arrows as she set them free, experiencing a swell of satisfaction when each one hit the mark.

In spare moments between her training sessions, Estel walked the city listening to conversations on the streets and in taverns. She was careful not to draw attention to herself and always wore her hood—it was easier not to be seen than to endure the curious looks from strangers. The citizens of Kvet seemed friendly and at ease with one another, but this only made her more cautious. It seemed careless that people shared personal matters without knowing who else was listening. Her ears were trained to catch anything concerning the province of Suha and soon she learned that the roads leading there were difficult to travel. Due to the increasing heat and the lack of natural water sources, taverns were few and far between. Suha itself was a place lacking in trees and plants and overrun with wild animals that roamed the mountain ranges and deserts. Small villages were scattered across this unforgiving land and the main mode of survival was the trade between Kvet and Vatra to the south. During one of her spying ventures, she overheard that after the contest, a caravan was bound for Suha, and she forged a plan in her mind. The money she was sure to win would buy her a passage on it, and she planned to offer her hunting skills to the caravan leader to secure the rest of her journey.

Estel spotted a handful of Greylanders in Kvet—with their ashen skin they were hard to miss—but she stayed away. It was unlikely they'd recognise her, but she wanted to avoid questions about her village. She doubted any of them knew about the Twilight Hunters and their invasion, but she was unwilling to test the theory. She hardly understood those events herself and whenever she thought about the dark-haired woman, the web of confusion spread wider in her mind. Who was she and why did she order the massacre? And the Twilight Hunters—how could such creatures exist? Ashk was the only one who would know, but a long road separated them.

The day of the contest found Estel calm and ready. She washed away the night's sleep with cool water from the basin and descended the stairs into the main room of the tavern, bow in hand. It was full of people. Zeal sat at a table by the window and waved her to join him. When she crossed the room, her bow turned heads.

Zeal grinned. 'They've come to see us make history today.'

Yari approached the table with a plateful of eggs, bread, and sweet rolls. 'The day's finally here.' He winked at Zeal. 'Are you ready to get your ass kicked by a girl? With a bow like this, she'll teach you a lesson.'

'She can try. Many did before, but even the prayer at the temple didn't help them.'

Estel lifted her head. 'Prayer?'

'It's a tradition in Kvet to make offerings to Vesta before big celebrations,' Yari explained, filling her mug with dark liquid that smelled of cloves.

Estel wrinkled her nose but tried the brew. It was warm and left a sharp taste on her tongue. 'I won't be making an offering.'

'But you must,' Zeal said in a firm voice. 'Trust me, you don't want to offend the priestesses of Kvet on a day like today. We'll go together, and I'll guide you through the rituals.'

She shrugged. Kvet's customs were unfamiliar to her and having to worship a boginya she didn't know felt like a waste of time.

When the food was gone, Estel followed Zeal through the city streets in the direction of the temple. He was his usual cheery self and whistled all the way there. The city was busier than before, full of laughter, and people dressed in festive clothes. Even Zeal looked smarter, with his copper hair loose and green shirt that intensified the gold and red of his eyes. Her simple black garb looked tired in comparison to the richly coloured lace, silk, and cotton of his clothing, but it didn't bother her. She wasn't here to impress anyone.

They joined the crowd heading for the temple and Zeal took her hand. When she pulled back, his fingers tightened around hers. 'Just follow my lead,' he said, close to her ear.

Wrapped in white robes, the priestesses of Vesta greeted them with warm smiles on the steps leading to the temple. One of them placed a white wreath on Estel's head. 'White for the boginya,' the woman whispered, and her blue eyes locked on hers.

'You're mistaken—' Estel said, but Zeal interrupted by dragging her away and through the tall doorway.

'The crowd is building, and people are getting impatient,' he said as a way of explanation.

The temple smelled of flowers, honey, and wax from the multitude of burning candles. Following the clamour of the street, Estel welcomed the calm inside that separated the world of the living and the world of the divine. Boginya Vesta watched her through the eyes of her many statues and icons that decorated every corner of the large chamber. Priestesses tended the tapers and incense, singing prayers in low voices. Chour's house of worship was a gloomy, serious place where priests scrutinised her with their beady eyes, condemning the detachment within her as if it would offend their bog. But here, in Vesta's temple, the faces she met were welcoming and free of judgement—in their boginya's eyes, everyone was equal. The assembled flock sensed her approval, and each face beamed with reverence.

They sat on a bench from which Estel had a good view of the lectern.

'Take your hood off,' Zeal said.

Estel shook her head. 'It's best if I don't.'

'Your face should be visible to all in the house of worship. It can be seen as lack of respect—'

'Follow your customs and let me follow mine.'

When the priestesses gathered in a semicircle and placed a leather-bound book on a lectern, all conversation hushed. The worshippers turned their eyes on them, waiting for the ceremony to start. A few moments later, a priestess in a blue robe emerged from the side door, heralded by a soft tune from a row of pipes set into a large instrument. The sound sent a shiver through Estel. Her eyes followed the blue woman as she took her place behind the lectern. Her hair was white and plaited around her head in a wreath, adorned with beads resembling flowers in a meadow. Her complexion was free of blemishes and so clear that even Estel's ivory skin paled in comparison. A blue jewel hung down her neck on a silver chain. She appraised the congregation and her mouth turned up in a sweet smile. A sigh of admiration ran through the chamber.

'Worshippers of Vesta, welcome,' she said, and her soft voice echoed through the temple. 'We have come here to ask for the boginya's blessing and thank her for the beauty and joy she bestows upon us. Let us join hands in prayer and open our hearts and minds so they can be filled with Vesta's courage and wisdom.'

People joined their hands and bowed their heads, whispering the words of invocation, while the priestess spoke them aloud. Estel ignored Zeal's tugging at her sleeve and her eyes remained focused on one of the statues of Vesta. Perhaps it was her imagination at play, but there was something familiar about the boginya. The way she inclined her head and the shape of her smile… The features reminded her of someone, another woman, but the memory was encased in a thick fog, and the more she focused on it, the more abstract it became. She snorted when Zeal gave a final warning tug but closed her eyes and listened to the monotonous litany of gratitude as the priestess thanked Vesta for her unconditional love.

You're one of us…

Estel's eyes flew open. She looked around the chamber, but the worshippers had their heads lowered and lips moving in a silent prayer.

'Did you hear that?' she asked Zeal.

He glanced at her through the corner of his left eye. 'Hear what?' There was annoyance in his tone, but she didn't care.

Before she could question him further, the blue priestess lifted her head and looked directly at her. The woman's stare was so piercing that it almost cut through the folds of Estel's hood, forcing her to cast her eyes down.

'Our merciful boginya welcomes everyone inside her walls and all she asks in return is love,' the priestess said.

'Without love there's no life. When you leave here today, carry your heads high and fill your hearts with gratitude. Blessings of Vesta to you all.' She looked upon the congregation one last time, and accompanied by the parting music, left the lectern.

'I need to speak to that woman,' Estel said, rising to her feet.

Zeal caught her arm. 'You can't. Outside of the temple, no one is allowed within ten paces of the high priestess. Besides, we don't want to be late for the contest.'

A sudden urge to speak to the woman warred with the need to execute her initial plan to earn coin for the caravan and to win the bow. Reluctantly, Estel followed Zeal to the exit.

Back in the square, the air was warm but fresh, and she inhaled a lungful of it. Her chest expanded, and her head cleared. She pushed the whisper from the temple from her mind.

'Are you ready to lose?' Zeal asked.

'Are you?' she retorted, watching his smile stretch into a wide grin.

X

The contestants were separated into groups and sent to await their turn in tents pitched at the edge of the main arena. From there they could track the progress of their opponents. In the commotion, Estel lost sight of Zeal and caught herself listening in for his familiar whistling. The people around her formed small groups and their faces spoke of determination to snatch the trophy. She found this tenacity to win oddly mystifying. It wasn't a possession of some decorative trinket that turned one into a good archer, but daily practice and challenging yourself against a more dangerous prey. This was a true test of one's abilities and no amount of trophies could change that.

She counted six contestants in her tent, but none of them was a native to Grey Lands, which didn't surprise her. Greylanders rarely left their homeland and it was unlikely that those who did would care to participate in such trivial events.

Two black-skinned women, with half of their faces concealed by veils, stood in silence, eyes fixed on the herald who read out the names of other hopefuls in a slurry voice. Their long and simple dresses suggested they came here from Suha.

Three men stood in a semicircle, and judging by their sideburns, all were natives of Kvet. During her exploration of the city, she noticed that many young men let their sideburns grow down and around the curve of their jaws. The men were engrossed in conversation, but Estel caught occasional words spoken too loudly—it sounded as if they disagreed with the part of the contest that involved a human target. The final contestant was a lone man in black leggings and tightly fitted jerkin. Slung across his shoulder was a bow made of dark wood she didn't have a name for. When he looked her way, his black eyes reminded her of the woman who burned her village. Estel expected that she would track her down by now, the fact that she didn't made her wonder about her intentions.

'Is this your first time?' one of the veiled women asked.

It took Estel a moment to realise that the question was aimed at her. She nodded.

'I'm Mila,' the woman said, and gestured at her companion, 'and this is my younger sister, Kara. It's her first tourney as well.' She smiled reassuringly at Kara as if trying to bolster her courage.

In other circumstances she would've ignored Mila's attempt at small talk— concentration favoured silence—

but if they were indeed from Suha, it could be her chance to gain more information. 'Do you hope to win?' Estel asked.

Mila pursed her lips. 'Against Zeal? I'd want to see an archer skilled enough to take the trophy from *him*. We came because the rumour had it that he wouldn't be competing this year, but it seems the gossip held little truth. Zeal's here and more determined to win than ever.'

'Is he really that good?'

'The best,' Kara cut in, her tone full of admiration.

A loud horn sounded across the arena, hushing the excited crowd. Shortly after, a man holding a scroll stepped forward to read aloud the rules of the competition. The archers would take part in four trials, and those with the highest marks would be admitted to partake in the next challenge.

'The rules are stricter every year,' Mila said. 'Have they no concern for human life?'

The use of human targets didn't bother Estel, and she wanted things to move along. The contest preparations dragged for far too long and the crowd was too hyper for her liking—betting coin, scrapping, and cheering in a drunken stupor. She tried to ignore the commotion, but the noise was like a shrieking bird trapped in the confines of her head, pecking away at her concentration.

‘How long did you travel to get here?’ she asked Mila.

‘Four weeks on horseback, but the journey wasn’t an easy one. Bandits ransacked a caravan near the western desert, so we had to take turns keeping watch every night. My bones feel like they’re about to snap, and I can’t stop yawning. Not the best start.’

‘Why travel alone? Despite the latest misfortune, wouldn’t it be safer still to ride alongside a caravan?’

‘The price for such comforts is too high even for me, and there’s my sister to think about.’

Estel pricked her ears. ‘How much coin does it take?’

‘It’s not coin I’m talking about, girl.’

A voice of the herald boomed, announcing the first round of the contest. The challenge was a test of agility and speed—to shoot as many sandbags in as little time as possible. The bags were the size of a large fist and would be hurled from makeshift catapults. One by one, the contestants were called into the arena and asked to form a straight line. Zeal stood at the opposite end and when he saw her, his hand lifted in greeting. Even from here, she could tell by a wide grin on his face how excited he was at the prospect of defeating her and claiming yet another trophy to his name. Her resolve tightened—she wasn't about to lose her new bow on his account.

At the sound of the whistle, Estel straightened her back and nocked an arrow. Its light blue markings caught the sun and glimmered back at her as if in agreement that this was an easy challenge to win.

The sandbags were released in a steady stream and the crowd fell silent; the only sound made by arrows swishing through the air. Estel forgot about the arena and the other contestants. Her mind and vision wound together and focused on the flying targets while the rest of her body carried out the mechanics of bow handling. She kept at it until her quiver was empty and the crowd's cheering rang in her ears once more.

'Challenge complete,' the herald boomed. 'Count the sandbags.'

The youths in charge of the catapults ran into the arena and shouted the scores back to him. He wrote in his scroll and after a quick consultation with his assistant, announced that out of the eighteen contestants, fourteen earned the right to the next challenge. Estel looked down the line—the people from her tent were still here, and so was Zeal. She expected no less.

The party readied itself for the second round: shooting a flock of live birds. Those who managed to bring the most down would be admitted to the next challenge. It required more precision than shooting at sandbags. Once set free, the birds were keen to seize their newly found freedom. When the whistle vibrated the air, Estel didn't move. Armon taught her not to kill animals without cause. The old trapper used to say that everything in nature was about equilibrium and every living being had a part to play in order to keep the balance. Even such predators as volks, no matter how feared, had their place in the circle of life. The birds she was about to shoot would be disposed of and benefit no one.

But she had a purpose.

Estel pushed back her shoulders and aimed. The locks on the cages were released and the birds flew out like pieces of torn clouds, wings flapping in a frantic attempt to escape. One by one, her arrows cut through the air, caught them in full flight, and brought them down. They plummeted to the ground like a shower of white rocks. The sight of them thrashing helplessly, eyes open, but dead, shrank Estel's heart and made her think of Srebro, trapped by hunters, her silver fur stripped clean. The image made her skin crawl. She took the lives of many animals in Grey

Lands for food, or to master her skills, but never before had she felt so disturbed by the act. What would boginya Vesta say to this? Would it please her to witness her birds treated with such disregard? She cursed Zeal for his foolish ways and her own stupidity at agreeing to his challenge.

The birds were disposed of by the very men who set them free.

'Ready your bows for the next challenge,' the herald called. 'Your aim is the concentric target. With each clean shot, you'll move back ten steps. Those who fail to claim the bullseye would go no further.'

Out of the fourteen contestants, ten remained. The bird challenge saw Kara and one of the three men from her tent leave the arena. Three archers separated her from Zeal. Estel drew her arrow and focused on the white and red target far in front. She stilled her breath and at the herald's mark, loosened her arrow. It travelled fast and hit the mark.

'Step back!' the herald called.

The crowd cheered Zeal's name and Estel wished they'd stop making so much noise.

Arrow after arrow, the contestants moved further and further away from the targets, until the quivers were empty again. The herald called upon his assistants to check the bullseye and make a verdict on who would be staying to see the fourth and final challenge.

When the names of the lucky ones were read aloud, Mila squeezed Estel's shoulder. 'You did well. May Yarilo bring you victory.' And with that she retired from the arena, leaving Estel with Zeal, the black-eyed man, and another woman who wasn't present in their original tent.

'It's the final challenge,' Zeal said. He planted his feet in line next to hers. 'I must admit, I'm surprised you've managed to get this far.'

'If I were you, I'd focus more on my technique and less on empty words.'

Four men wearing black vests lined up in front of them. Each had a round shield wrapped around his neck that rested against the higher part of the stomach. Painted white, they offered a good contrast, and Estel settled her eye on the centre of the one that belonged to her target. Even from eighty steps away, she sensed the man's agitation. He was right to be fearful, but luckily for him, he was appointed to be *her* target. The crowd went wild, clapping and screaming Zeal's name. They knew him for his unmatched skill and she had no doubt most of the betting was in his name. She looked forward to disappointing all of them.

The herald read out the rules of this challenge and a healer was called to be on hand in case an arrow went astray. When the whistle sounded for the final time, Estel didn't hesitate. The thudding of her target's heart reached her across the arena and she could almost smell his fear. She focused her senses on her vision to the exclusion of all else and centred her mind with a few deep breaths. The victory was eighty steps away and down to this last arrow. She drew her bow.

The symbol on her right arm shivered and her muscles rippled in response. The tip of the arrow quivered and it was no longer aiming at the shield, but at the man's chest. Estel ignored the uncomfortable sensation and repositioned herself. She had to keep it together for her own sake—and for the sake of the man who entrusted his life to her. With a final shake of her head, she aimed a second time.

Pain struck her arm like the spike of a pickaxe, dislodging the arrow that fell to the ground at her feet.

'Are you sure you're up for this?' Zeal asked her, lowering his own bow. 'There's no shame in walking away, and I'm sure the man ahead would be grateful.'

‘Walk away and let you win?’ Estel picked up her arrow. ‘I think not.’

The heat emanating from the sorrow mark intensified, threatening her with another vision. She knew that she had to find a safe place to wait it out, but refused to give in. The victory was in her grasp. With a sharp intake of breath, she mustered her strength and focused on the target. The first signs of headache spotted her forehead with sweat, but she ignored it and aimed. Her bow felt cool against her trembling fingers.

Two things happened at once—pain slammed her like a windstorm and she released the arrow.

She fell into a black and bottomless abyss.

***

‘She is gone.’ A woman’s voice reverberated from the walls of Estel’s skull. ‘I warned you, but you chose to indulge this game and now it is too late. Our last hope scorched to ashes.’

Estel tried hard to place the speaker, but her mind refused to listen. It felt as if her brain was an ocean and the woman’s voice a rudderless boat, tossed about by the waves and out of reach.

‘Quite the opposite.’ It was the man from her previous visions. ‘It’s her way of searching for the truth.’

'She is not ready for it. How could you be so reckless? You are risking all we have worked so hard to achieve.'

'Contain your anger, Lelya. Both your daughters are very much alive. But I agree. We mustn't let Estel misuse her gifts. Before the end, she'll need all her powers and more if she is to succeed.'

Estel opened her eyes a crack, but her vision was a blur. 'I have no powers…' She choked on her words as the pounding in her head resumed with force.

Lelya's voice grew closer. 'Save your words and reserve your strength. You must return to your world.'

Estel felt the woman's hand entwine with her own and the warmth radiating from it soothed some of her pain. Lelya's touch felt familiar, as if they had held hands this way before.

'Are you my mother?' Estel asked, but her dried mouth turned the words into a whisper. She clicked her tongue and tried again. 'Why am I here, and why the pain?'

Her vision cleared and Lelya's face came into focus. The woman's features were like Estel's: ivory skin, silver hair bound in plaits around her head, and eyes of the same colour.

'You're different from us in many ways,' the man said.

'But we look the same, and you said—'

‘We have not much time,’ Lelya interrupted them. ‘The longer you stay here, the more energy is drained from your physical body. You must focus in order to reunite with it.’

‘I won’t go anywhere until I get some answers. Are you my family? Is this place my home?’

Lelya’s face softened. ‘I cannot tell you all, but if it is of any consolation then yes, you are one of the Da’ariys, and I am your birth mother.’

‘Da’ariys?’ Estel struggled to keep her focus against that familiar tugging—her body calling her back.

The man drew his eyebrows together. ‘You’re a Creator, Estel. You won’t understand what it truly means until the trials are over and the choice lies before you. My hope is that, unlike so many others, you won’t fail us.’

‘I don’t understand.’

She rarely did. The visions were so muddled, and if not for her inability to dream, Estel would’ve mistaken them for one. But they were real enough—the touch of Lelya’s hand, the strong presence of the man, the sharp outline of the room with its mysterious tapestry.

‘You will understand,’ Lelya said, brushing her fingers against Estel’s cheek. ‘Ashk is waiting for you in the province of Suha. Find him before your sister does and he will show you the way.’

‘I don’t have a sister. I was Lea’s only child.’

‘Lea’s actions triggered her appearance,’ the man said. ‘Your adoptive mother disrupted the flow and your sister, Rana, came to seek you out and test your resolve. The creatures she forged, the Twilight Hunters, were meant to assist her in this task. As much as you’re the Creator, Rana is the Destroyer and she won’t stop pursuing you.’

Estel looked at them as if they were feeble of mind. The woman who came into the village surrounded by the violet beasts was a daemon. There was nothing human about her. To suggest that Rana was her sister was insane, but their time was running out and Estel’s mind became fuzzy. It was harder to resist the pull of her consciousness. She rolled up her sleeve and revealed the twisting symbol on her arm—the source of her pain. It pulsed with silver light, imbuing her bones with burning vibrations.

‘What is the meaning of this mark?’ she asked.

The man and Lelya exchanged glances.

‘Your heart embraced sorrow and the missing pieces are coming together,’ the man said. ‘When you open yourself to all of them, your destiny will become clear.’

‘It brings me nothing but pain and misery. Why would I want that?’

‘It is the greatest gift,’ Lelya said.

‘Emotions belong to humans,’ Estel said, but her tongue started wandering. Her eyelids grew heavy and she struggled to keep them open. ‘I don’t want to feel…’

‘Volh!’ Lelya screamed at the man and her voice was a thunder.

Estel drowned in confusion. The questions floated in her brain, but she was unable to form the words needed to ask them. Someone tugged her arm, causing more pain, and she jerked away. Dark fog hung low around her, suffocating, and no matter how much she clawed at it, it wouldn’t shift.

XI

When Estel opened her eyes, the night greeted her with the chirruping of crickets that drifted through the open window. Lost in the dark, a stray fly buzzed around the room in a confused frenzy. She was back in her bed at the tavern, and someone had covered her with a blanket. Her head was a smithy where the pain pummelled against her skull like a hammer against an anvil. Deep within her right arm, her flesh continued to burn, and her mouth felt like a dried-out cave.

She groaned and propped herself on one elbow. The room spun violently, and the nausea forced her back. After a few moments of stillness, the sickness passed and the fog in her brain shifted. The events of the contest came flooding back. Did she let the arrow loose? Too bad if she did, for her target was most likely dead.

The knowledge that Lelya was her mother and that Estel had a sister who wanted her dead made little sense. For whatever reason, her mother had abandoned her to a life in Grey Lands, amongst people who never accepted her as their own. And to what purpose? So she could be taunted and scoffed at by her peers? With a sudden pang, Estel realised that Lea was the only one who ever cared about what happened to her. Lea saved her life while her own kind abandoned her in the woods to the mercy of mrakes and daemons. And now, one of Da'ariys threatened Estel's existence.

The hushed voices outside her room interrupted her musings. She recognised Zeal's raised tone and Yari's urgent reply. There was a third voice, and it sounded familiar, but her brain was too taxed to puzzle together who it belonged to.

The door opened a crack. 'Estel?' Zeal asked, his voice soft with worry.

She was tempted to ignore him and pretend she was still asleep. No doubt he'd won the contest and couldn't wait to share the news with her. The last thing she needed was his boasting.

'Go away,' she said at last.

'She's awake,' Zeal informed his companions, and they entered the room. One of them fumbled in the dark and a flutter from a candle chased the night back out the window.

Estel watched them. The man she struggled to place was Juro, his face a mixture of worry and unease. Most likely he came to claim his bow back and she could do little to stop him—a bet was a bet. She waved at the table. ‘Take it and leave.’

‘You don’t remember anything, do you?’ Juro asked, and when she said nothing he slapped his thigh and laughed. ‘I’ll be damned.’

‘Did I kill that man?’ She didn’t care either way. If the man chose to take such risks, his life must have been of little value to him.

‘Girl, the man’s alive and the bow’s yours to keep.’

Estel frowned. Were they toying with her?

‘It’s true,’ Yari said with a grin. ‘The first person to see the legendary Zeal on his knees. I think his pride will need some time to recover.’

Zeal crossed his arms. ‘I was concerned for her safety. What would you have me do? Let her be and carry on?’

‘Whatever you say, brother,’ Juro said then he turned to Estel. ‘Everyone speaks of your victory tonight. When you’re well enough, there’ll be a feast in Vesta’s temple to honour it, and the high priestess herself will present the trophy.’

Estel could hardly believe it. Her memory failed to recall the last moments before the vision, but if what the men said were true, not only she had won the bow, but hopefully enough coin to continue her journey to Suha.

As if he read her thoughts, Zeal retrieved a small pouch and untied the knot. The jangling of coins confirmed her victory. 'Perhaps we can split them between us?' he asked. 'I saved your life, remember?'

'Give me that.' Juro snatched the pouch from him and gave it to Estel. 'It's yours to keep. You did me and my bow proud. Rest well, and don't let him bother you. We'll speak again at the feast.'

Estel inclined her head in thanks.

'I best return to my duties,' Yari said when the door closed behind Juro. 'The tavern is filled to the brim. All celebrate tonight, which means brawls after midnight. I'll send Tori up with some food and drink.'

Estel pointed at her pouch. 'Take what you need.'

'I'm more than happy to host the best archer in Kvet.' He clapped Zeal on the shoulder. 'Who would have thought?'

'Don't you have things to do?' Zeal said.

Yari chuckled and left the room.

Zeal pulled up a chair. 'What happened? It looked like you were dying from convulsions.'

'My hands trembled, and I kept losing focus. I must've passed out shortly after, so how did I win?'

‘With bow and arrow. As much as it pains me to admit, you’re a remarkable shot.’

‘What about you?’

‘Mine’s still in the quiver. When you fell, I dropped my bow to catch you.’

‘I guess you want my gratitude?’

‘Something tells me I’d have to wait forever for it. No. I want to know where you came from and why you are here. You owe me that much.’

And there it was. That human need to owe things to one another—life, coin, love, time—anything to hold one in a firm clasp of debt. Every Greylander owed something to another, and things seldom turned out well for any of them. She had to leave Kvet and Zeal behind before he trapped her in the same way.

‘I don’t owe anything to anyone,’ she said in a flat voice.

He cast her a solemn look. ‘I don’t know why your secret is so precious and why you refuse my help, but the world is an unforgiving place, and at times we need someone to face it with us. Someone who cares.’

‘And that someone is you.’

‘And what’s wrong with that?’

There was a lot wrong with that, but she had no desire to explain herself to him. Whatever it was he hoped to gain from their chance encounter, it had to end here. 'I thank you for your help, but you can't follow me. You must go back to your life and let me go back to mine. There's nothing more you can do for me.'

Zeal opened his mouth as if to argue but then thought better of it. 'If you want me to leave, just say so.'

'Leave.'

The chair scraped against the wood and he was up on his feet. The merry look in his eyes was gone, replaced by a cold stare. Estel expected him to challenge her, but he turned away and walked to the door. Without a backward glance, he raised his hand in farewell and was gone. As soon as his footsteps faded, Estel let out a sigh of relief—she reclaimed her freedom and was ready to focus on the final stretch of her journey. Her arm throbbed, and the pain that settled between her eyes didn't show signs of abating. Despite her weariness, she had to leave Kvet at once. She had no intention of attending the celebrations in her name. To do otherwise would be to encourage people to pry into her life.

Estel got up and walked to the window. The warm breeze swept in and out of the room, bringing a sweet scent of flowers and freshly cut grass. Music and laughter from the festivities vibrated through the air, and trees far on the horizon looked like ghosts wrapped in white and pink.

She longed for Srebro. Was the fox still out there? A silver shadow, skulking around the edges of the city. The thought sent ripples through her heart and fled before she had a chance to consider it fully. It was time to go.

Estel had little in terms of possessions. Even the clothes she wore belonged to Yari, but they were sturdy enough to last her until she crossed the border to Suha. She dipped her fingers into the pouch. She had no time to count the coins, but the weight of them assured her that the reward was generous.

There was a knock on the door.

'Enter,' she said, tying back the knot.

It was Tori with a bowl of stew, a thick slice of cheese and a flagon of wine. She thanked him and placed a silver coin in his palm. His eyes widened, and he shook his head.

'Keep it,' she said before he could refuse.

He stashed the coin into his breast pocket and looked around the room. His eye lingered on the bow. 'Why are you here when everyone is celebrating your win?'

'Sometimes your victories benefit others in a way they could never benefit you.'

Tori's gaze clouded as he tried to puzzle out the meaning of her words.

She felt a twinge of pity for the boy's lack of awareness. 'Yari is a good man and he'll see to your future. If you let him.'

'But all he does is order me around. While I'm with him, I'll never have time to pursue my interests.'

'You'll have plenty of time for that. But if you're not careful, the world will make a jest of your pursuits.'

'You're strange,' he said, and he left the room.

Estel ate the food as if it was the first meal she'd had in weeks. The meat was tender, and the spices tingled on her tongue and warmed her stomach. The bread was soft but had a nice crust on the outside and it complimented the saltiness trapped in the cheese. She finished off the meal with a cup of wine that tasted of plums and honey. Due to the weather, Greylanders cultivated roots and vegetables that ripened underground, safe from the ashy rain, so the abundance of edible fruits and flowers in Kvet came as a surprise. She could see why people worshipped Vesta. Chour offered protection in exchange for animal sacrifice, but the decimation of her village was a sign that some prayers went unheard.

She tied the coin pouch around her waist and found her bow. The quiver had a handful of arrows left in it, but they wouldn't survive her journey west. She had to make more. The blanket on the bed caught her eye and she folded it under her arm for extra warmth for when she camped at night. Her bundle made up of kindling, water skin, and a small knife—items she procured during her trips to the city—was still under the pillow. As the caravan didn't leave for Suha for another two nights, she had to abandon her original plan to join it, instead entertaining the idea of taking one of Zeal's horses. He kept them in the stables, under the watchful eye of Yari, but she decided against that. The man would no doubt question her about her sudden need for a horse and she wanted to avoid alerting Zeal of her plans. Not that he would care after their little exchange, but she didn't want to take chances. She stretched her feet—they brought her all the way here and would have to do for now.

With a final glance around the room, she stepped out into the corridor. It was dim, illuminated only by the light from two lanterns hanging at each end. As she walked to the staircase, the muffled voices of patrons floated from the adjacent rooms. Yari was right when he said that celebrations were underway. The main room of the tavern brimmed with people. A group of them sang at the top of their lungs, without any care for the song itself, while another was engrossed in a drinking game. Men and women danced in the corner where the musicians entertained them with their instruments. The crowd was too cheery and too drunk to pay any heed of her as she slipped past the tables. Yari was behind the counter pouring drinks from the large barrels, but he too failed to notice her untimely departure. Zeal wasn't among the crowd and she was glad she wouldn't be delayed by his questions.

When she stepped outside, the warm breeze rushed past her cheeks and into the folds of her hood. A dog howled in the distance and another answered with short barks. Despite the late hour, a few people still mingled on the streets. Torches flickered at the doors and in the windows, and the spires of Vesta's temple beguiled the moonlight. Even at this hour, the house of worship would be opened to those who sought blessings of the boginya.

At the gates, the guards acknowledged her with nods and she hastened past them. Beyond the stone bridge, her body relaxed. Free from the confines of human walls, her steps quickened, and her senses absorbed the sounds and smells of the night. The wilds of Kvet weren't that different from the wilderness of Grey Lands. Many animals coexisted here, dependent on each other for their survival, and she was a part of that cycle. The sound of her boots crunching gravel sent rodents scuttling away in the tall grass, and the air was fragrant with citrus, honey, and cherries.

It was unlikely that someone would follow her, so she decided to stay on the main track until sunrise, and with no possessions to hinder her, made good progress. The night walked the wilds alongside her, and soon Kvet was a distant dot. Far on the horizon the rivers cut through the hills like silver threads. Despite the beauty in Kvet's eternal spring, Estel sensed a lack of balance. It reminded her of human nature—overflowing with one emotion while lacking in another.

Mara, the girl who was the closest to being her friend, filled her heart with nothing but love for the man who betrayed her; Krag was proud of his ruthlessness; and Lea was full of kindness, worrying about those in need. Up until the experience with Arleta, Estel's own emotions were dead inside her. She feared little, hoped for nothing, and loved no one, but her experience of sorrow disturbed that balance, and she wanted nothing more than to restore it. If Ashk had the knowledge of the Da'ariys then he should know how she could clear her mind before her heart turned it into a quivering wreck. More than ever now, she had to stay strong and focused.

She caught a whisper in the grass that brought her to a halt. The stalks swayed from side to side as something moved between them. She shook the bow off her shoulder and pulled an arrow out of the quiver. With it nocked, she slinked toward the grass.

The stalks parted, and she lowered the bow with a sigh. 'It's you.'

Srebro's eyes flickered in the moonlight.

She crouched a few steps away and they regarded each other. Srebro flattened her ears and lowered her tail as if daring her to come closer, but Estel knew better. In all the years the fox followed her, Estel was never able to lay a hand on her. Srebro hovered at a safe distance, and the connection between them grew out of respect for each other's personal space. Despite her curiosity at how the silver fur would feel under her touch, Estel didn't want to test Srebro's boundaries.

'How did you find me?' she asked, more out of habit than hope of receiving an answer.

Srebro yawned and displayed her sharp teeth. Seeing the fox unharmed was a good thing, but her mind chewed on the question of how Srebro had managed to cross the sea and find her in Kvet.

'This will be a long trek, so I expect you to keep up and share your kills,' Estel said, getting up. The jest would be lost on the fox, but it made Estel feel better.

They resumed their journey in a quiet companionship.

***

The sun stirred from its slumber and began its steady climb across the sky when Estel left the road and ventured into a nearby forest. It was time to replenish her arrows and hunt for food. Luck was on her side. Thanks to the abundance of animals in Kvet, she wouldn't go hungry for long.

Srebro stalked after her, a silver shadow in the green grass. Her presence reminded Estel of sobakas tamed by Greylanders. These nimble animals were similar to volks in appearance, but smaller and less aggressive. Food scraps drew them into the village and a handful of Greylanders took advantage of that. With a promise of daily sustenance and shelter, they turned the sobakas into companions that, with their piercing howls, alerted their households of any strangers. Srebro had trailed Estel across the sea and through the foreign lands like a loyal pet, but unlike sobakas, she didn't crave Estel's attention. Estel knew that if the fox suddenly died, her heart would mourn her, but her mind would struggle to explain why. Greylanders gave love freely to their pets and family, but because of her birth, such feelings were denied Estel. It didn't bother her too much, since Srebro didn't seek her affection. But the reason was much deeper, and she intended to discover the truth of it.

Estel carved some arrows and managed to bring down a small sika, but it looked nothing like the sikas native to Grey Lands. This animal was lean, reaching her waist in height, and had white and brown markings all over its body. It was a perfect size to feed one person and a fox. As she skinned and prepared her catch, Srebro sat at the ready, tail wrapped neatly around her paws, waiting for her share.

When the food was cooked, Estel tasted the meat. It was succulent and juicy, as if the sika's flesh absorbed the sweetness of the land and released it under a touch of flame. Srebro licked her lips and regarded Estel as if disgusted that she'd go as low as to roast her share. Estel ignored the fox and licked the grease off her fingers. They washed their meal down with water from a nearby stream and Estel savoured the coolness as it cut a path inside her. Her water skin filled, she resumed her trek west.

Days and nights went by as they followed the road to Suha. The occasional travellers and merchants didn't bother Estel, and no one attempted to do her harm. She had plenty of food, and water was readily available from the many streams and rivers. Srebro disappeared from time to time, racing across the hills, among the white and yellow flowers, to return to her side with the setting sun. Far from the main path, she lit fires, and kept a tight grip on her bow even in her sleep. At first, she considered joining the caravan when it passed her, but changed her mind. Walking on foot and being in charge of her days suited her well and it was easier to keep an eye on Srebro. What would the caravan leaders do if they spied the fox? Hunt her down for sure.

The father away from Kvet she travelled, the hotter the sun. The occasional clouds fled the sky, leaving her at the mercy of its burning rays. As the heat intensified, it forced her to strip her cloak and hood and seek shelter in the midday hours to shield her fair skin. The landscape began to change: flowers were sparse, the greens on the trees turned deeper, and the patches of grass yellowed under the hot eye of the sun. The beauty of Kvet was scorched by the heat.

Sweat dripped down Estel's eyelids, distorting her vision, and she found herself lingering on river banks. The evenings and nights turned cooler, but the sweet breeze of Kvet was replaced by a stuffy and humid air.

Since her conversation with Mila at the contest, Estel counted the days of her journey by etching them on one of her arrows. According to the shallow strikes, she'd walked for eight days now, and considering it took the sisters a fortnight on horseback to reach Kvet, she still had a long way to go. The few settlements she passed on her way resembled the smaller villages in Grey Lands, but these were sprinkled with colour. She resolved to stay away from them for as long as her supplies of kindling allowed, but one look into her bundle told her that she would have to find a tavern soon. Srebro suffered from the increasing heat as much as she did. The swiftness was gone from the fox's step and she lagged behind just to reunite with Estel when the evening shadows covered the land.

Five days later, they reached a crossroad. The track to the west was straight and wide, with bare plains to either side, empty of trees and vegetation. To the east, a battered sign pointed to Willow's Hearth.

Estel hesitated.

Mila had counselled her about the lack of taverns along the road to Suha and the changing landscape warned her that if she didn't procure supplies, she'd run the risk of becoming stranded in the middle of nowhere. She didn't look forward to veering off course and incurring delays, but going forth without preparation would be foolish.

With a sigh, she followed the sign east.

XII

Srebro must've sensed Estel's intention to make a detour, for she raced ahead and disappeared over the ridge. They'd reunite when Estel's business in the village was concluded. She needed to secure a fresh supply of kindling, fill her water skin, and stock up on food in case the hunting grounds around Suha were as bare as the landscape. A clean bed and a good night's sleep wouldn't go unappreciated either. Spurred by the prospect of food she didn't have to prepare, Estel picked up her pace.

The old track was hardly visible through the mixture of grass and weeds, indicating that fewer people travelled this way. Flatlands on either side seemed devoid of life and silent, resembling some forlorn burial grounds in their emptiness. A few lone trees refused to mingle with the wind and stood like phantoms, motionless in their resolve. Suspicion tightened the knot in Estel's stomach and she put her senses on guard. There was no sign of threat and most likely the landscape was to blame for her unease, but her instincts urged her to watch her step all the same.

From atop a hill, she sighted the village. Willow's Hearth was a group of dilapidated buildings, clustered inside a fence that bore heavy signs of disrepair. The roofs didn't look any better, some partially caved in, others torn down, leaving houses exposed to the elements.

'So much for supplies,' she muttered and was about to turn around when she caught a movement. She scanned the village, but the sun's angle made it difficult to see, even shielding her eyes with the flat of her palm. Despite appearances, perhaps someone still lived in the village? It wasn't unusual in Grey Lands to see tiny settlements occupied by a family that refused to be part of a larger community.

Estel walked downhill and as she closed the distance, the signs of decay became more evident. Pocked with dry rot, the sagging houses looked grave. Doorways hung loose from their frames while windows stared vacantly at the neighbouring buildings. Wooden fences raised, once upon a time, for protection, had fallen apart. A forest of weeds wrapped the posts in a tight embrace. The trees growing inside the village were dead, their branches stripped bare of leaves and bark. Estel's boots stirred the gravel, waking dust that puffed about her like a cloud. Even the birds had deserted this place, taking their songs with them.

The sound of an opening and closing doorway stopped her in her tracks. She quested forth with her hearing, working hard to catch and follow the creaking.

'Is anybody there?' she called out into the ruins.

Nothing but silence.

A house further up the road looked to be in better shape than the rest, so she made her way to it. The roof sank in the middle but held its shape, and the door leading inside stood ajar. With her knife at the ready, Estel crossed a small yard and pushed it open with her elbow. It groaned in protest.

The smell hit her first: a musty stench of abandonment followed by another, stronger odour, reminiscent of a dead animal that had been left to rot in the sun. Dimness inside played tricks on her eyes and it took her a few moments to adjust. Apart from a hearth and a broken table in the middle, the room was empty. A thick layer of dust coated every surface, and spider webs laced the walls like intricate curtains. Desolation stared at her from every corner. Whomever lived here left long ago.

A narrow corridor led her to another doorway. When she pried it open, the smell inside washed over her like a wave of sickness. She choked and covered her mouth with her sleeve. Three bodies lay crumpled on the bed, decomposed beyond recognition, with teeth exposed in a ghoulish sneer. Their skin was dry as a husk, and from the way they clung to each other, she guessed they had come to this room to seek comfort in their final moments. The stench that lingered here was a mystery. The bodies looked dead for a long time, so the smell should've dispersed by now, yet it was as strong as if they perished only a few days before her trespassing. She backed away from the room.

'Your presence here stirred time, so it feels as if they died yesterday.'

Estel spun around, her knife ready to strike.

Arleta's small form filled the entrance to the corridor. She clutched her bear to her chest, blue eyes fixed on the corpses. Her lip quivered, and she looked as if she was about to burst into tears.

'What do you mean?' Estel asked, taking a step toward the girl.

Arleta peeled her eyes off the grim scene and trained them on Estel. 'You're getting stronger.'

'What would a little girl like you know about strength?'

'In my world, strength is survival.'

Estel couldn't shake the feeling that this girl was much older than she looked. 'You know things that girls of your age can't possibly know. You follow me, and yet I can't feel you the way I feel other beings. You've no weapons and no coin, and yet, you're here. By all means, you should be dead by now.'

'And I am, and you're the only one who can save me.'

'If that's so, then you must have the wrong person.' Estel pointed her finger at the dead. 'What do you know about these people?'

'Crimson Plague. They all died from sores, watching their flesh rotting before their very eyes. People don't come near this place, and without a proper burial, their restless souls can't find peace. They called out to you and you came.'

'I came because I need supplies.'

'You came because the voices of the dead lured you.'

Estel snorted. 'I've a long way to go and no time to spare for child's play. You caused me a lot of grief on the ship.'

'I saved your life.'

'That may be, but the price was too high. Whatever magic you used to pull me out of there, I don't want it near me again. Your tricks disrupted my inner balance and I'm still struggling to regain it. Now, stand aside and let me pass.'

Arleta's lips turned down, but she moved away from the door. There was something about the girl that put Estel on guard and her instinct urged her not to linger in her presence. Keeping her eye on Arleta's face, Estel slowly walked down the corridor and through the doorway.

Arleta snatched her hand. 'Some things are worse than death.'

The house was gone and the village with it as Estel plunged once more into the otherworldly expanse. Light and energy whisked her away in a rush of power she was helpless to resist. Seized by the current, she screamed in protest, but her lips uttered no sound, sealed by an invisible force. A wonder of crimson, blue, and emerald whirlpools sucked her in, taking possession of her limp body and stirring every drop of silver in her veins. The pressure mounted behind her eyes and in her ears until her head was ready to split open in search of relief. Her skin stung, as if subjected to a lightning shower, and her mouth tasted of scorched flesh. Estel shut her eyes and clenched her teeth, waiting for the inevitable end.

In a rush of energy and heat, she was hurled to the ground.

A cough rattled her lungs. The impact was like a barrelful of stones thrown at once to bruise skin and crunch bones. She curled and moaned while her nose throbbed and the tissue inside it swelled, obstructing the flow of air. What kind of daemon had the power to control another in this way? She should've killed that girl when she saw her singing by the campfire. So why didn't she? What stopped her from sending an arrow through Arleta's heart?

Estel dragged herself to her feet and dizziness swooped over her. Bile rose at the back of her throat and she retched strands of silver. Her lungs were filled with sharp nails that stabbed with each intake of breath. One look around confirmed her suspicions and for the second time she was propelled into the unknown place against her will.

The fog hung low and carried a chill that seeped right into Estel's bones, making her shiver. Ahead, a wrought iron gate with three distinct words running horizontally across it, beckoned her inside. Some part of her recognised the letters, but her brain was too scrambled after the fall to determine their significance. A white and red barrier blocked the entrance, but she couldn't see anyone guarding it. Behind her was nothing but bleakness.

Estel took a few staggering steps toward the gate and the fog thinned. 'You,' she said through gritted teeth.

Arleta stood beyond the gate, wrapped in the fog like a phantom from the Dark Nav.

'I won't hesitate this time,' Estel said, reaching for her knife. It wasn't there. 'What sort of foul magic is this?'

'Come,' Arleta said, seemingly unconcerned by her outburst. She stretched out her hand.

'Oh, I'm coming,' Estel said, passing under the gate. The girl looked so frail that Estel wouldn't need weapons. Her bare hands would be enough to force the life out of the creature. Estel looked forward to strangling this daemon spawn that was responsible for her suffering.

Her plan was cut short as the chaos of pain seized her. She cried out in surprise. 'What are you doing to me?'

Bright energy slammed her like a wave, flooding every vein in her body. Before she could react, another one sent her to her knees, bringing the familiar mass of emotions with it. The sensation ripped through her like the fangs of a wild beast, tearing into her right arm. She couldn't even scream, her voice lost in the emotional storm.

'Choose,' Arleta said, her little palm pressing against Estel's thrashing heart.

'I won't do it.' Estel's words came in coughs. 'You're tormenting me, stripping away my strength. What good am to you broken?'

‘You’re our only hope,’ Arleta whispered and the sorrow in her voice woke the sorrow in Estel’s heart. Her pain and burning anger fled like a dream before dawn and all she wanted was to hold Arleta close to her chest, to ease the sadness trapped in the girl’s soul.

‘My task is to put you back together. Please, make your choice.’

And so she did.

With her eyes closed, Estel opened her senses to the whirlpool of emotions that encircled her. She was the centre of it and once she exposed herself to receive them, they rushed her at once like a swarm of insects. But she remembered what Arleta said to her in the burning land—choose only one. Stilling her mind and heart before an onslaught, she fought and pushed away every emotion apart from the one that called out to her the strongest. With a touch of her hand she caught and trapped it.

The emotion surged through her, lifting hair on her nape and arms. Her follicles shivered all at once and beads of moisture stood out on her forehead. Moments later, it turned into pools under her armpits, soaking her skin and clothes in the stench of her own sweat. Her breath came faster, shallower, and when she tried to say something, all that came out was a stutter. A powerful urge to flee surged through her, and had her body not been imprisoned to the spot, she'd have given into it. The thrashing of her heart clouded her vision with black spots. Estel pressed her fists to her temples in a desperate attempt to still her thoughts and untangle her heart and mind from the emotion, but it refused to abandon its host. It latched onto her like an ancient weed, evading her efforts to pull it free.

Her right arm burned as if submerged in molten iron, while silver lines formed on her skin below the shape of sorrow. Carved by an invisible hand, the symbol marked her flesh in the guise of a scythe with jagged edges.

'Still yourself,' Arleta said, and her voice made Estel jump. 'The fear will drain you if you let it.'

The world turned into a hostile place, where even a whisper seemed a threat. Panic ate into her flesh and fear tightened its claws around her bones. There was nowhere to run and no one to help her. She'll die here. The realisation rammed into her and she bolted, then broke into a run. Ceding Arleta and the gate to the fog, she raced into the unknown, the sound of her footsteps echoing in the emptiness.

The buildings on each side of the road reminded her of storage bunkers in Grey Lands' harbour: tall and wide structures, fashioned from red stone with black window frames peering at her through the fog. Even in her flight, Estel sensed a menacing aura about them, as if a great sickness dwelled inside, trickling through the fissures.

She was a trespasser, thrust into this world against her will and struggling to separate reality from fear. Something brushed past her and she lost her footing and tumbled to the ground. It was a man, wearing a black uniform with a silver-grey braid on the collar. She swallowed the urge to scream.

'They can't see you.'

She spun around, every cell on high alert, to stand face to face with Arleta. In any other circumstances, she would've known the girl was following her, but the fear dulled her senses, deadening her awareness of the surroundings.

'Why did you bring me here?'

'The why is not important. Your task is to feel what these ghosts felt when every shred of their being was stripped away from them.'

'But why? Why would I want these horrible feelings inside me? No warrior would agree to this.' Estel shook her head as if to reaffirm the truth of what she said.

'Because without them, you're nothing more than a broken shell. The soul must be whole to lead the body into battle.' She must've sensed her confusion for she added, 'I can make you see and understand, but what you'll do with that knowledge is up to you.'

'What knowledge? I don't want any of this. Ashk is the one I seek… to help me find my past and understand my present.'

'And you will. But without your powers even he can do little for you.'

Before she could reply, another figure walked past—a woman, with a hardened face, a leash clutched in one hand. Straining against it was a large sobaka, ears erect and hackles raised like spikes on a spear. Estel watched as the fog swathed them.

Wind stirred the air and the trees waved their branches, bringing the chill and smell with them, a sweet and sickly stench of human flesh burning, writhing free of the world in a heat of flame and a cloud of smoke. The miasma filled Estel's mouth and forced her to her knees, retching.

Arleta rested her hand on Estel's shoulder. 'Nothing here can hurt you. The feelings are not your own, so walk free and see the future.'

'The future?' Estel asked in horror. This wasn't a future, but the blackest and deepest corners of Dark Nav. Was this a vision of her doom? Chour's challenge and a warning of what awaited her if she didn't change her ways?

Arleta led the way, and devoid of choice, Estel followed. Further down, a group of people dressed in striped shirts and leggings huddled on the ground, shielding their heads and bodies from a sobaka set on them by the woman she saw earlier. The animal looked nothing like the ones guarding the village in Grey Lands. With its fangs exposed and blood dripping down them in rivulets, it resembled a vicious volk. The body of a mutilated man lay on the ground, his face like a shredded ribbon, pools of crimson soaking into the ground around him. Estel grabbed for her bow, but her hand came away empty.

She seized Arleta by the shoulders and shook her. 'Where's my bow? Knife. Anything!' A sob broke into her voice as the horrific scene of what was to come unfolded in her mind even before it became real. 'We must stop them.'

The girl shook her head. 'There's nothing you can do.'

'So we're just going to stand here and watch as this sobaka rips them apart?' Without waiting for a reply and despite the throbbing of fear in her heart, Estel, with her fists curled, threw herself at the woman. Her blows went right through, as if she punched the air instead of a living being. These weren't real people but apparitions, ghosts of…of what? The future?

'But I can feel them just as I can feel you,' Estel said, staring at her wrists.

'The Creators have the power to move through time, and guided by their conduits, can relive the events of the past, or the future.'

A shriek tore the air. The sobaka was set loose and it was hard to distinguish who was who in the chaos that ensued. Estel screamed and the sound echoed in the deepest corners of her soul. The physical pain was less than the mental wounds inflicted by the hail of dread and terror that lashed down on her. She bent in half and wrapped her arms around her belly, body shaking.

Arleta wrenched her hand free and pulled her away, leaving the people and sobaka behind. Their dying screams reverberated in Estel's mind like the workings of an iron bell.

'I can't take it anymore,' Estel said. 'Release me from whatever spell binds us to this place. I beg of you.'

The girl said nothing but led her deeper into the settlement.

When they reached a low barracks, Arleta stopped, pointing her dirty finger at it.

Fog hung around the building like a curtain of dread.

'I don't want to go inside,' Estel said.

'But you must.'

An invisible force urged her forward and her feet were too weak to resist it.

Near the doorway, wrapped in a veil of fog, five female silhouettes awaited her, and despite fear holding her in a tight embrace, Estel was unable to look away from their sunken faces. Their eyes, wild with torment, were those of animals led to slaughter. As she crossed the threshold, the women trailed in her wake on their stick-like legs. She'd never known so much cruelty. How could such a place exist? Even her experiences with Krag and his crew paled in comparison to the anguish endured by the people trapped here.

She entered a room that was stripped of all furniture save for a chair and a round lantern fastened to the ceiling. It emitted a bright light and flickered at irregular intervals. A snapping sound, like sparks unleashed by a campfire, preceded each flick. A lone moth battered against the pellucid surface. Marked by a row of numbers on her arm, a woman perched on the edge of the chair, whimpering, while the other cut her hair with a pair of shears. Black strands fell to the floor in clumps, and after a few quick snips, the marked woman turned into a hairless ghost to join the sea of other hairless ghosts that roamed this place. The wave of her fear and sorrow washed over Estel and trapped her breath. She clutched her throat and hastened to the chair.

As if alerted by her presence, both women faded like a mist and Estel found herself in another room. It was filled with bunk beds made of red stone and wadded with a thin layer of straw. Hesitantly, she felt the stone with her fingers and the memories of those who slept here flooded her senses. Like a group of trapped animals, six women shared this cramped space, unable to move without disturbing those around them. When one of them died in the middle of the night, her body sapped the warmth out of all of them. Estel's teeth chattered against the chill of that memory—even in death, corpses clung to the living in this forsaken place.

'I've seen enough,' she said to Arleta, but when she turned around, the girl wasn't there.

Estel staggered back outside, hungry for a breath of fresh air, except the air wasn't fresh, and with each intake, it felt as if her lungs inhaled poison. She licked her lips and tasted bitterness on her tongue. A dirt track stretched before her and she hastened along it, searching for Arleta's familiar form in the fog.

The path ended suddenly, and she found herself hemmed in a queue of men and women that looked more like scarecrows in their striped clothing and worn shoes. Some held empty bowls and others hunks of bread the size of a human fist. A man with two pots headed up the line, dividing the contents among the eager procession. Estel approached and peered inside one—it held a soup with green leaves floating in it, but little else. She looked at the people and back into the pot and in that moment a new form of dread assaulted her. Slow death from starvation and thirst, feeling one's body shrinking to skin and bone as it consumed its own flesh to stay alive.

She fled, her heart writhing in her chest like an injured snake.

White flakes began to fall and the fog retreated. Estel stopped and caught a few on the flat of her palm—they felt like rain but melted when in contact with her skin. Soon the ground turned into a white rug and the wet chill that lifted from it seeped into her. Like a nightmare from which there was no escape, the ground before her transformed. One by one, corpses materialised wherever she looked—men and women who lost their battle against inhumanity lay sprawled on the ground. Their blue lips were parted in a final whisper as the frost sapped all life from their malnourished bodies. She stepped past them. Their accusatory eyes bore into her and their hands clawed at the invisible foe responsible for their fate.

Hovering at the edge of madness with the sound of her teeth chattering inside her skull, Estel left the gruesome sight behind and followed a lane between two red buildings. It no longer mattered where it led, for she was sure there was no way out of this grave. Arleta was the only link she had with Daaria and the girl had vanished. How long would she survive looking over her shoulder without her bow to protect her? Her strangled thoughts recalled Lea, dying from terrible wounds inflicted by the Twilight Hunters. Faced with imminent death, how loud was her scream? Did she cry out for her daughter to come to her aid?

'I didn't know what fear was, Mother,' Estel whispered, knowing that she could never undo her wrongs.

Screams mixed with the sound of music brought her to a stop. A string of people dressed in the same striped and tattered clothing walked in the direction of a large stone building. Paint flaked from its walls in layers, and dominating the triangular roof were two great chimneys, puffing out a dark cloud of smoke into the sky. The people on the path were covered in scars and lesions, their bodies like twigs threatening to snap at any moment. With their heads hung low, they trudged down the path as if the motion of putting one foot in front of the other was too much of a burden. The screams drifting from the building were muffled by music played by a band of captives, for now she knew that no free man would endure such savagery. Like a folly, the instruments jollied along those who walked their final walk.

Estel turned away from them. Her body felt like an empty vessel, filled with nothing but echoes of suffering and anguish. She no longer remembered how she got here, nor who she was prior to this place. Like a nameless creature, she dragged her feet to the gate, her flesh stifled by fear and heart choking on sadness.

When darkness encased her, she fell into it without a struggle.

XIII

A hand slapped her cheek again and again, and a distant voice called her name. The blows stung, and she swatted at the hand, but instead of retreating, it became more insistent. Estel hovered in a dark place, and in a way, it felt peaceful and cosy to be surrounded by nothingness. If only the hand would leave her alone. Piece by piece, her awareness flooded back, banishing the fog and darkness from her mind. She tried to hold on, but the pull of life forcing her eyes apart was too strong. As she came to, Zeal's frowning face was the first thing she saw. Memories rushed her at speed, like a waterfall cascading down the mountain face, and she shrieked. With swiftness she didn't know she possessed, Estel kicked him in the stomach and the heel of her boot sent him sprawling.

'Go away!' Her scream sounded feral. Waving her hands in a blind frenzy, she jumped to her feet and fell against the wall.

Zeal recovered from the blow. 'It's me,' he said, grabbing her ankle.

She lost her balance, but the need to escape drove her. The smell of threat and fear was thick in the air and Zeal was the source. She crawled away from him, kicking and snarling, while the room spun around her.

'Calm yourself. Let me—'

She staggered to her feet and grabbed her knife. 'Stay away from me,' she warned him, slashing the blade from side to side. Zeal's face was a blur, his silhouette multiplied from one to three and then back to one again. She rubbed her eyes, but the image before her didn't change. 'Let me be.' Another slash of the knife followed her words.

Zeal spread his palms open. 'I'm unarmed. Something happened to you and all I want to do is help.'

'I don't need help,' she cried out. A sudden feeling that someone was creeping up behind her clawed at her neck. Knife at the ready, she spun around and stabbed. There was no one there.

'Estel, please…' Zeal took a step and offered his hand to her. 'You've nothing to fear from me.'

Fear… Her world burned with it, her insides twisted at the mere mention of it. The snare of dread was set upon her and there was nowhere to run, nowhere to hide. Her thoughts trailed off and she collapsed to the ground.

Her consciousness slipped away.

***

A crackling of fire stirred her eardrums and snapped her back to the present. She opened her eyes to the night, and shadows were brought to life by flames. Through the slit in the door, she watched them writhe on the wall of the adjacent room like creatures from the Dark Nav. The moment before sleep and wakefulness is always the most peaceful, like floating in the air, blissfully unaware of the imminent crash. Estel wanted to stay suspended forever, but her mind disputed that logic, opening itself to the flood of events from the days before. She clutched at her temples, not wanting to remember any of it. After a while, she swung her legs off the bed and tried to get up, but the floor escaped from under her. Her dizziness refused to fade, and her tongue stuck to the top of her mouth. She squeezed her hands to stop them from trembling, but it helped little.

Zeal walked into the room. 'I thought I heard you. Feeling any better?' The candle in his hand danced erratically, the light from it distorting his shadow.

'Where are we?'

'In Willow's Hearth. You were unconscious, so I moved you here. This is one of the few houses that's empty of corpses. I stayed in case you needed help when you woke.'

Estel's fuzzy mind sorted through the events in Kvet: Zeal, the archery contest, her victory. 'Did you follow me all this time?'

'Not exactly,' he said, glancing around the room. 'I'm glad you're feeling better—'

'Answer the question.' Despite feeling like someone who took a great fall down a mountain, she kept her voice steady.

He placed the candle on the rickety bed stand and crossed his arms. 'After our little exchange in the tavern, I went back to see you, to apologise for my behaviour. It wasn't right of me to push you like that. You don't have to tell me anything and I realise that now. But when we met on the road, I felt this uncontrollable force drawing me to you… to your future.' He scratched his eyebrow. 'It's sounds foolish when I say it like that, and Agni knows I care little for such feelings, but it's different this time… important somehow. I had to follow through, and here I am.'

Exhaustion played tricks on her—Zeal's voice rose and fell as if they were in a deep cavern.

'And the contest?' she asked.

'That was pure coincidence. The way you looked at my bow made me curious and I wanted to know if you could wield one.'

'By issuing your challenge.'

Zeal gave her a quick smile.

'But none of this explains your presence here,' she said.

'I learned that you were bound for Suha, so when you left Kvet, I followed you. It took me a while to pick up your trail. Not only are you a great archer, you're very good at covering your tracks.'

Her mind struggled to keep up. How come she wasn't aware of someone following her? Her senses were sharp—sharper than those of any human—and yet Zeal had managed to track her without alerting her to his presence. Either he was an exceptionally skilled tracker, or she was losing her abilities. Neither conclusion was satisfying.

Zeal crouched next to her and cupped her trembling hands into his. 'You don't have to explain what's going on, but please don't send me away.' He helped her up and settled her back on the bed. 'I'll stay here until you're well enough to travel and then you can decide if you want me gone.'

She was too weak to argue. ‘If you seek connection, you won’t find it here,’ she said.

He let her hands fall free of his and stood up. When he picked up the candle from the stand and took the light away from her, her corner of the room turned black. Estel’s heart battered against her ribcage like a prisoner against the bars of his cell. She wanted to ask Zeal to keep the candle burning until she fell asleep, but that meant admitting her fears. Before she could think it over, her lips moved against her will. ‘I’ve never been scared of the dark before…’

Blackness came for her and her fears followed her into the void.

***

A stream of sunlight cascaded through the broken shutters into the room. Estel squinted as she tried to make sense of her surroundings. The room was a ruin. A makeshift bed was most likely assembled by Zeal while she was unconscious. Bundled up straw formed the base of it and pricked her back whenever she moved. The stand beside it looked ready to fall apart if she dared to set anything on top of it. A faint smell of dust, dried stalks, and old age lingered in the air. Despite the warmth, her lips quivered, and shivers raced up and down her body. Using the bed and walls for support, she managed to stand up and shuffled down the short corridor. When she pushed the door open and stepped outside, the contrast between dimness and light blinded her.

'Zeal,' she called out, her voice a croak. Her knees buckled under her and she had to lean on the doorframe to steady herself. Her breath came in rasps.

'You shouldn't be up so soon.' Zeal's hands wrapped around her as he pulled her upright. He touched her forehead. 'You have a fever. Let's go back inside and I'll get some water.'

Estel shook her head. 'No. The bodies. What happened to the bodies of those who died here?'

'In their homes, in their beds. Just the way the others left them. I didn't want to say anything before, but Willow's Hearth had been ravaged by a powerful plague. It's not safe for the living to walk among the dead. When you're strong enough to ride, we'll leave here. The sooner the better.'

He steered her back to the doorway, but she resisted. 'We can't leave them like that. They need a proper burial.'

'They've been left like that for years. When the risk of infection diminished, the priestesses of Vesta came by this place, and after a closer inspection, proclaimed that the best thing to do was not to touch anything, especially the flesh of the dead. They blessed the village and forbid people to come here. It was just my luck that you stumbled right in.'

She sensed that the last was meant as a jest, but she didn't find anything amusing in the situation. 'Without a proper burial, the souls of these men and women could never be at peace. For such a devoted land as Kvet, I'm surprised to see that no one questioned their judgement.'

'It was the boginya's will and who would dare question the divine?'

'To abandon those who worshipped her and let them rot in this forsaken place? Is that her will?' She looked around the empty house. 'If we don't do something, the dead will remain trapped here, without hope of ever entering the Light Nav.'

'Is this you or the fever talking? It's only two of us and the bodies are many. We can't do anything for them. Besides, you didn't strike me as someone who cares much about the feelings of others.'

'It's not about me or what I care for.' A rusty shovel propped against one of the walls, caught her eye. Fighting dizziness, she pulled away from Zeal. 'I need to do what must be done.'

'Are you out of your mind? You're too weak. And what if you catch whatever it was that killed them? Traces of the plague may still linger here. Why risk your life in such a foolish way?'

She didn't listen. Her muscles berated her for this sudden spike in activity, but despite the weakness in her knees and sickness rolling in her stomach, Estel dragged the shovel to a patch of clear ground behind the ruins. The earth was hardened by the lack of rain and constant exposure to the sun, and her shovel struggled to bite through the crusted surface. After a few digs, her body was drenched in sweat and heart ready to explode.

Zeal snatched the shovel from her. 'Stop this madness. You can't dig graves in this heat. You can hardly stand on your own. Rest tonight and if you feel the same way tomorrow, we'll think of a better way to do this.'

Estel sensed the lie on his tongue. It was common for humans to distract their kin and gain time by offering empty promises. She wrestled the shovel back from him. 'I'll dig until every corpse has a place to rest in.'

Zeal raised his hands to the sky and barked a laugh. 'She's delirious.'

Estel ignored him and resumed her digging. Was she the only one concerned about the souls of the dead? Didn't he know how much suffering was out there? She couldn't turn her back on these people, pretend that she never witnessed the devastation caused by the plague. She did that once and condemned her mother to a restless sleep for eternity. Now was her chance to right that wrong.

But these are not your people. Why concern yourself with them? You have a task to complete upon which rests the future.

Estel spun around, shovel aimed at the air. 'Who's that?'

Zeal cocked his head at her. 'Who's who?'

'The one who said…'

'Who said what?' He scanned the village. 'There's no one here but us.'

Estel listened intently, but apart from the humming of blood in her ears and a distant sound of cicadas, the air was still. She lowered the shovel and pressed her foot against the metal, her mind on high alert. Zeal left, just to return with a tool of his own—a wide scraper that had seen better days—and started digging next to her. His muscles twitched and flexed as he loosened the ground, rivulets of sweat forming on his forehead. Soon, his shirt was soaked with it.

'One deep grave should do,' he said between breaths. 'The bodies are mere bones in tatters.'

Estel looked aside. Her vision doubled and she had to use the shovel for support. If she fainted now, her task would be left unfinished. When Zeal offered her a water skin, she drank like a greedy beggar.

'You'll make yourself sick,' he said, taking it back.

'I'm already sick.' The words came out mumbled, as if her tongue was suddenly too large for her mouth. 'My soul is sick… My heart is sick… I shouldn't have left her for the mrakes to feed on, alone. She deserved a proper burial. All she ever wanted was to join Chour in the Light Nav. My actions denied her that.'

The blood of the Da'ariys flows through you. You're a Creator. Only you have the power to change the course of our world.

Estel sprang like a sika alerted by the hunter's presence, shovel pressed to her chest. 'Why are you tormenting me?' she screamed.

Zeal gaped at her, eyes wide, mouth half open.

Something wet trickled down her upper lip and she wiped it. The back of her hand came off a light pink, like the buds on Kvet's trees. She stared at it for a moment then looked at Zeal. 'I'm dying,' she whispered, and crashed to the ground.

***

Estel fell in and out of consciousness, vaguely aware of her body being moved from place to place. She was on fire, every part inside her burning. Someone set a cool cloth against her face, but it didn't stay cold for long. The visions came and went like strands of forgotten memories. One moment Zeal was leaning over her, calming words on his lips, and the next, the twisted face of a daemon sneered back, teeth snapping in a violent need to tear her flesh apart. She thrashed and yelled, resisting the hands that pinned her to the ground. In one of the flashes, Lelya spoke to her, the words quiet and soothing. When her mother's soft fingers caressed her cheek, for a moment, Estel knew peace. If death was the only way to reunite her with her kin, she was ready for it, but as soon as the thought occurred to her, Lelya transformed into Volh, who grabbed her shoulders and shook her back into consciousness. Images merged and came apart again, faces changed, voices sounded like the rumbling of distant thunder.

She was thrown back into the burning land where she walked amidst the scorched faces, forced to listen to the pleas for help and unable to do a thing. The air smelled of anguish and despair. She ran, desperate to put distance between them and herself, just to plummet right into fear's embrace. It took her through the fog and red buildings, filled with screams that rang in her ears long after she fled.

At some point, her eyes flew open. Zeal sat on the bed next to her, wringing a cloth over a bowlful of water. She grabbed his arm. 'The dead won't know peace until we right the wrongs,' she said in an urgent whisper then she fell back on the bed.

Before her consciousness slipped away, Zeal's voice brushed against her mind. 'To save your life, I must give up my own. Please, forgive me.'

The world was black again.

PART III
SUHA

Through shame we learn the fallacy of our judgement.

—the Seer of Da'ariys

XIV

Estel woke to the sound of voices and a sharp scent of herbs. When the room came into focus, her eyes caught strands of smoke curling across the ceiling and followed the rise and fall of their ribbon-like dance. It was a vapour from the many incense holders placed around the chamber, and each intake of breath scratched the walls of her throat. The light from numerous candles bathed the room in soft glow. A sculpture of the sun hung on the wall opposite and carved in its centre was a man with golden hair and beard, holding a rod. On the tip of it was an effigy of a smaller sun. The man's face radiated kindness, but the angle of his eyebrows held a hidden warning. Before her journey, Estel was led to believe that Chour was the bog above others, a deity worshipped and feared by all Greylanders, but her adventures on Daaria taught her that this belief was nothing more than ignorance of those who had never set a foot outside of Grey Lands. Past the borders of her village, people were as different from each other as the bogs and boginyas they worshipped, and everyone had a choice of paths to follow.

When she sat up, the sheets on her bed rustled and she ran her fingers through them. They felt soft, yet crisp under her touch—a long time had passed since she slept under fresh covers. Gone was the spiky straw and the smell of decay from Willow's Hearth. Someone had taken off her clothes and replaced them with a gown made of cream cotton. She looked around for her bow and knife but couldn't see them.

A faint ripple of pain in her right arm drew her attention, and she rolled up her sleeve to expose two silver marks. She traced the twisty lines of the first and the jagged edges of the second with her nail, and the memory of the harrowing prison clamped around her throat. Human hearts were wells of misery and pain, and by some cruel trick of fate, she was forced down into the chill waters to drink her share of it. She let her sleeve fall down. When her feet touched the floor, instead of beaten earth they found polished wood.

Guided by the voices, Estel made her way to a tasselled curtain that separated the room she was in from the corridor beyond. Wooden pegs clattered together as she let the curtain fall behind her. The conversation died down and she stopped to catch her breath. With her palm pressed against the wall, she assessed her situation. Her bow was gone, and she had no means of defending herself from whomever awaited on the other side of the hallway.

Her senses heightened, hair standing to attention on her neck in warning. Before her exposure to fear, she faced threats in her life with boldness and determination, her mind focused on the efficient way to eliminate them. But leaning in the dim corridor, with nothing to fight off the potential attackers, felt like standing in a den of volks and hoping to turn invisible. She reminded herself that she escaped the Twilight Hunters, braved the seas on a ship full of rogues, and stood face to face with a zmei.

A man wearing an orange robe stepped into the corridor and her first impulse was to flee, but she planted her feet.

He looked her up and down. 'It gladdens me to see you awake and moving.'

The wrinkles on the man's ivory face were as deep as ridges on the oldest bark. He was bald, and his forehead painted in white. His silver beard curved around his jaws, neatly trimmed and combed through. A string of colourful beads wound around his neck.

'You're Ashk,' she said, but didn't move to greet him.

He must've sensed her unease, for his silver eyes softened. 'You've nothing to fear from me. I awaited your coming for a very long time.'

'How did I get here?' The images of the events in Willow's Hearth were still fuzzy in her mind.

'Your companion brought you here, unconscious, and in a high state of delirium. I feared this would happen if Lea refused to fulfil her duty.'

'How do you know about Lea?'

'We've much to discuss, but it can wait. First, you must eat if you're to regain your strength. Come.'

Estel cast a final look at her chamber and followed him down the corridor, through another tasselled curtain, and into a room with wooden beams. A tapestry depicting wild animals pursued by hunters holding long spears hung on the wall above the hearth. The men wore amulets and had nothing but rags wrapped around their hips. A woven rug with black stripes covered the floor and guarding the door into a small garden was a statue of an animal, its brown coat spotted with black.

Ashk offered her a brown robe not dissimilar to the one he wore. 'It'll do for now. Suha is hot, but the winds from the desert bring chill at night. Rest here while I get us some food.'

Estel wrapped the robe around her shoulders. 'You mentioned my companion. Is he here?'

'I sent him away, but he'll return tomorrow.'

There was no denying that Zeal saved her life, but how did he know to bring her here? She recalled glimpses of their journey, the hazy conscious moments she fought for while pain and fever ravaged her mind. Each snippet that filtered through was like retrieving another piece of a puzzle, and she was transfixed trying to fit them together. Only the heady scent of a man's skin and a soft whistling penetrated all, and she could remember a pulse, a steady rhythm that shook her with each beat. She had been at Zeal's mercy, and now she was standing before a man she had never seen before. For all she knew, Ashk was an impostor, pretending to be a friend. Coldness washed over her and a droplet of sweat trickled down her eyebrow. That same feeling she had during her walk among the captives, where Arleta forced the fear upon her, threatened to engulf her, and she had to fight it. The last thing she needed was to lose control and let panic inside. If only she had her bow…

Ashk stepped through the curtain, a steaming bowl in one hand and a loaf of bread in the other. The aroma of wild meat and thick roots filled the air. 'Be warned, the stew may leave a bitter taste on your tongue. I've added some healing herbs to aid your recovery. While you eat, I'll brew us some chay.'

Estel didn't know what chay was, but the smell of hot stew woke her appetite. She lowered herself onto a bench draped with soft blankets and cupped the bowl in her palms, enjoying the warmth that touched them through the wood. One taste assured her that Ashk was right about the bitterness—the healing herb he sprinkled over the meat made her tongue recoil. A tiny voice in her ear whispered warnings of poison, but she refused to indulge it. If the man wanted her dead, he had ample opportunity to take her life while she slept. On the other hand, if he was who he said he was, perhaps he knew of a way to clear her mind and heart of these intrusive emotions.

Ashk placed a ceramic pot and two elongated cups on a square table and sat on a bench facing her. He poured some of the steaming liquid into her cup and invited her to try it. The chay was light-brown in colour and when she took a sip, its taste came as a surprise. It was a mixture of sweet grasses and strong bark.

Ashk sniffed his cup. 'If one knows how to mix the right herbs together, a lot can be achieved with a cup of chay when all else fails. Even the best healers in Suha resort to it at times.'

'I've never heard of chay before,' Estel said between swallows.

'I'm not surprised. Herbs are a rarity in Grey Lands. The earth is too hostile, the sun shies away behind the mist… But you already know that.'

'The question is how do *you* know that?'

Ashk remained silent for a moment then cleared his throat. 'I went looking for you, just like I looked for the other Creators who came before, but it was different this time. Lea was a mother in every sense of the word. She allowed herself to love you even though she knew your destiny. It was the first time that the seer failed to recover his charge.'

Estel put the cup aside. 'I knew nothing of this.'

'How could you? Lea guarded the secret with her life, but it wasn't hers to guard. She knew what would happen and yet she was fearless in the face of danger. Only a true human can sacrifice so much with nothing in return.'

'My village was burned down by the Twilight Hunters. No one was spared.' The memory of that night touched her heart in a way that the real event never could. She scolded herself in her mind—these were not her thoughts, but the regrets of those who wallowed in their emotions.

Ashk lowered his head. 'What happened was inevitable, and your mother knew the price.'

She wrestled with this new knowledge. Could it be that Lea knew all along that she'd die if she didn't let her daughter go? Was she ready to sacrifice her friends and neighbours just to keep Estel for a moment longer? It was too ill of an idea to be considered.

'What happened cannot be undone,' Ashk said, as if her thoughts were in plain view. 'All of us have choices and the freedom to make them. Lea had decided hers and let's hope that yours will be more heedful.' He got to his feet. 'Before we begin, allow me to light the hearth. If I neglect to keep it at bay, the chill seeps deep into my bones and only warmth can stifle it.'

He walked to the hearth and poked the ashes with a cudgel. She expected him to be more frail and unsteady on his feet, but for a man his age, Ashk moved swiftly. Soon the fire caught, and the familiar crackling chased away the silence. He wiped soot off his hands and sat back in the chair.

'Where do I begin?' he said, more to himself than to her.

‘At the beginning?’ she offered. Ashk had the answers she so desperately sought, but his slow demeanour began to grate on her. ‘Is Rana truly my sister?’

‘Indeed. But it’s not as simple as that for she’s also the Destroyer. As for myself, I’m Da’ariys like you, sentenced to my duty until it comes to pass.’

Estel took a moment to absorb his confirmation. ‘And my birth mother?’

‘You’re more alike than you might think. I’m surprised that you’ve managed to connect with your parents without any prior training. It’s quite dangerous for the Creator to use powers before they’re schooled.’

‘I don’t have any powers. My senses are sharp, and I take advantage of that when hunting, but I can’t control them for long. I have visions, but they too come and go, causing me much pain. I wish I knew the way to free myself from them.’

‘Free yourself?’ he exclaimed. ‘These are no ordinary visions, and it’s well within your power to control them. Estel, you’re not a simple being. You’re a Creator, born to change the course of the world. The Da’ariys were a powerful race of leaders and warriors, and they’re worshipped by the people of Daaria to this day. But the greatest of them all was Remha, the Father of all Da'ariys.'

Estel considered his words. The bogs and boginyas were her kin? It sounded like a sour jest. 'You expect me to believe that I'm like Chour and Vesta?'

'You surpass them in every way. What they lack, you have in abundance.'

Ashk rose from his chair and dropped another log into the fire. 'Have you met your conduit?' he asked after a time.

'You mean Arleta? She's caused me nothing but trouble.'

He turned away from the hearth and looked directly into her eyes. 'Show me.'

Instinctively, Estel clasped her palm over the symbols branding her arm. She struggled to look at them herself, not to mention showing them to a man she hardly knew.

'How many?' he asked.

'Two, and I'm certain they're the reason behind my sickness. I'm no longer clear of mind and sure of heart. My logic fails me. Can you remove them?'

'She wants to remove the very thing that's essential to her victory…' Ashk shook his head as if Estel were a woman devoid of all reason. 'I feared this would happen when Lea refused to let you go. She stripped away your chance at understanding the gravity of your changes. It's unfortunate, but too late to think about what could have been. We can't bring back yesterday, but we still have tomorrow to worry about.'

So, the reason why she never met Ashk was Lea's failure to curb her emotions. She was born with a purpose denied to her by human frailty, and now Arleta poisoned her with the same weaknesses. 'Why was I sent to Daaria?'

'To correct the mistakes made by Remha and our people.'

The way he said it made the task sound like an errand, hardly worth worrying about.

He scrutinised her over a long pause. 'Your quest is to undo what the Da'ariys worked so hard to achieve in their misguided pursuit of strength and control. There's only one enemy here: your sister, Rana. But killing her isn't your goal. Far from it.'

The more Ashk explained the less she understood. 'So I was sent to defeat the Destroyer.'

'Yes, but to defeat is also to create. Now that the Twilight Hunters caught your scent, they won't stop hunting you. Rana will soon realise that her assassin had failed, so we must use our time together wisely. Every moment counts.'

How could a woman she'd never met before want her dead? 'But what does Rana want with me? She doesn't even know me.'

Ashk paced around the room, hands clasped at his back, his shadow trailing close behind. 'When humans came into contact with Da'ariys, they were taught our ways, and soon, every conscious being on Daaria worshipped Remha.' The corners of his mouth twitched with a sad smile. 'But how can a man accomplish anything that requires heart if they're not emotionally connected? How can one truly fight injustice if they cannot feel the depth of another's suffering?

'After a time, those of pure blood abandoned Daaria and returned to their original home. With them gone, people began building altars in their honour. I've been stranded on Daaria for what seems like eternity, watching every Creator fail, and with them, the hope for a better future. Today, I'm a bitter old man.' His eyes settled on the darkness in his garden. 'You're of the purest blood, born with a very rare gift. The magic in your veins gives you the power to see into the future, to glimpse what awaits humanity if we don't correct the mistakes of our ancestors. The symbols on your arm tell me that you saw the world created by those of us who forsook balance to appease the order of our ravenous bog. You walked the paths of tomorrow, so tell me, what do you make of it, Creator?'

The question sounded simple enough, but Estel sensed there was a great weight attached to it. If what she saw when Arleta pulled her into the beyond was the future of Daaria, then even her confused heart shrunk with the knowledge that people will burn and mistreat one another in the way that surpassed the worst cruelty.

'If what you say is true, and these visions were indeed images of the future, then the people of Daaria have much to fear,' she said.

When Ashk opened his mouth to speak, she stopped him with the flat of her palm and said, 'My journey into those forlorn lands ripped out a part of me. The sorrow was worse than any sickness, and the fear more frightening than any threats to my life.' She pressed her hand to her chest. 'In those moments, my senses were numbed and I was but a feeble human, unable to control my impulses. These emotions are the greatest weaknesses and your account proves that Remha knew that. That is why he warned Da'ariys not to succumb to them.'

Ashk's face turned grim. He let out a heavy sigh, and the age that he kept at bay for so long seemed to catch up with him all at once. 'So many others before you chose the wrong path, too afraid to be one with their hearts. Emotions are what make us real. Without them we're nothing but skeletons in disguise.'

'Emotions are what makes us feeble. My experiences are proof of that, and as long as I'm alive and my mind is my own, I refuse to accept weakness into my heart.'

Ashk's eyes sunk deeper into their sockets and she wasn't sure if it was the glow from the hearth, or tears that filled them. A possibility of the latter filled her with disgust. This was the seer—a man who lived for centuries, who was meant to teach her and help her to save the world. Instead, he embraced human frailty and sought to convince her to do the same.

'Our people,' she said in an even voice, 'entrusted you with an important duty. To guide the Creator and to restore Da'ariys to grace. And here you are, wallowing in self-pity, comparing our race to humans. I don't know if any of the things you told me are true, but what I do know is that exposing my frail side to the enemy isn't the best way to navigate the world. If indeed I need to face Rana, I'll use my skill and logic to guide me.'

The flames from the hearth crackled and spat a shower of sparks onto the wooden floor. Ashk extinguished them with his sandal. 'The birth of a Creator brings forth a Destroyer. Two forces inextricably linked. You're her and she is you, but each with your own destiny and desires. Hers is simple: to keep the world the way Remha intended it to be. You can't defeat Rana with mere magic or an arrow from your bow. There's only one way to accomplish such a task, but you've rejected it already.

'Those places you've visited in your visions, the suffering you've witnessed, are doings of people who rejected their hearts. Perhaps like you, they believed that our feelings should be controlled. Emotions were seen as a handicap, something that if embraced, would hold them back. And look at the future they have created.'

'But if I kill Rana I could stop all that. If she's dead—'

'You possess something she doesn't. A place for humanity in your soul. Rana's heart is driven by one need only: to make you fail and tilt the balance in Remha's favour.'

Estel got to her feet. A sudden dizziness swept over her, but she braced herself against it. 'Teach me everything you know but don't ask me to turn into a weakling.'

Wrinkles on Ashk's face deepened, but he inclined his head to her request. The part of Estel that was tainted by human emotion wanted to assure him all would be well, that he needn't worry anymore. But the side where true Da'ariys lived cast those sentiments aside. She pushed her chest forward and answered his solemn gaze with what she hoped was a look of assurance and determination.

'Trust in me, Ashk. That's all I ask.'

'Spoke like a true human,' he whispered. 'It's a pity that my trust won't change the fates of those who will burn in the Dark Nav of our own making.'

XV

Estel slept well, her mind free of visions and pain. Following the hardships of the road, the soft bed brought comfort and peace, while the covers insulated her body from the chill that swept the room at dawn. When she opened her eyes, the sunlight spilled through the shutters, bringing flecks of dust to life.

Her energy was back and her giddiness was a thing of the past. Ashk left some new clothes for her: a white shirt with short sleeves, linen leggings, and a belt. The garments fitted her well, and even though she favoured leather, in the heat of Suha, the linen proved to be a wiser choice. She used water from a basin to freshen her face. The cuts and bruises from her time at sea had faded, and there was hardly any pain when she touched them. Her right arm felt numb, but it didn't hurt.

Her conversation with Ashk was not what she had expected. It seemed that her hopes for erasing the symbols would remain just that: hopes. Devoid of choice, Estel resolved they'd serve as a reminder that strength and skill would be her guides going forward.

She found her bow and quiver in the corner of the room and regarded them with fondness. The crystal weapon was as mesmerising as when Juro first showed it to her, and she fought the urge to grab it and run away into the wilds to test it against the beasts of Suha. But she had more pressing things to attend to. Last night, she ordered the seer to teach her everything he knew about the magic of Da'ariys, and she intended him to do just that.

The things he told her made little sense, and a part of her didn't fully trust him. The story of Remha and his might filled her with pride and regret that she would never meet the greatest leader of her people. Ashk's description of Remha's cruelty and boldness bothered her little. The seer had spent too many years among humans to understand the meaning of true strength. His heart was weak, no longer fit to support the ideals of Da'ariys, but she would change that by revealing the truth about bogs and boginyas. Somewhere above, where the stars swam in their colourful glory, her race had survived. She met Lelya and Volh and despite her lack of attachment, she wanted to meet them in the flesh. If all it took was to stop the Destroyer, then she was ready to face that challenge. With training and knowledge from Ashk, she'd utilise her skills, make a stand against Rana, and demand the truth. Through the centuries, the teachings of her people were lost, or altered to serve those who created the future, and she'd put it to rights.

But not in the way Ashk wanted her to.

As she made her way down the hallway, a string of agitated voices drew her attention. She thought she recognised one of them as Zeal's and picked up pace. At the end of the corridor, a curtain of pegs admitted her into a bright room where the light from the opened windows blinded her. A tree with long, jade leaves decorated one corner, and the floor was covered in black and white animal skins. A set of round boxes rested on a wooden table and among them a half-burned candle with wax blotches at its base.

'I ask again, walk away.' Ashk's tone was stern.

Zeal confronted him with his arms folded, face lost in a deep frown. 'Not until I talk to her.'

'Well, I'm here,' Estel said.

'Do you know who he is?' Ashk asked. He gripped a dagger, pointed the tip at Zeal. His cheekbones as well as his forehead were painted white.

Estel looked from one to the other. 'Yes, I do. We met in Kvet and when I fell unconscious in Willow's Hearth, Zeal brought me here. I guess by doing that he saved my life.'

Ashk waved his dagger. 'If you knew his intentions, you'd never allow him to walk free.'

'What intentions? He was never a threat to my life. Perhaps you confused him with another man.'

'That's what I told him,' Zeal said. 'Let me talk to her, old man. Alone.'

Ashk stabbed at the space between them, punctuating his words. 'A spy and a liar. How fitting.' He stepped in front of her, tripping on a wooden vase. It clattered to the floor and rolled down the uneven floor. The change from the wise and controlled Seer of Da'ariys to a wild man took Estel by surprise. Did her safety mean so much to him?

'Every flame-sworn brings deceit and death in his wake, Ashk said, curling his lip. 'Your presence here, assassin, is an insult.'

A sudden chill hit her core. 'Assassin?'

Zeal's crimson eyes bore into hers, and he opened his mouth as if to deny the accusation. While she waited for a flood of excuses to slam her, her mind berated her for not seeing the man for who he was. Her senses warned her all along, but she was too preoccupied with her injuries to confront Zeal and demand the truth. Looking back, his sudden interest in her, and the events in Kvet, were a clear sign that something was amiss. She was a fool who walked straight into his trap. Her muscles hardened.

Zeal must have sensed the change in her because the excuses never came. His shoulders slumped and he opened his arms wide. 'Yes, it's true. I'm an assassin, but I never wanted to harm you.' And with those few words, the mask of the happy and cheerful archer she had met on the road to Kvet fell away, replaced by a sharp stare and a clenched jaw.

'And not just any assassin,' Ashk said. 'He was sent by Rana, the very enemy you were tasked to destroy. Do you still trust him?' He directed the question at Estel, but his eyes never left Zeal's.

The realisation was like an avalanche of rocks coming down the mountain with her trapped at the foot of it. It took her a moment to gather her thoughts, and all the while, Zeal's crimson pupils searched hers in an urgent plea. But when she finally addressed him, a true Da'ariys spoke through her. 'My people would punish such deceit by death. What have you got to say for yourself, *assassin*?'

Zeal took a step toward her, but Ashk jabbed his dagger at him. 'One step closer and this blade will find your heart.'

Zeal let out a short laugh. 'You know who I am. If I wanted to kill you, you'd be dead already, and so would she.' He looked back at Estel. 'I won't deny that Rana hired me to track you down and kill you. When I picked you up by the side of the road, this was my sole purpose. Injured and without weapons to defend yourself, you were no threat to me, but I held back. Something about you made me wonder. You looked like Rana and yet you were different. It sparked my curiosity. My profession forbids questioning our contracts, but I couldn't slash your throat and walk away. I told you before that all I wanted was to keep you safe and nothing's changed.'

'You betrayed me,' she said.

'I was merely withholding the truth.'

'Liar's excuse.' The vein in Ashk's neck throbbed. 'You don't know who she is. If you knew, you'd never have accepted this assignment. But now, there's no going back. Each contract is given under oath and must be completed. Those who fail are shunned by the people of Vatra.'

'Is it true?' Estel asked in a calm voice. If it was, Zeal's inability to fulfil his assignment made her cringe. If she swore an oath to take his life, there would be no hesitation. Instead, his human heart held back his blade, and now he faced two choices: death at her hands or exile. Despite his skill, he was another weakling who succumbed to his emotions. A chance meeting with a stranger was all it took for him to form an attachment and fail his mission.

'Assassins of Vatra are trained to protect the altar of our bog, Agni, and his eternal flame. If used by someone with violent intentions, it could destroy whole provinces. We're flame-sworn, born and trained to guard it with our lives, to kill anyone who desires the power of the flame for himself. I was hired by Rana to track down a thief who wanted to steal the flame and I was intent on fulfilling my contract. Until now.'

'Fool,' Ashk said, 'it's Rana who wants the world to burn.'

'And why would I need the flame?' Estel asked. 'To what purpose?'

Zeal shook his head, as if struggling to grasp her ignorance. 'You must know that Zyma is the coldest place on Daaria and that Rana claimed the throne of Marena, the boginya of winter. People of Zyma fled to Vatra, some even as far as Suha. Only one who possesses the power of Agni's flame could hope to oppose Rana and her riders.'

'Twilight Hunters…'Estel whispered.

The image of her burning village flashed through her mind, the agonising screams of Greylanders as they fled the Destroyer's magic. Did they think it was Estel who led them? Rana was her twin and all the villagers would've seen was her pale face against the shadows. The familiar knot tightened at the pit of her stomach and she cast the thoughts aside. Now wasn't the time to indulge in sorrows of humanity.

'Your reasons mean little to me,' she said to Zeal. 'You've deceived me by pretending to be someone else. With my senses dulled by injury, I didn't see you for who you really were. A killer sent to take my life. I can't forgive you because my heart doesn't know forgiveness and if I let you live, the shadow of your contract would always follow in my footsteps. I can't allow that.'

'I saved your life, risked the wrath of my people… for *you*. I'd rather face exile than take your life. Don't I deserve a grain of hope that one day you'll learn to trust me?'

Estel felt a sudden urge to slap Zeal's face, to shake him. She wanted him to stand tall and remember his duty. He was a flame-sworn, Agni's assassin, but she knew that words would be useless. She witnessed it too many times in Grey Lands. Zeal formed an attachment and no amount of convincing would turn him against her.

‘Hope is but a foolishness of the heart,’ she said. ‘You saved my life and such a debt must be repaid in equal measure. Leave, assassin, and never come back. If our paths cross again, you won’t find me so generous.’

Zeal’s face dropped, and anguish stole over his eyes, but it only strengthened her resolve. When she gave no reaction to the pleading in his face, he turned around and stormed out, leaving the clattering of the curtain pegs in his wake.

Estel turned to Ashk. ‘There’ll be no more talk of humans in this house.’

***

Estel filled her days learning about Da’ariys, her destiny, and how to take control of her powers and use them without draining her life energy. Ashk was a strict teacher. To begin with, he forbade her to rely on her senses and cut short any interactions with Lelya or Volh. While she was under his roof, the visions that plagued her most of her life ceased, and she welcomed it with relief. He warned her not to use her magic without proper cause, for if she hoped to defeat Rana, she needed to conserve every bit of energy she had at her disposal.

'Your body is life and its resources are limited. If you keep draining them, you'll cripple your physical form and when that happens, no amount of magic will be enough to heal you.'

Ashk explained to her the inner workings of her mind and how it was different from that of an average human. Her abilities granted her a sharper sense of awareness, and if she was willing to stretch them, there was no limit to what she could access, from everyday sights and sounds to as deep as the intentions of another being.

'At peak performance, you may infiltrate the thought process of your enemy, and use that knowledge to tip the fight in your favour.' They sat on a hill behind his home, facing the setting sun. 'However, this level of hyper-focus requires many years to master. Regrettably, we don't have that much time.'

'Maybe I'll prove to be an exceptional student.'

'Nothing would please me more.'

Estel was wise enough to heed Ashk's warnings about staying clear of her visions, but a nagging feeling that she had left too many things unsaid when she last spoke with her parents wouldn't leave her. Despite her instincts urging her otherwise, she resolved to go against caution and meet Lelya and Volh one last time.

She found a remote place in the wilds where she was sure Ashk wouldn't look for her, and attempted to test her powers. She rested her back against a tree root, so twisted it looked like the veins of a giant. Suha was a dry place, with wilds stretching as far as the horizon. The vegetation consisted of the most resilient bushes and trees that continued to grow despite the lack of rain. Some had leaves stretching out like great sunshades, while others wore crowns made of thorns. A bunch of green plants grew in clusters, their thick stems punctured with needles and resembling forks pointed to the sky. There were hardly any flowers, and the land was made of dust and piercing rays of the sun. Far in the distance, the mountain peaks strung along the horizon like huge chimneys, smoke pouring from them in clouds. When she asked Ashk about them, he explained that they were chambers of flame that stirred in the bowels of the mountain for years only to erupt in pools of lava. The vapours they gave out were poisonous to humans and animals alike. If anyone was foolish enough to venture into their dominion, death was certain.

She closed her eyes and breathed deeply. Ashk maintained that learning how to connect with every cell in her body was the most important part of her studies.

‘Body must yield to the spirit,’ he said on a day when she’d grown particularly impatient with the slow progress. ‘If you wish to control your powers, first you must learn to control your body. If you force the energy you’ll lose the flow, and with it your balance.’

So now she sat, breathing in and out, feeling the tingling of sun on her skin, the rush of blood in her veins, the steady beating of her heart…

A rustling jolted her out of her reverie. Her muscles tensed and she opened one eye.

Srebro emerged from the bushes and cocked her head.

‘Can’t you see I’m busy?’ She swatted at the fox. ‘Go and catch us some food. Be useful for a change.’

Srebro stretched, shook herself, and laid down in the shade, nose between her paws. She watched Estel through eyes half-closed.

Estel snorted and went back to her practice.

Srebro had caught up with her when Estel first scouted the wilds of Suha, and she was glad to see the fox unharmed. Listening for the fox’s presence became something of a habit, and Estel found herself restless when Srebro went missing for a time. She couldn’t say why she felt this way and the only explanation that came to her didn’t please her. It was as if they were forming a bond, but this idea was unthinkable. After her expression of contempt for Zeal and Lea's feelings, here she was, questioning her own. Her deepest fear was the change the emotions wrung in her. She was more aware of human suffering and the frailty of her own life. If she planned to defeat Rana, this awareness was a disservice to the strong, bold parts of her nature. Like a parasite eating away at one's insides, the emotions Arleta forced upon her ate at Estel's soul, weakening her strength and resilience. Even something as insignificant as Zeal's betrayal weighted heavily on her. Until this revelation, she knew nothing of Vatra and the bog Vatrians worshipped, but the more she thought about it, the more tempted she was to discover more. If the flame was indeed as powerful as everyone thought, then maybe, combined with her skills, it'd be enough to destroy Rana. She turned this idea over and over in her mind until the answer became clear.

Estel had to find a way to steal the magic of Agni for herself and confront her sister with it.

The flow of her breath stilled her mind, and she concentrated her energy into one place until her focus returned. Ashk insisted that the heart was the best place to direct one's energy, for its steady rhythm brought one's body into balance faster than any other technique, but she demurred against his reasoning. To her, the heart was the weakest place, prone to illogical discord, a place where doubt was ripe and poor sentiments sprouted like weeds. Estel favoured her mind, for it bred logic and rational thought—two of her most trusted advisors. The seer scorned at that but ceased his attempts at persuasion. Even without him saying so, Estel knew he didn't believe in the success of her quest. He schooled her on the matters of Da'ariys magic, just as he promised he would, but his words lacked enthusiasm.

'To defeat the Destroyer, you must confront her with what she lacks,' he insisted. 'Apart from the darkest of them, most emotions are denied to her, but you can use that to your advantage. There's a reason why the future is broken. By refusing our deepest feelings, we turned our existence into mere survival. How does this make us stronger?'

She sneered, insisting her familiar method would ensure the end of Rana.

Dust settled in Estel's nostrils, bringing the smell of desert with it. She hovered at the edge of awareness, between the now and the spiritual connection with the beyond. After a time, the silver in her veins stirred, bringing the magic of her ancestors to life. When the blackness came, she no longer feared it, but mastered it, allowing it to fill her and take her where she wanted to go.

When Estel opened her eyes next, Suha with its harsh landscape and heat was gone, replaced by the room with the tapestry of the ship. Unlike in the visions that came before, she wasn't a bundle of pain huddled in the corner, struggling to make sense of her surroundings. This time she was in control, with her feet planted on the ground, vision clear, and senses intact. She brushed the coarse material with her fingers, feeling the wefts and warps weaved into objects and people. Da'ariys in their white robes were no longer strangers, but bogs, bidding farewell to those who left their homeland with the blessing of Remha to conquer Daaria and enlighten humans in the way of his creed. Estel wished she was one of the warriors boarding the ship of Da'ariys.

'You've found him.'

The voice startled her more than she cared to admit.

Volh entered the chamber, hands clasped behind his back. Like the bogs on the tapestry, he was dressed in a white robe that had an arrow-shaped gap instead of a collar, trimmed with gold. Estel stood taller at the sight of him, and met his silver eyes with calm assurance. Ashk told her that Volh was a healer and with his wife, Lelya, protected one of the many halls of Light Nav where warriors of yore were made and trained under the watchful eye of Remha. Her chest expanded with a sudden feeling of pride—she was his daughter and a warrior herself, with a destiny to fulfil.

'Ashk told me who I am,' she said. 'He taught me how to master my abilities and will continue to do so until I'm ready to face Rana. Fear not, Father, I'll bring back greatness to our race.'

His eye twitched. He crossed the room to stand beside her and pressed his palm against the tapestry. 'This was the day when Da'ariys set out to discover what lies beyond the stars. I wasn't among them, but even so, I knew that our race would bring doom upon Daaria. The humans who dared to oppose them died, and those who sided with them were taught the way of our creed and made to swear oaths of allegiance and obedience. Death would've been a wiser choice.'

His words cloaked her mind with confusion. 'But people of Daaria worship Da'ariys. Through prayers, they hope to find salvation promised to them by the warriors of Remha. There is a temple in every province where bogs and boginyas of wood and stone are revered.'

'Did Ashk tell you how to defeat the Destroyer?'

‘He’s a stubborn man with the heart of a frail human. His prolonged confinement on Daaria damaged him. All he talks about is emotions and feelings. He forsook his own race in favour of humanity and wanted me to follow the same path, but I refused.’

Volh drew his brows together. ‘Have you seen the future, Estel? What awaits the world if we can’t reverse the damage inflicted by our ancestors? You’re my daughter, and so is Rana, but I have never possessed the capacity to love either of you, and I never will. It means little to me whether you live or die. Your mother is the gifted one, her heart swells with affection and pride at the mere mention of your name. Sadness consumes her at the thought that her children must fight each other. I’m a true Da’ariys, of the warrior stock, and only by joining one such as myself was she able to give birth to the Creator and Destroyer. It was a great sacrifice on her part to enter a union in which she’d never know love or affection, but she was prepared to do it. The suffering you witnessed will be realised because of Da’ariys and the hardened way of our people. You must find the strength to cast aside the warrior and welcome the woman by embracing your human heart.’

His voice was calm, and his steady gaze searched her face, as if looking for that spark of understanding, but it was a wasted effort. He wouldn't find one. She took a step back. 'You speak like Ashk.'

'The Seer of Da'ariys lived many lives, but eternal rest is denied him unless he changes the course of the future, and he can't do it alone. Only a Creator can undo the threads of time and purify the hearts of the living. When we landed on Daaria centuries ago, we enforced our ways upon the human race and bred those without fear, without love, without hope. We followed the commandments of Remha and kept our hearts pure. We stayed true to our race, but in the process, stripped every soul that joined us of all feelings.

'This isn't my experience. If you could walk Daaria now, you'd see that humans are no different than before. Weak creatures, prone to impulses, devoid of logic. I grew up among Greylanders, where I witnessed love that cost lives, fear that bred failure, hope that blinded the truth. Is this what you want us to become? To forget our ways… and for what? To be crippled for the rest of our days.

'We're trapped in an eternal loop. A Creator is born when the world is on a brink, when the gifted ones balance those who are empty. Imagine scales where one deed could make all the difference. You've the power to tip the scale, but will you? The Creators who came before failed.'

Estel couldn't believe this was her father talking. He sounded like Ashk, but how could that be? He was the son of the greatest warrior, the guardian of Light Nav. Blood of Remha coursed through his veins like the purest silver, and he himself admitted his heart was free of emotion. Yet he urged her to accept the puny side of her. 'You're wrong, Father. I'll prove to you that we can have our victory and change the future without sacrificing who we are. You may doubt me now, but when the Destroyer falls, I'll return to celebrate with you in the halls of Light Nav.'

Volh laughed, but it was a hollow sound. 'She doesn't know joy, yet speaks of celebration.'

Estel frowned. 'Where's my mother?'

'She's grieving your death and that of the future.'

Estel's eyes flew open and she clutched her throat. Her lungs felt like a shrivelled plum, struggling to expand and let the air in. How long was she out? It seemed only a short time ago when her consciousness slipped away, but the night was in full force, with the moon as bright as the sun that preceded it. She spent up a lot of her energy and her limbs trembled while the world shifted in and out of focus.

Srebro was gone, abandoning Estel to darkness.

When her body calmed, and her heart resumed its normal rhythm, Estel got to her feet. Ignoring the waves of dizziness and nausea, she made her way back to the house. Her mind churned with Volh's words. She had risked her powers to connect with him, to hear his voice, and seek assurance in his strength. But instead, she found a man filled with doubt. Worse, he was sure she'd fail and die like the Creators before her. Seeing him was a waste of her time and energy. Da'ariys had become as weak as the human race, which increased the urgency of her quest. She had to save her people before it was too late and bring back the greatness of Remha. And while doing so, she'd stay true to herself by relying on strength and skill alone. The battle for Daaria had begun.

XVI

Estel never told Ashk about Volh and his warnings. The seer lacked faith in her and the last thing she wanted was to enforce his opinions by betraying that her father felt the same way. Instead, she concentrated on mastering the next level of her training and Ashk's attempts at teaching her how to separate herself from her body and re-join it again. He pushed her hard, even harder when she resisted him, and she suspected their differing opinions played a part in his behaviour.

'When you want to communicate through visions, you must become one with your body, but when you need to use your senses in the moment, you must learn how to separate from your flesh in a way that allows a smooth re-joining,' he lectured her.

At first, it seemed easy to concentrate her energy to reinforce a particular sense. She'd done it before, when Rana and her hunters invaded the village, but she struggled to keep her sight long enough to absorb more details of that event. Despite Ashk's explanations on how to control every part of her body, headache and dizziness cut her concentration short and it took her a while to recover. The practice required a lot of mental energy and left her exhausted by a day's end, but spurred by the visions of Daaria's future and her own plans of defeating Rana, Estel persisted.

Days merged into weeks and weeks into months of intense training, while her body adapted to the new regime and absorbed Ashk's knowledge. Estel learned the workings of her mind and its interactions with the body and spirit. Only when the three were in harmony was she able to see, hear, and taste things without moving a muscle. After a time, she learned how to use her skills with her eyes open and then when she was on the move. Her abilities were like a magnifying glass, allowing her to see the world in slow motion and greater detail.

One morning, when the sun scorched the cloudless sky and the heat was stronger than a working furnace, Ashk called her to join him in his study.

The cramped room was filled with shelves full of scrolls and letters, bound by leather strings. Inks and vellum covered a large desk by the window, and the smell of dust mingled with that of dry parchment. The seer leaned over a heavy volume bound in leather, and when Estel peeked over his shoulder, she found letters scrawled upon the pages in strange shapes and patterns.

'What language is it?' she asked.

Ashk rubbed his eyes. 'I'm trying to decipher it myself. This volume was a gift from a friend, a Vatrian merchant who knew that I've wanted to study it for a long time. Most in Suha know of my obsession with the matters of history and ancient writings. People call on me from time to time to tempt my purse with their latest finds. I pay them well and reserve the right to see their wares before anyone else.' He nodded to himself, as if pleased by this arrangement.

Estel had no time for trivialities. 'Why did you summon me?'

He leaned across his desk. 'Well, I believe the time had come for you to test your skills in the real world. It's all good and well to run about the wilderness and hunt the beasts who could never outsmart you in any case, but pitting yourself against people is a different matter entirely.'

'I'm sure there's much more you could teach me, but I've wasted enough time in Suha. While we indulge in ancient magic, Rana goes unchallenged.'

'You underestimate human capacity. The beauty of wild animals is their simplicity. Their focus on survival is absolute. People, on the other hand, are driven by a myriad of other desires and often don't hesitate to sacrifice all to pursue them.' He rummaged through the scrolls on his desk and pulled out a small parchment. He blew dust off it. 'There's something I want you to retrieve for me. It won't be easy, but if you succeed, I'll deem your training complete.'

'Why should I waste my time and energy on this errand? You yourself told me that I must use my abilities sparingly. The assassin failed in his duty and Rana will soon learn that I'm still alive—if she hasn't already. If so, I've no doubt that the Twilight Hunters will come after me. It's best I move on before your household shares the fate of my village.'

Ashk got up from behind his desk and waved the parchment at her. 'Indulge the old man. I've been waiting twenty years for you, surely you could spare me an extra day.' His gaze was alert and she spied a flicker of a challenge in it. 'This, here, is a list of names, but it's incomplete. I must procure the other half.'

'What sort of names?' she asked, taking the parchment from him. The names were scribbled on the left side of it in black ink. She didn't recognise any of them.

'The names of women and children of Suha. If you manage to get it for me, I'll explain its significance later.'

'What makes you think I care about any of this?' She put her hands on her hips. 'Besides, your magic is more developed than mine, so if the parchment is as important as you say, I'm sure you'd have better success procuring it.'

'But that's just it. I don't need to prove my abilities, for unlike you, I won't be facing the Destroyer. The parchment is important to *me*, but the challenge should be of interest to *you*. Every warrior would relish the opportunity to test his skills and prove himself worthy of Remha's magic.'

She looked him in the eye. 'Since when do you care about Remha and his warriors?'

He looked past her and carried on talking. 'The place where the parchment is kept is guarded by none other than the Keepers of Suha. Stealing it won't be easy. Are you up for the challenge, daughter of Volh?'

Connecting her name with her father's shifted something inside her. Volh was the guardian of Light Nav, the maker of warriors such as herself. Would he look down on her if she refused to put her skills to the test?

'Tell me more about the keepers,' she said at last.

'They're highly trained guardians who keep the secrets of Suha from falling into the wrong hands. I've lived in this province since my descension to Daaria and I found that some secrets should be exposed. The sooner the better. You haven't been to the city, so be prepared for a different experience. Suha is nothing like Kvet or Grey Lands. It may be viewed as alluring, but it's undoubtedly more dangerous. Not everything here is as it seems. Keep your face shielded and stay out of sight.'

Despite her doubts, Estel began warming to her task. If anything, this little venture would prove to Ashk that she was capable and worthy of trust. Perhaps if she succeeded, he'd be more inclined to agree with her way of confronting the Destroyer. 'Where do they keep the parchment?'

'There's a building in the northern part of the city. You'll know it when you see it. It's hard to miss. The parchment is kept in its lower levels. As well as the gates, the keepers guard the chambers inside, so watch your step and don't get caught. My involvement must remain a secret, which means that I won't be able to come to your aid if something should befall you.'

Estel acknowledged his words with a nod. 'I'll get the parchment, but no more delays after that.'

'Who knows, maybe you will learn things about yourself you didn't know prior to this errand? Either way,

I won't stop you if you wish to leave when your task here is complete.'

***

Estel snuck out of the house in the early hours of dawn. It was the best time for scouting. The streets of Suha would be quiet, and a handful of early risers would pay little interest in a hooded stranger. She left the back road and joined a wide and well-used track leading to the city. It was damaged in places by potholes as deep as her elbow. The morning air from the western desert reached for her, but she ignored the chill-induced shivers, knowing too well that in a few hours Suha would turn into a bed of embers.

The shrubs on either side of the road were dry and leafless, their stems spiked with thorns. Beyond them, flatlands stretched as far as the eye could see, silently waiting for the sun to raise its glowing head in the wake of another day. Despite the early hour, large animals with elongated necks and thick forelegs nipped at the crowns of the tallest trees. Even from the road, they looked magnificent, their coats, specked with brown patches, reminded her of an opulent rug. When she asked Ashk about them, he explained that rafas were the tallest species on Daaria, worshipped by the priests of Suha. It was believed their long necks brought them closer to the bog, Yarilo, himself.

Srebro announced herself through the rustling in a bush. Of late, she followed Estel whenever she stepped out of the house, and to Estel's surprise, some of the fox's weariness melted away. She couldn't say if it was a good or a bad omen.

'You can't follow me to the city,' she said, certain that Srebro would find her own ways to amuse herself while she was busy scouting. This wasn't the first time she had to leave the fox behind.

Srebro paid her no heed and trotted after her, staying away from the main track, but close enough for Estel to sense her presence.

The buildings on the outskirts of the city were unlike Ashk's house in appearance. Their walls were made of rusty-coloured clay, supporting round roofs made of straw, and circular doorways that dominated the face of each. Some were two-storeys with balconies running along the top half. The road changed from the beaten track to something resembling shavings of iron, spread evenly beneath her feet. Smoke from chimneys wound upwards in a tight string—a sign that she wasn't the only one with an early errand. Past the cluster of houses and further into the city, great pillars fashioned from red stone formed arches above her head, giving the path an appearance of a long hallway.

A flock of chickens clucked at the feet of a woman who sat on a bench at the entrance to a small house. She wore a colourful dress and a head band wrapped neatly around her head in an intricate plaited pattern. Her face was partially concealed by a veil. Never before had Estel seen such a headdress, and the bold orange shades of the cloth made her think of the setting sun. The woman's skin was as black as the skins of Mila and Kara, the archers who competed alongside her in Kvet's contest. The woman conversed with the chickens in a soft voice, feeding them grain from the hem of her dress.

Many buildings had carvings of the sun engraved on doorways and east-facing walls in honour of Yarilo. Considering the climate of Suha, it was fitting that its people turned to him for blessings, but Estel knew better. Yarilo wasn't some bog but a Da'ariys, sent to Daaria to speak the truth of Remha and his warriors. She wished Lea was still alive so she could ask her why she chose to worship Chour even though she knew of Estel's ancestry. Perhaps some habits, once practiced, overpowered even logic.

The flies began their daily humming, drawn in swarms to garbage cans, waste pits, and her sweat. She swatted at her neck, growing agitated by the constant need to keep them at bay, but in spite of their dying companions, the pesky insects kept on coming. The breeze stilled as the morning unfolded, and soon, not a leaf shivered in sight.

Estel walked through streets and alleyways with her head down, following the directions Ashk had provided. The houses and stores thinned, giving way to a wide track that ended in a clearing surrounded by a thick vegetation and a circle of trees. With tall grass for cover, she approached the clearing from the side. It led her to a square courtyard where pillars formed a dome above a fountain in the centre shaped into a stone maiden tipping a jug of water into a round bowl. Green vines climbed up the pillars and walls, and blooming among them were red and purple flowers, making the whole place look like a tapestry.

Across from where she crouched, a wide building with four sets of windows towered over the splendour of the courtyard. With its white walls and black roof tiles it looked out of place with the rest of Suha. The main entrance consisted of an iron doorway secured with a latch. The keepers patrolled the area—one circled the building while the other awaited his turn at the gates. They wore little gear except for the leather bracers tightened around their arms, and a cloth wrapped around their hips in a skirt-like fashion. The exposed flesh, as well as their faces, was painted with white and black letters Estel couldn't read. Ornamental chains hung from their necks, and each keeper held a curved blade. It was unlikely that she'd be slipping in through the main entrance.

Estel scouted the perimeter, but the iron fence separating the trees from the courtyard was well maintained and provided little in terms of entry point. When she was about to turn the corner to inspect the other side of the building, a clattering of hooves stopped her in her tracks. A cart pulled by two horses stopped at the main gate, and two men dressed in brown garb called greetings to the keepers in the courtyard. Estel was too far to hear the exchange, but after a few moments, the gates opened, and the keepers let the carriage in. It stopped beside the fountain, and two women, chained at their feet and ankles, stepped out. Their bowed heads and sagging shoulders told her they were captives.

The men in charge pushed the women along the path and into the house. When the doors closed behind them, Estel took her leave, but her thoughts remained with the chained women. The glamour of the house and the way it was guarded implied there was more to the story than a parchment full of names, and she intended to find out what Ashk was withholding from her.

***

'Tell me the truth, Ashk,' Estel insisted. 'You're asking me to risk myself for a piece of parchment. You of all people should know the value of the Creator's life. Or is it just an excuse to keep me here?'

They were in his study. The fire snapped and hissed in the hearth as if demanding confrontation of its own. Ashk leaned on a cudgel watching the erratic shadows cast by the flames that elongated his silhouette and turned him into a crooked man.

Returning empty-handed with more questions than answers from her scouting venture, Estel cornered him.

Ashk grunted and his face sagged. 'The women you saw were taken by force, ripped from their families to serve until their debt is repaid.'

'What kind of a debt? If it's a valid one, there should be no reason for concern.' In Grey Lands, debts were paid in full through labour, or a free use of one's skill. When times were hard, Greylanders turned to their own for help, and many times she hunted down animals to exchange the meat for favours from other villagers. If the women's family agreed to let them go, she saw no reason to get involved.

'Did it look just?' He swept the room with the cudgel. 'If so, why the need for chains? Surely, knowing their families depended on them, the women should have followed of their own free will. Nothing about it is just.'

'So I was right; this isn't about the names.' Her tone was sharp. As always, Ashk's primary concern was with humans. 'I've more pressing things to do than worry about debts and the manner of their collection. I should be on my way to Vatra, trying to find a way to steal the flame of Agni, but instead, I'm stuck with you and your human troubles.'

'Oh, just the opposite. The names contained on the pages of that parchment are those of debtors. I need to see them and warn the families. If I don't, more women will be taken.'

Estel scowled at him. 'Why should you? If the families you speak of indebted themselves willingly, you should let them settle their matters in a way they see fit.'

'There must be another way to repay them.'

Ashk was a stubborn old man and if he wasn't a Da'ariys, she'd have walked away and left him to wallow in his pity. 'What are the terms of their repayment?' she asked instead.

'Their bodies belong to the collectors who trade them for coin. The house is a burdel, a place where dignity means nothing. I saw women who left after their family's debt was cleared. Ghosts look more alive… You couldn't possibly understand the repercussions. The shame these women carry would never allow them to return to their families. They're banished to the wilds where most of them perish at the jaws of wild beasts.'

'Why would anyone surrender their flesh and blood to such fate?' For all their talk of love, humans were quick to betray their own. If it was her in place of these women, she'd have returned to Lea and resumed her life. Better still, she'd have found those responsible for her plight and hunted them down.

'Sometimes shame is stronger than familial bonds. But you wouldn't know that.' He stared at his hands cupped around the cudgel. They were the hands of a man who witnessed the passing of centuries.

'If that's so, then maybe you don't need me at all. Instead of worrying about the debts of others, you should think about the Destroyer and the future we're trying to prevent.'

'Oh, but this task has everything to do with the future.' He waved his hand as if chasing away an irritation. 'Never mind that, you promised to recover a parchment for me. Will you stay true to your word, Creator?'

Estel's instinct urged her to refuse him, to leave Suha, and follow her destiny, but something held her back. She couldn't deny that the fate of the women Ashk spoke of pulled on a lone string of sadness in her heart, but she refused to play its tune. Day after day, she worked hard to keep it silent and she wasn't about to give in. It was something bigger that held her in place. A promise given by a warrior was a promise kept, Ashk had once told her.

'There's no way to enter the burdel unnoticed, but—' she tossed her hair back and lowered her voice'—if I was to become a daughter with a debt…'

Ashk rubbed his hands. 'Excellent. Leave the arrangements to me. I'll call on you when all is ready.'

XVII

The following day, when the afternoon shadows stole over the fields, Ashk entered Estel's sleeping quarters with a square parcel under his arm. 'Try them on,' he said, placing it on the bed.

She cut the twine and unfolded the bundle to reveal a dress, not dissimilar to the one worn by the woman who fed the chickens during Estel's visit to the city. She ran her fingers over the cloth; it was light and airy and would allow for free movement. The flowers sewn on it were the colour of earth, sky, and fire. It had sleeves long enough to conceal the symbols on her arm.

'The headdress will disguise your silver hair,' Ashk said, pointing to a strap of cloth as colourful as the dress.

'It's ridiculous. Wearing it would make me look like an impostor. And not in a good way. Everyone will be able to tell I'm not who I claim to be.'

'As long as you play the part, no man would turn you away.' He brushed his beard and looked her up and down. 'You've a poor understanding of men, so I'm afraid you'll have to trust me on this one.'

At her questioning look, he snorted. 'Just remember that you don't want to be taken, and yet, you must go. Fill your heart with sadness and all will look as it should.'

'I'd rather not. I need my strength if I'm to walk away with the parchment.'

'No one who enters the burdel would look or feel happy. At least pretend that you're grieving.'

'This better be worth it,' she said through clenched teeth.

'Now, I want you to meet your escort,' Ashk said and he gestured at the tasselled curtain that separated her room from the corridor. The pegs clattered, and a girl stepped through it. 'This is Zoya. You're her replacement. I've arranged that her family's debt would be cleared in exchange for your services.'

Zoya bowed her head as if to express her gratitude and Estel gathered that she knew nothing about the real reason behind the change of her fate. The girl looked of a similar age to Estel, but that was where the resemblance ended. Zoya's skin was darker than a starless night, and her brown eyes harboured the thickest and longest eyelashes Estel had ever seen. The girl's teeth shone white, but her arms and cheekbones cried out for nourishment. While she stood there with her head dipped, her teeth worked on her lower lip, biting off tiny pieces of skin.

Estel preferred to go alone. Humans were easily distracted and struggled to keep calm when their lives were at stake. 'I'm better off on my own,' she said in a stiff voice.

'No, you're not,' Ashk said. 'For one, she needs to hand you over to the keepers to claim her freedom. Secondly, you need help with that dress. Something tells me you have never worn one before.'

Estel regarded the colourful cloth on her bed. As much as it annoyed her to admit it, she wouldn't know where to start with her makeover. With a shrug, she turned to Zoya. 'Well, don't just stand there. Help me with the headdress.'

Zoya hastened to her side and set about arranging the piece of cloth around Estel's head. Soon, her silver braids were gone, concealed beneath the sea of colours. Zoya offered her a bronze looking glass and when Estel peered into it, a woman with a smooth, ivory face and silver eyes looked back. A faint discolouration on her cheek was the only reminder of the wounds she had sustained at sea, and this too would soon fade. Her skin didn't scar the way a human's did, and it healed much faster. For all that, Estel didn't care about her appearance the way other girls in

Grey Lands did. Much to Lea's displeasure, she saw no merit in such pastimes after observing that they only invited more gawping and more trouble.

'You saved me and my family from shame.' Zoya's quiet words snatched her from Grey Lands back to Suha. 'May Yarilo guide your path for eternity.'

The girl's display of gratitude was pitiful. 'I'm not doing this for you.'

Zoya's face dropped. Estel saw the expression enough times on Lea's face to recognise disappointment, but there was nothing she could say apart from a lie, and she didn't have time for such niceties. 'If you want to earn your freedom, play your part tonight and let me play mine. If both of us are lucky, we'll still be alive come tomorrow.'

Zoya said nothing but focused her attention on helping with the dress. It was too long, but with the aid of some pins found in one of the drawers, the girl managed to adjust it. Estel never wore a skirt before and it felt odd to have all this cloth trailing behind and around her. Walking was even worse. Zoya had to show her how to lift the edges to allow free movement and to prevent her from tripping on the hem. Mere moments after wearing the dress, Estel missed the comforts and simplicity of leggings and shirts. She eyed her bow with longing. The afternoon light reflected off its bluish surface like a thing alive, and she couldn't believe her luck that Juro kept his end of the bargain and let her keep such a wondrous weapon. With a sigh, she forced herself to look away from it—she had to leave the bow behind or it would give her away. The only weapon she'd take was the small knife, which she hid in the rich folds of her dress.

Ashk entered the room and nodded his approval. 'Your beauty shines tonight. You look like a true Da'ariys.'

'I thought you favoured humans,' she snapped back. It was Ashk's fault that she had to endure this foolish garb. She struggled to understand why any woman would want to look like a meadow day after day.

'I'll take you as far as the market square, but then you and Zoya are on your own. She'll hand you over to the Keepers of Suha and explain that you've agreed to repay her family's debt. If all goes well, they should let you inside, but be ready for anything.'

'When I get the parchment, what then?' Estel asked, batting at a fly that settled on her sleeve. It wouldn't surprise her if insects swarmed after her through the whole of Suha.

'This is where your real test begins. Use your senses and find a way to escape. With your abilities, you should have no trouble avoiding the keepers. If you fail, we're both as good as dead.'

Estel berated herself for agreeing to this insane trial, but it was too late to back out now.

Outside, a red carriage was waiting for them. Two sets of wheels, back ones twice the size of those at the front, supported the main body consisting of a bench with canvas drawn over it like a hood to protect the passengers from the scorching rays of the sun. A white horse waited patiently for Ashk to take up the reins. Estel didn't ask who owned it, but she had a feeling that if not Zoya herself then her family had a lot more involvement in Ashk's plan than he let on. She concealed her suspicions and climbed into the carriage.

As the afternoon faded into shadows, the evening deepened but the breeze still retained its warmth. The seer knew the roads well and the horse must've sensed his confidence for it sped through the darkness as steadily as the potholed road would allow. Estel tasted dirt on her tongue and felt fine dust settle on her skin. Zoya kept her distance, huddled at the other end of the bench, her eyes fixed on the flatlands that stretched to either side of the carriage like the bed of a dried-up sea.

The wilderness gave way to the first settlements that multiplied to form the city itself. At this hour it was very much alive, with people taking care of tasks the midday heat had forced them to abandon. Those fortunate enough to steal an evening for their own pleasure filled the city taverns to drink away the day's labour, and those less fortunate rushed back to their families before the night's chill caught up with them. Lanterns flickered in the windows and above entryways, chasing the shadows into the darkest corners of the city.

The carriage halted at the marketplace. Besides a few beggars, they found it empty of people and trade. Suha wasn't safe at night, so merchants folded their stores long before the sun's departure.

'This is as far as I can take you,' Ashk said, scanning the surroundings.

Estel jumped off the carriage, tripping over the hem of her dress in the process. She cursed in Chour's name and felt a little pang of guilt. Lea would be aghast if she heard her now. The thought clenched her stomach. Why should she care what her adoptive mother might think of her? Chour was nothing more than a man of her race, albeit a powerful one.

She didn't wait for Ashk to depart, but ushered Zoya in the direction of the burdel. The clatter of hooves at her back announced that, from this moment on, she was on her own.

The dirt track brought them to the gates where two Keepers of Suha challenged them with their blades drawn. One had three fingers missing from his left hand while his companion had a ring pierced through his right nostril.

'State your business,' the man with the missing fingers demanded. Estel noticed a lift to the corner of his mouth when he appraised her.

Even though Estel wanted nothing more than to cut that smirk off the keeper's face, she had a part to play. She bowed her head while her senses took a measure of the men. With little concentration, she could hear their hearts pumping blood and smell the acid stench of their armpits. Their muscular arms and the way they handled their blades told of practiced skill. Ashk was right—it wouldn't be easy to slip past them, steal the parchment, and escape without raising an alarm.

Zoya, unaware of her companion's plotting and focused on her own survival, whispered the reason for their presence. The girl's body trembled, from excitement or fear, Estel couldn't tell, but watching Zoya stirred something inside her and her mind came alive with questions. What if she were walking into a trap that would cost her her life? If the keepers discovered her treachery, she'd die an agonising death. Pain and more pain awaited her for the sake of names of people she didn't even know. Cold sweat stood out on her brow and her breathing became shallow. The link her senses formed with the men was broken and she felt naked all of a sudden, exposed, and at the mercy of those serrated blades. It was the same feeling she experienced in the prisons of the future, where fear revealed its ugly face to her for the first time. She made a move to turn around and flee when a grip of Zoya's hand stopped her. The girl's full lips were flattened as she affirmed her intention with a curt headshake—if it was her life or Estel's, the girl made her choice.

Estel sensed Zoya's determination and berated herself for acting like a weakling in the girl's presence. Estel was Da'ariys, a warrior from a race that was above such lowly emotions as fear. It's her enemies who should be trembling, not her. And yet she cowered at the slightest sense of danger. Despite feeling lightheaded, she forced her chin up and stared into the painted faces of the keepers. No matter their strength and skill, she was the one with the magic of her people flowing through her veins.

‘The exchange is valid,’ Estel said, keeping her voice even. ‘I wish to serve instead of the girl. Will you accept the conditions?’

Zoya’s grip on her arm loosened.

The keeper with the piercing let out a short laugh, but there was no joy in it. ‘Watch your tongue, girl. We set the rules and decide the conditions here.’ He stared at her with bloodshot eyes, as if daring her to challenge him. Despite her best efforts to stay calm, she leaned back from him and earned a look of disdain. Two reactions warred in her—one part wanted to grab the knife and teach the man a lesson, but another urged her to flee. She dismissed both. She was forced to feel the fear through Arleta’s visions, but she refused to be a slave to it.

The keepers stepped away from the gate and exchanged words. Estel willed herself to listen in, but she was too rattled to keep focused. Using her abilities in the wilds was easy, but facing a real threat, with her brain obscured by a fog of dread, was another thing. All she could do was control her breathing and conceal her quivering fingers. The men seemed to have agreed on something, and both of them walked back to the gate.

‘The master isn’t here,’ the fingerless man said. ‘He’ll be back in the morning to inspect the goods.’ He pointed his blade at Estel. 'You may enter. As for you,' he nodded at Zoya, 'return to your family and wait for a word from us. If the master approves of this exchange, your family's debt will be erased. If not, however, both of you will be held responsible for tonight's intrusion.'

Zoya's eyes doubled in size and she backed away from the gate, bowing. Further up the dirt track, she broke into a run, willing dust to life with her sandals.

'Come with me,' the keeper with the piercing commanded, opening the gates.

When Estel went through, his fingerless companion shut them with a clang behind her then resumed his guard duty. Her muscles tensed at the finality of the sound. She followed the pierced man down the courtyard, past the fountain, and up the steps to the main entrance. For all its vines, flowers, and glamour, the burdel looked like a tomb with its soul still trapped inside it, regarding her through the many windows. The keeper urged her through the doorway into an anteroom where two lanterns threw soft light on the walls painted in shades of rich wine. Even in the dim light, Estel could tell that the house was opulent. An armchair and a curved desk were fashioned from thick wood and polished to shine, and past the anteroom, she caught a glimpse of a winding staircase. To each side of it, carpeted hallways led to right and left wings of the burdel.

The man yanked her back and grabbed her face. Estel caught the inside of her cheek and the bite filled her mouth with a taste of silver.

'And what do we have here?' He turned her face from side to side then ripped off her headdress.

She jerked away from him. 'Master won't be pleased.' She tried to replace the headdress, but without Zoya's knowing hands, the cloth refused to cooperate.

The keeper laughed—a deep and eerie sound that lifted the hair at the nape of her neck. 'I don't think Master wouldn't begrudge me a closer look before I hand you over.'

Her mind considered different options. From her days in Grey Lands, she recalled the men who made advances toward her, and in her experience, they were weak creatures, easily outwitted if one knew how to manipulate their urges to one's advantage. Mara tried to teach her the ways of seduction, but at the time, Estel had little interest or need for such trivial knowledge. Why would any woman want to waste her time attracting a man's attention? But the situation she was in demanded this foolish approach, so she swallowed her distaste and pulled the strands of her memories. With a flutter of her eyelashes she said, 'I wouldn't mind so myself.' She kept her voice intentionally low and inviting.

'A willing one,' he said, chuckling. 'That's a surprise. Your lot moons about for most of the days they're here, as if that would make a difference. But you…' He sniffed her neck. 'We can have fun with you.'

Estel stretched her lips into a smile.

The keeper grabbed her hand and pulled her into the adjacent hallway lined with thick animal furs in stripes of black and white that prickled her exposed toes and made them itch. As they hurried down it, Estel found the blade hidden in the folds of her dress. The feel of it close to hand filled her with courage. All she needed was an opportunity. They passed a row of doors with golden knobs and numbers chiselled on the front of each one. Murmurs and garish prayers to every deity in Daaria drifted from inside—debts were being repaid throughout the house.

They stopped at the end of the hallway and the keeper retrieved a key from under the rug. He opened the door to the last room and pushed her inside. It was dark and smelled of men and sour spirits. Their breaths and the shuffling of his feet were the only sounds. The man moved about the room and she heard him fumbling with a candle.

Soon after, a dim light penetrated some of the darkness, revealing a square room. Hefty curtains, drawn over the window in the north wall, blocked any daylight from entering. Four wooden posts supported a large bed in the corner with a veil stretched over it like a house roof.

It was as good a time as any. Estel edged closer to him and brushed his arm with her fingers. 'What do you want me to do?' she purred in his ear.

'Take it off. All of it.' His voice was coarse and his breath heavy on her cheek.

She hooked her index finger round the hilt of her knife, pressing it against her bare wrist. With her other hand, she began loosening the dress around her shoulders. Impatient and overcome with lust, the keeper drew closer, his hungry gaze following her fingers as she pulled her arm free of the cloth. The sweat of his skin permeated the air and in the dimness his eyes looked like pools of murky water. Estel's breath was coming on fast and she tightened the grip on her knife.

With a brutal force, the keeper grabbed her arm and pulled her to the ground. Estel couldn't stop the small sound in her throat as he pinned her down with the weight of his body. The more she struggled, the more her resistance excited him. His hot palm pressed against her thigh and he forced her legs apart. The knife pricked at her wrist as she fought to clutch it, but as the man's tongue slid across her cheek, her blade plunged deep into his jugular, as fatal as the bite of a poisonous viper. Estel pressed her shaking palm against his mouth to hold in his dying scream, then pushed his body off of her. She lay there for a while, staring into the ceiling, trying to calm her ragged breath. No man had ever forced himself upon her. Such behaviour was intolerable among Greylanders and she assumed that others followed the same rules. Now she knew better.

When her hands ceased their trembling and her heart settled back into a steady rhythm, she got to her feet, wiping her knife on her dress. The keeper's blood merged with the crimson flowers on her hem, leaving a permanent mark of her kill. She adjusted her sleeve then searched the body for keys, but her hands came up empty. The soft rug on the floor masked all sounds as she dragged the keeper into the corner of the room and pushed him under the bed.

With the keeper dead, all that remained was to find the room with Ashk's precious parchment, steal it, and escape before the other keepers realised what happened. She wasn't sure how many of them walked the hallways. The seer mentioned a basement, so she needed to find a staircase leading down. Estel edged through the doorway and crept down the corridor back into the anteroom. The kill stirred adrenaline in her body, lifting the fog off her mind. Her thoughts were sharper and her senses more in tune with her surroundings. She listened hard, shifting through the menial sounds of men and women behind the closed doors, and looking for the more purposeful strides of the Keepers of Suha. A quick scan of the anteroom assured her it was empty. She crossed it and entered the hallway on the other side. It was dimmer and curved to the right. The walls were laden with paintings of orchards and busy markets, both depicting skimpily dressed women and men. With her back against the wall, she inched down it until she came to a window covered on the inside by a wooden screen. To the left of it was a narrow alcove, but no sign of a staircase.

Estel retraced her steps. Somewhere, a door opened and closed, and she couldn't tell the direction of the sound. When she neared the anteroom, a conversation between two men made her halt. With her eyes closed and breathing even, she directed all her energy to expanding her hearing. The voices grew sharper and she recognised that one of them belonged to the fingerless keeper. He sounded agitated and the responses he gave his companion were short and snappy.

'I told you she went with him,' he said. 'I saw them enter the house.'

'Where are they then?' the other man asked. 'I told the master the man wasn't worthy of his time and title.'

'Let's find him before you judge him too harshly.'

'I'm too lenient as it is. He should be on duty instead of whoring away his time.'

Estel's senses were so in tune that even the thick carpets couldn't drown the sounds of footsteps heading in her direction. Her eyes flew open and she scanned the hallway. If she stayed here, the men would come upon her and all would be lost. It was one thing to defeat a lone, lustful man, quite another to fight two keepers who already sensed trouble. Her only way out was the window at the back and she hastened for it.

The footsteps were closing in when she yanked the screen. It rattled but didn't give. A little chain linked it to the hooks on the other side—she'd need more than strength to pry them open.

As her options dwindled, panic shook her. She fought hard to keep the fear from spreading.

Maybe she could try one of the doors in this wing.

She ran to the first and pulled the knob.

Locked.

She tried the room opposite, but the door didn't budge.

The voices grew louder. It was too late to try other doors. Even if she ran, the keepers would spot her before she had a chance to turn the knob.

With her only way out cut off, Estel planted her legs firmly on the ground and reached for the knife.

A whisper reached for her, 'This way.'

She turned her head but couldn't see anyone.

'Hurry!'

Estel narrowed her eyes at the alcove then took a step toward it. A set of blue eyes stared back at her and Arleta's small hand reached for hers. Estel hesitated. Last time she touched the girl, she was thrust into a terrible vision of the future where her heart tasted terrors beyond belief. But the keepers rounded the corner and the only other choice was to fight them with a puny knife. Even before her hand met Arleta's, she regretted her decision. A familiar pain licked the symbols on her arm and spread through them like venom, but the girl pulled her deeper into the alcove.

Her feet found a channel of corridors, musty and covered with cobwebs, once hidden from her in the darkness. They moved down it, quieter than a whisper.

'Why are you here?' Estel asked, trying to free her hand, but Arleta's grasp was surprisingly strong for a child.

'You should know. You summoned me.'

She didn't recall summoning anyone, and least of all the girl who caused her internal disruption.

Arleta led her through a maze of corridors, taking left and right turns. Each hallway looked the same as the last, and soon Estel lost her sense of direction. Her arm throbbed, and the heat caused by the girl's touch was growing stronger, which could only mean one thing: another trip to the future. If she wanted to protect the pure part of Da'ariys in her, she had to get away from this cursed house and Arleta before it was too late.

'I know what you're trying to do,' she hissed at the girl, jerking her arm free. 'But not this time. You hold no power over me.'

Arleta stopped and lowered her head, fingers of her other hand wrapped around her brown toy. She carried that thing everywhere as if it served any purpose. It was dead—dead and useless as the girl herself. Estel yanked it away. One button regarded her in a pitiful expression, as if it were trying to prove its own worth. Sudden and uncontrollable anger swelled inside her and Estel ripped the button out, pulling loose strands of straw with it. Arleta let out a cry at the sight of the gaping hole. Her hands flew to her mouth as she watched the button land on the soft carpet.

'You're too old to carry this… this foolish thing,' Estel snapped at her. She would have rather faced the keepers than Arleta's shocked face. The toy was a burning coal in her hand and she let it drop to the floor. It landed at the girl's feet.

Arleta reached for it. Her every movement was torturously slow. She stared at the eyeless toy and all colour drained from her face. Her blue eyes filled with tears.

'Which way is out?' Estel asked, averting her gaze. She couldn't stand tears. 'We shouldn't linger here. If you knew about this passage, so would they.' She didn't say it loud, but if the keepers discovered the dead body before they had a chance to escape, they'd be trapped here.

Arleta dropped down to her knees, eyes fixed on the toy as if the damned thing was more important than life. Estel regretted not burning it when she first saw it in the forest, back in Grey Lands. It seemed so long ago. Grinding her teeth, she grabbed Arleta's shoulders and shook her. 'You'll get us killed. Which way is out?'

Arleta sniffed, tears streaming down her cheeks. Her finger pointed to the door at the end of the corridor.

Estel's head pounded and she swayed from dizziness. The corridor was so narrow and suffocating. Was the door there before? She couldn't be sure. 'Come on,' she said, stumbling forward. She couldn't afford to lose herself in this place, not with the Keepers of Suha on her tail. Leaning against the wall for support, she felt her way to the door. There was light coming through it. Was it daylight already? Was she trapped in this house all night? She lost all sense of time. She pushed against the door and it gave way. The light pulled her inside.

XVIII

The pain was like an army of axes, hacking and chopping in quick succession, without a moment of relief. Darkness swirled at the edges of Estel's mind, pulling her further and further away from consciousness. The world was on fire and so was her flesh. Her tongue felt too big for her mouth and her eyes rolled inside their sockets. The flames were everywhere—behind her eyelids, in her throat and stomach, searing the insides of her brain. Her cry was that of an animal trapped in a snare, and all this agony came from one place: her right arm, where a new symbol carved itself to life. She begged the girl to stop it, but the words came out as a gurgle.

'You know what you must do.' The voice belonged to Arleta, but Estel couldn't see her anywhere.

Whatever was happening to her was different than before. There were no stars or galaxies, no magic or sky wonders, only heat and the terrible realisation that yet another piece of her was being ripped apart. The light was gone and she was back in the burdel's corridor, but the place looked more run-down. Water marks stained the walls and there was a heavy smell of mould in the air. A surge of energy slammed her like a rogue wave slams a boat. She shut her eyes and pressed her cheek to the ground, certain that the impact would be the end of her.

More voices echoed in her ears. 'Don't forsake us. Free us… Free us all.'

'Where are you?' She scrambled to her knees and fell against the wall. The pain in her arm blinded her.

'We're everywhere, if you're willing to look. Open your heart and see us.'

'I can't. I won't.' She had a choice in this. She was a descendant of bogs and boginyas, stronger than any human. 'I'm a Da'ariys,' she said as if that was her one and only salvation.

But the voices refused to be silenced. They pushed at her from all directions—women and children begging her to save them. She shut her mind and focused on her pain—it was the only way to keep her sanity. If she lasted long enough, maybe this world would fade and she'd wake up in Suha.

Someone tugged at her sleeve—an insistent pull that wouldn't be ignored.

She pushed the hand away. 'I'll never be a human. I'm a Creator.'

The hand continued to tug and when she looked up, she saw Arleta's furrowing brow. The girl's eyes were rimmed with red, but her lips pressed together in a way that told Estel the girl wouldn't be dismissed so easily.

'You want to destroy what's pure in me,' she accused the girl. 'Why? Why do you want me dead?'

'Choose one,' Arleta said.

'No!'

'Choose one.'

It was like listening to an echo and Estel knew that no matter how hard she fought, Arleta would force her will upon her. It was her world, her rules, and Estel had no magic strong enough to withstand the girl's. Despite that, Estel waged war against the emotions that pushed their way inside. She didn't want this, any of this, but her resolve was powerless against the force that challenged it. Estel was a tree at the mercy of a hurricane, rooted in her beliefs, but unable to protect the parts of her exposed to the emotional winds. Her heart trembled with fear then shrank with sorrow and flared with anger. The whirlpool sapped her strength until she was drained and her guards crashed down, exposing the human part of her that craved to feel.

And she made her choice.

Like the first breath of a newborn, the emotion filled her. Her nerve endings sparked and carried a message back and forth between her heart and brain, changing her, morphing Da'ariys and the human side. Estel pulled her arms and legs close to her chest as the heat blistered her face and neck. It wasn't the pulsing heat of pain but something hotter, stickier, and far more sinister than live fire. She pressed her clammy palms against her cheeks and swallowed the nausea that threatened to choke her. She wanted to sink into the wall and fade forever, wishing everyone would forget she ever existed.

'We must go,' Arleta said, pulling with more force.

Her small voice stirred Estel's memories. 'What have I done?' she whispered, unable to meet the girl's eyes. When she saw a child in a dirty dress, hunched over the dying fire, she was ready to shoot her and told herself that Arleta was nothing more than a mrake, hunting for a taste of her flesh. 'I left you there, alone, at the mercy of Grey Lands' daemons. I didn't know what you were…'

'Doesn't matter about before,' Arleta said. 'You must follow me now.'

'Follow you where? I can't bear to face Ashk again, to live, knowing what I am and what I've done. To you, to Lea… to Zeal. He risked being shunned by his own people to save my life and what did I do? I threatened to kill him. And for what? Is that who Da'ariys truly were?'

'All of us are privy to foolishness, and you're no exception. The shame is a part of us and if you want to become whole again, you must feel it and accept it. The more you fight it, the more it'll mar you.'

'No child speaks this way.' The girl looked like a mistreated child but spoke the words of wise men.

'I'm no child, but a conduit, a bridge connecting the present and the future, so my Creator can witness events through time and change them, for better or worse. Don't you remember?'

Estel searched her aching brain for a memory that would make sense of Arleta's question, but her mind came up blank.

'When you were six years old, Lea made you your first dress. It was grey and blended well with the landscape but called attention to your ivory skin. When you went outside, the children in the village made fun of you—'

'And they threw rocks at me…' The memory of that day emerged from the mists of her mind with a sting. She remembered walking along the stone wall when two boys and a girl ran up to her and poked at her dress with sticks. When she refused to react to their mockery, one of the boys picked up a small stone and threw it at her. It cut the skin on her arm, releasing silver bubbles to the surface.

The girl laughed and stuck out her tongue. Estel's eyes and cheeks felt hot then, the way they did now, and she never forgot that day, but she was only a girl herself.

'You can feel, Estel, but you choose not to. You embraced the emotionless part of you, and so the human part faded. But it hasn't been lost. It's where the real magic lies, but you must be ready to accept it.'

'Isn't my destiny to stop the Destroyer? If she dies, the future you all fear won't be realised and the race of Da'ariys will be restored. I don't need shame or sorrow to make this happen, but skill and a clear mind.'

Arleta sighed. It was strange watching a child and listening to an adult at the same time. 'Your purpose is not to restore your race, but to balance the world. Your magic allows you to touch minds with your ancestors, but they aren't really here, nor there. Da'ariys are long gone from the world, but their deeds remain. For you, there's no past, present, or future. As a Creator, you're stuck in a time loop, a moment in which the events of tomorrow could be altered, and you're the only one who can alter them. But an unbalanced heart can't create equilibrium.'

'So my life is a lie?' Estel asked in astonishment.

'It will be if you fail. We must go now. I can only keep you here for so long.'

Estel pushed herself to her feet. Her knees felt weak and the thickness in her throat strangled her. 'What is this place?'

'You need to see what happens to women and children in the future created by your ancestors. Maybe then you will understand.'

Gripping her right arm, Estel followed Arleta along the corridor, wishing the floor would open up and swallow her whole. Despite the strength of it, a part of her knew that the feeling wasn't hers, but radiated from people who inhabited this place. She could almost see the eyes staring at her through the walls, accusing, and full of contempt for who she was. She angled as far away from the walls as the narrow space allowed. The corridor felt impossibly long and faded in and out as they moved under the lanterns that flickered with bright light. They looked nothing like the ones in her world, and she struggled to comprehend how they could work without a live flame.

They stopped by a red door. It was ajar, and Arleta invited her to see inside. Estel trembled all over and wanted nothing more than to curl into a ball and cease to exist. Whatever hid behind the door, she didn't want to see it, but Arleta's world didn't care for her needs or desires.

Her instincts told her that once she crossed the threshold, there would be no way to unsee whatever awaited beyond.

Even before she could consider the implications, her hand pushed the door open.

The room reeked of spirits and unwashed body parts. A woman was strapped to a bed, panic wrinkled every inch of her face. Her left cheek was the colour of a ripe plum and most of her naked body was covered in lacerations. Her pain was almost palpable. A man wearing nothing but a pair of leggings stood in the middle of the room, a transparent cup in his hand. The nails on his toes reminded Estel of predators she used to hunt in Grey Lands. He swished the liquid and took a swallow. His mouth turned downwards.

'It tastes as bad as you,' he said, and threw the cup on the floor. It smashed with a ring. The man undid his belt and wrapped it around his knuckles.

The girl cried out and so did Estel. She ran out of the room and slammed the door behind her. She couldn't bear witness to this savagery, but the thin walls weren't a barrier to feelings. They poured out from the trapped girl like blood from an open wound, forcing Estel to receive them. The self-loathing overpowered her, writhing beneath her skin like a worm on a hook, followed by a desire to end it all. Estel's thoughts blended with the girl's and she struggled to tell them apart. Maybe she deserved pain? Maybe it was her fault that she was strapped to a bed with no control over her own body?

Arleta's light touch snapped her back into herself. Somehow, the corridor was no longer a corridor, but a cramped room. Clothes and rubbish strewn around made it look more like a waste pit than a living space. The air inside was stale and made her gag, but what she sensed the most was Arleta's sorrow. It hung about her like a storm cloud, filled to the brim with acid tears.

Despite her own torment, Estel embraced the girl in a tight hug. Her body protested against this sudden closeness by going rigid, but her heart screamed for more. 'I'm so sorry this is your future.'

For the first time, she was ashamed to be Da'ariys. How could Remha mistake such dominance for greatness? Was this what Ashk warned her about? The future where emotions were chained and denied seemed worse than the Dark Nav.

Arleta pulled away from her and her blue eyes went still. 'Your pity can't help me, but your actions can. Your choices in the days to come will seal the future, and with it, our fate.' Her round chin motioned to the pegged curtain in the corner of the room.

Every inch of Estel screamed at her to get out, but where would she go? Arleta bound her to this place like a master binds his slave. No amount of pleading would release her. Skirting around the clutter, she crossed the room and reached for the curtain. The pegs clattered as she moved them aside and peered into the chamber beyond. In a dim light, cast by the same strange lantern she saw in the corridor, the place looked and smelled like a sea cave. It was cold and damp. A stained bed occupied one side, with an armchair in the opposite corner. Paper with little rusty flowers hung off the walls in tatters, revealing bare stone. Lea's simple hut in Grey Lands was a stately home in comparison.

A boy Arleta's age sat in the armchair, feet dangling above the floor. His face was dull, shoulders sagging, as if he carried the weight of the world upon them. Estel's heart squeezed at the sight of his grubby arms and sunken cheeks, and despite the knowledge that there was nothing she could do for him, she rushed to his side, wishing her presence alone would strengthen him. There was a rift of time between them, centuries separated his world from hers, but even so, she had to try. She grabbed his hand, but it was like grabbing air—the boy was there, and yet he wasn't. His feelings were what connected them, his powerful need to flee and hide superseded all else. Estel felt his regret at being caught as if it was her own. He shamed himself for the way he wandered off at night, despite his mother's cautions, his sense of adventure stronger than any warnings. By the time he grasped the danger he was in, it was too late. The men caught him and brought him to this house, and since then he wanted to burn it to the ground.

Shame warred with desperation as Estel turned to Arleta. 'There must be some way to free him. I can't just leave him here and carry on.'

'There is a way, but you're not whole enough to see it.'

A sudden surge of energy passed through her and a man entered the room. Like the boy, he looked real, but she knew better than to challenge him—you can't reason with phantoms.

He swayed on his feet and stank of liquor. With a whistle he appraised the boy. 'You'll fetch a fine price.'

Estel backed away from the room. She felt ill, and it wasn't an illness brought on by spoiled food or high fever, but a sickness of the soul. Her shame returned in waves—for herself, for her race, and for those weak enough to embrace the Da'ariys who came to lead them. Was she like them? Driven by the needs of her own and blind to the plights of others? To rid herself of weakness, she denied the strongest and most painful of human emotions, until they died inside her. She had the power to wake them, but to do so would be to forsake who she was forever. Was she ready to make such sacrifice for the good of others? The part of her that now craved humanity was ready, but the warrior of Da'ariys was stronger still. Can you declare a war with yourself?

Arleta stood next to her, looking down at her sandals. The little flower on one them was missing, ripped away like the eye from her bear. Estel's own conflict wrapped her so tight that she missed the transition, for now they stood back in the corridor.

'I can't take any more,' Estel said. 'It's my people who created this world.' She felt weak at the knees and her bones were like snapped branches on a dead tree.

'And you could be the one who heals it.' And with those words, Arleta faded like a mist touched by sunlight.

Estel groped after her, but her fingers came away empty. Her time in this world ran its course and Suha was calling her back. She sought the blackness and answered it.

XIX

Estel's eyes fell upon the image of Yarilo in Ashk's bedchamber. It took her a few moments to clear her thoughts before the memories of the burdel came flooding back. The events she witnessed there resurrected the heat of shame.

With her face on fire, she rolled up her sleeve. It was just as she feared. Another symbol marked her arm in faint silver: two halved circles regarding each other at a distance like two sides of repelling magnets. They looked as if they once fit together to form a perfect sphere before something separated them permanently. The shame and humiliation she experienced through Arleta had marked her forever. Estel wanted to scream. Her resolve to reject her human side was trampled and the choice ripped from her without consent.

She clambered off the bed and scanned the room for her bow and arrows when a smear of blood on her dress caught her eye. It was the keeper's. Cringing, she wrestled the dress off and kicked the colourful cloth away from her. Her actions were unstable, jerky, and she struggled to control her usually calm and collected mind. She was changing. The human side of her grew stronger, greedy for more, while the warrior of Da'ariys shrunk and faded.

Estel searched for her knife but couldn't find it. She must've dropped it during her escape through those cursed corridors. On a table by the side of her bed she spotted a small pocket blade for sharpening the tips of incenses, and she grabbed it. It was short, but it would do. She stabbed her wrist with the point and pulled it across. After a breath, blood filled the wound and seeped down her arm, and she couldn't stop staring at the tracks it left in its wake. The once silver liquid was now a river of deep pink, with only a tint of its original metallic hue. Even the beautiful shimmer was gone. Estel dropped to her knees, watching the pink droplets hit the floor. Without the blood of her ancestors, who was she?

She didn't know how long she sat there, numb and lost inside herself. The house was as quiet as a tomb and she wished she could use her powers to melt into that silence. Like the wreck of a ship that had lost its captain, she could no longer tell what her course was. To destroy Rana? To save tomorrow? To give in to Ashk and Arleta's pleas and accept the human inside her? Da'ariys whispered in her ear, accusing her of weakness and betrayal, and then there were the voices of Lea and Lelya, two mothers urging her to make the right choice.

When she got up at last, her movements were slow and precise. Neatly folded, her clothes rested on a chair where she left them what seemed like many moons ago. She put them on, taking care to tighten each strap. Her steps sounded deliberate when she walked down the hallway to Ashk's study. The colours of the late afternoon painted the rooms and walls with orange, and the heat felt like a blanket against her skin. The seer awaited her by the window with the view of Suha's dry flatlands. White paint was gone from his forehead and he seemed to have aged a hundred years since she last spoke to him.

'You're awake,' he greeted her without meeting her eyes.

'You lied to me,' she said, advancing on him. 'There's no parchment and never was. It was a lie—all of it.'

'If I had told you the truth, would you have gone?' he asked in a flat voice.

'To witness the worst of human nature? You tricked me.'

'It may not seem this way, but I want you to succeed. That's my only purpose, to prevent—'

‘Don’t lie to me!’ She was losing control again and as difficult as it was for her to admit, her outbursts made her too human. The thought enraged her further. ‘You knew she’d come for me, force me to see it, to feel it.’

He said nothing.

‘You’re so scared of who you’ll be tomorrow that you forgot who you are today. Our ancestors weren’t afraid of the world. I admit, there was a lot wrong with Remha’s order. I can see that now, but together we could change our laws and return Da’ariys to grace. You keep telling me that I can create a better future, but why does it have to be at the expense of who we are?’ She rolled up her sleeve, exposing the three silver marks. ‘Why do I need them to prove my strength and worth?’

Ashk’s lips twisted into a bitter smile. ‘After all you’ve seen, you still cling on to the foolish hope that you could defeat the one born to destroy. No power exists in this world that could kill Rana. The magic you seek is not in the flames of Vatra, or on your arrowheads. It’s inside you. The real strength resides in your heart, but you deny it. It’s the Da’ariys like you who brought damnation upon the world.’

Her stomach heaved at his words. ‘If all Creators failed before me, perhaps the fault lies with you. Maybe you’ve become too blinded by your human side to understand what we seek. How could shame help me to stop the Destroyer? How could fear fill me with strength? How could sorrow assist me in making the right choice? Our ancestors knew the answer to that. Only by controlling our emotions can we achieve the clarity of mind to lead the warriors to victory.'

'And lose our ability to understand and share the feelings of another,' he said.

A heavy silence followed his words, broken only by the humming of blood in her ears. Estel's fists clenched and unclenched as she tried to gain control of herself. It wasn't an easy task. The images from the burdel were like ghosts creeping around the edges of her mind. She didn't want them to sway her, but she couldn't ignore them either. If Rana's only purpose was to uphold Remha's laws and destroy anyone who would challenge them, even her own blood, then she'd find her sister and use whatever magic she inherited to stop her. With Rana gone, the balance would be restored and the old laws cast aside. Perhaps then Ashk would join with her and help her restore Daaria to what it was before her race intervened.

Ashk broke the silence. 'You're not a Da'ariys, Estel, and not a human either, but a Creator with the ability to become both. If you refuse to accept it, you'll fail. Your heart is pure, and you want to do right by our people and Daaria, but so did the Creators before you. I should know. I've seen them all and mourned their deaths more times that I can recall. I don't blame you for thinking I'm here to hinder your quest, to force changes upon you that you aren't ready for. But I'm immortal, for such is the burden of the Seer of Da'ariys. I can't die until a Creator fulfils her destiny. I'm bound to this life, to this moment in time, for eternity, forced to relive the same story over and over again.

'Perhaps you're right. I failed in my task and my punishment is well deserved, but I still have hope. You'll fade, but I will not. Another Creator will be born and take your place, and the day will come when the Destroyer will be defeated. I'd like that Creator to be you.'

His words struck her heart. 'If I accept my human part, I could never go back,' she said.

'You wouldn't want to, but to understand that, you would have to become whole. I wish I could tell you more, but no two Creators are alike, and each has her own path to travel and her own choices to make.'

After a few moments of silence he added, 'The burdel was destroyed last night. A powerful explosion decimated everything, along with the adjacent parts of the city. This is what you can do when your mind and heart are aligned. You can't wield magic without both.'

She jerked her head back. 'Decimated? I don't remember doing anything…'

'What you witnessed must've had a powerful effect on you. To resort to magic at such times is dangerous, but no less effective. The possibilities are limitless.'

Estel was about to respond when Ashk stopped her with the flat of his palm. The wrinkles on his forehead deepened and he cast a quick glance at the window. Far on the horizon, the setting sun coloured the world in shades of red and orange.

'They have found you,' the seer whispered.

And then she saw it—a faint haze that shimmered in the air. The same purple mist that stole over Grey Lands when the Twilight Hunters burned her village and took Lea's life.

'The Destroyer knows of the assassin's failure,' Ashk said, and then, 'You must leave. Now.' He ushered her into the hallway and through the back door, leading to the stables.

The twilight grew thicker and more intense, twining around her arms and ankles. It writhed after them like living smoke, saturating the world in purple. Ashk opened the stable door and led out a white mare. The horse was ready for the journey, with Estel's bow and quiver strapped to the back of the saddle.

At her questioning gaze, he explained, 'I knew you'd want to leave Suha after you had learned about my betrayal, and I didn't want you to travel unprepared.'

Estel mounted the mare. Her last experience on a horse wasn't her best. Her thoughts strayed to that ride with Zeal and his joyful whistling. She killed the memory before it took hold.

'Ride fast,' Ashk urged her. 'Don't stop. The horse is well rested and should carry you through the night. You'll know Vatra for its cool air and the cinder trees. May Yarilo guide you, daughter of Da'ariys.'

The mare shifted uneasily at the touch of the twilight ribbon. 'What about you?' Estel asked, stilling the horse with her boots.

'It's not me they are after.'

She wanted to ask him about the trees, but Ashk slapped the mere's rump and it took off at speed, into the unknown.

PART IV

VATRA

Hate poisons the heart and only love can purify it.

—the flame-sworn

XX

As twilight lost its battle with darkness, the night turned the wilds on either side of the road into a void. Heeding Ashk's counsel, Estel rode at full speed. Freed from the constraints of the stables, the mare was eager to gallop and sped away from Suha like a loose arrow. If the Twilight Hunters tracked her, they were far behind. She pressed on southward with the crescent moon as her guide, taking comfort in seeing the violet haze dissipate. The warm air gave way to a cooler breeze that dried the sweat from her arms and face.

When the mare showed signs of weariness, Estel slowed her to a trot and sharpened her own senses. Enduring cramps in her arms and legs was easier than ignoring her mind as it conjured up images of what would become of her if she were caught. What if the Twilight Hunters moved at twice the speed of an average horse? They would outrun her in no time, and armed with only a bow, she would make an easy target. Would she meet the same end as the people in her village? Turned into mist and absorbed by translucent flesh, or abandoned, half-dead, for the wild animals to feast upon? Such punishment would be fitting for someone who left her mother to the same fate. The memory stabbed her like a prong and she ordered her mind to focus on the road; the last thing she needed was to get lost in the darkness and unknowingly skirt back to Suha, straight into the arms of her pursuers.

The road to Vatra stretched onward like a sandy-coloured river, while the horse's hooves stirred dust that found its way into her mouth and nostrils. Soon, her throat was parched, and she was glad to find a water skin attached to the saddlebag—Ashk made sure she had enough supplies to carry her through.

She had mixed feelings about the seer. He was a descendant of Da'ariys, but unlike her, didn't stay true to their race, choosing to embrace his human side instead. He refused her way of seeing things, too stubborn to accept that maybe she could succeed where others had failed. If indeed her powers were connected to her emotional side, she was sure they would hinder her progress rather than make her victorious. Each exposure subjected her to pain, and the madness that followed it rendered her immobile for days, so how could any of this be of help when she faced the Destroyer? From what she understood of her sister, Rana embodied a true warrior of Remha, not bound by emotional constraints and unhindered by weakness. To rise against someone like Rana, Estel would have to match her mind and skill, and yet, Ashk and Arleta were convinced that was a path to defeat.

With her arm maimed by symbols of significance she didn't understand, Estel refused to sacrifice any more of herself. What she needed to succeed was the strong and independent Estel who left Grey Lands, determined to find answers to her origins. Now that she had them, they didn't bring peace, but instead, thrust her into a battle for the future, and after all she had witnessed, it was too late to turn away from the path set for her by her ancestors. Despite her resistance, her encounters with Arleta, her visions, and the markings on her arm brought upon changes she couldn't undo. But the final choice was hers and hers alone, and when the time was right, she intended to make the correct one.

When the outlines of the mountains to the east became clearer, and the mist of dawn spread across the flatlands, the mare's energy was spent, and it refused to take her any farther. It was time to find shelter. Not used to long hours on horseback, Estel's muscles were in knots, crying out whenever she tried to stretch them. She found a crevice between two hills wide enough to conceal a woman and a horse. She knew little about horses and even less on how to care for them. Her flimsy attempts at removing the saddle and loosening bridle bits would have earned her a scowl from Zeal. The thought made her wonder how he fared. Was his punishment for failed assassination as severe as he feared it would be? Most likely, she would never find out.

One of the saddlebags held grain, so she offered it to the mare. The horse dipped its head into it and began munching. Estel sat with her back against the rock and chewed on dried meat and fruits she found in her pack. She chose not to light a fire in case someone spotted it from the road and came looking for her. The mist was dissolving, and the morning sky opened before her like a pink and yellow canvas.

A lone shape slinked through the mist in the direction of the crevice. Estel grabbed her bow and pulled an arrow out of the quiver, every move measured and silent. She pushed the nock of the arrow onto the string and pulled it back. Her first thought was of a volk, attracted by the smell of the horse, but there was something familiar about the way the shadow moved—low to the ground, ears pricked. She quested toward it with her senses and lowered her bow.

‘I thought, you went back to Grey Lands,’ she said as Srebro came clear of the mist. The fox managed to sneak up on her when she least expected it. Each time they parted ways, Estel was sure it was forever, but every time, the animal proved her wrong. Whatever bound them allowed Srebro to track her down no matter distance or unfamiliar terrain, and despite her strong senses, Estel couldn’t see her coming.

The mare snorted as if disgruntled by this new addition and moved away.

Estel offered Srebro a strip of dried meat. Before, she would throw it to her and be done with it, but this time, she held on, curious to see how the animal would react. Srebro always shied away from physical contact, never coming closer than two arms’ length. Estel held her breath and waited.

Srebro watched her for a long while, silver eyes gleaming like polished silver, head cocked to one side as if considering how sincere the offer was. Time came to a stop while they appraised one another—two silver beings, surrounded by a morning mist, two lives linked by twenty years. Was there a meaning to this bond, to the way the fox followed her everywhere she went? If it was so, the significance of it escaped her. Or could it be that what she shared with Srebro was nothing more than a simple companionship, born out of routine of sharing in one's life for so long? There was no way to ask.

Srebro took a few steps toward her outstretched hand then hesitated.

'You must know by now that I don't mean you any harm,' she said, waving the meat.

A few more steps and the fox was within arm's length. A thin layer of sweat broke out across Estel's brow. The flatlands, the crevice, and the possibility of the hunters on her tail all fled her mind as she waited. Her eyes didn't leave Srebro's, as if through sight alone she could convey her intent.

The fox reached forward with her snout and sniffed the meat. She was so close that Estel could almost feel the softness of her silver fur. But just as Estel thought the animal would make the final leap, Srebro backed away, shook herself off, and trotted into the morning light.

Estel sagged against the rock and took a bite of the dry meat. Srebro's rejection pinched more than she was willing to admit.

When the first sun rays ripped through the clouds in the east, she removed a blanket secured by Ashk to the back of the saddle and wrapped it around her shoulders. She needed a well-rested horse to continue her journey and she herself could do with a nap. Estel closed her eyes and emptied her mind of thoughts, but despite her efforts, sleep wouldn't come. As the sun reared its golden head and its warmth spread across the land, the chirruping of insects grew louder, followed by a trill of birds greeting a new day.

She wondered about Vatra and what she planned to do once she got there. Since she learned about the Flame of Agni, her mind had been working over an idea until it was fully formed. If the flame was as powerful as Zeal claimed it to be, then maybe, combined with her skills, it could be enough to put an end to Rana. The question was how she would steal something that was revered and protected by highly skilled assassins. Zeal was one of them, a flame-sworn guardian, trained for one purpose only: to safeguard Agni's power at all cost. By sparing her life, he had failed in this duty. It was a sacrifice she couldn't comprehend.

Her mind wouldn't still. Instead one thought grew into another like links on a chain, and before long, she was up and ready to go.

The morning air was crisp and fresh, and there was still no sign of the violet haze. Maybe Ashk managed to mislead the Twilight Hunters and they gave up their pursuit? She doubted it. The creatures were not of this world, created by magic that far superseded his own. Despite what the seer told her about the part she played in the destruction of the burdel, Estel doubted that she would be capable of calling upon her powers at will. More time was needed to fully hone her abilities. Time she didn't have.

The journey to Vatra was a long one, but unlike her trek to Suha, less arduous. She didn't have to worry about shelter and provisions. Taverns were plenty and thanks to the money she won in the contest, she was able to afford a bed and warm food. The tavern keepers she encountered were friendly and cheerful, most bearing the markings of Vatra: russet hair, red pupils set against gold, and freckled skin that reminded her of Zeal. Wherever she turned, she thought she glimpsed the assassin who saved her life, only to discover it was just another Vatrian. Despite the contrast between her looks and their appearance, no one commented or challenged her in any way. It was odd to accept the hospitality of people who she intended to wrong.

The Vatrians worshipped Agni and the signs were everywhere: in the candles that burned continuously before the wooden statues of the bog, and in the carvings that adorned the walls and doorways. Even mugs and bowls carried his image. Unlike Yarilo and Chour, the bog of fire had a smooth face, free of wrinkles and hair. His cheekbones were strong and defined, and his deep-set eyes had a hard look to them. In the cup of his palm rested the flame—the very one Estel planned on stealing. But how could anyone take possession of a live fire? She didn't know, and not wanting to draw attention to herself, was reluctant to ask.

Vatrian cuisine was very different from anything Estel had tried before. They favoured sweet things over savoury. A particular favourite of the region was pastry twisted into a bun, with a sticky cinnamon paste spread between the layers. It was offered free before every meal, and after a while, she came to enjoy the sugary taste. A fluffy yellow bread was another novelty. In Grey Lands the dough was dense and dark brown, but here, it tasted of honey and biting into it was like biting into a pillow of feathers. It was served with milk made from a local nut called migdal.

The closer she drew to Vatra, the more changes she observed in the landscape. The barren flatlands were things of the past, overtaken by forests and valleys in shades of sunglow, fire, and copper. The grass wasn't green like in Kvet, but yellow and sharp to the touch. Estel welcomed the change in weather, the cool air that smelled of churned earth and curtains of fog at dawn. The clouds swept across the sky in wisps, some light, while others fraught with drizzle. On some mornings she would wake to find the world transformed into a water pool, with rain glittering on the leaves and meadows. Her ivory skin enjoyed these moments of respite from the blistering sun of Suha.

Set against this striking landscape were clusters of barns and cottages. Farmers ploughed their fields with horned and muscled creatures Estel didn't have a name for. Unlike the withdrawn Greylanders, Vatrians took their hats off in greeting to any who came to admire their colourful homeland. Halfway through the journey, she was forced to trade her horse for another more likely to survive the long stretch of road before them and was surprised to find that she regretted letting the old one go.

Srebro re-joined her from time to time, following at a safe distance. Her presence gave an illusion of companionship and Estel caught herself talking to the fox on more than one occasion, as if telling someone about her turmoil would make it go away. She would ask questions aloud before answering them under her breath.

When the city loomed into view, Estel dismounted and led the horse to the gates of a long stone wall decorated with paintings of Agni at various stages of worship. Above the central archway, a line of torches burned like a live circlet. She couldn't see any guards. One look over her shoulder assured her that Srebro would stay behind—the fox never followed her into human settlements.

Beyond the gate she was met by a line of houses made of white brick, with flat steel roofs. Each window was set in a red frame and every doorway shaped from iron. The smell of baking dough and cinnamon lingered in the air. Deeper into the city, she passed orchards heavy with apples and pears, where fallen leaves covered the ground like a blanket of fire. Men and women teetering on tall ladders picked fruit from the very top of the trees, filling their woven baskets with glistening gold and crimson spheres.

Her brown horse bolted at the sight of an orange cat that leapt from the fence and onto the street in front of them. When Estel tried to shoo it away, it came closer and rubbed against her legs, meowing. She had seen a cat only once before—a black creature that accompanied a pedlar who visited Lea's hut to trade. The cat's green eyes regarded Estel with so much contempt she was sure that if the creature could speak, it would hiss nothing but insults. But the Vatrian cat looked harmless enough.

The deep red spires of the city could be seen from afar, piercing the sky with sharp spears of immoveable force. Giant bells within the towers were manned by priests in scarlet robes, and within the city's walls, Estel struggled to believe there could be a more pious region. She never saw so many shrines dedicated to a bog, and even Kvet's lustrous temple was no match for the miniature altars erected at every corner. A golden statue of Agni stood proud among the candles glowing at the feet of each, while red priests walked the streets, replacing the ones that burned down with uncanny efficiency. Now that she knew she was a descendant of bogs and boginyas, she wondered, if she managed to turn the course of the future, would people of Daaria erect shrines in her honour and write laws around her worship, until the story of Estel would be greater than the woman herself?

She stopped a local man with a young boy at his side and asked for directions to a tavern. The wrinkles on his face betrayed the years of his life, but the fire in his pupils was as vivid as the flames that rejoiced at the feet of the golden statues surrounding them.

'What's the purpose of your visit? Taverns are many, and each one caters to the needs of patrons in its own way. Share your intentions and I'll gladly offer my knowledge.'

Estel considered the man for a moment while her brain sieved through the possible lies until it settled on one. 'I came to Vatra to learn the way of Agni's faith in the hope to become initiated as one of his acolytes.'

The man raised his eyebrows. 'Good. We, Vatrians, are always eager to welcome new retainers into the fold.' He joined his fists and bowed. 'I'm Sovran and this is my nephew, Argon. I'd be honoured to show you the way to a tavern best suited to your needs. A relative of mine works as a stable master there.'

Estel would have preferred go on alone, but refusing his gesture of good will would no doubt offend Sovran, so she followed him and Argon through a maze of alleyways.

They crossed what looked like a merchant district, with shops and stalls taking up the full length of the street. Keen to attract business, the shopkeepers bellowed greetings to those passing by in an attempt to lure them into their stores. The street opened up into a round square where jugglers dressed in golden robes entertained viewers by tossing burning torches into the air and catching them without extinguishing a single torch.

'Don't you fear fire?' she asked Sovran when one of the jugglers put a flaming torch into his mouth.

Argon clapped his freckled hands at the spectacle.

'Fear it?' Sovran clamped his lips together as if to contain laughter. 'You've much to learn if you're to become an acolyte. Fire is life. Vatrian children are born blind and we baptize them in flames so Agni can bless them with sight.' He looked at his boy with a soft smile. 'Fire is blood and blood is fire.'

She said nothing, toying with the idea of revealing that Agni's blood was in fact silver. What would he say? What would all of the Vatrians do if they knew the truth of it?

A woman with a cage full of copper kittens barred Argon's way. 'Buy one,' she said, grabbing one of the kittens by the scruff of its neck. She brought the meowing thing close to his face. 'You would be hard-pressed to find better in all of Vatra.'

Sovran came to his rescue. 'Leave the boy alone, we aren't here to barter for your cats.' When they moved away, he added by way of explanation, 'Soil in Vatra is rich and grain grows well here, which in turn attracts vermin. Good hunting cats are sought after.'

They crossed a few more streets before stopping in front of a long stone building with arched windows.

Candles flickered invitingly in each one. The man approached one of the outbuildings and pulled on the iron handle. When he was about to step inside, the stable master appeared from a different doorway. The two men exchanged greetings and embraced one another, clapping their shoulders and thanking Agni for their health and that of their families.

When the stable master lead Estel's horse away, Sovran turned to her. 'I hope you'll find Vatra to your liking and earn Agni's favour.'

She thanked him, and they parted ways. She watched the man and his boy as they crossed the street and merged with the crowd. What would he do if he knew her true purpose? Would he attempt to talk her out of it, or turn her in, so she could be burned by the same life-giving flame? From her times in Grey Lands she found there was a fine line between reverence and hostility. Any criticism of Chour would earn her a severe rebuke from Lea.

When Estel walked inside the tavern, the sweet aroma of cinnamon and wine filled her nostrils and her stomach answered with a gurgle. Walls of jagged red brick encircled her, making her feel as if she was trapped in one of Grey Lands' caves after an ashfall. Men and women crowded stone tables, drinking and singing along with a band of musicians that occupied the far corner of the room. Copper pots and pans dangled off the beams, reflecting the light from the candles, and behind the counter, stacked into square holes, rested bottles of dark wine. The length and height of the rack took up most of the back wall.

The tavern keeper was a woman who looked twenty years older than Estel. She wore a green gown with an apron strapped around her lean waist. A pin secured her rusty hair at the back of her head. Her golden-red eyes smiled at Estel from behind the counter.

'What can I do for you?' she asked with a sidelong glance.

Estel requested a room and feed for her horse. After the payment was settled, the innkeeper called upon a helping girl to show her to her quarters. Estel followed her down the corridor and into a room that was as cavernous as the tavern itself. Candles burned everywhere: along a stone shelf above the hearth, on the window, and in the candelabra suspended from the ceiling. Their warmth battled with the chill from the stone.

At Estel's questioning glance, the girl hurried to explain. 'No safety without firelight. The burning candles protect us from wicked spirits.'

‘Or consume you in your sleep,’ Estel said, placing her bow and quiver on the berth. It had a stone base, layered with blankets to take the edge off the chill.

The girl gave her a puzzled look. ‘Stone can’t burn,’ she said then turned around and left the room.

‘But I can,’ Estel said under her breath.

There was fresh water in a round basin and she splashed it on her face, enjoying the touch of coolness on her skin. It was time to tend to her empty stomach.

As soon as the innkeeper saw her coming, she cleared out a table and gestured her to sit down. Shortly after, buns, migdal milk, and a jug of honey cider appeared, followed by a plateful of cheeses, yellow bread, and chutneys. The smell of it made her mouth water and the taste made her want to forget her ordeals and settle in Vatra for good.

Once the worst of her hunger was satiated, she turned her attention to the chatter of people around her. The musicians indulged in a melancholic tune, making it easier to catch strands of conversations. Estel cleared her mind and walked the room with her ears. Some men were plain drunk, babbling about everything from their wives’ bad temper to the state of the world, but the women among them were more coherent, thrilling one another with the latest gossip. It was from them she learned that a celebration was underway to bless the marriage of a high-ranking official to the head of Vatra's daughter. Out of respect for this new union, the Flame of Agni would be lit every night until the vows had been exchanged and the marriage consummated. Estel stored this piece of information and licked the last of the honey cider off her lips. By the time she retreated from the tavern's main room, the night took hold of Vatra.

She found her way down the corridor into her chamber, and when she removed the shutters from the window, she saw the city transformed. Flames burned everywhere she looked, lining the cobblestone streets like glowing embers. Round lanterns nestled in the tree branches and hung off the roofs, while priests carried torches, using them to relight any dying candles at the shrines and altars. Golden statues of Agni reflected all this fiery splendour, and it was a wonder that Vatra didn't go up in smoke. It resembled one huge bonfire.

But the biggest of them all was a flame that burned in the distance, so high and vast it seemed as if the whole sky was consumed by it. Its colour didn't match the orange from a torch or yellow from a candle, but instead, it was a rich crimson, such as could be seen flowing from a freshly open wound.

The Flame of Agni was closer than she thought.

XXI

Guided by the crimson flame, Estel made her way through the red night in search of a way into Agni's temple. It wasn't an easy task as each alleyway looked the same as the last, bungling her sense of direction. Questing ahead with her senses didn't do much good, for she found the heady smell of melting wax and smoking wicks distracting. After hours of wandering the streets, she was no longer sure if it was the candles that flickered, or her vision. It looked as if Vatrians forgot all about sleep in the face of the upcoming celebration, eager to commence the festivities long before the big day. Estel knew little of Vatra's customs, but if the city was this crowded every night, her task might be impossible to accomplish. And she still had the assassins to contend with.

The elusive flame beckoned her from afar as she took wrong turns and stumbled in the dark, trying to find her bearings. She wondered if Agni would condemn her efforts to steal his glory, or would he share in his power and aid her in her pursuit of Rana. Ashk implied the flame alone wouldn't be enough to challenge the Destroyer, but she had to take her chances. No other Creator had attempted this feat, so none could predict the outcome.

Maybe joining her skills with Agni's power would be enough.

At last, the street widened, parting the orchard trees on either side to reveal a temple that put to shame everything she saw on Daaria since leaving Grey Lands. Like the rest of Vatra, the length of the structure was illuminated by candle fire that quivered upon its walls like leaves in the wind. A single staircase, chiselled from a crystalline rock, proceeded the building before her, climbing several levels all the way up to a central tower of shining red stone. The walls on either side of it were shaped by a set of multi-layered and elevated steps, each narrower than the one before it. From where she stood, the whole thing resembled an open chapel atop a mountain. A line of smaller statues of Agni adorned each side of the elaborate staircase, with the biggest of them gracing the entry to the red tower. Beyond the statue, upon a round altar, The Flame of Agni danced in its crimson glory, and despite the distance, the heat emanating from it pressed upon her cheeks like the searing hand of a giant.

'Magnificent, isn't it?'

Startled, she spun around with her bow at the ready. When she realised who spoke the words, a sudden coldness came over her. 'How did you find me?'

‘It’s my duty to find people who are a threat,’ Zeal said, not taking his eyes off the flame.

‘So, you’re here to fulfil your contract?’

He looked at the arrow pointed at his chest. ‘We’ve been here before.’

‘Answer the question. Are you here to warn them?’

His red and golden eyes bored into hers. ‘You should know better.’

‘So why then?’

‘Always with the questions.’ His voice was flat and vacant of his usual cheerfulness. This wasn’t the same man who taught her how to ride a horse. Dark circles framed his eyes and his face sagged with resignation. In his black clothes and hair tied at the back, he looked more like a pedlar at the end of day’s work than an assassin sworn to protect the fire of the almighty bog.

‘I knew you’d be coming for the flame,’ he said. ‘I saw it in your eyes when I told you of its power. You want to use it to defeat Rana.’

When she offered no response, he carried on. ‘After you sent me away, I came back to Vatra to find my family already informed of my failure. They cast me out. I had two choices: surrender to my fate and die with honour, or flee to Kvet and start a new life there. I chose the third option. To wait for you.'

'Are Vatrians known for making bad choices?' she asked, lowering her bow. Zeal's insistence on playing a part in her life grated on her, but she couldn't understand why. It wasn't as if she cared for the assassin—Estel didn't have to wrestle with such feelings—but his presence and the lingering looks he sent her way unsettled her. She wished she'd never met him. 'If you came to stop me, I suggest you leave.'

'I've come to realise that coming between you and a task you set your mind to would be like coming between a bear and her cub.' His mouth quivered at the corners. 'Come to think of it, I'd have more luck attempting the latter.'

'And what of your duty? How do you think your people would react when they discover the identity of the thief?'

Zeal looked down at his boots. 'I hope to be far away from Vatra when they do. But stealing the flame won't be easy.' He shook his head as if to convince himself that he was making the right choice, then he looked back at the crimson fire. 'Besides, to contain it, we'll need a vial blessed by an exalted priest.'

This was a new complication she wasn't ready for. 'Any ideas?'

'The vial is kept in the tower, but the priest is another matter…' He trailed off as if weighing their options.

Her mind made its own deductions. 'Surely we can steal the vial, find the priest, and force him to bless it.'

'If it were only that simple.' He pressed his hands to his temples. 'The blessing must be done voluntarily. Only then will it transform the vial. Forcing the priest would gain us nothing.'

They stood in silence for a time while Vatra glowed all around them like a blushing maiden dressed in smoke. The fire from the numerous candles and lanterns swished on the breeze that snuggled Estel in a blanket of warm air. She didn't ask about the flame's true power. Zeal said that it was capable of great destruction, but how would one know how to wield it? She had a suspicion that even the assassins who guarded it didn't really know. Around them, people clustered at the base of the temple, talking in hushed voices, chanting prayers, or simply admiring the crimson wonder that was the Flame of Agni.

Estel broke the silence. 'What about the upcoming marriage?'

Zeal scanned the people around them. 'I've considered it, but it's too risky. We'd have to dispose of the assassins and reach the tower unnoticed. Marriage blessings are held at night, like other important ceremonies, but even in the dark it'd be a hard task to accomplish. If we're exposed, the bells would ring and every Vatrian would join the hunt. We'd never make it out alive.'

Estel scrutinised the shadows to either side of the stairway. Did the flame-sworn assassins watch them from beyond the veil of dark? They guarded the flame under an oath and she imagined how great would be their fury if that oath was put to the test. Perhaps the plan was doomed from the start.

'We need to take our chances,' she said. 'I came here for the flame and I intend to get it.'

'Why am I not surprised?' He reached into his breast pocket and pulled out a kerchief. He tied it around the lower part of his face, covering his mouth. 'The blessing ceremony is in two days and there's much to do. While you admired the wilds on your way here, I've made preparations of my own.' The kerchief concealed his face well, but she caught a smile in the corners of his eyes.

Zeal didn't know about her destiny—how could he? Rana hired the best assassin, fed him full of lies, and ordered him to track her down. In her haste to get the job done, her sister overlooked one little detail: human nature. Humans were unpredictable creatures, and even the smallest thing could throw them off their chosen path. Zeal was an example of that. He left Vatra a flame-sworn assassin only to return as a faithless thief. And all for her, a woman he knew nothing about.

'I buried them, you know,' Zeal's whisper was quieter than the breeze. 'I buried every one of them, just like you begged me to. But now, they haunt my dreams with their mournful cries.' Anguish stole over his face. 'Even when I'm awake, I can hear their echoing breath inside my head.'

Her heart lurched in her chest at the memory of Willow's Hearth. Following her vision of the enslaved future, she insisted they bury the bodies of those who died from the Crimson Plague. It was delirium that conjured desire, but even so, it was a powerful desire. Suddenly, she wanted to share it all with Zeal. Explain who she was, her destiny, and why ensuring her success was so important. But how would he react? Would he be appalled by the idea that she wanted to overthrow the very side that shaped him into the man he was today?

'I'm running out of time,' she said.

The longer she waited, the more human traits she absorbed. In Grey Lands, and shortly after her departure, she was able to block most of her emotions, but now they snuck up on her, striking the core of her soul before she had a chance to guard herself.

***

'How long have you been hiding here?' she asked, inspecting the items laid out on the berth: a set of short knives encased in a sleek black sheath, a grappling hook, two lightly curved swords, brass knuckles, and other tools of the assassin's trade, all polished and ready for use—his wondrous bow among them. She traced its curves with her fingertips and the flamewood glimmered at her touch. She drew her hand back.

'It's imbued with Agni's magic,' Zeal said, and he picked up the bow.

After their exchange at the foot of the temple, Zeal had led her through Vatra, navigating the streets as if he had a map of them etched into his brain. They took left and right turns, scaled fences, and crossed through orchards before arriving at his hideout on the outskirts of the city. It consisted of a small room in an abandoned stone building, dimly lit by a set of two lanterns fastened at the corners. Apart for the berth and a low table that served double duty as an eating and a sitting area, there was little else in the room. A map with black crosses marked in charcoal hung off the wall above the fireplace. Estel noticed the absence of Agni statues and was curious as to why Zeal didn't worship the bog of his homeland like the rest of the Vatrians.

Zeal pulled the bowstring then eased it back again. 'I shouldn't have it. Anyone who fails in his duty as a flame-sworn is unworthy to wield Agni's bow.'

'I wouldn't give up mine no matter the rules. It was made for me, like that for you. Besides, I wonder how you can think yourself inferior to it. You say it's imbued with magic, but you use it like an ordinary bow.'

'There's nothing ordinary about it,' he said, reaching for one of the red arrows from his quiver and setting it against the string.

Estel watched his face as it sharpened into focus. He aimed at a wooden mug set on a bench across the room. The more he concentrated on the target, the more alive the bow became. The deep red of the wood glinted the way it did when she touched it, but it was more animated. Like blood coursing through veins, it brought the decorative black grain to life. But the most striking change occurred in Zeal's eyes. His red pupils burned like a bonfire against molten gold, transforming him into an otherworldly being. Estel stared into them, mesmerised. It was like looking deep into the Flame of Agni itself.

Zeal drew the arrow back and the fire in his pupils caught the tip of it, setting it aflame. It happened so fast that even her swift senses struggled to catch the moment. He let the arrow free and as it flew past her, the heat from it brushed against her cheek. With a clang, it struck the mug and set it alight.

'That's the power of my bog and my people.' Zeal quenched the fire with a bucket of water. It hissed, smouldered, and died.

She looked at Zeal through different eyes. 'I need it for a good cause. Rana must be destroyed and my bow, however skilful I am with it, won't be enough this time.'

'You can do the same, you know. When Juro entrusted you with the bow, he knew that you could wake the magic sleeping in the glasswood. I don't know how, but he knew.'

Estel shrugged the bow off her shoulder. It felt cool against her palm and shimmered with a bluish light, as if enticing her to consider Zeal's words.

‘The glasswood is a special type of wood that grows in the province of Zyma, where moonlight is the only light source.’

‘How do you know this?’

He shrugged and reached for the bow. ‘May I?’

She handed it over, but when his hand closed around the glass, a puff of smoke escaped from between his fingers and his skin began to sizzle like flesh on a spit. Zeal thrust the bow back at her and she glimpsed a set of tiny blisters that formed on the inside of his palm.

‘Long ago, Vatrians waged war against the people of Zyma, for their attempt to enslave us and make use of our fire abilities. If they came peacefully, I don’t doubt that we would’ve aided them, but instead they arrived armed with weapons forged from glasswood and imbued with the magic of Marena, the boginya of ice. Like a swarm of snowflies, they passed through Vatra, killing men, women, and children. Those who managed to survive the onslaught went up to Agni’s temple and prayed for help. It was then that we learned the true power of Agni’s flame.’ He rubbed the blisters on his palm. ‘The slightest exposure to glasswood burns our skin. We made peace with the people of Zyma long ago—mostly because very few of them survived. The province is a barren land, with nothing but cold and snow. Those who live there fashion their homes from the ice itself and hunt foki for meat and fur. If it's there that you're bound, I don't envy you the task.'

Estel regarded her bow. Even if she could wake the power trapped in the glasswood, how would that aid her in defeating Rana? Her sister chose Zyma as her home, so the magic that came from there would have no effect. It was Zeal's bow that she needed, but only flame-sworn could evoke fire magic at will. Would the same be true for the Flame of Agni?

'I got you some clothes to help you blend in with the night,' Zeal's voice broke into her thoughts. 'Let's hope they fit.'

Black shirt, similar to the one he wore, and leather leggings hung off the back of the chair. She took them and looked around the small space.

'Give me a moment to get my things and I'll leave you in peace.'

When his remark registered, her muscles went rigid. It was Zeal's way of telling her that she could change in private, without feeling embarrassed by his presence. A defiant thought crossed her. Why would she care if he saw her naked body? Before her misadventure in Suha, such things never bothered her. Memories of the burdel echoed in her mind, and her insides writhed with shame and humiliation at what she had witnessed there. No, she screamed at her mind. She wouldn't be coerced into feelings that were no use to her.

With clothes pressed to her chest, she turned to Zeal. 'You can stay.'

The lines on his forehead deepened. He looked like a hunter about to walk into a trap. 'What are you saying?'

'It makes no difference to me if you stay, or go,' she said, ignoring the wave of heat that swept through her. She was stronger than that, in control of her feelings and impulses. Baring her body in front of Zeal wasn't a cause for concern.

'I don't understand…' he started but trailed off. His face was a mask of confusion.

'And you don't need to.'

Pretending to ignore him, Estel proceeded to untie the laces of her shirt, but her fingers refused to come together. Instead, the simple task turned into a clumsy effort at tugging and straining. Zeal's chest rose and fell as he followed her movements.

When she was about to pull the shirt over her head, he grabbed her elbow. 'Hold on. It's not that I wouldn't enjoy having you all to myself—quite the opposite. But this isn't you. The Estel I remember threatened to kill me and I very much doubt she'd want me near her. Not like this, anyway.'

His words woke fury in her. She offered him a chance to see her, but he refused with feeble excuses. Despite the anger, a little voice whispered that maybe she was mistaken about him. Maybe human desires ran much deeper, but some were able to control them. Was such a thing possible? A human in full control of his emotions? It was hard to breathe all of a sudden, but she didn't want him to see that she cared about his rejection. 'Isn't this what all men want? To indulge their desires without restraint?'

Zeal's body stiffened, and he took a step back from her. 'I don't know what men you speak of, but I sure am not one of them. I won't deny my attraction to you, but you misjudge me. You should know by now there's more to my interest than just plain desire, and something tells me if I indulged the latter, you'd be lost to me forever.'

She stared at him, waiting for a burst of laughter or the shadow of a teasing smile, but his face remained serious. He wanted more from her, invited her to dance a lover's dance to which she didn't know the steps. But worst of all, he was in the dark about her. If he knew who she really was, such thoughts wouldn't cross his mind. Lea had schooled her on how to recognise and fend off the lustful advances of men in the village, but she failed to teach her how to dismiss a tender heart.

'I hear you, but your words mean little to me,' she said, keeping her voice as soft as possible. 'I can't feel emotions the way you do. My ancestors came here many centuries ago, a group of warriors who settled among humans and changed Daaria. Their hearts were forged from strength, without a drop of weakness in them. They brought new laws and forced humans to follow them. I could never give you want you want, because there's no place for love in my heart. I can remove my clothes in front of you without shame, or charge into danger without fear. If you die, my eyes won't shed tears at your passing.'

She said the words knowing they were lies. Sorrow choked her when she walked the burning land, shame scorched her when she crossed the burdel's threshold, and fear sunk its fangs into her when she lost her senses in Willow's Heart. But if she denied the emotions out loud and often enough, perhaps she could rise above them and free herself.

Zeal gaped at her as if she'd lost her mind. 'Are you the same person who mourned the dead and insisted on burying age-old corpses? The same woman who feared being left in the dark in her delirium? Even now you stand before me with burning cheeks. Aren't these the acts of humans?'

'I knew you wouldn't understand.' Anger simmered in her, for he confirmed her deepest fears. The Da'ariys part of her was fading and there was nothing she could do. The choice was taken from her the moment she was proclaimed the Creator.

'Think what you will, but don't fool yourself. I don't know who your ancestors were, and I don't care, but let me prove to you that you're no different from us.'

And with that he cupped her face in his hands and pressed his lips to hers. Estel stood frozen while her mind sifted through the sensations. She could feel his rough fingers against her ears. His lips tasted salty and were warm and strong at the same time. In his search for connection, he pulled her closer until she felt his heart beating against her chest like a drum. No one ever got this close to her before and having Zeal in such proximity made her feel like a jik trapped in a snare.

She pushed him away with force that made him stagger. 'Don't attempt this again.' Her voice quivered and she fought to keep it even.

His eyes were pools of fire and dismay, and the hurt in them was the one she saw in Lea's when she told her that she wasn't her daughter.

Zeal didn't grace her with a response but spun around and left the hideout.

XXII

While Vatra spent the next two days preparing for the marriage blessing, Estel and Zeal drew up a plan of their assault. They spoke little, and there was no mentioning of the kiss. She thought it was for the best. As soon as they succeeded in stealing the flame, she would be on her way to Zyma to confront her sister, and her interlude with the assassin would be over. Zeal kept his distance and spent most of his time away from the hideout on errands of his own. On the afternoon before the celebration, they went over the strategy for the final time.

'We'll join the procession to the temple and separate there.' Zeal leaned over the map and traced the route with his gloved finger. 'I'll take the right side of the staircase.'

'How many assassins should we expect?' she asked.

'No less than five on each side and more up the top of the tower. The presence of the exalted priest will draw more flame-sworn assassins. He must be protected at all costs, especially on such an important day.'

'You know that I won't hesitate to kill him if I have to.'

Zeal pinched the bridge of his nose. 'Let's hope it won't come to that.'

Discussed in the confines of a small room with no windows, the plan sounded simple enough. They were to eliminate the assassins on either side of the staircase, apprehend the priest at the tower, procure the vial, and contain the flame inside it.

'Remember, without the priest's blessing, the vial will be of no use to us,' Zeal cautioned her one last time. It was the trickiest part—they would have to judge their time and wait for the exact moment to strike. An instant too early, or a second too late, would doom the whole plan to failure.

The night of the blessing transformed Vatra into a crimson carnival. Music vibrated the air from all directions, disturbed from time to time by outbursts of laughter and screams of joy. Wrapped in flowing skirts and red robes, excited crowds mingled on the streets, dancing and singing to the festive beats. The smell of meat roasting over an open fire blended with that of freshly baked bread, as local cooks showcased their skills under the open sky. The candles and torches burned so bright that even stars reflected their glow, and the night hummed with anticipation—there was no soul in this city who wouldn't hope to catch a glimpse of the bride during her ascent into Agni's temple. As the procession heading for the temple grew in size, Estel and Zeal joined the crowds in their celebration.

With all the commotion Estel found it hard to concentrate on the task at hand, and the bustle reminded her of the first time she entered Kvet. The amount of people there made her dizzy, and if not for Zeal's guidance, she would have never made it through. As if sensing her thoughts, Zeal squeezed her hand briefly and let go before she had a chance to scold him. Despite the task before them, he found a way to enjoy the carnival, pinching snacks from the food stalls on the way and exchanging jokes with drunken Vatrians. Estel watched him grin at her from across the street and wondered why he insisted on forsaking all he knew to aid her. Lea had spoken to her of love as something so profound that, once experienced, changes one forever, but all Estel could see was sacrifice. To her, love seemed more like a force that took away people's choices, a current pushing left to right, back and forth, leaving them to struggle against an irresistible force, and just when it eases, and they might catch their breaths, it pulls them back under.

Deep inside, Estel knew she wasn't worthy of Zeal's affections. For one, she couldn't reciprocate them, and even if she could, what good would it do either of them?

She was bound by the Creator's fate, tasked to change the course of tomorrow.

Lost in the grimness of her thoughts, she didn't see Zeal until he grabbed her waist and whirled her about in a giddy circle. They were in the market square where a band of musicians cheered people with their tunes. Around them, couples and children danced like red ghosts in their flashing robes and painted faces. Estel tried to pull away, but Zeal only tightened his grip.

'You can't deny me this final moment with you,' he whispered in her ear as he led her through the dance with uncanny skill.

'Stop this foolishness,' she hissed. 'Our task—'

'I'm about to betray my land and people. Don't I deserve one dance?'

Estel frowned. 'I can't dance.'

He pulled her closer and took charge of her in a way she would never let anyone else. Her body, stiff and rigid to begin with, relaxed into his grip as he led her in line with the flow of music. Her feet moved like a pair of puppets without a master to pull the strings, and she kept tripping over his boots and stepping on his toes. The more she struggled, the louder he laughed, but there was no malice in it. She was soon out of breath and berated herself for letting him sap her energy this way. She should be concentrating, getting in full command of her senses, but instead, she was prancing around the square like a sika in season.

'Enough,' she said, and this time he let her go.

'Now it's time to enjoy a different kind of dance,' he said, and the last traces of smile fell away from his lips.

In the throes of their mad spin, they'd managed to scale the whole square and find themselves at the back of the procession heading for the temple. Bound by the confines of the narrow street, the crowd formed into a line, crawling toward its destination like a crimson snake in the wake of a fat meal. Impatience was written on every face.

Zeal tied a kerchief across his face and pulled the red hood over his head. She followed his lead. When their eyes met, he gave her a nod. This sudden change in his manner threw her—one moment he was grinning like a youngster, and the next, his face was a mask made of stone.

'I'll see you at the top,' he said, and he melted into the masses.

With his departure, a strange feeling came over her. The crowd became too dense, the air too heavy to breathe, the noise too overpowering. As hard as it was to admit,

Zeal was like an anchor in the sea of crimson, and without him, she was like a boat at the mercy of shoving elbows and irritable grunts. She didn't like the course of her thoughts. Zeal's presence weakened some part of her she had no access to, while unsettling the stronger parts. It was best to forget him now and focus on the task ahead.

The procession neared the orchard and Estel weaved through the queue and picked her way along the outside edge. At the base of the crystalline staircase people clustered in a semicircle, ready for the bride's ascent, while her mate awaited at the peak to receive her. Four assassins stood on each side, as motionless as the temple itself, but Estel wasn't concerned about them—their task was to keep the overzealous crowd in check. She found the whole spectacle foolish. Why anybody would choose to be joined in front of so many people was beyond her. The wilds outside of Vatra made for a much greater venue. Tying yourself down to a man was bad enough, but doing it surrounded by a pool of staring faces would make the event unbearable.

The farther away she got from the staircase, the thinner the crowd. The walls of the temple were shaped from wide, stepped platforms that soared above her like a mountain. Each step was illuminated by torches set between the statues of Agni. She counted at least five of the sculptures upon each—a much-needed cover on the otherwise open blocks of stone. According to Zeal, the flame-sworn guardians resided in the alcoves built into the walls, but difficult to spot without daylight. Unlike her, they had a great view of the city and those who approached the temple itself. Far atop the red tower, the Flame of Agni set the sky ablaze.

Estel detached from the crowd and walked all the way to the temple's corner where the shadows were the thickest. With her shoulder against a tree, she steeled her mind and inhaled the night. It tasted of fire and smoke. The black clothing from Zeal disguised her well, making her one with the shadows. Ashk taught her to calm her senses before any undertaking and she followed his counsel. The task before her wasn't a ruse devised by the seer to trick her into another vision, but a real test of her abilities. During the preparations, she went through Zeal's stash of weapons and selected a few that would prove the most useful.

Equipped with a set of steel daggers and a grappling hook, with leather wrapped around the metal to deaden the sound, she was ready to take on the temple. Zeal urged her to leave her bow behind. It would be too cumbersome, he reasoned, and even though she agreed, she couldn't bring herself to follow through. The weapon was a part of her, and without it strapped to her back, she felt incomplete. Like a token of good fortune, one arrow was strapped to the bow. During her time in the wilds, she had learned to rely on her hearing the most—her prey would make noise long before it came into view—and she planned to employ the same strategy here. It was her advantage over the highly skilled assassins. The burning torches transformed the shadows into living beings, crawling and fluttering against the stone, and Estel looked forward to becoming one of them.

She unstrapped the grapple and measured the distance between her position and the height of the first block. She'd never used such a tool before, but Zeal taught her the basics. With her foot on the hook, she wrapped the rope around in a wide loop. Aiming for one of the Agni statues, she swung her arm out and let it fly.

The crowd around the temple, and the music that drifted from the city, drowned the clang of it as it wrapped itself around the stone foot. Estel stood motionless, waiting for any signs that she'd been discovered, but all was quiet. With a sharp tug she checked that the hook was in place, and bracing her feet against the wall, began her ascent.

The muscles she had developed climbing trees in Grey Lands assisted her in this task, while the leather gloves eased the rope's chafing. She made good progress, and soon, the edge of the first block came into view. Suspended in the air, she listened. Wind swept across the platform and the torches quivered in its wake, sputtering in their iron holders. In the trees below, crickets stirred the night with their chirruping. Satisfied with the absence of human activity, Estel pulled herself up. The statues along the platform were half her size and she crouched in the shadow of the closest one, scanning the wall in front for an alcove. Decorative images of Agni's life from birth to death, painted in red and copper, embellished the stone, and the burning flames breathed life into them.

Estel slinked across the block and hugged the base of the next platform. It was as tall as the one below it and required the use of the hook. She judged the distance and spied another statue to grapple on to. Her second throw was more accurate and didn't make as much noise. She climbed the rope, but as her elbow touched the top of the block above, she realised her error. Zeal was right—the alcoves blended with the temple and it was hard to tell them apart from the wall itself. If not for her sharpened vision, she would have missed the indent and walked straight into it.

She hung from the edge, taking stock of the situation, keenly aware of her deadening fingers. The smooth stone didn't offer much in terms of a grip. Her only choice was to employ an act of surprise and risk the assassin sounding the alarm if she wasn't quick enough in her ambush. To give herself more room, she shimmied away from the statue and pushed her feet against the wall, while pulling her chest in. With one fluid motion she sprang up the wall, drew her dagger, and threw it at the shadows inside the alcove. There was a whoosh of air and a thud as something heavy hit the ground. She remained hunched over for a while, listening to the sounds of celebration that drifted on the breeze like a multitude of chiming bells. Agni's statues on this level held round candles that conversed with the wind in soft whispers. She edged to the alcove to find the assassin with her dagger thrust in his chest. She dislodged it and patted her bow—luck hadn't abandoned her yet. A quick glance across the stone assured her it was clear.

The next platform was lower down, and the wall leading up to it was furnished with ornaments in the shape of leaves and vines. Dyed in the colours of the setting sun, they looked like an image out of a scroll, proving to be a great support for her hands and boots. She clambered up and surveyed the block above.

The next indent was to her left, hidden in the shadows, some distance away from any torchlight, but due to its angle she couldn't tell if anyone was inside. The night brushed against her cheeks like cool fingers, drying moisture off her forehead. She wished all distractions away and let her hearing explore the area.

At first there was nothing but stillness, mixed with the crackling of flames, but then, her sense picked up another sound—a slight ripple that stirred the air as someone inhaled and exhaled. Estel's nostrils detected a whiff of human sweat. The assassin, no matter how well trained, couldn't disguise his scent, or the way his lungs rose and fell with each intake of breath. Her power was a gift not of this world and so very few could hide from it. Her mind absorbed the details and filtered them through her other senses until she had an image of the man's position and the best way to strike. He stepped out of his hiding place and stood with his back to her, half of his body outside the alcove, surveying the area. When she leapt onto the platform, time itself slowed. Her boots crossed the distance at the speed of a Vatrian cat, and she closed her daggers around the assassin's neck. The blades were as swift as her approach and she killed the man's dying scream with the flat of her palm. She lowered his body onto the stone and hauled it into the darkness of the alcove. The kill pleased her. All the talk about the flame-sworn made it seem as if they were indestructible, but here lay proof that they were no match for Da'ariys. Agni's guardians bled and died as any other human.

A high-pitched squeal tore the air and Estel froze.

Her stomach tightened, and she waited for a stab of steel, but then another scream joined the first, followed by a third. She swivelled and swept the platform for the source of the commotion. Her vision narrowed and centred on the people clustered around the base of the crystalline staircase. They parted, making way for a woman wrapped in a white, strapless gown split in the centre to reveal a crimson underskirt that made it seem as if she was on fire. A belt of the same colour hugged her slender waist, and trailing behind her was a translucent veil, embroidered with golden flames. With her gloved hands clasped in front of her, and eyes set upon the Flame of Agni, she began her ascent. Time was of the essence.

Marking the bride's progress, Estel made her next climb. The wall was full of carvings of burning fires and

Vatrian priests in various stages of worship. She found their bodies with her feet and grabbed the stone-chiselled flames with her fingers. Before scaling the edge, she quested with her nose and ears for another clue. This time, her task was much simpler. Entranced by the ascending bride, the assassin stood outside his alcove in full view, facing the central staircase. Estel sprang onto the platform and clasped her hand over the man's mouth, drawing her fist back before plunging the dagger into his chest. She held his slackening body against hers and felt his final heartbeat. She disguised the still warm body in the shadows and wiped sweat off her brow. The climb and the focus required to remain undetected took its toll on her. The spasms in her muscles increased in frequency and dull aching at the back of her skull promised a severe headache later. Did Zeal face the same difficulties on his side of the temple? She wanted to believe that he was as highly skilled as he claimed since his capture would mean her failure.

Estel cast a glance at the bride in her imposing gown and snorted; the woman had no idea that her blessing would not be realised tonight. Or any night for that matter.

High above, the Flame of Agni was a blistering inferno, pulsating heat in every direction as if to mock her intentions and scold her arrogance. Her face was damp with perspiration and her clothes clung to her like a second skin. Unlike the lower levels of the temple, the middle ones and those higher up had more firelight to brighten them. More torches burned on each platform and fewer shadows lingered between the statues, ensuring that her task would be more gruelling.

The flame distracted her a moment too long and she almost missed the assassin crouching atop the next platform. His silhouette looked like a black rock against the burning sky. At first, she thought it was just another statue, but then his scent betrayed him—human skin mixed with a sharp smell of sage. His location and the torch burning in close proximity gave Estel little room to manoeuvre, and even less to deliver an accurate blow. Crouching behind one of the statues, she surveyed the block and decided to try her luck by climbing up the higher step and surprising the flame-sworn from above. She crept away from him, into the blackness of the opposite corner, then began her climb. The carvings on the wall dug into her chest and a sudden urge to cough came over her. She paused and stifled it by clasping her hand over her throat. Her vision blurred a little, but she maintained her concentration with a few deep breaths.

Once at the top, she slipped along the edge, quieter than a whisper. Her position gave her a good view of the man below and she aimed her dagger. It swished through the air and sank into the rock that was the flame-sworn. The man toppled on his side. She was preparing to jump down and retrieve her weapon when cold steel pressed against her throat.

'It was my brother there,' the muffled voice said in her ear.

His voice paralysed her. How could she have not seen the second assassin? The man's knife cut into her throat and a slightest move on her part would slit it open. Out of the corner of her eye she glimpsed the bride and her veil, sweeping the staircase in her wake. If she wanted to get to the priest before her, and procure the vial, she had to think fast.

'Who sent you?' the flame-sworn asked, and the knife pressed harder against her skin.

She felt a trickle of blood run down her neck. She needed to distract the man. By asking the question, he gave her an opportunity and her answer would either end her or gift a precious moment to wriggle out.

'Your father,' she said. 'Your father sent me.'

There was a sharp intake of breath. 'Impossible—'

Primal instinct was all she could rely on in that moment. His confusion offered her a split second that she could not afford to waste, and in one instant, she lodged her hand between his bicep and her shoulder, gripped tightly at his flesh, and pushed back as hard as she could until they slammed into the wall behind them. His hand, streaked with her blood, flew out at the force of it, and the blade fell, spattering flecks of red against the stone.

She drove her elbow into his flank and lurched away from him, turning back only to see him unsheathe a second blade, longer and far deadlier. He raised it high above his shoulder and circled around her. She licked her lips and followed his every step, her own dagger at the ready. Her body and mind thrummed with tension—only agility would save her now.

The assassin sprang, and she hopped back, almost tripping off the ledge. He came at her again and she crouched, missing the edge of the blade by a breath. Her own dagger connected with his thigh. The slash made him stagger and he clasped his hand around the wound, lending her an opportunity to strike. She didn't hesitate and delivered another stab to his lower abdomen. He let out a sharp cry and bent in half.

‘You can join your brother now,’ she said and kicked him off the platform.

She clasped her palm against her neck. The assassin managed to deliver a deep gash that bled more than she wanted it to. She’d relied on her abilities for too long and they failed her when she needed them the most. Estel focused on her primary target to the exclusion of all else, and now she would pay the price for her blunder. It made her realise how undeveloped her powers were. Ashk warned her that more time was needed to uncover her full potential as a Creator, cautioned her that going against wild beasts was quite different than taking down a human prey, but she dismissed him. It was the worst moment to learn he was right.

She untied the kerchief from around her face and applied it to the wound. It would have to do for now. Her breath was coming in rasps and her hands shook. One look at the staircase told her the bride was out of sight. There was no more time to play hide and seek. She had to hurry and take her chances with whatever awaited above.

Abandoning all caution, Estel scaled the blocks ahead as swiftly as her climbing skills allowed. High above, in the red tower, the groom in black robes reached for the hand of his wife to be. The altar with Agni’s flame loomed closer while the air around her felt as if she'd stepped into a blacksmith's forge, assaulting her face with heat. Only three more platforms separated her from the power of the fire bog.

The priest wrapped in crimson stepped out with his hands wide open to receive the joining couple. Hanging around his neck was a vial that glittered in the firelight like a glass full of embers.

'Stop her,' someone yelled at her back.

A hand grabbed her, and she met it with a wild kick, but the movement unbalanced her and she fell, hitting her chin on the stone. There was a crunch inside her mouth as her jaw bounced off the hard rock, the impact filling her mouth with a taste of iron. She scrambled to her feet, oblivious to all pain, eyes locked on the priest who was her only concern. The platforms ahead were low, and she scaled them with ease while more cries chased after her.

A couple of dark silhouettes blocked her path. Two against one didn't bode well and she knew she wouldn't be able to fight them off in the open. She had to seize the priest before the assassins overpowered her. She snatched the rope with her grappling hook and threw it at the first man. It caught him square in the chest and he stumbled back. The second assassin advanced on her with his sword drawn and Estel pulled the rope with all her strength. The returning hook connected with the man's blade, the impact shoving him sideways. Estel crossed the distance and smashed her boot into his back. He flew atop his companion and she charged past them without looking back.

One final leap landed her between the joining couple and the exalted priest. Zeal sprang from the shadows to her right and cut down an assassin that reached for his sword. Blood spattered the bride's glorious gown and the couple shrieked in unison.

The sound of a horn blasted through the air and other horns answered the call.

Estel grabbed the priest and set the dagger to his throat. With a sharp tug, she ripped the vial off his neck. Five assassins formed a circle around her while another two closed down on Zeal.

'If you do anything foolish, the priest will die,' she roared. Then quieter, 'Now, bless the vial.' Free will or not, she had to chance it. Applying more pressure with her dagger, she steered him to the altar where Agni's flame burned in a crimson cloud. The heat emanating from it scratched the walls of her throat, making her cough, and the strain widened the wound on her neck. Blood loss made her head spin.

'You're committing a grave—'

'Just do as I say.'

The priest's heart rammed against his ribcage like an animal in the confines of a cage. With trembling fingers, he pulled the stopper of the vial and began chanting. The intensity of the flame didn't seem to affect him. A sound of steel clashing against steel reached her ears and she heard a mocking laugh. Only Zeal could laugh at a time like this.

The blessing ritual went on forever and the tension of keeping him at knifepoint sapped most of her energy. When the priest pushed the stopper back, she snatched the vial off him. It glittered in her palm like a red jewel.

'How do I contain the flame?' she asked.

At the base of the temple, more and more citizens assembled to witness this impious onslaught, screaming curses and yelling for the protection of the flame-sworn. But Estel held the priest in her power, rendering the assassins useless.

'No one has ever attempted such sacrilege,' the priest whispered. He appeared to be more afraid of Agni's wrath than her knife. 'You can't contain the power of the bog. His holy fire will devour your soul.'

'Let *me* worry about that,' Estel said. 'How do I contain the flame?'

'You… you must offer the vial to the flame… without letting go.' He reeked of fear.

The golden statue of Agni beside the flame altar watched her as she pulled the stopper off the vial with her teeth, still gripping her captive. She stepped closer to the flame. The priest, the assassins… the whole world held its breath. The vial shimmered as if beckoning the fire to seek shelter within its glassy walls, and the Flame of Agni stirred like a living, breathing thing. Estel stilled herself against pain and thrust her hand into the crimson inferno, all the way up to her elbow. It licked her flesh and it felt as if the heat peeled her skin off, scorching her very bones. She gritted her teeth but didn't let go of the vial.

The priest gasped and the assassins cried out in chorus. The flame changed forms, stretching and shrinking, morphing into wild shapes of beasts, humans, and birds. Only sheer determination kept her from dropping the vial and fleeing. As the flame's heat touched her soul, she recalled everything that happened to her since she left Grey Lands—like a reminder of what she must do and why she must do it. The death of Lea and her unconditional devotion, Arleta's faith in her and the future she had a power to create, Ashk's fate if she failed, and many more thoughts rushed through her as the flame cleansed her soul of doubt and affirmed her duty as the Creator. The one who could create was the one who could deliver the world from the brink of desolation. The flame grew weaker and shrank further until it reduced to a smoke-like string and wound its way inside the vial. Estel slammed the stopper back on.

One by one, every torch and candle that lit Vatra died, and the temple plunged into darkness.

There was no time to think, no time to tend to her throbbing arm. She pushed the priest aside and broke into a sprint, passing the altar and leaping with only a prayer crossing her mind: *Let my feet meet stone, Chour.*

It seemed like eternity before they connected with the platform. The vial in her hand was a beacon, emanating red light that assisted in her wild descent. She couldn't afford to be captured, not when she had just obtained the power to kill the Destroyer, not when the reasons why she must were so clear in her heart. She didn't need more revelations, or other emotions. If her task was to save Daaria for future generations then she would do it, and with the power of Agni in her grasp, she was sure of victory.

She picked up speed, leaping from platform to platform like a mountain goat. The kerchief around her neck managed to stifle the bleeding from the cut, but her escape was tearing it further. Estel ignored the searing pain shooting up her throat with every intake of breath and continued running.

The sound of her pursuers echoed all around her as they staggered in the dark, tripping and falling down the platforms they so dutifully guarded only hours ago. She wondered if Zeal made his escape and, like her, was dashing down the temple as one of the shadows. It was impossible to tell in this darkness, but even if she could, there would be no way of helping him. The flame was her priority now.

The last two platforms were too high to jump down from, and her grapple was lost in the scuffle with the assassins. Below, the people of Vatra fumbled in the dark—black shapes flailing like ghosts in the night. Panic stirred in her stomach. She had no choice but to lower herself into the masses and let their bodies cushion her fall. With the vial safely tucked in her pocket, she adjusted her bow, grabbed the edge of the platform, and hung off it, legs dangling with no grip to support them.

Heart pounding, she squeezed her eyes shut and let go.

The flight was short and uneventful. When her body collided with the people below, the force of the impact knocked a few of them down, providing a much-needed cushion. Her bow didn't snap, but her ankle twisted under her and something fractured inside it. The pain of it travelled up her leg and through her midsection, only to reverse and race back down to its point of origin. She untangled from the less fortunate Vatrians, and in the confusion managed to limp her way into the trees.

'It's her!' someone shouted. 'Don't let her get away!'

Estel tried to run, but the stabbing ache in her ankle made it impossible to gain speed. Using the trees for support, she transferred all her weight onto her fit leg and hobbled faster. The pursuers were on her heels. Twigs snapped to her left and right, and the yelling and cursing grew louder. They needed to recover the flame, but most of all, they wanted her blood. She felt her belt for the dagger. Apart from it and the lone arrow at her back, she had nothing else to fend them off with.

The trees thinned, and she came out into an open street. Her pulse quickened and dread seized her. She spun around, but it was too late. The first of her pursuers was ten steps away and his companions were closing in.

Vatra would be the end of her.

'Hop on!' A scream, followed by the clattering of hooves.

She would have recognised that voice anywhere. Zeal rode down the street in her direction. He held out a hand and she grabbed it, just as the first man reached for her. She clambered up the horse and wrapped her hands around his waist. It was a second life she owed him.

They galloped across the darkened city and she was glad it was Zeal who held the reins. If anyone could get them out of Vatra it was him.

As if sensing her gratitude, Zeal laughed, spurring the horse to greater speed. She didn't blame him for this outburst, for she too felt a wild sense of elation. They'd managed to achieve the impossible: to steal the Flame of Agni and shake Vatra to its core.

'I'm coming for you, little sister,' Estel muttered.

But their joy was short-lived. As the city zoomed past them, the air began to change. It was subtle at first, only a ribbon that wound its way through darkness, but then it divided. Like a pair of greedy fingers, it grasped the night in its clutches and suffocated it with a blanket of violet mist.

The Twilight Hunters were coming.

XXIII

'Faster!' Estel cried into Zeal's ear. The last time she faced the hunters, she was curious, but unafraid, watching as the villagers were slaughtered and their houses burned to the ground. But that was before Arleta stirred the fear in her, and now it dragged its razor-edged claws down her spine. The horse took sharp turns, frothing at the muzzle and skidding across the cobbled streets. Zeal was a good rider, but was he fast enough to outrun hunters created by the Destroyer herself?

The city gates stood wide open and they raced past two stricken guards. Estel caught a glimpse of their faces—furrowed brows, eyes darting, as they tried to make sense of the unfamiliar twilight. The mist grew thicker, the violet trapped in it, more intense, heralding the approach of the beasts that spawned it. Estel pressed her cheek to Zeal's back and tightened her grip on him. The wind whipped the side of her face and the mist wound itself around her like a smothering cloak. Wilds to either side fled alongside them in a blur of hills and forests.

A clatter of hooves made her want to look back, but she fought the compulsion. This was no longer a quest to escape with the Flame of Agni, but a race for their lives.

But no matter how hard Zeal pushed the horse, the Twilight Hunters caught up with them, flanking them on both sides, their violet stallions faster than the wind. Visible through their translucent skin, their veins and organs pumped jet-black blood. The hunters were one with their horses, joined by a ribcage that held a charcoal heart. It gave life to the abominations, and Estel couldn't tell where one ended and the other one began. The rider closest to her turned his head and pierced her with an eye of violet jewel. Swirling inside it was the same mist that spread across Vatra in the all-encompassing twilight.

The presence of the hunters panicked the horse and it halted in mid-run, digging its hooves into the ground, waking a cloud of dust. The grit filled Estel's eyes and particles found their way into her nose and mouth, choking her. Zeal tried to assert his control over the animal, but it went up on its hind legs, kicking at the air and throwing Estel off the saddle. As her back hit the road, Estel felt a sharp stab to her chest and the impact knocked the air out of her lungs. Zeal flew sideways, meeting the same fate, and the horse, freed from its burden, bolted into the safety of the rusty wilds.

Dust settled around them and Estel struggled to her knees. Black circles danced in her eyes and she more sensed than saw the Twilight Hunters surrounding them. She shook her head to clear away the fuzziness brought upon by the fall and blinked numerous times to disperse the darkness. Her bow lay far to the side, snapped in half, alongside the arrow that she carried all the way from Vatra as a token of good luck. Regret twisted her gut—it was like losing her closest companion. The twilight cast a violet shawl over the riders and their stallions, while they snorted and kicked the ground in fury, breathing out the purple smoke through their nostrils. Estel counted six of them. Zeal crawled toward her in a daze of his own. The dive split his cheek open and blood gushed down his face; his copper hair matted with it. One of his arms spread beside him at a strange angle. In his Vatrian eyes she saw a reflection of her own fear. The world of Nav beckoned them, but she wasn't sure if it was the Light or Dark side of it that would await them once the hunters devoured their flesh. Either way, they were going to die.

Estel clambered to her feet and the earth rocked beneath her. She extended her arms to keep her balance, and after a few moments, the vertigo passed. The Twilight Hunters watched her like a predator watching prey but didn't make a move to kill her. She felt for the vial in her pocket and found it intact. A plea formed in her mind. If

Da'ariys shared a bond of any kind, then now would be the time for Agni to acknowledge it.

The hunters parted and out of the violet mist came the cause of this chaos.

Rana smiled from atop a black stallion that put to shame the hunters assembled around it. The stallion wasn't a magical beast, but a horse of such pure blood he seemed like a beast out of the tales of yore. His coat gleamed like polished obsidian and in his eyes resided night itself. The energy that flowed through the beast was darker than the blood in the Twilight Hunters' veins. Estel could sense it, for it hung around the horse like a reek of a putrid flesh.

'Welcome, sister,' Rana said.

'I am no sister of yours,' Estel replied.

Rana dismounted. Her leather clothes matched her horse in colour. 'This is no way to greet one of Da'ariys.' She took a measure of Estel and a half-smile stretched her lips.

For Estel it was the strangest feeling to see her likeness in another's face. Her sister's features mirrored her own, distinguishable only by the blackness in her hair and eyes. Staring into them was like staring into the pits of Dark Nav. Rana's skin was as ivory as hers, lips as thin, cheekbones as high, but the resemblance ended there.

Since the beginning of her journey, Estel denied her human side together with the emotions it contained, holding on to the pure side of Da'ariys, but looking at Rana now, she questioned her reasons. If Remha looked anything like the Destroyer, the future Arleta had shown her made sense. Rana's features were sharp and raw, without traces of mercy or compassion in them. Her face was that of a statue, carved from the darkest stone, smooth and free of warmth or affection. It was the face of the guards who abused the captives in the prisons, the face of the men in the burdel who traded in the bodies of women and children. It was the face of the warrior of Da'ariys and the face of tomorrow.

The resolve to destroy Rana strengthened within her. Like earth that bears the seeds of all life, her sister carried ruination in her womb, and if Estel failed to stop her the darkness festering inside it would spill across the land and devour the world.

'You're changing,' Rana said while her black eyes lingered on Estel's neck.

Estel brought her hand to the wound and it came away bloody. The blood wasn't the shade of silver or pink, but the deep red of a summer wine.

'Oh, don't look so surprised,' Rana said. 'It's the price you pay for becoming one of them.' She pointed at Zeal and recoiled, seemingly repulsed by his mere presence.

He was still on the ground, laying in a pool of blood from his face, moaning softly. Estel wanted to tend to his injuries, but there was no way to do it. She wiped her palm on her leggings and challenged Rana with a stare. 'I'm no human, but a Creator, sent by our people to witness your end.'

Rana's laugh filled the air, stirring the violet mist. The Twilight Hunters shifted in response. 'You could never destroy me. You're too weak, and like those who came before us, you will fall. No Destroyer has ever been defeated, for my purpose is stronger than your reasons to kill me. My blood is Remha's blood—pure, untainted. He created us, gave us a new world where we could create warriors of our own. Instead, we brought it to ruin by mixing the silver of our ancestors with the red of the unworthy, breeding half-wits who can't even stand on their own.'

'Da'ariys are nothing like you,' Estel said, wanting desperately to believe that. 'You disrupt the balance.'

'I *am* the balance. Da'ariys' legacy will tip the scale of the future in our favour. My purpose is to bring Remha's glory back into the world and see his commandments fulfilled. When your quest ends in failure, our creator will no longer be a memory, but the most feared bog who had ever ruled these lands. I'll make sure of that. All will bow to him and follow his rule. We'll root out the weak and purify Daaria.'

Rana's reasons were similar to those Estel presented to Ashk but hearing them from the Destroyer's mouth lanced her soul with shame. One thing she was certain of: she'd never want to see a future where her sister had any power.

Her fingers tightened around the vial. 'You speak as if you've already won the battle.'

Rana regarded her as if she were an insect about to be squashed with a shoe. 'I've claimed the victory from the day I was sent to Daaria. Your future is sealed.' She jabbed her finger at Zeal's crumbled form. 'If not for this useless piece of meat, I wouldn't need to waste my time by having to watch you bleed like a human wretch. This race is weak, vulnerable, easily manipulated. By siding with them, you betrayed your bloodline.'

Zeal raised his head. Blood and dirt smeared all over his face, left eye so bruised that it disappeared in the swollen folds of his lid. Despite that, he showed his bloody teeth in a grin. 'Letting Estel live was the best thing I ever did,' he croaked. 'She is the stronger one.'

Rana bared her teeth at him. 'You're nothing but a failure to your family and land. You think by defying the rules you proved yourself worthy of her? No, with your love and devotion you ensured her failure. My sister can't feel it yet, but the walls of her heart are coming undone, and *you* will be her downfall.' The words had barely left her lips before she advanced.

In four brisk steps, Rana crossed the distance between her and Zeal. She grabbed him by the collar and jerked him to his feet with strength no woman could possess. When Estel rushed at them, the twilight itself trapped her feet in a violet quagmire while the hunters closed around her. She fought the mist, but it was like trying to escape a bottomless mud pit—the more she struggled, the more it thickened around her calves and ankles.

Rana seized a handful of Zeal's hair and yanked his head back. Estel fought harder, thrashing against the fog like a bird in a cage.

Zeal's eyes locked on hers but there was no panic in them. His red pupils burned with silent calm, as if he knew this moment was written long ago on the pages of his destiny. His swollen lips stretched into a soft smile. 'I took an oath to serve Agni, but now I know it wasn't his flame I was sworn to.'

Rana drew a dagger of black steel, and with one swift move she sank it into Zeal's chest, all the way to the hilt. His eyes widened, but never left Estel's. The fire that burned in them slowly died until there was nothing left but a black void where his pupil was. Fresh blood trickled down the right side of his mouth and he went limp.

Rana pulled her dagger out and let his body fall to the floor. 'An end befitting a flame-sworn who failed his bog,' she said, wiping the blade on Zeal's shirt.

During her journey, Arleta forced Estel to experience a myriad of emotions: sorrow, fear, shame… but all of them belonged to someone else: a prisoner, a woman, or a child she encountered in the visions of the future. She absorbed them into her soul and they altered parts of her, reshaping her view of the world. But what she felt now, watching Zeal's motionless face, was hers and hers alone. It was as if a giant fist punched through her ribcage and ripped her heart out, leaving a bleeding hole in her chest, a hole that would never heal. The whole world, including her own existence, dissolved, leaving her stranded in a place where time and light were no more. She wanted Zeal's final breath to also be her own. At first, she hardly felt the searing pain that spread through her right arm. What was another symbol in the wake of desolation?

Estel let out a cry, a raw shriek that echoed through the valley.

'Love… Humans call it the greatest emotion,' Rana said, sheathing her dagger. Her voice was a mixture of pity and disdain. 'Does it feel as good as they claim?

'Get used to it, because he's gone forever, and you weren't strong enough to refuse him. This ache will follow you in every waking moment, and there's nothing you can do to soothe it.'

Estel's body shook and Zeal's voice echoed in her ears: *I'd rather face exile than take your life…learn to trust me… to save your life, I must give up my own…* The words were like shards, each stabbed deeper than the one before. Her senses called out to him, but the only response was silence. The link between them was gone.

Rana watched her, head cocked to one side, eyes like black pools, a shadow of a smile across her flawless face. Just seeing her standing there, unaffected by the events, filled Estel with a different kind of feeling. It pounded against her chest like a pestle against mortar, once, twice, thrice, until her cavity was nothing but a pulp of muscle and bone. And from that shapeless mass something darker was forged, an emotion that saturated all others. It guided her hand to the vial concealed in her pocket. The Flame of Agni swirling inside it was the colour of blood, and it had one purpose only. To burn.

Estel pulled the stopper off and set it free.

It was like opening the gates of Dark Nav and releasing fires from its deepest pits. Freed from the confines of the vial, the Flame of Agni turned into a shapeless, roaring beast that called forth a firestorm of such magnitude that it set the land, sky, and the air itself ablaze. The violet mist that held her captive writhed and squirmed as the burning wind devoured it. Estel fell to her knees. Her blood simmered in her veins like a pan of water over a hearth fire, while her flesh braced against the inferno.

The red beast charged the hunters, its hungry fire setting their violet flesh aflame. The riders screeched—a sound so unnatural it didn't have a place among the living—and sought to free themselves of their stallions, but they shared the same heart, and it refused for them to be so easily parted.

In moments, the Twilight Hunters were no more, and the earth they stood on, scorched to the core. The Flame of Agni lost its heat and shrunk in size until only a string of smoke remained—a red haze that dispersed on the air.

I leave the final task to you, Creator.

The words were no more than a whisper on the wind. Estel looked across the scorched land to where the Destroyer leaned on her black stallion, both untouched by the firestorm. It was all for nothing.

'You fool,' Rana said. Her face was satisfaction mixed with pity. 'You can't kill me with the magic of our ancestors.' She mounted her black stallion. 'My task here is done. When you come for me, you *will* take my life.'

Estel's consciousness fled and she fell into the arms of blackness.

***

A hand stroked Estel's cheek, soft and cool against her burning skin, while a soothing voice filled the chamber with a song. She wanted to stay like this, suspended between worlds, her consciousness split between Daaria and the realm of her ancestors. Never again having to worry about past, present, or future, but remaining forever in the now. But this was a wish for the blessed, and she was one of the accursed. When she opened her eyes, the song died on Lelya's lips. Her mother sat on the floor next to her, robes spread around her in a white fan. Her silver hair shimmered like stardust in the light of the chamber. If Estel squinted, she could imagine Lelya to be a part of the tapestry on the wall behind her, one with the Da'ariys encircling the ship. Time separated them and there was no magic powerful enough to break the barrier and unite them.

'You shouldn't be here, and yet, I can't take my eyes off you,' Lelya said.

Now Estel knew the meaning of such words. 'If that's so, where were you when I needed your help?' she asked, pushing away her hand. 'Where was my mother when I cried into the night in a wicker basket? Abandoned at the edge of the forest. You brought me into this world, but it was Lea who was a true mother to me. I've lost everything…'

A gentle smile played on Lelya's lips. 'That what is lost can be found again, if not by us, then by those who come after. I'd want nothing more than to be a real mother to you, but such luxuries are denied to me. Your father and I were chosen to bear Creators and Destroyers until the future is restored, for such a feat could only be accomplished by the joining of the gifted and the untouched. Every time I give life, my children are taken from me, and I'm forced to watch them stumble in the dark, hoping they'll find their path and gain a deeper understanding. But each time they face themselves and fail, and the cycle of loss continues.'

Estel's heart was a heavy rock wrapped in raw hurt. 'Maybe because you abandon them? Leave them to their fate, to be torn apart piece by piece, until there's nothing left in them to fight with.'

'You speak as if emotions are your enemy, but they're there to shape us. They inform our actions, form our character, and if we learn how to utilise them, they can gift us freedom. Our feelings equip us to face the greatest trials of life. We shouldn't lock them away but examine each one and gain a greater understanding of their purpose.'

'Before I acknowledged my emotional side, I was a strong and capable hunter. But then my life fell into ruin. I've never felt so weak. My reason and will to live are gone. I failed, and the Destroyer will have the future she desires.' She grabbed her mother's hand. 'Release me from my bonds. I want to die with him. If you have the power to take my life, do it.'

Lelya said nothing for a time. Estel closed her eyes, sensing a faint call of her body laying amidst the wreckage of her life. Her mortal shell awaited her return, every inch of it cracked like the surface of a frozen lake, where one step would tear it open, plunging her deep into the icy waters for a never-ending torment. She wanted to hold off as long as she could before reuniting with that broken being and facing Zeal's death.

A soft touch of Lelya's hand pulled her away from her grim thoughts.

'Come with me,' she said, raising to her feet.

Despite her lack of energy, she followed her mother's example. They crossed the chamber, and Lelya stepped through the doorway. On the other side, Arleta awaited them, the eyeless toy clutched in her dirty hand. Her sandy hair was more dishevelled than the last time Estel saw her. She looked more like an abused child than a conduit capable of constructing bridges across time.

Seeing the girl's mournful face brought back memories of all they had gone through, and Estel took a step back.

'I'm a part of you, so why do you refuse me?' Arleta's voice was imbued with hurt and loss.

'You know why. You're the reason I've lost my own self.'

'Is that what you believe?' Lelya asked. She took the soft toy from Arleta's grasp and offered it to Estel. 'Don't you remember?'

Estel took the toy. It was as dead as it ever was and now it lacked the eyes to see. Shiver of a memory ran through her. She looked from the toy to Arleta. A faint image of herself floated to the forefront of her mind. Wearing a dress with striking colours, Estel too held something close to her chest... Could it be?

Lelya cupped Arleta's chin in her hand. 'Her purpose is to guide you, so you could become whole and fulfil your destiny. Her magic is that of an innocent, but it's dying and when the last of it fades, you'll be on your own. Take her hand and let us join our strength.'

Lelya and Arleta held hands and waited for her to joined them, but she hesitated. Why did she need more visions? Hadn't she witnessed enough? There was nothing in the future worth seeing. It was a wasteland, filled with dark deeds and people who forgot their own purpose. They waged wars, punished one another, sentencing each other and their world to a slow and agonising end. What could she possibly learn from a race that sought life's meaning in destruction?

But then her eyes met Arleta's and in them she saw a willingness to believe that not all was lost. The little girl who followed her through Daaria, and time itself, believed that Estel could heal the wounds inflicted upon her world.

She wrapped her fingers around Arleta's small hand, and one last time, the three of them stepped into the future.

***

There was no fall, no excruciating pain, no stars, no harsh thrust into reality. All it took was one step to breach the barrier between worlds. The transition was seamless, and when Estel looked around, half expecting to see the aftermath of some terrible tragedy, her eyes met with quite a different sight.

They stood on a street lined on either side by a row of sharp-edged buildings, with so many windows there wasn't enough fingers to count them. Glass replaced shutters, catching sun rays and reflecting them back on the sidewalk of grey stone. The beaten tracks of Daaria turned into a smooth road with white lines painted across the middle, separating the left side from the right. Tall black poles were fixed alongside the road at regular intervals, with an occasional tree in between. The street looked so orderly it was hard to believe it was real. Even the air smelled different, heavy with smoke that was stronger and more palpable than one born out of a campfire.

'Is this…?' Estel asked.

'So far, in your visions of the future, you witnessed only pain and misery,' Lelya said. 'But not everything here is woeful.'

Estel rubbed her right arm. 'It doesn't hurt… Why doesn't it hurt?'

'You've come a long way. Some parts of you are whole and it makes you stronger.'

Stronger? How could this be if her world collapsed mere moments ago? She felt anything but strong. When this vision faded, she would wake up and be forced to deal with Zeal's death. The thought was like a rock in her abdomen, crushing her innards. She turned her mind away from it and regarded a small crowd of men, women, and children at the edge of the road, holding poles with square boards nailed to them. Some had strings of words written across them, and others depicted red flowers and animals drawn by a child's hand. The air around them throbbed with anticipation.

At her questioning glance, Lelya explained, 'These are welcoming messages, written in the language of this land.'

Before she could say more, a shiver of excitement ran through the crowd and everyone turned their attention to the road. Estel squinted at a square shape that appeared in the distance. It was yellow and resembled a low house with windows fastened to the front of it, except it wasn't a house but a moving structure that closed the distance between it and the crowd at a remarkable speed.

Estel backed away from the cluster of people, panic spreading through her as the roar caused by movement reached her. What magic was this? The crowd seemed unaffected as every person stepped closer to the road to welcome the bellowing creature.

Lelya must've sensed her dismay for she placed her hand on Estel's shoulder. 'There's nothing to fear. These machines will replace horses in the future. They're controlled by magic of a different kind. It's human-made, and only humans are capable of wielding it.'

The machine rolled down the road on a set of black wheels, smoke gushing out of its rear end. Despite her mother's assurance, Estel wasn't convinced it was trustworthy and it took all her resolve to remain still.

The people gathered by the sidewalk joined hands and cheered on the beast, beckoning it with waving hands and broad smiles. The most surprising thing of all was the absence of negative emotions. There was no darkness among them, only warmth and a peculiar breathlessness Estel wasn't accustomed to.

'Why can't I feel them?' she asked Arleta.

The girl took her hand and squeezed it. 'Let's do this one together,' she said with a smile.

It took her by surprise. She was used to Arleta's solemn and cast away look, but seeing her lips stretched wide softened something inside Estel. It made the struggles of her past trials worth it. Like a touch of air on her skin, an invisible hand pulled them both to the assembled crowd and Estel's consciousness brushed against that of the people. A wave of excitement hit her, so powerful that her chest struggled to contain her racing heart. The eyes she looked into beamed and the grins on children's faces stretched from ear to ear as they bounced around, unable to contain the joyful energy that suffused every inch of their being. The air was rich with laughter and hooting. Women clasped their hands under their chins, craning their necks to see down the road, while men, with their hands wrapped tightly around them, bit on their lips, stifling the emotions that surged through them.

Estel's chest swelled with the joy flowing from the crowd, and to her surprise, the corners of her own mouth lifted. It was an odd sensation. She had seen others smile before, Lea and Zeal among them, but she could never find a reason good enough to try this for herself. She felt around her lips with her fingers. With the shifting of her mouth, she could feel the shape of her face change—her cheekbones rise and her eyes narrow—but the strongest change occurred inside her. It was as if the act alone cleansed her soul, wiping away all traces of pain and grief. Was this how Zeal felt when he whistled his happy tunes, while she begrudged him this little pleasure? She looked down at Arleta, an understanding passing between them, such as could only be experienced by two souls who descended into darkness and came back up to face the sun.

At last, the yellow beast pulled up along the curb and ceased its roaring. When its double doorway parted in the centre, a shiver stirred the hair on Estel's nape, and she held her breath along with everyone else. Arleta's fingers squeezed around hers and she sensed Lelya's presence, joining them to witness the event.

One by one, men in green uniforms filed from the gap in the doorway, large bags strapped across their shoulders, flat hats covering their heads. Some of them bore scars that spoke of recent injuries to their faces and limbs, while others leaned on metal sticks with a crosspiece at the top for support. As soon as the men emerged, smaller children ripped free of their mothers and ran to greet them, yelling the names of their fathers with glee. They collided and united in a storm of laughter that vibrated the air. Women followed their example, unable to stop the flow of tears.

‘Why are they crying?’ Estel asked, baffled by this sudden shift.

‘There are different kinds of tears,’ Lelya said and wiped her cheek. ‘But like rain after drought, every drop brings relief. Just standing here and sharing in their joy is enough. It’s a promise of what the future could be like.’

One of the men embraced his woman and swirled her around. They looked to Estel like a pair of children at play.

‘But even in such a joyful moment, unseen sorrow lingers. For some, the homecoming is filled with joy, but for others, it brings an unspeakable grief. Those who smile today may be weeping tomorrow, for such is the cost of war. The war that you have the power to prevent.’ Lelya’s face went slack. ‘I know that your loss is deep and you’ll have to face it alone, but remember this: if you prevail, he’ll be reborn into a better future.’

A reminder of Zeal’s fate filled her with anguish. Even if he was born again, she wouldn’t be the one to own his heart. He wouldn’t even know of her existence. Estel couldn’t decide what was worse—losing him or knowing that he would belong to someone else.

‘The world could be a beautiful place,’ Lelya said. ‘Today, it lacks equilibrium. Our race unbalanced it when we came to settle here. By stripping it of emotional attachments, we broke the human race. Those who opposed us and managed to escape the sword of justice turned to self-sacrifice in order to prove that Da'ariys held no power over them. But those who sided with us shaped the future you saw in your visions. But two halves can only become whole when they come together. If you tip the scale too far to one side, you create disparity.'

'If emotions are so sacred, why does it hurt so much?' Estel asked.

At her side, Arleta, with her eyeless toy pressed to her chest, stared wistfully at the children jumping and clapping at their parent's feet. Perhaps she too wanted to join in their excitement, but instead, she was bound by the magic of Da'ariys that drained her life with every trip into the future. And all for a Creator who refused to follow the path set before her.

'It only hurts if the hope is lost,' her mother said.

'But how would I know what to do? Everyone keeps telling me that I should forsake my own race and embrace the human part of me, for if I don't, all would end in defeat.'

Lelya took Estel's hands, and the warmth of her touch sent a soothing current through her daughter. Looking into her mother's soft eyes made Estel feel as if nothing could break the bond between them. Now she knew the emotion. It was the same one that emanated from Lea when she nursed her and watched her take her first steps. Estel wished she knew the feeling then. If she had, Lea would never die alone under the rubble, and Zeal would leave this world with the knowledge that her heart belonged to him.

'You misunderstand. This isn't a choice. You don't have to choose between human or Da'ariys. Seek balance and let hope be your guide.'

Estel's throat felt raw and each swallow was harder than the next. The people around her began fading, taking the joy and laughter with them. Lelya's face turned into a blur, her gentle smile nothing more than a ripple on a lake's surface, until it disappeared completely.

'Arleta?' Estel whispered, but the girl was no longer there.

She looked down at her feet where smooth stone gave way to scorched earth. The present collided with the future, taking her back to face the world where Zeal was nothing but a memory. The evening shadows licked the land, attempting to disguise the damage caused by Agni's flame, while the setting sun burned the western sky. Silence and despair walked hand in hand, waiting to ambush her.

Weakness spread through her legs and she sank to her knees. Her heart was a lesion, swollen with infection that no one knew how to heal. As a Creator she was able to withstand Agni's wrath, but nothing remained of Zeal's body apart from a handful of ash in a human form. Choking sounds escaped her as she crawled on hands and knees to the spot from which he graced her with his final smile. Now she knew the meaning behind it, but it was too late. The person who chose exile to save her life paid with his own, and she failed him. Estel ran her hand through dirt and her chokes turned to whimpers that exploded into sobs. Her eyes felt hot and itchy, as though something had tried to scratch its way out, and the more she resisted, the more persistent it became. Grief closed its suffocating fingers around her throat, and her lungs refused to expand and take in more air. Her body gave up on her like she gave up on Zeal when she sent him away.

Tears spilled from her like a saline river, and once unleashed, there was no stopping the flood that poured down her cheeks and hands, turning the ash between her fingers into slough. If the feeling that ravaged her soul was love, then she didn't know why people called it the greatest emotion. Lying in the dirt and wailing into the earth while her insides crumbled into ruin softened even the cruellest visions of the future. There was a hollow in her chest, a black void where regret and loss danced in a tight embrace.

Over and over, the voice in her head whispered that Zeal was gone, taking her chance at redemption with him. She realised, with her breath caught in her throat and her stomach rolling with regret, that she would give up all her powers just to hear his voice one last time, to share the feelings his death awakened in her.

But the dead cannot be summoned at will, and even if there was a way to bring him back, how could she even begin to convey her shame? She was the reason his life was taken, and nothing could make this right.

Nothing.

Something soft and moist pressed against her cheek. Estel lifted her head, and from the blur a pair of silver eyes looked back. Srebro stood over her, her black nose sniffing Estel's face. It was the first time the fox dared to approach so close, and Estel's heart swelled with affection for one thing that stayed true to her. She reached out and buried her fingers in the softness of the silver fur. Srebro's presence didn't stop the tears, or make the loss of Zeal less painful, but it brought peace to her shattered heart. Lelya was wrong, she wasn't alone, for her companion watched over her.

Srebro laid down next to her and rested her head on Estel's neck. She smelled of the forest and feral animals—a deep and musky aroma of the wilds Estel had grown so fond of over the years of her life. She could feel the fox's beating heart, and the warmth of her breath against her neck filled Estel with calm. Estel's tears dampened Srebro's fur, but the fox didn't seem to mind, as if she sensed that her presence soothed the anguish in Estel's heart.

Night found them curled up together like two parts of a greater whole.

***

Estel stood still for a while, feeling the wind on her face, watching it play with a sea of red and yellow leaves. The silence that fell across Daaria echoed that in her soul. She was reluctant to move or think, afraid that despair would return and sink its claws into her if she did. But her memories were relentless creatures, scratching at the edges of her mind, demanding she let them in to wreak their havoc. Each wore the face of someone she knew and lost in her quest to prove she was stronger and better than all of them.

Mara, her first friend, who confided her anguish in her, only to have Estel turn her away with a careless remark. Was that what pushed Mara to take her life? She would never know.

Lea, who found and raised her, left bleeding and alone in the darkness of Grey Lands for mrakes to feed upon.

And Zeal, a man who cared for her more than he did for his own life. He forsook his flame-sworn duties and broke his oath to Agni so he could follow her to his death. And what did he get in return for such devotion?

What did all of them gain for their trust and affection? From every corner of her mind, each of them looked at her with deep regret.

Her right arm bore another symbol, one that resembled two vertical pillars with ragged edges, connected through the middle by a horizontal one. Four silver marks, each representing an emotion she fought so hard to keep locked away. Now, she had no desire to resist them anymore. The Destroyer awaited her, deep within the snowy mountains of Zyma. Estel still didn't know how to defeat her, but it was time. She had learned all she could, and she was ready to face Rana and make her pay for every life she took.

Following the night of sharing Srebro's warmth, Estel woke to face a new day with another feeling brewing inside her. It wasn't the shy breath of affection for the fox, nor the pressing guilt over Lea's death, or Zeal's passing. The new sensation that spread through her swept aside all these emotions, replacing them with another, one Estel didn't have a name for. It was dark and filled her soul with toxic vapours. Its voice was a roaring in her ears, urging her to cast aside the past and march forth in search of retribution.

She closed her eyes and centred herself. The task entrusted to her as a Creator would change the course of the future, but despite its significance, her mind was preoccupied with the Destroyer. She knew that she wouldn't find peace until her sister paid in full for her deeds. Human or not, she would find a way to avenge Zeal and Lea, and those who suffered before them as each Creator failed to fulfil her destiny. Now she understood what it was to be human. Despite the fear, you couldn't turn your back on the people you love, were they alive or dead. She would face Rana and seek justice.

Srebro was at her side and she leaned and stroked the spot between her ears. The fox didn't shy away. Somehow, Estel's loss deepened the bond between them, removing the barriers that stood in their way for twenty years.

Having Srebro trot beside her to Zyma filled her heart with courage—she wouldn't be facing the Destroyer alone.

'Our final task awaits, my friend,' she said. 'Come what may, we will avenge the dead and restore balance to the world.'

PART V
ZYMA

Only those who wield the blade of forgiveness can conquer the future.

—the Creator of Da'ariys

XXIV

The days that followed Zeal's death were filled with hunting, sleeping, and running. Estel didn't have a horse and didn't need one. Her swift legs carried her across Vatra at a speed that even a grey sika would find imposing. There was freedom in racing the wind and feeling her lungs expand and contract with each intake of fresh autumn air. Srebro matched her pace with ease, trotting beside her day after day. Before, the fox would vanish from time to time, coming and going as she pleased, but since that fateful night, she didn't leave her side. There was a new connection between them, forged through the sharing of her pain and loss. She didn't know why Srebro would care about her feelings, but she did, and her presence kept Estel centred and focused. Like a silver beacon, the fox was her guide through red forests and over copper hills.

Estel made a new bow and more arrows. Unlike its glasswood cousin, this bow was a simple one, but sturdy and reliable, such as she was used to in Grey Lands. She hunted alongside Srebro. Vatra was rich in game and rodents so they never had to go hungry, and the woods provided plenty of fuel for campfires. In the evenings when Estel skinned their kills, Srebro, with her nose tucked between her paws, waited for her share.

Before Rana decimated her village in Grey Lands, Estel spent most of her days outdoors, in the wilds, with her bow as her only companion. She relished solitude and indulged in it as often as she could, much to Lea's displeasure. Her adoptive mother wanted her to forge bonds with people and find her place in the world. It caused discord between them. But now, trekking across Vatra with only Srebro for company, Estel found the isolation hard to bear. Something that gave her so much pleasure before had become a hindrance, and she fought hard against the feeling of loneliness that bit her when she least expected it. She ached for Zeal and his joyful demeanour. Her heart forever whistled his cheerful tunes, but her lips remained silent. She couldn't bring herself to acknowledge his passing aloud. Only keeping the memory of him locked inside allowed her to carry on.

Her nights were restless and filled with ominous dreams in which she pursued a dark figure of a man through the streets of some unknown city. She never had dreams before and it was an odd sensation to race across cobbled alleyways that were nothing more than vivid hallucinations caused by restlessness. Despite the knowledge, she pursued the man relentlessly, but every time she caught his shoulder and was about to expose him, the dream ended, leaving her awake and breathless.

When the first snowflakes touched the ground and the air shivered with chill, Estel left the land of fire and crossed into the realm of boginya Marena. Zyma lay before her like a maiden wrapped in white, silent and waiting. The sun stayed behind, as if the very idea of entering this frozen land repulsed it, and the full moon took its place, surrounded by an army of stars. The deeper she ventured, the heavier the snow. Srebro struggled as the white dust restricted her movement, forming balls around her feet and muzzle, and Estel had to stop often to loosen them from her fur. After a while, the fox began to sneeze and lost some of her stamina, but it didn't deter her from moving onward. As she skipped from snowdrift to snowdrift, her silver ears appeared and disappeared like arrow tips.

Rugged mountain peaks perforated the distant horizon, issuing warnings to those who dared to enter their domain. The cold intensified and the snow deepened, until running was no longer possible. Estel's jaw went stiff and her breath was a living fog that clung to her lips. Her clothing provided little protection against the bitter chill, and she walked with her hands tucked under her armpits. There was a reason why Marena was worshipped as the boginya of snow—her presence was all around, and her icy fingers kept a tight grip on the land. It was a strange place, illuminated only by the moonlight that fell across the snow, turning it into a bed of fallen stars. The path ahead wound into a mountain pass, disturbed only by a set of hoof prints. Estel didn't know where Rana resided but felt confident the tracks would take her right to her sister's doorstep. Their confrontation was inevitable, and no distance could keep them apart.

After a time, her teeth began to chatter and the cold formed icicles inside her brain. She didn't see any farms or households, only fields of white, with no sign of animal or human activity. The silence was deafening, as if all sound was cast out from this land of vast emptiness. A forest of glasswood glittered ahead, with trees of hard, translucent bark. Her broken bow was made from the same wood and she decided to use this opportunity to stop and fashion herself a new one.

From afar, the wood looked rigid and unyielding, but upon closer inspection, the branches proved to be soft and nimble. She placed her palm against the glassy surface, and the chill radiating from it spread through her veins. She wished that Ashk, or the previous owner of her bow, Juro, were here to explain the origin and properties of this strange wood. A deep sigh escaped her. She'd had so many opportunities to interact with people but chose to reject them all. It was only fitting that she found herself in Zyma, with only its oppressive silence for a companion. Despite the abundance of glasswood, she couldn't use it to build a fire. It was too hard and icy to entice a flame, but perfect for making a new bow and arrows to go with it.

'No rest for us, my friend,' she said, then leaned down and rubbed Srebro's chest.

The fox yawned and shook herself, covering Estel in a fine dust of white. Srebro's eyes shone in the moonlight like a pair of silver jewels and Estel saw her own reflection in them. Her chest swelled with affection—Srebro claimed her own place inside her wounded heart.

It took her a while to strip suitable twigs to shape the arrows. Despite their solid appearance, her knife scored the bluish wood with ease. To her dismay, the shavings fell on the snow and melted into it as if they were nothing more than softened ice flakes. Working with glasswood was easier than carving dab or olshas from her homeland and soon her quiver was full of sleek arrows.

She pressed on. And all the while something baleful followed them, leaving invisible footsteps in the snow, a dark form that took shape when Rana plunged her dagger into Zeal's heart. It spread through Estel, hotter than a fever, baring its teeth like a savage beast at the mere mention of the Destroyer's name. It wrapped her in a black mood that only Rana's death could lift, and despite the wind and snow, it spurred her onward.

The lack of sunlight made it hard to tell the time of day, and Estel's body wasn't the best indicator. Worn from the long trek across the snow plains, and chilled by the ice, her limbs were stiff and skin no longer ivory but red. She could see the veins on her wrist—dark blue branches that carried the blood of humans. It was a sign that she had lost her inner battle, but the awareness didn't fill her with dread. Her changes made her feel closer to Zeal and Lea, and accepting her transformation was a way of honouring their memory.

The hoof prints took them to the base of the mountain pass where the path turned steep and winding. She examined the snow—a set of hooves alongside two impressions left by a female foot—Rana dismounted here and walked the rest of the way. Estel began her ascent. The effort warmed her limbs and even Srebro recovered some of her grace. She trotted ahead and halted every so often, as if to check that Estel still followed. The higher they climbed, the more of Zyma spread before them. The glasswood forests shone with bluish light in the all-encompassing whiteness, the vast lakes to the east resembled black ice pockets, surrounded by jagged peaks that rose and fell whichever way she looked. There were no temples devoted to Marena, and no bells rang out to call upon the worshippers. It was as if Estel had gone back in time, walking across Zyma even before her ancestors came to claim this land, bearing with them the eternal change that cast the world and its future into oblivion. What would Zeal think of her if he knew the truth and the burden of her destiny? Would he be so willing to give his life for a person whose ancestors unbalanced the world? Or maybe he knew all along, but still chose her. They ran out of time to get to know each other.

She clenched her wrists. No.

The time was taken from them.

The climb seemed never-ending. Higher up, the wind turned bitter, slapping her cheeks and pulling her hair in all directions. She shielded her eyes from the snow, but it found its way into her nostrils and ears. Breathing became a chore. The air stabbed the walls of her throat and spiked her lungs, but she climbed on. At the top of this merciless mountain, the Destroyer awaited her punishment, and nothing would stop Estel from delivering it. She owed Zeal that much. Lelya said that her victory would grant him a new life and he deserved to live it out in full in a better world. She hoped she was strong enough to grant him this final gift.

At last, the path opened up before her and a steel gate loomed into view, covered in thick frost leaves. Jagged icicles hung off the arch like a line of spears pointing down. One side of the doorway was ajar, like an invitation. Srebro sat by the opening as still as a statue, eyes squinting against the gusts of snow.

They made it to the top and were about to enter the Destroyer's domain.

Estel placed her hand on the hilt of the dagger at her hip—apart from the bow, it was the only weapon she had. Zeal gave her two of them before they set out to steal Agni's flame, but one was lost in the assassin's chest halfway up the temple. During her mad descent, she managed to keep hold of the second dagger and was glad she did. It was the only thing that remained of Zeal and with it in her possession, she was ready to face whatever her sister threw at her. It was as if the man himself walked with her to witness the Destroyer's end.

She lifted her chin and crossed the threshold.

Beyond the gate was a vestibule with walls and floor of black stone, so refined that she could see her own reflection in it. Lining either side of the central walkway were tall columns that met in the centre to form arches above her. A torch was affixed to each pillar, flickering with a silver glow, and she wondered if it was the magic of Da'ariys that gave it life. Moonlight trickled through a set of windows, embellishing the walkway with spear-like shadows. The echo of Estel's boots was the only sound in this lifeless structure. A second gate, ajar, awaited on the opposite side. She turned around to find Srebro sitting at the other end, tail wrapped around her feet.

Estel's stomach clenched and she whispered, 'So, I must walk this path alone.'

She retraced her steps back to the fox and hunkered down in front of her. She stroked the silver fur, trying to fix in her memory how it felt under her fingers—like hair on a soft brush. Holding back tears, she whispered, 'Farewell, my friend.'

Srebro locked her silver eyes on Estel's and pressed her cold nose into the girl's palm. There was a time when Estel would have dismissed these little gestures as insignificant, but now, each warmed a place inside her. The Creator's quest was a lonesome journey and she wanted to get it over with. Win or lose, she was ready to face her fate, for what was life when you had no one to share it with? She got to her feet and drew her bow. It was time to honour those who languished in the terrible future. Arleta believed in her and so did Lelya. Estel couldn't change her present and bring back people she loved, but she could try to secure a better tomorrow for those who lived today.

Without looking back, she crossed the vestibule and walked through the doorway. It opened onto a long and narrow bridge made of pure ice. Each side of it was exposed, bereft of any railing to guide one safely to the other side. Beneath the icy structure, she found herself staring into a gaping chasm. If she fell into this seemingly endless void, there would be nothing but blackness to ease her descent. Her breath caught in her chest and she had to use the gate to steady herself. To the far right, trapped in mid-air like a snow slide, sat the city of Zyma. Its glacial structures were built into the walls of a mountain that formed a part of the chasm. Round, glasswood dwellings dotted the face of the rock at various levels, connected by a chain of ice steps and bridges.

But even from here Estel could see that the city was dead. Apart from the light cast by the silver moon, darkness swept down the mountainside, where wind and snow were the only occupants. The absence of life stirred something inside her. Rana must have killed the last dwellers of Zyma—but for what purpose? So she alone could rule the mountain peaks? The memory of the Twilight Hunters descending upon her village made Estel clench her jaw so hard, it felt as if her teeth would shatter. Had the same fate befallen the residents of these snow-covered houses?

She stepped onto the bridge and the wind slashed her cheeks. It was much stronger than in the valley, and it tried to push her off the ledge with each gust. The icy surface was slippery, and she struggled to keep her balance while the chasm with its city of ghosts beckoned her from below. She refused to look down, and instead fixed her eyes on the bridge. It was slow progress, but she pushed onward, her mind focused on the task of staying centred. She didn't climb all this way just to tumble down into a void.

Near the end, the bridge widened, and she gave out a sigh of relief. It brought her to the base of a mountain, with its face carved to depict an image of Marena. She stared in awe at the size of the sculpture. One of the boginya's eyes were larger than Estel herself and filled with the snow of the land. Ice clung to her brows, and the protruding rocks formed spikes around her face that brought to mind wisps of hair. Her wide lips were parted to form a doorway into the mountain, enticing Estel to see inside in a mocking shimmer of light and shadows. Looking at Marena's sharp features, Estel felt like an intruder. Unlike Vesta, who brought abundance to the people of Kvet, the boginya of ice wasn't here to provide comfort to those who chose to settle in her realm. To the contrary: only the strongest survived in her kingdom. Her white gaze reminded Estel of Rana, and the way the Destroyer looked at her when she plunged her knife into Zeal's chest. She sneered at Marena.

'No bog can deny me my vengeance,' she uttered, and walked through the opening.

'Welcome, sister.' Rana's voice rang off the walls, but its echo lingered long after the words themselves died out.

XXV

The sound of Rana's voice set Estel's soul on fire. The Destroyer was here, in the heart of Marena's mountain, marking the end of her long and cold journey. Rana sat in a glasswood chair looking as if nothing in this world could harm her.

'I bring death with me,' Estel said in a bold voice, pulling an arrow out of the quiver.

Rana's laugh was like chimes. 'I would expect no less from you, Creator. Your hatred burns so bright, I can almost feel it.'

The chamber was a stifling dome illuminated only by the blue light of torches mounted on the walls. Everything was sculpted from ice and glasswood: the floor, the walls, the wide steps leading to Rana's high chair. Frost had found its way inside through the main opening and showcased its talent by decorating the surfaces with gardens and orchards. The air was as bitter as it was on the outside, travelling up and down Estel's arms and raising gooseflesh. Her fingers were numb from exposure to the cold and she struggled to nock the arrow.

Rana got up and descended the steps. She wore the same black garb as when they'd last met, and her image plunged the spike of hate deeper into Estel, twisting her stomach. This was the creature who murdered Zeal as if he were no more than an expendable part of a game he never knew the rules to. Estel was ready to fight her to the last arrow.

The Destroyer pulled a long, curved blade from the sheath at her hip. The light from the torches danced on the steel. 'Your bow is useless. This sword is alive with the magic of Da'ariys. Nothing can escape its wrath.'

Estel circled the bottom of the stairs, trying to find the best position from which to release her arrow. The bow gave her an advantage—she didn't have to be close to make her move. 'You speak of Da'ariys, and yet you claimed Marena's temple as your own and killed the last of her people.'

'Please,' Rana waved her hand, 'I did the boginya a favour. Her people were cowards who fled before the Flame of Agni and hid in their snow houses like children behind their mothers' skirts. Marena gave them ice and all its power, and they squandered it. None of them deserved to live and so I fed them to my hunters.'

'And I fed *them* to the flame,' Estel said and loosened her arrow.

Rana calculated the movement and the position of the arrow in less than a second, adjusting her stance just enough so that it brushed past her shoulder. In a few strides she closed the distance between them and slashed the air with her sword. The tip of it sliced Estel's cheek before she had a chance to jerk out of the way. Her long trek across Zyma, combined with the numbing chill of the region, disabled her mind and crippled her abilities. Movement in her arms and legs was slower, delayed, and her concentration waned. The stabbing chill of the chamber didn't help matters. Crouching, she wiped the cut with the back of her hand and it came away crimson. There was no trace of silver in her blood.

'Nothing of Da'ariys remains in you,' Rana said. 'When you embraced the human soul, it was over for you. You surrendered your victory, and it is mine for the taking.' She sprang like a wild cat and Estel brought her bow up to meet the sword, fully expecting the wood to splinter, but when the blade crashed against it, the bow held its shape.

'Glasswood,' Rana said, pressing down harder. 'It's strong, but won't last forever. Nothing can resist the steel of Da'ariys.'

Estel gathered all the strength she could and pushed against the blade. As Rana stumbled back, the pressure was released and Estel leapt to the side. She ran up the steps and climbed the high chair. From there, she nocked another arrow and set it free. The Destroyer was fast on her feet and the arrow glanced off her blade like a stick. Trapped in the chamber, and with no way to retreat, Estel wished she took more time to prepare for this battle. Driven by her need for revenge, she didn't consider the hardships of Zyma and Rana's skills. A lone dagger and a bow were feeble weapons against the powerful sword that came as swiftly as a flash of lightning in a storm.

Rana advanced again, clearing the steps in a few quick strides. Estel leapt off the chair, evading the blade that came down in full force. The tip of it wedged into the glasswood. The Destroyer continued her pursuit without showing signs of tiring—a predator in her prime with prey only just able to elude each pounce. The floor was slippery, and Estel's boots struggled to find a grip. As the sword chipped the ice around her, she staggered and tripped.

'Your human heart turned you into a coward,' Rana called after her, chest heaving. 'You can't outrun me, and you can't defeat me. You'll die just like your assassin.

When my blade entered him, I felt his despair. His love for you bled through my fingers, as useless as his life.'

Zeal… His name roared in her ears like the flame he was sworn to. Even when he knew his life was over, he didn't falter or plead for mercy. Instead, he smiled at her. The memory of that smile punched Estel's heart like a gnarled fist and she shrieked. Blood spots flooded her vision and she stopped in mid-run.

'Good,' Rana said, laughing. 'That's good. Let your heart swell with hate. I destroyed him the way I'll destroy those like him in the future. That's what I was made for, to lead the true followers of Remha and bring the weak to heel. A new race will rise under my command. Generations of Creators couldn't stop me, and neither will you.'

Estel focused on the words, letting each of them stab her in the deepest of places. She cast aside the love and fear that burdened her, and let the darkest of human emotions into her soul. It filled every cell in her body like tar, thick and black with her need for vengeance. Rana turned her world upside down, took away everyone she knew, without a scrap of remorse. She recalled the power unleashed by her that crumbled the burdel back in Suha. If she could tap into that magic, maybe she could defeat the

Destroyer and give Zeal and Lea one more chance at life. Wasn't that her destiny? To offer the gift of a better future to all, and right the wrongs of Da'ariys?

She drew her bow and let the arrows fly. Like deadly stings they travelled across the chamber. The clatter of glasswood against steel bounced off the walls as arrow after arrow met with the Destroyer's blade. Rana was fast, her moves those of a skilled dancer, staving off the arrows with her sword, or avoiding them all together, until all that remained was air in Estel's quiver. She cast her bow aside and unsheathed her dagger. With a scream of fury, she ran across the chamber to meet Rana. They exchanged blows, evading and charging all at once—silver braids warring with black locks. With Zeal's image fixed in her mind, Estel focused her senses on her heart, searching every inch of it for that hidden power that once unleashed, would consume everything. Her chest expanded, her moves were faster, deadlier, more difficult to dodge. Something surged inside her like a high wave nearing the shore. Rana's sword became more hesitant. She staggered, then fell back.

Her dagger stabbed Rana's arm. As black liquid burst through the wound, she uttered an air-piercing scream. Estel charged again, but an invisible force shoved her aside as if she were nothing more than a leaf caught in the throes of a hurricane. Her body flew across the chamber and hit the wall. The impact knocked the wind out of her and blood filled her mouth. She choked on the taste of iron while the room spun.

Rana ripped the sleeve off her shirt, exposing ivory flesh. The stab was deep, and the blood oozed in a black river down her arm. She pressed her palm to the wound and started whispering. Estel was too dazed to make sense of the words, but they sounded like a chant of some kind. When she lifted her hand, the stab was gone as if it had never been there.

Using the wall for support, Estel clambered to her feet. The chamber swayed.

'Do you see now?' Rana's voice was painfully loud inside Estel's skull. 'There is no fight to be won, sister. The black blood of Remha flows through my veins, for I am to uphold his legacy as his warrior. The cycle will continue as though you never existed, and you'll know in your dying breath that destruction is a force stronger than creation. Da'ariys like our mother can't grasp the futility of their undertaking because their emotions make them blind to the truth. You can't save the future because it doesn't need saving.'

Unlike Estel, Rana was in control of her powers. Her heart didn't ache for Zeal or Lea, and she was unencumbered by human emotions. Before defeat took root in her, Estel recalled Ashk and Lelya and their insistence that her power dwelt in her feelings. If she could only understand what it meant. Instead, all she had was a dagger that could do no damage and a hope that somehow she could awaken her own abilities and use them to sway the victory in her favour. She tightened her grip on the hilt and prayed to her mother and father, and to the other bogs and boginyas of Da'ariys for guidance.

'Why would you want to live anyway?' Rana asked, raising her sword. 'The people you loved are dead. You're all alone in a world where no one awaits your return. Those we fight this battle over don't even know we're fighting it. Now that you're a human, loneliness will follow you wherever you go, until death knocks on your door. The Creator who saved the future will turn into ash, and the world you fought so hard for will crumble under the rule of the weak.'

Rana made a sweeping movement with her sword but Estel was ready for it and rolled to the side. The blade glanced off the wall and Estel sprang and ran the length of the chamber, back to the wide steps. The Destroyer hissed then followed, but her steps were measured, as if she had no reason to hurry. Her blade scraped against the glasswood wall, filling the chamber with a shrieking peal.

Estel clutched her dagger, watching Rana climb the steps one at a time, and knew that her time had come. Regret washed over her. Ashk was right, she was destined to fail like the Creators before her. She thought of Arleta and her unwavering belief in her, of Lelya and the hope in her eyes when they watched the soldiers coming home from war, of Ashk and his destiny. He would be trapped here for another century, watching the world go to ruin again and again.

And Zeal. If she lost now, his sacrifice was for nothing. By choosing her he chose death.

A nagging feeling scratched at her heart. She knew there was something she had to beg of them, something significant that would ensure her absolution, and bring peace to her wretched soul. But, like a fleeting shadow, it eluded her.

The Destroyer was upon her, and Estel lifted her dagger to meet her sister's sword. As their eyes locked, her body stilled. They stared at each other as if trying to mark the weakest point—two sisters, each fighting for their own vision of the future. Estel was the first to strike. Her dagger fell upon Rana only to change direction at the last moment and deliver a surprising stab to her side. It sank all the way in. Estel let go of the hilt and rammed into Rana with her shoulder.

Her sister roared her fury, black eyes whirling. She grabbed the hilt and pulled the dagger out. 'I'm tired of this game,' Rana said through clenched teeth. 'Let's end this.' Her palm was already at work to seal the new wound.

Estel felt around the icy floor and her fingers came upon one of the arrows that missed its target. The glasswood shimmered with the light from the torches and she tightened her fingers around it. Her bow lay on the other side of the chamber, but as she sprang forward, cold steel scored the lower part of her calf. She buckled under the burning pain that spread through her leg. Another slash met her shoulder and she cried out. Crimson gushed from the wound and she had no magic to stop the flow. Her bow beckoned her from afar, calling for the arrow in her grip, but the distance between them was too great. She could never hope to cross it in time.

Rana struck at her side, but it wasn't her boot that kicked Estel. Her own shame delivered the blow. She failed everyone. Ashk warned her, Lelya and Volh counselled her, Arleta pleaded with her, but for the need to prove her strength, she refused them all, and now she was the weak one, staring into the abyss of Dark Nav. There would be no salvation for her, no trials to find her place in the afterlife. Only black pits awaited her for her foolishness. Her birth was a waste, and Zeal's love and sacrifice was for nothing.

But then the symbols on her right arm began to throb as if urging her to stay strong. Her nostrils flared, and her knuckles turned white against the bluish sheen of the arrow. A sudden jolt of adrenaline made her grab the Destroyer's ankle and throw her off balance.

Rana's head bounced off the floor, leaving a black smear where the skin hit the ice. The sword clattered away from her.

Estel rose to her knees. She forgot all about the bow, her mind focused on the obsidian eyes that reflected her own rage. Silver light flooded her arm and her chest swelled with a sense of purpose. The Creator of Da'ariys would not be so easily defeated. The arrow in her grasp began to shimmer. A chill rose from it in a swirl of smoke, freezing the tip with ice. The blue mist sneaked down the length of the arrow, and shards wrapped around her arm, imbuing her blood with the magic of Marena. She felt the curtain of ice being drawn across her eyes to make them look like those of the boginya's at the entrance. Her skin tingled all over, and never before had she felt so alive. As her mind cleared and her senses sharpened, the weariness fled her, replaced by exhilaration that filled every inch of her—the victory was so close she could taste it on her tongue.

Rana's laugh filled the chamber and her face beamed with triumph. 'So, you've found your power.'

Estel raised the icy arrow. 'The reign of Remha ends here.' She aimed it at Rana's heart.

'But you're wrong, sister,' Rana whispered. 'His reign has just begun.'

Estel let the arrow fall.

Rana's eyes narrowed while Estel's ears filled with the pounding of her own heart.

'No!' A scream tore the air. Time stilled and so did the arrowhead, inches from its target.

Lelya stood at the mouth of the mountain, Srebro at her side. Her white dress wrapped around her like a protective cloak, her silver hair tied in a tail that cascaded down her shoulders, the tip of it brushing against her hip. Her skin shimmered with silver and for the first time Estel thought that from afar, Lelya looked like an older version of her.

Estel blinked the image away and tried to drive the arrow through the Destroyer's chest, but her arm was locked, as if cast in stone. She stared Lelya. 'What are you doing? I'm so close.'

'You don't understand,' Lelya said, her hand pressed to her stomach. 'If you kill her now, it's the end.'

Rana's face was motionless, but the mocking smile never left her lips, as if she couldn't wait for the arrow to find her heart.

'The end is all I care about,' Estel said and pressed harder, but the magic that held her was stronger than any physical force.

'Not this end.' Her mother crossed the chamber to stand next to them, but Srebro stayed where she was.

'What then? Have you come to kill me? Or maybe you're the reason why all the preceding Creators have failed.'

'There's no place for us to be but here,' she said and opened her palm. 'Let us unite for the last time, then I'll leave you to make your choice.'

'What choice?' Estel asked, red spit flying from her mouth. 'With this arrow, I can defeat Rana, avenge Zeal's death, and save the future. Isn't this what everyone wants?'

‘You’re about to destroy the future, not save it.’

And just like that, Estel was out of her body, staring at her own image frozen in time, with her arrow still pointing at Rana’s heart. Her first reaction was to reunite her flesh with her spirit, and find the strength to impel the tip of her arrow as deep as it would go, but Lelya’s magic held her in place.

‘What have you done?’ she asked, inspecting her hands. In her previous visions she fled her body to another dimension, seeking connection with her ancestors, but now, it was as if time itself had stopped.

‘Arleta knew you would falter but insisted on following you into your final vision, but I couldn’t allow that. She did all she could for you and now it’s my turn. The four of us are one, but only the one in the present has the power to decide who will make the final choice.’

Estel’s head was spinning. None of this made sense. Her eyes found Srebro’s, but the fox was locked in time with the rest of the world. ‘What about my fox?’ Estel asked, fearing to hear the answer. Everything she believed in was coming undone. Was all her life on Daaria an illusion she assembled together so it could lead her to this frozen wasteland?

Lelya frowned. 'After everything you went through and all that Ashk taught you, I expected more wisdom from you. The fox is a vessel for your essence. You've become a human to fulfil your task, but your place isn't among them. You're the boginya of Creation and you belong with your ancestors. You've been born and reborn, just like the Destroyer, to fight this battle until balance is restored. Unless you prevail, the cycle will never end. Our kind inflicted enough damage and we can't allow for the suffering to continue.'

'If that's so, let me complete my task. Release my body and let my arrow serve justice.'

'For better or worse, you've become too human and the need for vengeance blinds you. In Rana you see a woman who tore away your heart, but to recall your purpose you must look beyond that. That's what makes humans so resilient. A river of possibilities flows through them, and what they pull from it shapes everything around them, including themselves. By stripping humankind of emotions, we disrupted that flow, and your task is to restore it. But you can't do that unless you're whole again.'

Before Estel could answer Lelya took her hand and pulled her into a vortex of time, where all possible pasts and futures collided in a pool of blue energy. It was like stepping into a vast lake with no shores. The force from it flowed through Estel as if her physical body was no barrier. It was a place with all possibilities, a moment in time where everything could be altered, and Estel was the one with the power to realise those changes.

'Let us find the missing piece,' Lelya said, pulling her deeper into the pool.

XXVI

Estel found herself at the base of a hill overlooking grand vistas of pale rocks. The sun bled over the western horizon and the air on her tongue tasted of iron. The whole mound was wrapped in a tight cloak of anguish, so palpable that it settled around her throat like a hand ready to choke the life out of her. Lelya awaited her at the top and Estel began her ascent along a curved path. After a few steps, her breathing become laboured and she had to stop to catch her breath. Someone walked this road before with a heavy burden, and as a part of her vision, Estel shared the weight of it now. Her shoulders slumped as if something pressed upon them, heavy and uneven. Her throat turned into a dried creek, but she struggled on. Despite the setting sun, the heat was hard to bear, and her body radiated with pain that didn't have a source.

When she reached the peak, her energy was spent and her legs swayed beneath her. The walls of a city loomed on the horizon, beyond which fires burned as bright as those in the city of Vatra. But the hill itself sagged with mourning.

And then she saw him.

Her hand flew to her mouth, but she couldn't distinguish if it was her own scream she tried to kill, or that of the man in front of her.

He was tied to a vertical pole, twice the length of his body, and fixed into the earth with a set of spikes at the base. His hands were spread to either side, tethered to a horizontal pole, and his head rested at the intersection of the two. His ribs were so prominent that she could count them, but the worst of all was the state of his skin—she couldn't find a spot that was clear of lacerations. From the shape of them, she judged that the man was beaten, or whipped. Thick blood oozed from the cuts, dripping down his arms and legs in a path of crimson. Angry flesh festered around the wounds. What deed would sentence a man to such punishment?

Lelya beckoned her to come closer. The man's chin rested on his collarbone, his face covered by locks of matted hair. He looked unconscious.

All the emotions she witnessed through Arleta, together with the memories of the cruel events, tore into her like a flock of savage birds. Were Da'ariys truly responsible for so much misery? And to what end? So they could create a perfect race, strong enough to torment those weaker than them, empty enough to not to comprehend the pain they inflicted upon others?

She looked at Lelya. A great sadness was trapped in the corners of her eyes, and for the first time Estel felt proud to be a human. The ability to understand and share the feelings of another was a gift, not a burden. Lelya was right when she tried to tell her that, but Estel wasn't ready to listen then. She fought and killed before: the sailors on Krag's ship, the Keeper of Suha, the flame-sworn assassins on her way to steal the Flame of Agni. Taking a life was easy. One stab in the right spot, one well-executed thrust, and the deed was done. The man before her was an example of the frailty of human life. But if those who beat him in such a violent way could experience his anguish with each fall of their whip, would they still carry on? Feeling what she felt now, would they still think it was a just punishment?

'He was the first man to defy Remha,' Lelya said. 'A Da'ariys who refused to believe that the only way to become a true warrior was to cast aside one's heart. He chose his human side and walked Daaria teaching people to weave the emotional tapestry hidden in all of us. The threads we choose will shape our lives, and if some of them are lost, the image becomes distorted, until we can no longer distinguish the purpose of our existence.' She walked closer to the pole and looked up at the man. 'His death served nothing. By killing him, they created a deeper rift, and instead of uniting the world, they divided it further. The only way for him to escape his fate is for you to embrace yours. Unless you make the right choice, there will be many like him in the future.'

Estel looked at the man, at his injuries, at injustice of it all. 'But I still don't know what to do…'

A slow and agonising moan filled the air and Estel recoiled from it. It was a sound of despair that would haunt her to the end of her days. The man raised his head and the face that looked back at her was so battered she struggled to see where one eye ended and another began. His lips were cracked, and his nose was a lump of bloody flesh.

A whisper quieter than a sigh escaped his lips, 'I forgive them for they are lost, and there is no one to save them.' His swollen eye met hers. 'You're the Creator, so create, and give back what was taken from them.'

His words expanded every cell in her body, imbuing her blood with the magic of his wisdom. The walls that held her back crumbled, and she understood her part in the creation of a better future. Lelya was right, if her arrow took Rana's life, she would be embracing Remha's future.

She couldn't bring about change by taking a life, but by giving it back. The man nailed to the pole was an example of this. If she let the anger and hatred for the Destroyer fester in her, she would never know peace. It took all parts of Estel to bring her to this moment in time.

She was whole at last, ready to cleanse Daaria from all traces of Remha's deception.

Lelya inclined her head and her image faded. She fulfilled her duty, leaving Estel to fulfil hers.

The time resumed its flow and Estel found herself back in her own body, about to plunge the arrow into the Destroyer's heart.

'Do it,' Rana said in an urgent voice, as if she sensed the change in her sister. 'Do it for Zeal, for Lea.' She grabbed Estel's hand and pulled it down.

Estel wrenched the arrow back from Rana's grip and threw it aside. Her arm throbbed, but she didn't have to look at it to know that a new symbol worked its way into her flesh. She rose to her feet.

'What did she say to you?' Rana demanded. Hate took possession of her face, twisting her lips and distorting her perfect features.

'Nothing I didn't already know. Even though I can't recall it, we've been here before, and every time you took the victory away from me because I was too weak to stop myself. Now I know what you meant when you said that I will take your life. I did for many centuries, but no more. This time I intend to give it.'

Estel found Rana's hand and pulled her to her feet. She looked deep into the black pits of her sister's eyes. 'You've done well to lead me here, so I could face my final trial. You've fulfilled your task and I forgive you, sister. For everything.'

Rana struggled against her grip, but Estel's strength was no longer of this world. The power of the Creator coursed through her veins. She pulled the Destroyer inside her as if she was nothing more than a feather caught on a breeze, and their bodies merged like dawn with the morning light in the wake of a new day. The five symbols on Estel's arm expanded then burst open, releasing silver energy that filled every part of her. The brilliant light surging through her grew stronger, brighter, until it consumed everything in its wake. She opened herself to it and let the magic absorb her. Her final thoughts were of Zeal and Lea. She asked their forgiveness and offered whispers of gratitude for their love and for the lessons they taught her along the way. The act brought her peace and severed the chains of anguish that had been locked around her for so long.

Like rain after a century of drought, the Creator's magic spilled across Daaria in a shower of silver, touching all of its creations, restoring the missing pieces to every soul that walked the earth until each was complete, and balance was restored to the world.

***

The sun rose over the eastern sky in a blush of pink, waking every part of the valley with a promise of a warm day. Dew glimmered in the morning light like beads of silver, and the flowers across the meadow shivered at the touch of a light breeze. Silence hovered over the plains, but it wasn't the silence that descends upon a battlefield at the fray's end. It hummed with calm, infusing the hearts of those it touched with tranquillity.

From a hill overlooking the valley, a fox sprang to its feet. It shook dew free of its silver coat and stood motionless, ears pricked, searching the ground below.

Two young hunters ran between the trees, their hair flying in the wind like strands of copper. Each held a flamewood bow. Their pupils were aflame, sparked by the pursuit of their prey, and their chests swelled with laughter.

The fox followed their progress, and when the forest claimed them, its silver eyes squinted with pleasure. It sniffed the air and with a soft bark, trotted down the hill toward the rising sun.

Acknowledgements

I would like to thank Phillip Athans for his advice, support, and encouragement, but most of, all for making editing fun. Many disasters were averted thanks to his sharp editorial eye.

My reader, Lauren Nicholls, for cheering me on and sharing her creative wisdom with me. Her ability to see beyond the words on the page is truly admirable.

Mario Wibisono for bringing Estel to life with his magnificent cover art.

My brothers, Paul and Andy, for their phone calls and continued support. When you truly care, distance is no barrier.

Printed in Great Britain
by Amazon

38286881R00272